Jonathan Mallalieu was educated in Wales and now lives overseas. He is 27 and this is his first collection of stories.

Patty Devlin McCullen
1.50 Irish at Easons Galway
9/8/96

The Prince of Wales and Stories

JONATHAN MALLALIEU

PHŒNIX

A PHOENIX PAPERBACK

First published in Great Britain by Phoenix House in 1993
This paperback edition published in 1994 by Phoenix,
a division of Orion Books Ltd,
Orion House, 5 Upper St Martin's Lane,
London WC2H 9EA

A CIP catalogue record for this book is available from the
British Library.

ISBN: 1 85799 098 6

Printed and bound in Great Britain by
The Guernsey Press Co. Ltd, Guernsey, C.I.

CONTENTS

JACKS
stories

MEN
Jack and Edna   5
The Church   39
Mother's Day   52
The Reluctant Millionaire   65

WOMEN
To Annia   81
Our Marya   94
Martha   108
Of Saphira   122

TRANSCRIPTS
I   139
II   148
III   155
IV   165

THE PRINCE
OF WALES
a novella
175

DEDICATION

I DREAMED OF JACK – one evening on the beach. Awoken twelve times, I dreamed twelve dreams. And diving, like Swansea Jack, to rescue corpses from the Bay, I reclaimed bits of Jack. And, clasping them as stones, scurried to write: to resuscitate the bitty corpse. And as I wrote, the stony pieces, juggled in the hand, piled to this bitty book. He is still in pieces. Books are arks of covenant, storing stones etched with the doings of a god. And these standing stones are a clock, a horoscope cast to read the mind of Jack. And in this book, passed from my mother to me and now passed back to her, Jack (a local here in Lotos-land) may be sniffed, but probably never known. For references are not to actual places, nor to actual people. Any similarity is accidental. There are no secrets, there are no echoes, there is no representation, there are no Jacks.

JACKS

stories

MEN

Jack and Edna

I

Christopher Fishen ran away from home on his seventh birthday. Kidnapping Oscar the guinea-pig, he set off at a waddle across the marshes. No one followed, his family was too busy squabbling to notice, arguing over who spent most money on their youngest's present.

Christopher returned within the hour, unmissed. Distress at not finding himself pursued drove him home. He wanted to be indispensable.

The Fishens lived on Llanrhidian Marshes. The Loughor estuary soaks the land to a sponge, flooding once a year, softening the Gower to mudflats. Dykes irrigate the marsh, a moat surrounds their plot, a firebreak.

In the upstairs bedroom of their tithe cottage, Jack Fishen straddled his wife. Edna inflated with child then popped – as she put it. Belinda, their firstborn, set up a caterwauling in the front bedroom. Jack escaped the noise, clomping out in boots to douse fires and pocket snooker-balls. He lolled in the common-room at Loughor fire-station, avoiding the struggles of mother and child.

Julia was conceived and born within two years. Edna, marooned eight miles from town, hankered after company. She manufactured friends. And while her efforts to conceive paid off, her efforts to slim down after each birth did not.

Congenital obesity, reluctantly received from her gigantic mother, was passed to her two daughters. Julia ballooned from birth. Belinda, believing she had escaped, mocked her podgy sister, then to her horror found an immovable wad of flesh accumulating about her thighs.

As years passed, the wad inflated, spreading about her waist, her

5

arms and neck. Terrorised, she watched her mother's jowls grow and flap beneath her own jaw. She saw her future self as Mum. As mother waddled so she waddled – and the family waddled with heavy lumbering movement. Jack raced on ahead and was shouted to slow down, so paused to rejoin his breathless, staggering women. The large move slowly.

Julia followed, a progress decided not by choice, but by a silent conspiracy of cells. Deep within and on the surface, both girls could see their enemies – in a skin, a patterned flesh that refused to be constrained.

II

As if the cellular conspiracy had exhausted itself, Christopher was born puny, weak and deathly pale. His mother frowned. Father peered glumly at his imitator, a pathetic sliver of soft bone and gristle.

Ah – he's nothing but a runt! exclaimed Edna, hugging him to her breast. The infant was dwarfed by the gland. To soft enormity it sank, pampered by three elephantine girls.

Edna, Julia and Belinda fought to master the boy. Jack was ignored. No one much bothered if he was at the fire-station, roasting in the fires or, beslippered, snoozing by the Aga.

Give him, give him, give him me – spluttered Edna, thrashing out at rival mothers.

Mum – let me! chimed the other two.

He's *mine*! she snapped.

Mum – I hate you –

Belinda could squash Julia to submission. It was always the way. If the younger rebelled, her elder would simply slam her loathed advantage into Julia's shoulder. Staggered, the girl fell flat on her rump. Belinda sat on her face, rubbed buttocks to the screeching gob and rose to fondle little Christopher.

Edna seethed at such appropriation of her property. She regretted having girls first. She wished the boy had inherited the fleshy genes, been big at birth. Girls should come later, pretty as he was pretty, slender as he was slender. Besides, she would have liked a little bit of time alone with the kid.

It's no good my schooling them, she argued to a snoring Jack. No good me telling them what to do! – they're just like you – it's all inbred it is – all their bad behaviour – nothing I can do!

But for him, her youngest, she reserved the hope in perfectibility. She set him to speak at two, read at three, write at four. She grew pregnant with ambition for him. But he stubbornly refused to accept her raging urgent aspirations.

He wanted to be a fireman.

Edna snorted her disdain.

A what! – why your father's a fireman! a bucket-carrier, a hose-mender, a snooker-player!

Jack worked his jaws and turned up the telly. Christopher clambered to his knee.

Instead, by circumlocution, her preaching reached the bitter rivalrous girls. Belinda and Julia were their mother's daughters. And with obesity came a desire to influence, to be adored despite a surface grossness, and to rule.

Belinda soon tired of ruling Christopher. She needed larger, more defiant males to cow.

Once in school, the Primary in Crofty, she set about subduing the idle natives. With all her mother's natural fire she rose from being class bully to class monitor. Aged ten and considering herself inferior without a boyfriend, she took to clubbing Jamie Jones with an egg-beater. He conceded to her greater size. He consented to be her drone. Any mockery he suffered was reported back to queen- bee Belinda. The scoffer was subjected to a season of bullying, the type of which the poor mite had never dreamed.

I'm the boss, Belinda declared. I am – I am – I am – and anyone who says no is dead!

It was a simple gospel, easily grasped and quickly promulgated. Backed up with violence, it became law. That is, until she rose to the barbarities of Senior School in Olchfa.

Julia suffered. Beside her larger, more conspicuous and better established sister, she was eclipsed. Friendless, she wilted. Set upon by skinny wits, she collapsed to tears. Poked with needles and drawing-pins to see if she would pop, she burst into a stream of self-abuse.

I know I'm fat I do! she shrieked to the teacher's alarm – leave me alone, Jason – I know it was you – I'm horrible, I know, but leave me 'lone!

Edna and Belinda stoically ignored Julia's decline. Weakness was despicable. An eight-year-old would weather the storm. The strong inherited the earth, they believed. Julia stormed to her room, an agnostic. She sided with oppressed peoples everywhere. Her heart reached out to the mocked, the humiliated. While Belinda wanted only to captain industry, to storm government, Julia wanted to nurse the mentally handicapped. Theirs was a mind she understood. And Jason Darnley was horrible to them as well. His enemy was her friend.

Secretly, she clung to her family.

III

Edna, a local Methodist preacher, boomed from the pulpit each Sunday morning. On the circuit, she drove to emptied chapels across Glamorgan. From Tuesday through Saturday she compiled her five-point sermons amongst the baking-tins. While plucking potatoes from the garden she murmured one-liners to the sprouts. Stomping back into the steamy kitchen, she scribbled them on an envelope, pinned it to the corkboard and, kneading dough, memorised the phrase.

Years before, Jack watched her majestically ascend the mahogany stairwell. From the heights of a chapel lectern she hurled the gospel of Jesus to where he sat quaking in a back pew. Her bloodshot eyes seemed to ignite his to flame, her jowls to blow the fiery word of God into his cheeks.

On her call, he stumbled to the front. Edna's growl resembled mother's. A weak man, he was subject to a nostalgia where mothers were concerned, a sentiment which shut his mouth and got from him mesmerised obedience whenever their voice hit a certain pitch. Like crystal wineglasses, some men have only to be assailed by a screech of the correct pitch and they will disintegrate into selflessness.

8

Converted, Jack hugged Edna – or rather he was hugged, squeezed into her bulk so hard it seemed she never wished them to part. He was less than confident in his decision to convert. But her indomitable will overrode his vacillation. He silenced inner voices. She kept up a busy monologue for the first decade of their marriage, a rattle which drowned murmurous sedition in his heart.

And I saw Mrs Pwll – what's her name? – she's so thin! she'll vanish – her husband walked out on Tuesday – probably lost sight of her – left a note on the stairs – and her a god-loving woman – she was in tears – I prayed with her I did – she laughed – isn't the Lord good, Jack?

He sidled to the shanty-hut workshop at the tail of the garden. Their plot wandered to a distant fence. Grasses crowded to peer over to the estuary. Woodruff, hollyhock and foxgloves flourished on the damp soil. The kitchen-garden fed the family its vegetables. Jack stooped to tend sprouts, spuds, cauliflower, runner-beans, carrots and rhubarb. In a rotting greenhouse, he nightly sprayed tomatoes, wall-flowers and cucumbers. And on a sheltered plot beneath a hawthorn, he jealously guarded a clump of alpines and a verge of daffodils.

In a smaller shed, a lawnmower and clippers, a rake and shovels jostled for space with the family bicycles. When the war in the kitchen became too fractious for his simple nature, he could rest here and smoke a cigarette.

Had he not been subject to occasional vicious needs for intercourse, he might have lived alone in such a place. He might have survived on his navy pension, caring only for plants and lawns and men. Instead, he subjected himself to Edna's divine eye and rule. He could not now conceive life without her. Nor life with her without the lads at Loughor. And the bar to which – unknown to her – he slunk each night before driving ten miles home.

Is that drink on your breath, Jack? Edna squealed. I'm sure I can smell drink!

It was the lads, dear – the lads had a party – terrible smell in the station.

She came at him in repentance.

Give us a kiss – Mmm, that's better – and another.

9

And he slouched to stand in the centre of the lawn and stare to where the river slunk to silent union with the sea.

The ridges lay dark in thick marsh grasses. Dykes criss-crossed the plain. A shrub here and there bent in permanent obedience to the driving wind – like the smoke from the Aga, a long low dark cloud firing the south.

Above him glowed planets, trapped in the hemisphere of heaven, circling a vast gas axle.

IV

Christopher was unborn on the occasion of their first serious fight. He lay, barely formed, inspired by God (Edna announced) in the deep of her, squashed by a poundage of flesh even the most gargantuan frame found difficult to bear. He probably heard every word.

It arose, as all things, from the most atomic of beginnings. Jack voiced his dissatisfaction with sleeping on the south side of the bed. Edna, disbelieving his motives, refused to swap. He claimed the mattress would be softer, more broken-in, on her side. She said Yes it was *her* side. He had *his* side – couldn't a woman have *her* own space? Whatever next? The row smouldered.

Jack was offered lateral promotiom – a position on the nightshift at Llanelli station. Edna objected, arguing the family prayer hour (the highpoint of her evening) would suffer. He disagreed, the sessions (his lowpoint) would benefit from an earlier timing. She commanded him to remain in Loughor. He dissented. She said God had given her a word. He disobeyed God.

She kept a peace, surprisingly but archly. A quiet reigned for ten days. Jack began his nightshift, sleeping through the day, rising at three, tending the gardens, collecting the girls from school. He avoided his wife. And, most heinously, he connived to have his name entered for the Saturday night roster. His need to sleep through her sermons was given a solid grounding in reason.

Edna was not slow in her revenge. Virtually ordering the women of the vicinity, she set up – with haste – a coffee afternoon, a bazaar and women's groups. She hosted these in the lounge and garden. Ten, twelve, sometimes twenty godly women congregated in the house. Jack's sleep was disrupted. His moods sank, his irritability became a characteristic.

I'm only doing God's duty, Edna sniffed. And seeing as I've a husband who won't stand by me – what's a wife to do? – I obey – the long and the short of it – I obey!

Who? enquired her husband.

My Lord – you know that Jack – no need to be difficult.

No no, Edna – who do you obey?

I told you, Jack – now, get the kids in.

Edna, we're having this out – I'm damned –

You *are* if you speak like that in this home – my God, you are – now, I'll have no more of your backchat – get the children in – Girls!

And he retreated to gnaw his upper lip, to feel the bile squirt to his gut, to despise every square centimetre of the woman. He quenched the fires in himself, turned and orbited the room.

The girls silently watched the dumb-show. The inanity of an inspirational-music tape concealed the silence. In the thick liquid brimstone, the family's elements floated, maintaining strict distance from each other. Like the atoms of which they were made, this family was a cluster of charged particles revolving about an invisible centre – the pressure to depart, to run, was countered by a tortuous elemental need to remain.

Edna nursed these grievances in her heart. She adored Jack with a fine blend of hatred and desire. His woolly-headed weakness, his white white body, his large hands, their filthy fingernails and his hug which squashed her to a smaller girth, all warmed in her a lust she preferred to call love, a need which could only speak itself with greed.

The children observed, piercingly.

V

To mark Christopher's entry into the house, Jack finished his table. While Edna was lying in and recuperating at Morriston General, he took time off. The old blue veneer fold-down table would go, he sliced it to fragments with an axe. There was no alternative – he must finish his long-planned circular table.

Uneven lengths of inch-thick oak and pine had been gluing and drying for months. G-clamps clasped the crosswood to the planks. Epoxy resin dried in the seams. A black circle was drawn on the wood.

With a jigsaw he sliced the tabletop from the beams. On the night before their return, he lathed the single leg. He had a touch of love for Edna, a need to see her impressed. After the girls were in bed, he fitted a block to the leg, struts to its foot and laid the disc of beams on top.

Edna was delighted. She had hennaed her hair at hospital and bought red-framed oval glasses to match. And with flaming orange jowls she bounded to squeeze him and take her seat at table. Christopher, born without complications as the sun entered Aquarius, screeched his hello.

For a while, they squabbled over places. There was no head, Jack had too many rivals. Christopher was enthroned on a highchair. Belinda and Julia fought over the seat at his right hand. Mother always sat to his left, Jack beside her, passing dummies and napkins, towels and bowls.

On the table, Julia copied Belinda's homework, Jack reassembled his newspaper, Edna scrawled her sermons, Christopher wriggled and finally fell.

His fall cracked open his skull and engraved a scar on his forehead. As he grew, so he emboidered the tale of his drop – how, because he had no wings, he fell to the stone floor while mother clouted father for paying no attention to his son.

Christopher adored his father, much against his mother's wishes. She considered herself the only wholesome influence in the house. She dreaded seeing the child clamber over the bough of his thigh to claw the precipice of shoulder and swipe at his bristled chin. His mother was a bother, a vast sun bearing down on him, swathed in a linen smock. He slapped her away. She drew him up from father's leg to bury him in bed. Father vanished, to fight fires.

Fire fascinated the boy. The great cast iron doors of the Aga would clang open. Orange and the flash of sulphur roared within.

Ooh, what are you standing there for! Edna cried. Where I'll tread all over your toes and you'll burn your little eyebrows off – get away!

And he retreated, staggering backwards from the slammed door. He had seen the future.

As soon as he was able he set cones of copper leaves afire. He torched bugs and dragonflies. Far out on the marsh he lined aerosol cans on a log and fired air-rifle pellets to see them explode. Running wild across the bogs, he dreamed he had a flame-thrower and scorched the wilderness to desert. And on a dank November afternoon, Christopher destroyed the shed.

He had – he claimed – been playing with matches. It was not known why the lean-to disintegrated in a cloud of flame. Some suspected a liquor still was hidden there. Others, that little Christopher had imported unstable liquids to the hut. Jack was not on hand. Edna flapped, shrieking. The boy hauled buckets to pour water over the shattered jars and smouldering bicycles. It was his first blaze.

And afterwards, in commemoration, his mother bent him over the log of her knee and walloped some sense into him.

You – little – scamp! she shouted, punctuating each slap – I – leave – you – for – five – minutes! You – raise – hellfires! – What – am – I – going – to – do – with – you!

Jack entered while she was admonishing the boy. He tore the frail lad from her grasp, his anger foaming, his violence unrestrained.

With the rear of his hand, he knocked his wife half-conscious. Upstairs, he soothed the lad.

There, don't.

He rearranged the golden hair.

You did good – putting that there fire out – like a man, you did.

Christopher moaned, sucking a finger, vowing to avenge himself on mother, vowing to repay his father.

The girls laughed at the demolished shed – it was typical of the Fishens! They couldn't leave anything standing. No sooner had you got used to something than one or another of them blew it to bits. Edna nursed the bruise, a purple stain to her right cheek. She prodded it and dug at it, willing it to last so questions would be prompted from her ladies as they swarmed in the tiny lounge and kitchen, bewailing husbands.

13

VI

For Christopher, a father was an absent god, a mystery who, when at home, slept or snoozed by the fire. When Jack doffed wellingtons and strode to dig the garden, or laid a rug under the car and vanished beneath, or clambered up a ladder to mend the gutter, his son invariably padded after him to learn.

With a hot, palpitating heart, Christopher chased after his father's commands. He routed out a chisel or a spanner while Jack bled tubes or tested levers. Quivering with hope, the lad waited at the boots of his mechanic-father. Passing him his tea or smoothing grease from his broad brow. It was enough. It made him feel required.

When he tripped into the steam-clouded kitchen with some request from Jack, the girls and mother would cry:

Oh! so here's daddy's boy!

At last – never thought we'd see you again!

Got your marching orders? What does he want now?

Christopher trembled with embarrassment. He had been beaten by all three women, their lardy hands had swiped at his thin skin. Father never struck him. He was a friend, gone most of the time, but a mate.

For his seventh birthday, the girls clubbed together. They cycled into town of a Saturday, shrieking their rival ideas to the wind. Belinda wanted to get him a watch, Julia an atlas.

Then he can find his way around!

He can't tell time, though – how's he going to know when to come back?

Exactly – we never see him again!

They bought a watch, a watch that had to be taken back for it did not tick. And without a tick it was no watch. But on the day, they proudly jumped on him to wake the celebrant. They poked the watch into his mouth.

Mother grew worried at his indifference to her. A distant guilt troubled her, a concern at her dislike for him, if anything a faint hatred of his weediness. She had no thoughts on the matter. But her revulsion from his bowed, powerless, white limbs disturbed her. She sought God on the matter. He said to buy Christopher an extraordinary gift.

Here you are, my darling, she purred, descending from the heights to offer him a box. Mummy loves you.

Christopher turned away to peel the present. It was a small oblong box containing a gold-nibbed pen. From her pocket, Edna withdrew a bottle of ink.

So you can write me lovely long letters when you're all grown-up and gone.

He forced a sickly yellow grin to his face.

Edna beamed, a deep gorge widening through her cheeks, a rumble of laughter shaking her breasts and rising to nod her head.

He likes it! – he likes it! don't you, darling!

Jack sidled in between them, sheltering the boy and clutching a podgy guinea-pig, dappled white and brown. The girls squealed.

Oh Daddy, is it ours?

It's yours, Chrissy – what are you going to call it?

Christopher blinked to let the pleasure colour his face. He placed the pen behind him. The guinea-pig raced to the far fence. Jack paced about, irritated.

It's tame, it is – I made sure.

Get it!

The animal quivered far away, then ran hectic through the cabbages. The family, hectic, followed.

Jack had built a cage from an old pallet, fronting it with wire. Two hours later, Oscar was jailed for life. After another hour's drubbing he settled. Christopher poked carrots to the detainee.

Mother dressed down her husband for not telling – how dare he connive to upstage them all! He could have said something! He had not breathed a word. Was she sharing a house with a stranger, a rebel? Had she known, she would have bought a wife for Oscar. Jack blinked, inscrutable. His relations with his son were a separate affair.

Belinda and Julia squatted sullenly on the swings. The brat ignored his watch. It lay, stopped, on the kitchen table. They disliked boys in general, but had lowered themselves to be nice for this one's birthday. And look where it had got them. Men, they had heard Mother preach, were uncaring, mindless slobs. And even when you did their thinking for them, they showed no gratitude.

15

Christopher sidled indoors to get some more carrot. In the hallway, Edna stood jabbing the air beneath her husband's nose.

And if you ever tell me how to treat my son again, she hissed – I'll – I'll – I'll tell you what I'll do – I'll leave, I will – I'm sick of it, do you hear?

Be quiet woman.

Don't you tell me what to do – I've had it up to here . . . She sliced her neck with a palm. He's your son, so get out there and make his birthday a good-un!

Christopher snuck from the kitchen, scooping up the guinea-pig, and took a secret exit from the garden. The girls silently watched, sucking thumbs. He vanished into a drainage trench. Occasionally a golden head bobbed in the bent grasses. He could go, for all they cared, the ungrateful wretch.

He stopped, wearied, in the shadow of an alder. Tying a noose about its neck, he let the pet flounce in a circle about a stake. He squatted and dabbed at a wound – Oscar had nipped his wrist. The blood flowed freely over white skin, It wasn't Oscar's fault, he just hadn't been trained yet. He was bound to hate people around him. It was his way. He might change, he might not. It didn't matter. A heron stood knee-deep in a dyke, its wild head flicking a gaze across the flats. The boy watched as the bird stabbed water, retrieved the silver muscle of a fish and beat the air with great grey wings. It was nice to be away, to squat and watch nothing. To feed Oscar handfuls of torn grass. To lick a finger and taste the tang of blood. But he grew lonely and bored with being still. He could not move, the guinea-pig was not ready and he might be seen. He had to stay till they wept over him. And he wanted to prolong his absence for ever, to punish them, to get the girls a telling-off. If only it was just him, if they had never been and he was big and strong. At this rate he would never equal Father. He wrapped a finger and a thumb about his upper arm. It was measly and seemed to be thinning. The blood must be sapping from all his muscles and soon he would be no bigger than Oscar. Seven years growing, down the drain! He leapt up and released the guinea-pig. There were no figures chasing him or shouting on the plain – only the tree and the distant smudge of house. The sun was moving. If the sun moved they'd all move! He stumbled across the gluey marsh. One day, he would run away and, before leaving, set off a big bang to pay them back for all their sins. But he loved Daddy and wanted most of all to have Daddy look at his cut to stop the loss of blood.

Edna had gone upstairs to have a lie-down. Jack stood, sullenly stirring her a pot of tea.

Your mother's tired, he mumbled to the boy. What's with your finger?

Oscar bit me – doesn't hurt.

Jack stooped to wipe and tie the wound. He held the quivering skeleton of boy for a moment, then roused him to think of delights to come.

There's a cake and some sweets and a treat I'm not to tell you about – and you'll never guess what I've got . . .

But Christopher did not trust the man, he stood back and wondered why they had not chased him, why he was not needed. And why his father seemed sad and was lying to him. He obliged him and played along.

The girls swung back and forth in their Sunday best, lace and ribbons scraping the mud, backs bowed and the folds of stomach gathered beneath straining buttons.

He's back.

He'll go again.

VII

Belinda started at the Secondary School. For a year the sisters were divided. A minibus trailed about the hamlets and the cottages, collecting children for classes at Olchfa, eight miles away.

School became less an escape from home than a cockpit in which the jabs and digs of mocking kids riled her to violent resentment.

At home, a calm unhappiness descended, a misery which, unspoken, festered in the hearts of the women. Belinda felt it most grievously, a winding to her stomach, a sudden breathlessness at her plight. Jason Darnley and his mob had ascended, a year before, and

17

marshalled about themselves a brotherhood of boys. On Belinda's first day, they made their presence felt.

Get your tits out, big sister!

Or are they flab like the rest?

She was ashamed in a new way; a sexual intelligence now ridiculed her: the language of repulsion. A half-formed consciousness of attractiveness stirred in adolescent minds. Belinda was not just fat, she was ugly and she made you feel sick.

Urgh! I saw Belinda Fishen in the nod! Guess what! She hasn't got a fanny! Eurgh!

She overheard and, broken, limped to the toilets to sob. Avoiding the mirror, she hurried to a cubicle and wished herself dead.

Edna guessed as much, within the year – she guessed the root of the unhappiness. Julia, unprotected by a bigger sister, subsided to morose silences at dinner. Occasional explosions from both girls left slammed doors shivering in their frames, shattered vases reeling on the tiles.

She tried to talk it out, recalling her own tormented youth. Neither daughter was impressed. Their resentment lay much deeper: that she had, knowing this, then happily borne more like herself, that was the fault. Why couldn't they have been born to someone thin?

This could not be said, so smouldered in unquenchable moods. Edna prayed for them both, calling on the Lord to destroy their oppressors. She locked up all her pills.

Dr Davies, the family GP, was told in secret of Belinda's troubles. He looked gravely at her plumpness and pronounced her obesity hereditary.

It's big bones and your glands, he advised. Nothing to be done I'm afraid – just learn that folks is made all different – no one's better than another – those boys are rude and horrible – you ignore them.

It was muddled advice and Belinda's muddle worsened.

Julia followed a year later and, the weaker of the two, retreated into silence in class, broken by outbursts of sobbing.

Oh, there's two of them! Look, look! *Two* bouncing bubbles – boing, boing, boing! Is that a mirror, B'linda?

Belinda learned to fight back. When mocked, when called 'Balloon' or 'Sponge' or 'Tubs', she bitterly avenged the gibe. She made it her business to gather dirt on the ringleaders, gossip to throw like acid in their laughing faces.

Gorgeous arse, Belinda, cried Jason Darnley, to jeers.

Little dick, Jason – what size are you?

Damn sight smaller than you, lard-arse!

Damn sight too small for anyone, I've heard!

But the return blows never raised the laughs. They only made her feel less paralysed, less helpless. Worse still, Jason Darnley had develped a beauty which all the girls admired, even her. His blond boy's bowl-cut had been styled and centre-parted. It fell in golden curtains over each temple, quivering as he denounced her as a hog.

Wiggle, woggle, butter-belly, he chanted, pointing her out, his vivid eyes electric under dark brows.

He was taller than his mob – they clustered round him like lesser plants hungry for sun. And he steered them up to the heights of the playground from where all could hear the chants.

There she goes – look at bus-bum!

Fuck you, Jason Darnley! you and your small-penis mates – suck them off, do you?

Besides, Julia added, momentarily bold – It's big bones that does it, not fat, so there!

And to the chorus of hyena squeals, Belinda led her sister downhill to the lea of the wall where they soothed each other, swearing God would take vengeance. Skinny friends laid arms around them, murmuring consolation, secretly relieved mockery was not fired at them.

Jack cleared out the attic and furnished a further bedroom. Edna said it was best the girls share a room no longer, not with the phase they were going through.

He pasted to the wall cream paper dotted with tiny oak-leaves. Edna hung thick linen curtains at the foot-square window. A candlewick spread covered the bed under the eaves. Edna gave up her dresser and mirror for the room. Belinda won the fight over who was to have it – she was bigger and older and more grown-up.

From her desk, she could see the soft pewter of the river and the railway ridge, a pencil line across the mud at Burry Port. She dreamed herself beautiful, always the feminine and silver-blonde beauty in the tales of Enid Blyton, Arthur Ransome and Laura Ingalls Wilder. Isolated, in the wilderness of marsh, hidden in the pale cream loft, she could be anyone, she was slim – there were no boys to blush at her weight or girls for her to envy or sister and mother to remind her what she was and what she would be.

And as if hard dreaming would bring it to pass, she wished and wished to lose her weight. Then, committed to the idea, she undid her dressing-gown, raised her nightie and inspected the mass of cells in the mirror.

It was a full-length glass. Jack said there was nowhere in the house where Edna could stand and see herself entire, reflected. She must remember bits, then alter angles and memorise the rest. So, Jack said, his wife only saw herself in pieces. She was a collage not a portrait, an exploded sun.

Belinda started way back across the room, flashing as it were, opening the flaps of gown and her eyes simultaneously. She moved closer. It was the light, the light that made her ugly. She switched on a small side lamp. A rosy hue coloured her thighs and stomach. It was a little better. She stared again, but it was so difficult to hold your own gaze, to recall what you had seen. She had to keep staring. But it was hideous, so she could stare no longer. *What* was hideous? She grew angry at herself. She must not be prejudiced. And she looked intently at each part, the swollen belly, the broad white thighs and the double chin. Breasts were barely visible around each nipple, but mother said they were there and she must start thinking about a bra. Her upper arms could not rest vertical, nor could her knees meet without squeezing. She was deformed, leastways when you looked at Marya she was – Marya and her elegant poise, her willowy arms and flat stomach! And all the rest – she could handle being fat like Sian, the one who had a problem with her size but took some tablets and is better now. If only Dr Davies had said Here's some pills – knock them back – you'll be six stone when you wake up in the morning. Why couldn't you choose to be fat? Then fat people would be happy. Then the taunting would be fair. But it was useless. She would stop eating for a while. That was one thing she could do. And she would not look in the mirror for a year. Mirrors were useless ways to see yourself. That way she might forget.

Edna found the bags of uneaten meals at the foot of the garden. Belinda fainted twice in one weekend. Mother worried, bought a book on anorexic Christians and celebrated her size all the more.

VIII

The lease was up on the cottage. The council, who let the property, had held the rent artificially low. Upon renewal, the holding would triple in price.

Jack and Edna had lived there for fifteen years. Children had been conceived, born and raised under its tiles. They had pebble-dashed the lower half, whitewashed the upper. Its vegetable-garden was a rich development of the soil. They could not leave.

I'll have to work, moaned Edna. You never allowed it but –

I'll not allow it, Jack responded weakly.

So? So we move! – we leave our lovely home?

Her lower lip and chin set up a wobbling. He knew the signs and, after a show of disgust, capitulated. She would take a job in an office. It dismayed him, set an anger aflame in his core, a dread that she would cease to work for him. He needed her, but secretly assuaged the pain with thoughts that now he would see her even less and the ladies' days would come to an end.

Christopher bounded in, froze and stared – his father lay sprawling across the bulk of Mother. She had her arm about his neck and was pulling his head to her open mouth. The boy backed off.

What is it? Jack softly said.

Nothing.

Never seen me kiss Daddy before?

The boy shuddered and loitered in the kitchen.

Julia's got a boyfriend!

No I haven't. Shut up, B'linda!

She had not got a boyfriend, but was most desperately in love with Allen Griffiths. His family attended their Baptist chapel. To Julia's mind, God had shone a torch from heaven, its beam had alighted on Allen's scalp, the man was to be her husband.

Yes you have – you said.

What's his name Julia? asked Edna. Jack uncoiled himself from her arms. He grew disturbed at the stirrings of sex in his daughter, she was doomed as he was doomed. Sentenced to years of need, latching-on to the nearest and easiest supplier.

He's not anyone!

Edna stomped about the kitchen, provoking Julia to greater anger. She advised the girl snatch him before he had time to think. Remember, men are donkeys – take a sharp stick.

Mummy I'm not! It's just Belinda.

Jack assembled his kit for the evening shift. Belinda appeared, pins and grips in wet hair, a helping of mascara under each eye, blusher tinting every cheek.

You're not going already! moaned Edna to her restless husband. It's barely five.

Uh-huh.

Every night – rush, rush, rush – as if you can't wait to get away – aren't we pretty enough?

What does that mean?

A girl had started at the station, Edna had heard a name twice. Two syllables stuck like barbs in her midriff. She howled with pain.

Don't you try and cover up – we know your high jinks – never could keep a secret from me, Jack Fishen – read you like a book, I can!

Hush, woman.

I will not hush – not when my husband's running off like he's no responsibilities – not when me eldest daughter's gadding round bars like a common tramp.

Mummy, wailed Belinda – I'm not a tramp – what did you call me?

Running around with that Marya what'sherface – up to no good, I'll be bound – flinging yourself at anyone who glances!

I'm not – I do not.

Yes you do, B'linda, corroborated Julia.

And a daughter of mine, wailed Edna. Dressed up like a tart – how short is that skirt? You look like a hippo – well someone's got to tell you – if your mother doesn't who will?

I'm off, murmured her father, going.

You're not going anywhere till I've had my kiss goodbye – and a promise that you'll keep your eyes off that skinny witch.

22

She grabbed his donkey jacket, hauled him to within a foot of her, rearranged his collar and proffered her cheek.

Here . . .

He planted a kiss and raced to the door.

And . . .

I'm not going to go looking at another woman when I've got enough woman for ten men around here, am I?

Never can be too sure . . . answered his wife. These modern women – Mrs Lessing's run off with another man – and he's a deacon!

Jack sighed, smoothing his laquered black hair to his scalp.

Have you done?

Daddy, Daddy – can I have a lift? – wait!

Not until you tell me, interjected Edna, exactly where you're going, my girl – when you'll be back – who you're going to meet – whether they're Christians and why they're out on a Saturday night when there's church in the morning . . .

Mummy . . .

Lord knows, woman, you'll give yourself a heart-attack with all this nagging. If you want a lift, Belinda, make it snappy.

Christopher scrutinised his mother's misery, her concern, her nervousness. High up on a chair, he saw and felt her fear, knew that she wanted to hold them all to her, but could only stand and screech at the fission in her kitchen. And he felt happy that he had no need of her himself.

Edna took a part-time position as a secretary to a firm of defence contractors. She typed letters and sent bills to the M.o.D. The company made capacitors for use in missile targeting systems. It did not go with her principles, but she kept hush about it. The job let her leave at three to pick up Christopher from school.

IX

Christopher noticed before anyone else, before even Jack saw it in himself. The boy saw how his father no longer needed his wife. He knew they were at last the same. It had taken his father a while, but he had grown out of it. They were free. He knew, as they worked by

23

lamplight in the garage, on the car, that Father no longer cared and, like him, was excited by dreams of running away.

Thing is . . . his father murmured in his continuous, absent way . . . you've got to stay free – spanner.

Christopher knelt low and passed the tool.

Jack felt an urgent, thoughtless need to impress on the boy his terrors. He dribbled his quiet monologue. Increasingly, he felt the constriction of family. He was committed – the words scared him. It was a passive action – done to him, not by him. Edna – no, it was not a person, it was a sense – had been a friend, now she was a wife. He saw too much of her. They abused each other. Friends were wonderful things, the best. Wives were serpents coiled about you.

You got any friends, Chris?

Lots.

He was an isolated boy, speechless. He was quickened to listen, not to speak. Silence urged his father on.

My mates at work – you know? The boy nodded. They threw this party for me – don't tell your mother – she'd have a fit.

On his fortieth birthday, the lads staged a mock call-out. Racing to a supposed blaze, they drove him to a mate's flat. Inside, the entire squad – including Iris – were dressed up to the nines, popping champagne. He got wasted and did all sorts . . .

Who's Iris?

Woman at the station – telephonist – don't mention it to your mother.

The boy shook his head with vigour, the conspiracy flamed between them. He wanted more secrets, he wanted their covert world to flourish. The knowledge would hold them together. He had vague ideas of bribery. He was ebullient with pride.

Nothing really – just friends – she knows me.

And that was it, but between the sounds the boy imagined worlds. He divined how it was. The word 'Iris', muddled by him with his father's bloodshot eyes, took on the magic of liberation. Iris would see them all right, away from here, on their voyage. Iris would run away with them.

Under pressure of their worsening finances, Jack grew to hate the plaster walls of the cottage. The constraining fences and boggy marsh

24

jailed the wanderer. The rains which swelled the dykes sentenced him to the lounge.

Rebellious against the weather and his wife, he would gallop up Ryer's Down. He clambered the rough grass incline to peer through the mists to Sweyne's Howe, Llanmadoc and the watercolour sea. The hill was dotted with burial mounds, Arthur's Stone smudged a distant hill. Overhead, planets skidded, barely restrained from flying outwards to oblivion. And between Landimore and Oldwalls he found Samson's Jack, a huge pillar of rock erected as a memorial of what no one knew. Just the stone, a memorial to itself, its own tombstone, leaned from the turf, shielding him as he sparked a cigarette.

The tumultuous lounge, with its angry mother and nervous daughters, the flashing fire which threatened to blow up in their faces, the nagging debts – all this troubled him so much he came to wish for the soothing syrup of another, the laudanum of a voyage. He was a sea-going man.

Dad why don't we run away to hers? Christopher blurted impetuously.

Jack exploded.

Don't you go saying that – anybody could hear! Do you get me? Fool!

Christopher reeled as if struck by shrapnel. The abrupt response chilled his nerve. He doubted his own optimism. They seemed separate. Jack shuddered on hearing his own most guarded fantasy given words.

Each evening, he arrived two hours early for his shift. He loitered about the office. He lolled at the duty officer's desk. In the restroom, he pretended to read a paper. Then, with kindled lust, he stomped to the office.

Iris leaned back on her chair to read a paperback. Occasionally, the bank of lights ignited to flashes. Alarms sounded and he was thrown from her company.

She was Edna's age, a cynical forty-one, seeming to peer down on him from a year's advantage. He suffered it, she had a lulling eye, she was an opiate to his worry.

Slender, with a bush of dyed chestnut hair and eyes magnified by thick glass lenses, Iris was the widow of a fireman, Archie. She quietly mourned his passing and suffered Jack's obvious affections as a sedative.

So, they doped each other, dulling the ache of mismarriage. But there it stopped. Tormented by precedent, neither could accept the other. Superstition made a mockery of Jack's fantasy – he wished against Archie's ever having been, his being a firefighter, their having met. Because it had happened before, it could not happen again.

He waited in silent hysteria.

Edna knew in her heart, but could not admit it to her mind. She knew he did not believe in her god. She knew he did not believe in her. There was nothing she could do – so she made more noise, chatter and busying to cover the glances, voids which told of his indifference. She did not despair. He would not leave – he loved Christopher too much. And on thinking that, she spontaneously burst into tears, with hands in a bowl full of potato peelings. For moments, she shuddered with terror, tears running over the moraines of her cheeks. Then with violent reproaches she upbraided herself. He was a weakling, a puny runt, and the puny runtish men of the house would wilt without the women. And so she nurtured the beginnings of a false desire, a desire for Pastor Parsons.

The recently drafted minister had moved from Rochester to Penclawdd to be near his mother. Edna met him on two occasions. She preached at his chapel. With distinction she waged war on demons. He glowed in adoration from the front pew. And she had coyly ignored his gaze. She refused his invitation to share lunch. She had been a good girl, and not many girls would have been good in her position! She wiped beneath her glasses with the tea-towel and sniffed.

As she had told the girls, many men adore big women. She celebrated the beauty of the enormous. Her size was her great beauty. If a man adored a woman, he would welcome her immensity – she could be his shield and protector, his vast unlimited planet. Pastor Parsons was obviously a reasonable man. He saw that there was no finer woman than a strong one. And why only have an illimitable spirit? The girls had stared in horror at her words. But they would see, they would understand.

On her next visit to the Pastor's chapel she accepted his invitation to lunch. Boisterous with desire, she flirted with him on the short journey to his house. She slapped his buttocks as they entered the door. And she felt a sudden overwhelming lust. She was about to tweak his bobbing earlobes when she noticed the gardenful of pensioners and Youth League kids. The welcome had been general. She sank to desolation and made her apologies for leaving so suddenly.

X

The round table dispersed its family. Christopher fell off his chair and, again, cracked his skull. Julia refused to eat with the family – saying Christopher's filthy habits made her sick. She relocated before the television. Belinda joined her, picking at her meals, stowing them in plastic bags to be hidden later. Jack was rarely at supper – Sunday lunch became an occasional affair, posed for guests, not observed by family.

They could not bear the sight of each other. They separated to rooms and hovered alone, traipsing across a patch of carpet, listening hunched to the radio, escaping into a book, dressing up in different outfits.

Jack took Christopher fishing of a Saturday afternoon. He met Edna to conduct high-tempered squabbles over money – how were they to manage? Rarely did he see the girls.

Belinda had fallen in with a bunch of contemporaries in Gowerton. About the marketplace and war memorial, they leaned, shouting, smoking, snogging. In the bus-shelter, they flagged down buses till they stopped, then waved them on. In high anxiety, they waited for something to happen. At nine of a summer's eve, they would disperse. Belinda caught the bus home, staring furiously at her ghost in the window, hating the sun for dying.

She had come to hate even Julia. Her sister was a double conscripted to follow her around. When the irritant asked to come along, Belinda told her she could not.

Why not, B'linda?

Because you're not like me – I don't like you anymore – so shut up!

Wounded, Julia retreated to her room and dreamed Allen Griffiths would ride up on his motorbike and sweep her off to the centre of Swansea, buy her a martini, kiss her gently, then hard, then gently again, and show her what a Frenchie was. She thought she saw him one evening. As she stared from the prop of her hands out to the furnace of sunset, a Yamaha 750 moaned past. But it couldn't have been him – a girl was on the back and Alice said he definitely had not got a girl.

Belinda met Mark just after Christopher ran away again. Her brother blurted out some reference to his father's unhappiness, Edna struck out at him. He left in the night. Police found him forty-eight hours later, sleeping in a dustbin on Swansea docks. He had been ambitious to work his passage to America but they said no boats ever went to America now. Edna couldn't see why he wanted to go there – the Americans wouldn't put up with his rudeness.

Christopher was subject to occasional outbursts of obscenity. Edna tried to have this clinically diagnosed as a syndrome. Doctors said he was simply a quiet child who stored up all he heard and repeated it at intervals, mangled, perverse, shocking yes, but just like a spoken dream.

You know Dad's unhappy but you just ignore it – and we're going to run away one of these days and never come back, see if we don't – you drive us to it, you do, and the girls – Dad says men shouldn't live with women they should rent them . . .

Edna whacked him good and hard, more for the reportage than his insolence. He was not an insolent child, rather just taken with speaking out what he had heard, saying how he saw things. And that he did see things a little odd – well, she could do nothing about that. But, by God, she could belt him one, knock it out of the poor mite.

It's best to let him grow out of it, Dr Davies said. Leave him be.

Edna saw a legion of demons possessing her boy and thought it best to get them out of him quick sharp. She was certainly not going to leave them be. She prayed over him, took out a book on DIY exorcism from the church library, and said the necessary over his head.

Oh Lord – relieve this your child of all who is possessing him – take the unclean word from his mouth – strip it from him, Lord – wipe it out – send those demons back to where they came from, Lord – they've got no right interfering with my boy!

Christopher stared at the distant guinea-pig and the distant river and distant America and planned his next getaway and his next blaze.

Jack heard little of the fracas, he was too overjoyed to see his prodigal son, too eager to extract promises the lad would not do it again – not without his daddy anyhow.

Belinda sniffed haughtily at his loss and return. Celebrations on his being found were not enjoyed by either sister. Edna cooked Christopher's favourites, lamb chops. Fatty, greasy lumps of meat were a thin person's food. Belinda chewed and secretly stowed the morsels in her pocket. She was watching her figure.

For in Gowerton town centre she had met Mark. She had fallen in love. She willed herself to it, urgently, feverishly forcing the donkey of her desire to feel, feel, feel like she had never felt before. She baptised herself in emotion, wallowing and snorting joyously in the mudbath. This was a new indulgence, a self-willed delight drawn up from the well of her self. She could sit and say his name as a mantra and, silently, slowly, the slopping bucket of feeling would rise to her throat. She paused to let the stars burst in her head, then subsided to a murmur and a soft oily smile.

He was a dolt-headed youth, a reprobate and a waster, a wanderer and good-for-nothing – all in the opinion of Edna, who snarled at him when he was first announced at the kitchen door.

Mark Sharp was a dull-witted fellow, illiterate in all languages save those used on motorbike petrol-tanks. He was able to spot and name a make, the year and engine size at 500 yards.

'Lo, Mrs Fishen – my name's Mark.

Mummy, this is Mark – isn't he nice!

Hullo, Mark – you be careful with her and keep your hands clean – do you hear me? If you want a word with Jack he's in the shed.

Mother!

Belinda strutted belly out for the first time in years. It mattered not a jot what she looked like, she was loved and she loved. Beneath the apple-trees, she reclined and read to him the Song of Solomon. He upended his Suzuki on the lawn and stripped the gearbox down.

Julia stared with fury from an upstairs window – somehow prayers had got mangled in the saying. Belinda had got the biker and not she. Anxious to deduce the magic ingredient from Belinda's wardrobe, she tried on outfits, make-up, handbags, shoes and turns-of-phrase.

When Belinda saw her in a favourite dress and heard her use a pet saying she rounded on the girl:

You! You always tried to copy me, you did, and now you won't let me alone – stop trying to be me! – I hate it – it's like having a shadow that lives!

Julia cowered. She did not like being found out, her life went on in secret. Discovery of her disguise shamed her – especially in a full kitchen.

Mark made no attempt to rein in his girlfriend's savagery. He was a man of few words and fewer thoughts. Those he had, revolved principally around two-cylinder internal-combustion engines and his girlfriend's genitalia. Belinda adored such a man. Unconsciously, she obeyed her mother's sermons and provided the thoughts for him to put in his head.

He was not a Christian fellow – he was enamoured of the ancient mysticisms of pagan England as passed down to him by those musicians bikers admire. And Belinda was no evangelist. But she persuaded him to say the requisite words so he could enjoy Edna's shepherd's pie and peas of a Thursday evening.

I love the Lord, Mrs F, he announced stiffly. I do.

He did not develop the point. Edna looked at him, then at Belinda. She tried to detect the hoax but decided not to disbelieve.

Mark had his uses. His resurrecting Belinda from violent self-hatred did not go unnoticed. However, Jack's decline concealed the shift in family atmosphere. On another occasion, Mark raised the alarm when Christopher ignited the daffodils – the boy had doused the patch with petrol before lighting the lot. He said, sometime later, in an outburst, he wished to see how the yellow trumpets would respond to flame.

Have you ever wondered, Mummy, how yellow flowers and yellow flames would look just for a moment, a quick safe bang, have you, Mummy?

Edna thrashed him good and hard for torching her prize daffs, but later learned the value of tuning in to his mad monologues. They gave him away. Similar to Julia's *faux pas*, they revealed the soul under the make-up. His interminable silences were the batteries charging. They gave up their solar energy in a flash of emotion.

Mark ignored Christopher, never acknowledging the pale wisp of a boy who stood observing all he did to the motorbike.

Go 'way, Chris! whined Belinda.

The boy backed off, hands behind back, then remained thoughtfully scrutinising the bowed mechanic.

He guessed before Belinda and Mark knew it themselves, that they would run away, return penniless, move into her room together, give birth to a child and marry only when Edna threatened suicide if they didn't. Christopher had a way about him.

When Mark's motorbike was fixed, Belinda suggested they take a holiday, ride to Pembroke or Tenby, with a tent on the back. She did not wait for an answer, made arrangements and, with the sleeping-bags rolled on the back of the bike, she told Edna.

You're what! You are going no such place, my girl – you're staying right here until I'm good and ready and not before! Get off that bicycle!

Mark blinked glumly at the woman, Belinda goaded him to try it on. Fearing the larger of the two, he dismounted.

You're a lily-livered fool, Mark Sharp! screeched Belinda. She ran weeping to the house.

She had promised to give herself to him in his one-man tent in a field on Overton Cliff. That was to be their first time. Instead, outraged by her mother's draconian edict, she stomped upstairs, removed her knickers and waited with knees raised for him to come and get her.

Later, she discovered Edna had sent him home. And the simpleton obeyed her mother. Belinda retired, in the heat of composition, to plot their getaway. Edna placed her in purdah, gated until her sixteenth birthday – seven weeks off. Julia silently rejoiced – having lovers under her nose was bad enough, having them joyriding along the coast, unspeakable. Her imagination would have made it a hell.

Edna flagrantly rejoiced, telling her Friday evening ladies' group she had saved her daughter from barbarism, from the devil himself. She barred Mark from the premises. He mended his bike on the opposite verge, hailing Belinda at her top window, watched by Christopher from the lawn.

XI

Allen Griffiths was a pious man, a seventeen-year-old protégé to Pastor Parsons, a youth of God. His prayers were the longest in the Youth League. His motorbike was the largest. He stood in Pastor Parsons' study, hands held high, making war in the heavens. Julia gawped at him, never sucking her thumb in his presence. He, a man of God, would be the perfect lover.

Oh Lord – bring down your glory on this evil town – sweep clean these dens of vice – fill them with your majesty – use us, Lord, use us!

Julia cried Amen, raising her voice to drown out Amelia's mumbles. Allen was seeing Amelia, but not for long.

Julia tried to catch his eye, his bug's eye, the one which drifted off centre, parted company with the one staring at Amelia. The errant eyeball seemed to search to find her out, sliding round the pebble-lens of his glasses and shivering at her. Surprised to meet her stare it would flick away to centre on Amelia, then drift again . . .

She made up God's mind that she and Allen Griffiths should marry. They would take a chapel in Mid Wales on her eighteenth birthday. To this end, she used Edna's concordance to confirm it in God's word, to find every Bible reference to love and sing them out at his prayer meetings.

You stupid goose! Edna cried. Any fool can see he's gooey over that Amelia – stop making a laughing-stock out of yourself, girl!

Julia retorted that God had said so and did she doubt God's word? She had put her faith in God and look what she got for it! A rebellious mother!

At Bible Studies, Youth Group and Sunday afternoons at the Pastor's house, Julia would plonk herself next to Allen. There was no point in hiding your light, she reprimanded Alice Bishop – who also nurtured a fiery passion for the godly Griffiths. Best to speak out God's word, not whisper it. That was what Allen had said anyhow.

Allen . . . she asked gravely. Do you think Ezekiel was right when he said . . .

She looked to her Bible.

As is the mother so is her daughter?

Why – of course it's *right*, Julia – it's the word of the Lord, Julia – it's God speaking through Ezekiel.

His left eye twinkled at her, his right drifted off to find Amelia.

But, but it can't be! she cried to lure the right eye back to her. Amelia's mum is an atheist!

Julia wanted him to say it was and it was not right. Her sense of doom was magnified – she was becoming a replica of her own mother. Life was just waiting to see how you would evolve into your parent. Before any more damage was done, she wanted Allen to sweep her away from Edna.

She calculated the days remaining until her sixteenth birthday –four hundred and eight. To Alice she cited Isaiah – 'In that day seven women shall take hold of one man.' Edna always preached that a man needed many women. Amelia was a weak and colourless thing, tiny, limp, she would snap in pregnancy. What a preacher needed was a house of women, like Jesus, a team of seven – well, maybe three –wives.

Alice mentioned that her uncle was a Mormon and Julia told her to stick to the point. It was important. But when Julia suggested it to Allen, his condemnation was complete.

That's rot! he cried. Amelia, Amelia – little Julia reckons I should take seven wives!

That's not very nice is it, love? simpered his girlfriend.

Julia felt the words 'little Julia' and 'love' like crossbow bolts. She staggered to the lawn and began to walk home. She pleaded with God to avenge her humiliation. She would devote herself to a celibate life if only, if only he would see off that Amelia, make her really unhappy. And when, a year later, Allen Griffiths passed under the forty-foot trailer of a juggernaut at the crossroads on the Carmarthen road, travelling at more than sixty miles an hour, and parted company with his holy head, Julia recalled her prayer and praised the Almighty that he had heard her lamentation.

Our Julia's really come out of her shell! remarked Edna after his death. She's talking of going to Bible College – her mother's daughter!

The second of her daughters worked her first miracle in the Sixth Form college Christian union – healing in a remarkable fashion the earache of a bystander – this was followed by a series of talks given by Julia, on the subject: 'Miracles in the Modern Age'. Her audience at Youth Group were sufficiently awed to assist her in organising a Healing Meeting – two headaches were cured, thirty backsliders recommitted their lives to the Lord and a woman believed she was going to be relieved of a boil on her neck. At twenty, Julia would devote her life to healing the mentally handicapped of Senegal and her mother would swell.

XII

One evening, Jack was found to be drunk on the job. He was suspended for one month pending an inquiry. He did not tell Edna.

This, like much of his life, grew out of a mangle of absurd and inept plotting. In a spiral of hopes he had scripted a pledge to Miss Iris. The sermon-notes, less a letter, more unintelligible points about which to talk, fell into enemy hands.

The lads were not ignorant of his desire. They considered it in bad taste – setting out to bag a dead colleague's old lady. One approached Jack with advice to back off, ignore the woman, find another if he wanted so badly to cheat on his wife.

Jack recoiled. He presumed Miss Iris had been told. He steeled himself. And, necking a small bottle of whisky, loped into her office.

Iris – can I have a word?

She welcomed him in, he had meant outside. He sat down.

It's like this – am mad for you – I am – don't know what they've told you – I can't do a thing about it – will you. . . ?

She had been shaking her head for some moments. He rose, apologised as if he had asked for a raise from the boss, and limped out. The alarm was raised, a house fire in Llangennith. The duty officer smelled his breath as they boarded the engines. Jack denied he had been drinking. He was barred from the job, breathalysed and suspended.

To pay the rent and buy a car for Edna, he had taken a set of unsecured loans. He had arranged a fourth to supplement his pay, to fund his drinking.

Now, on half-pay, with six nights each week to kill, he had furtively to find a job.

He took work on the taxis, driving an unlicensed cab throughout the night. Mostly, he waited at the station or took a call from the rank. It was unremunerative, but it gave him a place to hide.

A police officer checked his licence. The authorities had enforced a ban on unlicensed cabs. After only ten nights' work, Jack was taken off the road.

For two nights he worked alone, picking up odd fares from street-corners. The practice became suddenly dangerous when he carried a friend half-a-mile. He let him off without charge. That, he hoped, would kill the rumour.

On his twelfth night in town, he sat for ten hours in the car, reading a manual on explosives. Every thirty minutes he walked the block. The volcanic frustration mounted.

In a fit of sexual fury, he telephoned Miss Iris. His desolate mood was complete. He hadn't spoken to his family in months. His wife – he wanted to murder his wife. His son, he loved his son but couldn't understand a word he said. Would she. . . ?

Out of sympathy, Miss Iris offered him the key to her flat, on condition it was vacant by her return at six a.m. Jack thumped the glass of the telephone booth with joy.

Promise me, Mr Fishen – please?

Iris – I'll be out at five – I love you.

Six is fine, Jack – you love your wife – that's quite enough for one man.

He mooched about her pale, plain flat. He could not sit still for more than an hour. A painting of a lily particularly disturbed him. It was her. He vacuumed the carpets, he polished the woodwork and, at four of a morning, dug her rosebed. At dawn, he stood – with lights out – staring at the street till the vivid violet light blinded him. Then she appeared, tall and beanpole-thin under a velvet hat. And he checked everything and backed out, running pell-mell down the fire escape. He was her protector – the part charged him with eroticism. He stared deep into the violence of sunrise and wished for a reincarnation as guardian to one as serene as Miss Iris. It would be nice.

Of course, it was she who protected him. Almost, that is. For Edna called the station to contact her husband at ten o'clock on the Wednesday of the fourth week. His wife asked Iris if she could get a hold of Jack. It was an emergency – his son had destroyed the kitchen. The oven had exploded. The fire was out now, but in the panic his daughter had escaped with her good-for-nothing boyfriend.

Iris said she would tell her husband, they were out on a call. Iris telephoned her flat. Jack, ordered not to answer the telephone, remained obedient to his protectress. Iris flapped, not being able to up sticks and go tell him. She had gone soft on her housekeeper, the man whom she never saw, the man who spring-cleaned every night, who dug her garden, who left simple notes declaring adoration about the place.

For eight hours she let the matter rest. Oh, she telephoned the flat at intervals. But never rang for long – she was impressed by his solidarity to her commands.

At dawn, she returned early, caught him before he left. He blenched and embraced her. He admired his son's ingenuity. He envied Belinda her freedom. He grew dizzy, telling Miss Iris how he couldn't return. His wife would brain him. Despite her coolness, he knew she liked him. He could tell that much – could he come back later, before she went to work? He needed to speak with her. She nodded.

Edna had rung a colleague of his. She had discovered his fiction. On his bleary-eyed arrival, she tore his head off. For four hours, the volcano simmered and raged and simmered again. He lolled, careless, against the broken kitchen door. The insurance would take care of the kitchen. Belinda could take as good a care of herself as anyone. Let her be.

And you'd just let it go, wouldn't you! raged his wife. Whoosh! Bang! Up in smoke! All we've laboured to build!

Ah, there's nothing built, Edna – don't kid us any longer – Chrissy can't wait to get his wings and fly – I've had it – I got debts up to me eyeballs – our Julia's gonna be off soon – I never get a moment's peace – Belinda's gone – see it!

God . . .

Edna wept, staggering, from foot to foot, her smock swaying from her breasts, sufficient room beneath to hide the entire family. She blundered about the wrecked kitchen, her hair flat, without her glasses, her eyes red and swollen. She was extinguished.

It's that Sheila, isn't it!

There's no Sheila, Edna – no Sheila – only Iris and you – and right now I'm as good as finished here.

He spoke dully, disinterested, weary.

Iris! Iris! Who's this Iris? This devil woman who's wrecked my home? Who is she? I'm going home to me mother!

Edna wandered bewildered from corner to corner. But her mother was little good to her, quivering with imbecility in Morriston Hospital.

Jack drove Christopher to school, then on to visit Iris. She awoke to his knock and peered, reptilian, from behind the door.

Aw Jack, don't, we can't!

He pleaded, but she was insistent. He couldn't run away to her, he must go back home, say he hadn't meant to leave, sort it out. There was no point, she had learned that. All her life she had wanted to run away, but there was no point.

Iris . . .

Jack – go home – go to bed – wake up – start it all over – I want to sleep.

Outside, the roses were in bloom. The town wailed in its dirt-brick corridors. Christopher stood at the corner of the playground and told fortunes, Julia talked to Alice about boys. Belinda, to her terror, mislaid her virginity. Edna slept. Jack stumbled, sleepless, through a precinct: a mobile axis to the whirling, orbiting, fleeing, chasing shoppers pooled about him – starry galaxies in nebulous chaos, running home. He looked to the clouds. Two swifts, embroiled in flycatching, turned tail on the wind, hung in ovals, floated sideways and flapped forever to stay in the same place.

He found his car, after a day's searching. The door was open. The boot was closed. The swifts were stuck on the glass. In the blue of the clear distance he could see America. He drove to the sun. And a sign led him the wrong way. He tried to steer back. But it's difficult, going back when you're going forward at such a speed. And all to stand stock-still.

XIII

They brought him home six months later. The runaway car had been crushed to a cube the size of a table. He was honourably discharged from the service, pension intact. The hospital treated his burns as best they could. But there was nothing to be done for a snapped spinal column. A crack in the head had stripped him of speech. But he was alive all right, no doubt about that – you could see from the blinks of his bloodshot eyes, and the dilation of his pupils and the vigour of his irises, and look – a tear!

It was good for Christopher to have his father at home all the time. And it was good for Jack to have his Christopher. What with Belinda's unholy racket and that lout Mark crashing around, a man needed a man he could listen to every now and then. He'd go crazy otherwise.

And as for Edna, well, now the Lord had taken his beauty away and left him a crusty old hulk, she felt – well, liberated, liberated to be herself – and all in all, yes she meant this from the bottom of her heart, she thought it was for the best. It's funny how you can see the Lord's handiwork in everything. Sometimes Christopher wheeled his father on the marshes and carried him across the dykes so he could see the river and the railway and the house and the town. He liked to be able to see – he liked living in a flat world.

And watching the slow shuffle of boy and man, she rejoiced that leastways now, her men could not run away, but must shuffle with her and her bad joints, and Julia and her veins, and Belinda's sickness, so like a family of walruses they shuffle – all together – families ought to be together – if the cells could hold together, the body would remain – imagine if all the planets suddenly decided to go their merry way! What on earth would happen to the sun?

The Church

I

Jack saw the pink house from the beach. Waking from a nap, he thought he dreamed the stucco walls and twelve sash-windows, savaged roof and central door. Though he daily traipsed from Newton to Blackpill, he had not noticed it before.

On the beach he piled sandcastles half-heartedly to pass the time. In contest with the sea, he re-sculpted the bay. The sea won over Jack, the city council won over the sea. Each autumn, bulldozers nosed the retreating sand back to the waves. And so it was that a man, a city and the sea came to be at war.

Besieged, he patrolled the bay. Napping on a different dune each day, his dreams of guerrillas thrusting petrol bombs under his canvas coat awoke him regularly at four. Mockery from passers-by did nothing to dent his war effort. He was a lone partisan against the city council, a terrorist in hiding from the law. In a daily concession to civilisation, he walked along the Oystermouth Road and into the White Rose for opening at five.

That afternoon, he paused to consider the unthinkable. He would alter the pattern of a life's monotony. He would adventure.

He tramped up and over the dune and verge. Perpendicular to his habitual trudge, he walked thirty paces. And by the high flint wall, he pissed a claim on wall and house and yard.

He had plans, he had faith in plans.

Having urinated at each corner of the derelict, he ventured over the border wall. He approached from the back. Avoiding the twelve-eyed glare of the mansion, unobserved by all save you and I, he trespassed.

The garden frothed to fill the walled plot. As he valiantly adventured, snapped grass-stems and broken elderflower sent up a pungent incense to his nose.

His nose, not bald, sipped the air, wary for antagonists. He sniffed for assailants. He had once been set upon by brigands who stripped boots and cap and coat. Muggers regularly turned him over, as he slept, to see what lay beneath. Thugs booted his behind as he waddled on a curving course from the bar to the bay. The city and even the dogs were his enemies.

Jack was not naïve about the imperfectibility of man.

The house had been bombed. Its eyes blown outwards, its roof scattered about the plot, it had rotted since the war.

A single ordnance dropped from a scarpering craft landed smack-bang in the upstairs loo. It tore balustrades and cornices to shards. It whipped the busts and statues to a moment's fission and left them mouldering on the lawn.

Beneath boots, he ground the nose of Apollo to dust. He stomped to a window. Peering through, he appreciated the total ruin.

Adventurous ivy had populated the premises. The spine of the plant had rent a gash in the wall. The house had been sliced into estranged halves, a cheese cleft by the wire of the plant.

Jack gained a purchase with his boot-toe on the stalk. He hauled himself aloft. He mounted step by step, handhold by handhold, up the sturdy plant. From the vantage of the roof he viewed the bay.

Five miles distant, the cement cubes blurred. A gust blew meringues of sputum from the waves. It flicked a lick of brylcreemed hair from Jack's nosy scalp.

As a rule, he frequented only the city's older districts. Those which bombers had gutted and architects had rebuilt held for him no magic. In his tramp from bed to bed, he elected to nose in only magically ancient worlds.

A sudden blast of wind as from a detonated device threatened to put a stop to both this tale and Jack's ambitions for the house. The gust nearly swept boots and their occupant from the ledge.

He was weary. He dismounted, not without caution.

Once down from the clouds, he rested in a grove of rhododendron and speculated on property in the air.

His voyage had tired him. Like all men of a certain age, he was anxious for a place of rest, a home to lease for his confinement.

He did not rush to secure property. He spent decades making notes on all sea-facing houses in these parts. Mother taught him well: the business of speculation was nine parts dozing, one part haste. Accordingly, following her death, he dozed for twenty-one hours and forty minutes each day. Most prudently, he divided the two hours twenty minutes haste between his afternoon constitutional and the stampede to his bed.

He had never owned property, not having capital. He had not inherited wealth, having thriftless forebears. He received a modest income from the state which with farsightedness he invested in his potential as a seer.

While dozing in the shading shrub, Jack foresaw the renovation of the house, how with his skills in architecture, painting and design, the shell might live with him in momentary rejuvenation, a flame coaxed reluctant from a dying coal.

He pulled up the coatsleeve from his one forearm. Mysteriously, his other had been misplaced in the trauma of birth. He set about a hasty start to his life's task.

Sixteen minutes remained before the landlord of the White Rose threw open his double doors and welcomed in the world. And Jack's appetite was greater than his ambition.

It drove him from his Eden as autumn gloom arose, evaporated from the hocks. He clambered over flints and in a half-run fled to where pump-handles drew half a quart of ale to his glass.

II

Jack discovered that through astute management of resources he could pay his way in the White Rose each morning and evening of the week.

To his inventor's mind this discovery was as great a leap forward as the devising of the wheel. It eased his passage from snooze to snooze and, as such, he preached, possessed all the ingredients of entre-preneurial genius.

Afternoons busily taken up dozing, wandering and speculating left only nine hours of night to organise. These could be obliterated in sleep, the location for which remained his bugbear.

He devoted his life to the solution of this puzzle.

Appetites for food, alcohol and sleep forced him into the exploiter's arms. To eat and drink and doze he must pay good money to a snitch. Pickpockets thieved his hoarded wealth, trumped up as landladies, barmen and waiters.

Life was a slow coming-to-terms with this reality. He made savings, he was no squanderer. Fleecing the feckless for drinks, shoplifting loaves and frozen fish, begging from the foolish pedestrian, flitting from lodgings, sleeping in the comfort of Oystermouth bus-shelter – these economies preserved monies for his great invention.

He was by necessity an early riser. His tormentors awoke him at dawn. Officious bus conductors commanded he move to less salubrious surrounds.

Big Barney Bucks sympathised but, with the incomprehension of the housed, could offer only poor advice to his mate.

Jacko, he slurred, I always said you should get yourself a place, haven't I? Haven't I?

Jack said that he had got himself a place.

He stared mournfully at the vastness of his mate whose generous contours gave him the look of a man jammed in a council bin, his head shivering with conversation, his arms like lagged pipes reaching to neck a half-pint of ale with each swig.

Barney, Jack said, in hope of cutting short the flow of bad advice – I have found meself a place – down road, biggish, nice – it needs a little doing up.

How you got that, then? Sold your arse?

Just renting – just renting.

Rentboy! Barney spluttered, victoriously repeating the wit so it should not escape the note of all. All ignored him. Jack continued to apologise for finding a property despite his sermons against ownership.

Barney, I need some advice.

Barney Bucks, plumber, master builder, tax evader and oracle was placed in his element. He laid his arms about his sides, having no alternative.

His expertise covered all continents of the construction world, his globe of a body all sites of renovation in the town. He could lay twenty bricks a minute in a cool climate. He could plane square a twelve-foot length of four-by-two without geometrical aids. He had built more than one hundred houses in the vicinity, tombstones to his having been.

To Jack's description of his designs, Barney whistled by inhaling several litres of air through clammed lips. Shaking his head, he dismissed ideas to roof the house with old slates, fit new floors, leave old beams be, paint over sodden plaster, frame glass in ancient slats. His scepticism was complete.

S'pose you could, he began sadly, you could – at a pinch – strip walls – start again – you'd bring the whole lot on your head – not worth putting a penny in a derelict . . .

Again he inhaled. He was a black-capped judge passing sentence. It was a solemn moment. Jack fled to refill tankards at the bar. On his return, Barney's head was still shaking in mournful half-revolutions.

Knew this bloke once. Never guess what he had planned – build a detached three-up two-down slap bang in the middle of that there beach! – that there beach there! Course, council wouldn't have it – imagine! mid the boats and surfers – tides each morning and evening – a home! Imagine raising three kids and a wife in that! – Wouldn't rate his chances of them or the house staying – and look: the lot vanished by morning!

Barney giggled, or rather he vibrated as a laugh exploded deep in the core of him.

Jack sipped beer and wondered at the man who conceived such a plot. He toyed with asking his name. He envied the imagination that saw no barriers to where man might build himself a hut, that did not bow to the gods of the common-as-muck mob, to common sense, to common law.

He vowed to press on, to ignore doubters' voices. At worst, he would become a story told by Barney Bucks in the White Rose bar. He offered his oracle a pistachio nut.

III

He moved his kitbag from a hole in the hills above Langland and stowed it in the hut at the end of the garden.

After clearing the ivy from within, he hacked with a stolen axe and clippers at the great stalk which clutched the back of the house.

With a scythe, he harvested grasses and elderflowers, convolvulus and dock. A lawn emerged. He broke into a gardener's lock-up in Newton Road and borrowed a mower. In bleak gloom, he brushed stripes on to the vast patch. Beneath the tangle of runners, briars and clematis he discovered paths, flagged stones testifying to an earlier civilisation. He pruned and cleaned, then in sudden glee hopped from stone to stone about his land.

Under cascaded ceilings, upper floors and ornament he found a tessellated floor, the marbles pure and unbroken. A layer of earthy debris concealed black and white squares from the damp.

Clearing this mosaic floor cost several days' labour. He put aside his mother's dictum on the division of his time. Mothers could not be obeyed in matters archaeological. Were she here, she would put up a fight. In her absence, he could alter the rules. Obedience to a dead goddess resurrects that divinity, restores her rule, relieves the obedient of the terror of making up their mind.

In courageous autonomy, Jack found a new serenity. He worked for six days without ceasing, save for sleep and recuperation in the White Rose bar. In the solitude of his walled plot he reconstructed earth. Safe from the sea and the city council, his pyramids remained in rockeries and castles, unobserved.

On the sixth day, having wheeled, in a barrow, all the rubble from the house and made of it a hummock at the foot of the lawns, he set to puttying paned glass into the sash-frames.

Smoothing paste along the crumbling bevels he fell to dreaming, mixing the tiled floors and moulding walls with the ghosted reflections of garden shrubs and path.

His eyes looked at themselves, traced the scorelines and crow's-feet, the gape of astonished mouth. As the light caught them, his few teeth mirrored cream, his ears eclipsed the distant wall. The silhouette of head was crowned with the swell of slickered silver hairs, and in the depths of the glass he swore he saw his double, a miniature resting on the garden wall.

He turned to scan swiftly the boundary. With terror, he feared he might be being watched. A cloud obliterated the sun, shadows dulled outlines. He laid the trowel and putty on the earth.

Wiping hands on thighs he patrolled. It was vital he convince himself not a soul was watching.

Even in the highest mood, Jack could not suffer for long the scrutiny of crowds. He lay on the sand for hours with closed eyes or sat entombed within a public loo just to stop being for a while.

Now here in this sterilised enclave it was more vital than ever to ensure he went unseen. If he could be without being seen, so much infliction would be relieved him.

He built up flints where they had fallen on his entry. With gates lashed more firmly together, house and garden were made impregnable.

He concluded his circuit and warily sat to lunch.

While working at a second-storey window he heard a voice:

Wha'choo doing that for?

He pretended not to hear, then grew fearful his unresponse would draw the curious close. He turned.

A brown figure insolently sat on the wall. Its head lolled to its chest, its arms splayed to support it. Legs without knee-joints pointed large feet at the mocked.

Jack stared boldly, then turned to work.

Don't want to go doing that, you don't!

The heat of the sun drew sweat to Jack's brow, the glass shone vivid blue. He slaved on.

House is finished, it is – di'n't nobody tell you?

A bird screeched in terror from the shrub. Jack turned, instinctive. The figure picked at stones, scattering fragmented flint to the soil.

Oi!

What!

Stop!

Why?

I said so!

S'not yours!

Tis!

How?

Jack had broken his silence, he clenched teeth in regret. Mockers, scoffers and cynics had distracted him all his life. Opening dialogues legitimised criticism. He would say no more.

But Jack was an impressionable man. He had no character to speak of, but what he had was chiefly formed from the jabs of the impertinent. He reeled.

You don't want to go doing that, mister – house is falling down – nobody worked that house for fifty years – you's behind the time! Ha! Bin ripped off, you have!

In the glass Jack could see the figure rise and tread the length of the wall. It paused, turned, then balanced along another perimeter. Closer to him, it leered, intent on seeing what was being done.

Go away! Jack whispered the stones.

He dropped inside the house to a scaffold made from stolen irons. He sweated vigorously. The onlooker had rattled him. He thought murder, but remembered mother's opinions on the matter. It would not do to bloody his hands in this his hermitage.

He moved to other windows to peer at his tormentor.

The brown figure scampered along the wall, stopped, looked up for several moments, scrutinising the house, then ran again.

Jack scuttled about, vainly searching for a weapon. He had not expected attack. He toyed with the axe, rejected it and crouched to view the figure. The sun peeped for a better look from behind a cloud.

It seemed to be a man by the crop of russet beard which frothed from the duffle-coat hood. And it could not be older than he, it had an agility he had not enjoyed for decades. It jumped fearlessly along the wall's crown, never venturing into the plot, searching for a view in the windows.

Jack grew agitated, racing from peephole to peephole. He feared it would actually venture further into the property, confront him, assault, or worse, rape his handiwork. It was most certainly an agent from the council, sent to terrorise him. He lost forever his serenity, the work had been seen.

The figure vanished. Jack spent the evening searching the gardens to determine it was gone, that it was not infesting the plants, that it was not hidden in one of the crab-apple trees.

That night he avoided the White Rose, staying instead to fortify the premises, to line the tops of the wall with shards of glass, to board up lower windows, to secure the doors. He stole a ladder, entered a first-floor window and hauled up the steps behind him. He was at last permitted sleep.

IV

The rains came with autumn.

To shield his work, he stole a vast tarpaulin from a lorry park. He bore it on his shoulders to the house. With ropes he slung it like a tent out of view below the ribs of shattered roof.

He sealed its edges with an ingenious guttering. The great sail of ceiling flapped in the storms, as if with flapping it might lift the house airborne or drive it out across the prom and on to waves that boiled in the bay.

The house resisted flight or launching. Jack worked dry and gloomy in the ark to the rattle of the roof. The rains sluiced along guttering and fell to the beds.

The lighting was the key, the way to perfect the illusion. He occupied days with wiring a set of fourteen lamps, carefully shaded to conceal the green canvas ceiling. The circuit was connected to the mains on the tenth day. The cavernous hold of the house blazed yellow.

He slung blackouts at every window. As if bombers might again cause catastrophe and render his world a shell, he flicked on lights only when each pane was shielded by a veil.

Desire to perfect the closed interior drove him. Taking Barney's counsel he stripped the rotten plaster from all walls. The labour cost him many exhausting hours, the obsession his evenings in the bar.

He was neither young nor old, nor ever had been, but the toll of labours such as these hastened ageing in his insufficient limbs. His arms grew muscular but scarred. His hair, ungreased, flowed thinly upwards in a cloud of silver; his eyes, reddened by the oyster's itch of dust, saw less well the vaulted ceiling and instead scrutinised the beauties of the floor.

Weeping at the hopelessness of ever plastering all four walls alone, he wished for sons, three sons with whom he might share the insane labours of his muddled mind.

But his numerous deformities dissuaded any woman from consenting to his plaints. No girl let him mount her to dispose of his cumbersome virginity. His chance to rear sons died with his youth when, one girl seeming inclined, he had refused, thinking another might respond. To refuse a hinted possibililty is to refuse the woman, and no others ever offered Jack a hint.

He waited, life-perpetuating optimism hoping for a chance. But his only company for decades took the form of Barney Bucks, a certain Mickey Bocks and a rapist, Mr Charlie Bick.

The three visited Charlie in his lodgings at the city jail – here he passed much of his not unhappy adult life, doling out observations on the female sex to Barney, Jack and Mickey Bocks.

Knowing him to be of an impressionable cast, Charlie suggested to Jack that he simply grab a woman and ignore her finer feelings on the matter. Jack failed ever to let this ideal become an act. His admiration for his mother, added to his own dread of brigands, fiends and thugs, made rape an inadmissible crime against himself.

Jack was exiled from the sexual world. As his appetites were most highly developed, this testifies to a resilience of character I had not thought he possessed.

Barney, Mick and Charlie wasted no time telling him of the difficulty of woman-handling. But with soft affection for his mother, Jack recalled a time when a woman had shown more fascination for his soul than all the men he had ever known.

And in a moment of extreme fright, he remembered that he had no friend in the world, that he had forgotten the years of his solitude, that aloneness only pained him when he looked back over its many years.

He suddenly wanted to befriend his antagonist. The brown-coated figure appeared every evening in the arbour, materialised from the tawny alders then faded to a cone of leaves awaiting bonfire.

It was insanity, to want an association with his scoffer. And yet if they could come to some agreement or better, familiarity, the dream might be realised.

Jack had not stopped ruminating on the figure since its first appearance. He loathed it, he adored it, he wanted only to murder it, he wanted it to become a friend. While labouring he feared it would bring the house crumbling about his ears.

Worry at this end drove him harder, as if by erecting his inner vision he would quash the ambitions of his twin.

Jack has, his doctors tell me, always suffered from delusions of oppression. They insist he is a free man, to his disbelief. He is free to do just as he wishes, he has no enemies. He begs to disagree. He knows of the evil in man.

He hung white sheets over the blistered walls, great shrouds through which the pale light of unshuttered windows made oblong murals. The cosmetics were almost complete.

To furnish the palace, he exceeded himself. On two nocturnal raids, he burgled antique shops. Four studded Regency chairs, a huge vase and a Persian rug were smuggled into the cathedral of the house.

In disturbed solitude, he sat enthroned, bored by completion, smoking a cigar butt, farting inaudibly to himself for want of company.

V

He looked over what he had created.

With parts of it he was not displeased. He paid particular attention to the stone outside the rear door on which he had intended of a night to dry his boots.

He felt, however, considerable distress at the shoddiness of the prior artificer's work. Poor beams, inept plastering and a lazy choice of window woods excited his disdain.

And closer inspection of his own incautious stringing of the roof, his hurried wiring, his rush to fortify the lower floors, his forgetfulness where kitchens and servants' quarters were concerned – all these brought on a fit which left him shivering on the floor.

He despised his workmanship. He loathed his impatience. But

most of all he regretted his wish to see his reverie made real in wood and stone.

That was the folly. To have presumed his vision might be duplicated in stiff, resistant elements, that was idiocy – a child's hope at recreating for his mother an illusion that had gripped his mind.

He took a hold on drifting sheets and strapped the hemp of it about his wrist. He repeated the distracted action about his stump. He would hang for a while.

Murmuring regret to his half-hearing ears, he let himself become suspended on the veils.

He kicked his feet and shrieked without enthusiasm, part hoping some invader would burst in and laugh. Then he fell.

A small fire was started by the explosion of fourteen lanterns. On striking the tiles, they disintegrated, the heated coils igniting oiled canvas, cotton and Jack's hairs.

For some time he thrashed about beneath the descended roof in a Samsonian struggle with the cloth.

Emerging, he found the ropes and wires and sheets of his most temporary world about his feet. Deprived of his silver hair and the uppermost layer of facial skin, he howled and bawled as if his shrieks would make his melodrama great.

No one wept, no one stirred with empathy. No one visited to calm his noise, nor to bathe his wounds. The curious were blocked by sealed gates and barricaded doors. The echoed squeals set off a sympathetic howling among local hounds. A while passed and neighbours grew relieved at the quiet.

Much later, on discovering the hidden ladder, Jack clambered from the charred but largely unchanged house. From without, it remained as it had been, a shell mocking interior decorators.

He expended much excess energy by many times kicking an inner wall. It remained intact, unlike the larger of his ten toenails.

The mutilation of his face and hand was aggravated by an over-eager mounting of the wall. Forgetting his farsighted installation of sharded glass, he rent the blistered palms and chin as with a slap he hauled himself aloft.

Without a bed, he slunk to the beach and, with much emotion, reunited himself with the sand. He burrowed a shallow grave and with the excavations built a modest pyramid to mark his presence. He laid his bruised decrepit body in the pit and buried all but a hooded head in beach.

And as he slept, the muddied waves corroded the contents of his kitbag, his mother's photograph and his spare boots. Gnawing gently at his tomb, waves ate round his ankles, under arms and behind his neck. In his first good wash for weeks, the sea lapped at his lugholes and plucked the wax from nose and eye and ear. He dreamed, smiling.

Totally immersed, the baptist failed to see the dove descending to the flooded beach.

Mother's Day

I

It was finished. After near-death in birth came the waiting. Jojo, a seven-pound complex of cells, was born.

Doctors hauled him from the womb to find the twisted toffee of an umbilical cord a noose about his neck. The face that would sprout a beard and discolour with forty winters was blooded blue. Egg-white eyes were lustreless in the fat flesh.

Execution stayed, his mother's son lay beached between towering thighs. Administrators of birth unknotted sausage-cords. With tubes of blood throttling his jugular, Jojo had been swiftly passing on to a perpetual womb.

Disentangled, scythed with broad bladed scissors and reknotted to a navel, his well-meaning lifeline shrivelled to a yolk.

Jojo wailed. Rich with oxygen, blood flooded his skull's cavities. The oiled face took on the hue and resilience of a peach. Mother murmured prayers. He was hoisted high by the heels. For his toils in the amnion, the doctor castigated him with flat of hand.

Shrouded in swaddling crochet, Jojo continued to waul. He shrieked, he sang, he mustered objections to his rescue. Nurses blushed at the vociferousness of his complaints. Brothers born that day craned necks to peer at the malcontent. Cots shivered with the rebellious load. And with one almighty explosion of rage, Jojo blasted liquid effluvium to dye his loincloth black.

Mother raised him in the profession of happy man. In pursuit of this end she told him new histories of his birth. It was a happy birth, just like those of blissful fellows, rounded human beings, pillars of the community.

With suspicion, he heard how his birth had been marked with an oleaginous ease. Mother told how her first and only son had sprung from the womb at a gallop, his feet working the great strides of the ambitious at the tender age of fifty seconds. His face had bloomed a visionary's grin the likeness of which she could not quite place – but had seen beneath haloes in lithographs of gods, angels and saints.

Jojo was destined for Olympus. He would go up in the world. Ambitious corpuscles bubbled through the arteries of his genealogy. In her recitation of histories Mother would cite the precedents of Uncle Joe, Great-grandfather Johnny, and his Great Auntie Mary's second counsin Jonathan the Astronomer who had written a stargazer's column in the rear of a national newspaper for twenty years.

However, such ambitious corpuscles seemed to have been plugged by surgeons in the back half of his umbilical cord, from where they retreated to his mother's veins, and gave up their oxygen to breathe a dew on Jojo's carmine brow.

He rose, solicitously. He grew to marry a Mary and father a Mary and strove to perfect the noble art of civil service.

In a small town in the South, he struggled forty hours weekly to maintain the town council's records of births, marriages and deaths. A system he had devised described the entrances, unions and exits of forty thousand citizens, avoiding investigations into such vulgarities as their state of mind, a detail to trouble the purity of the record.

Then, unaccountably, he abandoned his little-respected position and, claiming to have seen a 'gap in the market', founded the first firm to rival Joseph & Son, Funeral Directors to the Populace Since 1765, working, aided only by a second-hand hearse, from the front rooms of the family semi.

Mary, his mother, swelled with pride at his ingenuity. Mary, his wife, sank to misery at his morbidity. Mary, his daughter, fended off mockery in the playground. She made threats that her father would bury their fathers head-downwards so on Judgement Day arses would fart at the swarming gods who, rankled, would rocket their mouldering corpses to a flaming core's crematorium.

II

This was the age of entrepreneurial adventure. And what better business for the morbid than the perfect planning of internment? Individually, he reasoned, he might manage other people's deaths with an ease denied his own.

The story of his mismanaged decease came to him from his daughter.

Mary enjoyed the ribaldry of her grandmother's Saturday evenings. With whisky breath, Grannie Mary stuttered to her namesakes the indignities marking Jojo's incipience.

Transmitted, the tale fostered funereal ambitions in the registrar Jojo. And, within weeks, he conceived, incubated and brought to unreluctant birth the rest-home for the successful dead.

Two front rooms were swiftly turned to good use as reception and charnel house. Net curtains mournfully concealed the bereaved from the curious street. Rouge velvet sealed the powdered deceased from urchins' leers.

Marys, mother, grandmother, granddaughter, reacted angrily to cohabitation with perfumed and lathered cadavers. They preferred to squabble between themselves than with the stoical funeral director. Jojo heard nothing from them.

Jojo – full name Johnny Jack Jonathan, contracted to the less historicized 'Jo-jo' in his eagerness to be rid of predecessors – advertised his discreet and sympathetic services in suitable journals. He donned a tall black hat, trim with silk ribbon, a matt black suit and patent brogues with requisite squeak of instep.

Beneath a black hispid brow, his forehead paled as befitted his vocation. As if inner comfort with his house guests occasioned a change in his haematic composition, the iron in his blood seeped out through inattentive kidneys, leaving his skin pallid, etiolated, until he seemed monochrome.

Charcoal grey underlined each eye, an adornment given up not by soft black pencils but by the pigment of his skin. A sombre mood marked all he did, the dysthymia inherited from his birth now having a profession to excuse it.

In the ebullience of the kitchen the women baked foods, stoked the black furnaces of the Aga, boiled chicken-bones free of flesh, and spent much time reclining in a muck-sweat about the dining table, chewing tales.

Mary, Mary and Mary maintained a cheerful kitchen, quite separate from the parlour that presented a shopfront to the world. While corpses gathered dust under thin sunbeams, the three women chattered and gossiped, told *memento mori* and laughed out loud. It was a rare occasion when they ventured into the Stygian gloom of Jojo's mortuary.

A boy came to help him load and unload coffins. Coffins were stored in an unlit lean-to, filled in the parlour, lidded, and ferried in the hearse to their final destination. The apprentice swapped monosyllables with the obmutescent master, learning only that muteness was next to cadaverousness.

Once, seated beside his stone-faced employer in the silent hearse as it passed through the land of the nearly living, the boy glanced at Jojo and noticed a rare blush staining his chalk skin.

The man's teeth clenched, his eyelids winced, the blush blossomed and then, with what was perhaps the most expressive sound Jojo ever passed on to his apprentice, the funeral director eructated with three sharply pronounced farts.

The emissions filled the perfumed carriage with a foul odour, reaching a level of diffusion that seemed to threaten even the deceased's continued incarceration in his crate. Then, the mephitis faded as did the blushes colouring both man and boy.

Business was conducted in silence. Preparation was conducted in silence, being administered by Jojo alone. Transport and burial would have been conducted in total silence were it not for the occasional coughs of the boy. Jojo would have worked alone had he been allowed to bear a loaded coffin on a trolley.

The transport of grieving relatives demanded a second car. A local taxi operator was called upon to drive his black Granada to and from the cemetery several times weekly. Jojo found dealing with the quick the most arduous of his tasks.

III

Embalming – a suitably beautiful word for beauty's preservation – was Jojo's joy, a quiet ritual enacted in solitude. Accompanied only by a tray of fragrances, fluids, drugs, he worked. Left alone with the cool dead, he grew to savour the rare pleasure of sharing air with those not rivalrous for its consumption.

Noise was obliterated (the parlour had been soundproofed). Arguments fell away to soliloquy, love met no resistance. That is not to say I am accusing this reputable operator of ancient practices. Rather, that his affectionate ornamentation met with no coercive response. No objection was made to his taste in colour of eyeshade, no flippant backchat when he mentioned with relish oil of jasmine.

Clothed and arrayed with flowers, the body of the lifeless was adorned so as to sustain lifelikeness until all due ceremonies were done with.

In the case of cadavers wanted for a wake, special oils would anoint odiferous zones guaranteeing fetor-free nights for waiting memorialists.

Plugs were inserted in orifices to prevent complications.

Whenever necessary, wigs were made to specification, correcting the ravages of illness or the faithlessness of follicles.

Teeth might be inserted if dentures had been misplaced in transit. And in the final rite accorded him, the decoration of the body would begin.

With crayons, pencils, buff-pads, mascaras, and lipsticks, Jojo delicately infused a lifeblood to the slack çapillaries. Cheeks gone pale shimmered with Rhododendron Gloss. September Morning fired white lips with orange fit for osculation. The penumbra beneath closed eyes was erased with Pale Flesh. Treated to a brush of Woodland Violet, it seemed eyelids tremored on the verge of resurrection.

Hair would be dressed, blown dry and glossed with gel. And as his own ingenious addition, the funeral director placed some personal memento in praying hands.

Jojo would then congratulate himself: he had created a being more perfect than the deceased had ever been. Arrayed with several dressed and embalmed corpses, his parlour resembled the heart of a pyramid.

For hours, he sat with sweatless hands prayerful on his lap. Velveteen curtains sealed, he supervised the dead's departure.

Though he had tutored himself out of superstitions, he often found such beatific notions as heavenly fields, prepared mansions, reincarnation, and perpetual bliss, strangely seductive. Despite his immersion in the industry of the dead, Jojo relished such myths.

He did not face the lifeless with cynicism. Rather, he identified with their impassivity, their bloodless tranquillity and, frustrated in such identification, found it altering to envy.

The dead left excessive love behind them, love that had been lukewarm in life. The dead were unmoved by eruptions of state, home or soul. The dead lay like gluey-eyed sheep deep in thick grasses fearlessly awaiting a storm.

IV

Possessed of a job but rarely employed, Jojo's boy found himself accepted into the kitchen, the heart of the house.

Mary grandmothered him, Mary mothered him, and Mary sistered him. Sweetmeats, fat fresh loaves and home-made juices were his for the consuming, made for but ignored by the invisible undertaker. And in the glow of continual attentions, he flushed with blooded life.

It was only when he began to explore the breasts that had swollen to meringues beneath Mary's blouse that he fully appreciated the perks of his fortunate appointment.

On extended walks in the woods, he mapped the entire region. He dug thin fingers deep into the warren of her groin, painted her cheeks with saliva, drawing a peach blush to her lips and cheeks.

Mary, feverish with these attentions, conceded ground inch by literal inch. She permitted the frontier to be extended week by week as this brave pioneer searched out the savage in his new-found land.

A favourite glade was returned to, loved for its secrecy, made more secure by the fountain of rhododendron leaves that plumed with the spring.

On the soft humus of the hiding-place, he laid her out and began his ministrations. She closed her eyes and recalled last week's borderline. As his cold digits inched lower, she held her breath and drew his explorations upward.

Such is the nature of desire that the boy wished for her resistance. Each week he dreaded the prickly touch of pubic coils. The hidden, the veiled, the forbidden, exercised the strongest fascination over him.

One week, when with excess enthusiasm he blasted a groinful of seed into his underclothes and felt that coincident betrayal of desire, he dreaded further the moment when orgasm within her would end the blissful erotics of discovery.

The moment came sooner than he would have wanted (which was both never and now).

One September morning, a certain arrangement of the planets did and did not exercise a surcharging influence over the undertaker's daughter. With the sun in Virgo, Mary took to stripping every stitch as they brushed into the grove.

Laying herself out, she closed her eyes. The boy traipsed about her, crushing violets. Orbital, he viewed every aspect of the pale body, memorising flat breasts, engraving the fall of flesh on thigh to resistant retinas.

Shaking with fear, he stooped and crumbled over her. He smoothed dust from her eyelids with his tongue, fixated by a gaze that was and was not there.

Mary refused to open her eyes throughout the enthusiastic episode, concentrating instead on tightening and loosening the muscles deep at the base of her spine.

With urgency she wanted to hold him there for ever, in spite of her agony. In panic she dreamed he would get trapped and, siamese, they would stumble through a life conjoined, umbilical. Then, without knowing herself, she disappeared into a momentary unlife, a non-being, a vacuum at the heart of the vortex whipped within her.

The boy dismounted, shivering with hatred. She opened her sticky eyelids. She saw him, fringed with light, scrabbling with a zip, muttering guilt.

V

Jojo sacked the boy upon the announcement of Mary's matin nausea and slapped the girl viciously about the jaw.

She was held in purdah for eight weeks. Meanwhile, annual accounting had revealed the absolute failure of Jojo's adventure with the burial of the dead.

Greater movements than those confined to the kitchen and the parlour dictated that certain loans taken to purchase licences etc. were withdrawn. Accountants, solicitors and courts ruled that the ambitious but inept funeral director should declare himself bankrupt.

With inherited fortitude, Jojo refused to do as instructed. And for some days, he kept alive his embalming parlour, place of rest, haven for the unhurried.

Customers, not knowing of his fall, continued to supply their dead. Jojo continued, with excess care, to prepare them for the hereafter. But receivers, like births, cannot be staved off for ever, once procedures have set fatal wheels in motion.

Dates for foreclosure were announced, ignored, squabbled over and finally enforced. Mary, Mary and Mary knew nothing of the growing storm.

Mary, benefiting from her father's distraction, enjoyed a period of relaxed tyranny. This subsided into full-blooded enjoyment of the forthcoming child.

As her womb and breasts swelled, so did both mother's and grandmother's lust for the child's birth (some four months distant). Chatter turned to reminiscence, tales of tortured labours were re-enacted with dumb-shows, horror stories of death in birth were poured forth to steam with excavated loaves. Motherhood was extolled with litanies.

Jojo heard them and buried himself in paperwork, changing toilet-rolls on the *Titanic*. He despised such glorying in motherhood. Part of this fury (that may have been envy) lay behind his corrective blow to Mary's cheek.

He wondered if, by a different coagulation of chromosomes, he might have been a girl, a woman, a womb. Instead, he was contained by a repulsive, sterile masculinity, condemned to fail at whatever he had begun, damned to questing for frail success, born an acolyte to the hieratics of womanhood.

And on Mothering Sunday, he awoke before the womenfolk, placed modest gifts and understated cards upon the breakfast table and settled himself for a day in the dark of his study. The sun roared low in the east, enthusiastic for March.

VI

He had thought much on his own imminent death, preferring euthanasia to the interminable waiting on good fortune. One brush with death's ineptitude had convinced him that, contrary to popular myth, death, though much personified, had never been a person – it knew nothing of the finer feelings endured by the sensitive.

Best to control such matters oneself and leave no note, give no reasons.

For some days he had, with a calmness new to him, been scientifically devising the purest manner of self-sacrifice. Several factors bore down on this science. He was not operating in a sealed vacuum, much as he would have wished.

To prostrate himself before the onrushing meat-slicer of a train's wheel would be too messy. His mother had an unimpeachable reputation in the town.

A flight from the heights of a channel steamer went against the grain of all his undertaker's professionalism. He imagined fragments of his cadaver spoiling a distant beach-picnic. This was not how he dreamed of his future.

It would be done in the confines of his own parlour. The little expertise that his women had gleaned from having dead tenants in the house would aid them in dressing his throttled carcass. In the comfort of his own morgue, his ingenuity would complete the work his mother's doctors had failed to do.

The light-fitting would become his mooring. A length of fresh three-core cable would be attached and beneath it a chair: his diving-board into oblivion.

Calculating the length of the piece of flex proved irksome. He had never professed a delight in, nor a command of, mathematics. The finer art sat poorly amongst his clouded cells. Figures scribbled on a receiver's envelope did nothing to clear the matter.

But for those who have mastered figure-grubbing, here are the specifications: Jojo (1778mm long, 77.11kg mass, 372mm neck, age: 21,056,400 minutes since birth; 21,419,280 minutes since conception), the study (4144mm long, 2743mm high, 3333mm wide), the flex (3–core, 6mm bore, 1201mm when unknotted, 750mm when moored and noosed), broom-handle (1220mm long, 33mm bore), light-fitting (75mm steel plate bolted to 102mm joist through 20mm plasterboard, G. Baker [Master-Builder], 1976), chair-height with four legs perpendicular to the globe-surface (914mm back, 460mm seat), windspeed (negligible).

He had practised looping the flex to a noose some twenty-four times when the door burst open and his daughter launched herself at his stooped form, arms flailing a Mother's Day card.

You remembered! You darling! You remembered!

She pressed herself against him, the swell of her maternity wholly perceived by his compressed elbow. Breasts slithered on his shoulder, arms locked a minute-long embrace about his neck. He gasped for air. Hair fell to his teeth and was chewed with splutters. Overcome with unwelcome emotions, he clasped her waist, lightly slapped her buttocks and coaxed her from the gloom.

His card to her she had dropped to the carpet. He did his finest to ignore his own distended writing on the interior. Its protestations of wonder at her looming maternity mocked him. He blinded himself to his glib signature of adoration, his name.

Jo-jo.

His name, bisyllabic mockery of a title! a stutter coughed by the scoffer, a lunatic's gasping for breath. No name.

Tying the cable to the steel bracket set into the plaster was quickly accomplished. For a silent minute he gripped the flex to let his weight fall speculatively on vacant air.

It held. Creaking, the knot tightened. A thin powdering of ceiling motes salted his eyes.

Then the boredom as he paced the room attempting to assign a time to the act.

It should be done at a ceremonial time, a time that had importance. He looked at his watch, but could not recall the hour of his birth. Asking his mother would demand egress from the sanctuary, egress from the tomb.

So, he dismissed time as an inadmissible excuse for the procrasti-nator. Clearing his throat, arranging his tie with a swift tightening clench, he stepped to the mock-pulpit of the chair.

But it was too soon, too soon. Too soon for what? But his hands had gone cold, icy in anticipation of bloodlessness as if his fingers knew they were to be deoxygenated, as if his nails knew they would grow uncut to scratch the toes of the coffin.

He took another turn about the room, fiddling with curtains, afraid urchins (his phrase) might spy his indignity. Absently, he began to think of Ireland.

In a vague trance he stepped again to the chair, arranged the noose comfortably about his neck, made the knot taut, inserted a broom-handle through his sleeves so his arms were extended (preventing any fiddling afterthoughts with the knot), obliterated thoughts from his mind, raised a knee, placed a foot on the rear of the chair and waited. For a long while, he waited.

In mockery of his scrupulous plans for this moment, the fall occurred by accident. He was engaged in lustrous recollection of a nude swim in the sea off Sligo Bay twenty-three (or -four) summers earlier. He tapped a toe to the memory of an aria. He giggled.

And his leather sole slipped from the varnished chair seat. Skipping lightly in the air for a panicked purchase on wood he dropped, and felt the snag as a tough embrace about his throat.

There was no death, only acute consciousness of the present moment. It revolved as he revolved, second by cruel second, apprehended in luscious colourfulness with every beat of the blocked vein in his jaw. Pale light hung about him. A shadow hung on the globe beneath him, the shadow of a ludicrous scarecrow, arms cruciform, twisting in chaos. Chained-up from the belly of the ceiling, slung where the light-bulb should burn its hollow globe, he suffered the most intense thoughts of his dulled life. Eyes glared, widening as if, like boils lanced, they would any moment pop from his head. They would bounce about mocking his suspension above the concrete. He wished again for time so that he might know how long it was since he had drawn breath. A countdown, somebody, a countdown! Best laid plans thrown awry. Perfect death flung back in your face. Typical. And he revolved, seeing moons and satellites orbiting. His globed head dreamed a world. Alternately the space turned black with distant waters millions of millimetres below, and brilliant blood-red so he presumed himself to have exploded in a rude redecoration of his universe. Then, without warning or intention, the spasms began, involuntary attempts to rid himself of the crucifying broom-handle, the constricting suit, and an itch on the ball of his foot he would have killed to scratch . . . The itch, the itch spread, engulfing his turning torso with a volcano's magma oozing to nerve ends until they frazzled, hairs jiggered in their roots, eyes were blinded by vibrations and in one dazzle of exquisite sensation he simultaneously ejaculated the brewing contents of both his bowels and his scrotum. Then, the crackling of the cord as, twisting, it slowly hauled its burden higher, higher in a continuous ascension, with a low scream for death.

VII

Mary came into the sweetly scented study, minutes after the sun (roaring behind a veiling cloud) had slithered to a grave in the west.

She spent a moment looked at her suspended son and laughed. The twitching face was able only to lick the air with a dry tongue. Her son forgave the giggle, compassion in his egg-white eyes. Black mucus dripped from his trouser-leg. In imitation of a planet, he revolved to face away from her, then reappeared, blue tongue shivering, arms perpendicular to his jacket.

She moved, now with tears, now with laughter, to the foot of him. She gently clasped his ankles. With a slow haul his mother pressed him towards the earth. The cable creaked. She clicked her tongue on her palate. She whispered regrets to his brogues. Releasing his feet upon which she had exerted her whole weight, she marvelled at the builder's fine work. She stepped back to vomit on the carpet.

It was some time later when the women ceased pitying, perhaps midnight, perhaps dawn. The body was removed to the parlour. All blood seemed drained from his body.

With a professionalism previously reserved for their own ravaged masks, they dressed his face, his hair and his stretched flesh. Then, fragrancing the carcase with all that remained of his perfumery, all three wound him in spiced linen clothes and laid him in a pine coffin of one-inch board.

They hoisted it to trestles, four feet from the maroon carpet tiles. And with cautious ritual, his daughter hauled back the velveteen veils from the glass.

The boy (Joseph A.) was requisitioned to drive the hearse on its last voyage. Mary, Mary and Mary sat three abreast on cowhide seats and stared death in separate directions.

The boy said nothing, concentrating on successful pall-bearing to the sepulchre, but was convinced he could smell a familiar breath of advice as if the coffin were already on its pyre and the empyreuma was ghosting an oracle foretelling bliss.

The Reluctant Millionaire

If he permits me, I shall tell the Life of J. K. L. Wedge, that local philanthropist who is generous with all but his history. Generously, he has allowed me to lie about him. He will stop me when I go too far. He is sitting in censorship beside me as I write, nudging and smudging his Life.

In our part of the earth, there is gold in the hills. This is well known, it is the talk of the town. There is gold in the sea and gold in the cracks of the flagstones and nuggets buried in the beach. And there is not a head in the city that knows how to get it out.

No head, that is, save one. And it is a considerable head at that – a particularly well-rounded head, a world of a head.

Mr Wedge has thanked me for this metaphor. He says it sums up his feelings for himself and I need go no further.

Apologising, I press on.

Jack Wedge prospected, tramping across hills to join a rush on wealth. Two hundred thousand migrants settled around him, a prospector's city burrowed itself into the mud.

And on the beach he sat and dug at sand. In the streets, he tramped nose earthwards, scanning the stones for gleams. Knee-deep in sludge, he panned the waves.

Mother Wedge lived on the edge of the quarry, the crater burrowed by speculators hungry for lodes. The city spawned in the crater flourished. No gold was found, but still it flourished. Cities flourish in the hope of gold.

Jack dreamed he too would flourish, that he would grow to marry, spawn and ail in the city's crater.

He was young, he had prospects.

And a vision came to him: he had become a millionaire, the first to

65

blossom from the golden soil. And in the first flush of wealth he tramped, nose skywards, to celebrate with Mother.

Mother said, You don't wanna go spending it all at once, now, do you, Jack! You put some away. Put it in a hole.

And, sagely, Mr Jack Wedge creamed off a little of the bullion and had a cavity in his tooth plugged with it. He, being a seer, foresaw the rotting of his molars and thought best to stow a saving for their future.

For celebratory supper, be bought Mother Wedge a pie, a kidney pie which oozed its ore of rubber flesh to a plate of chipped potatoes.

Don't wanna go wasting your money on me! his mother cried. Find yourself a girlie. Find yourself a wife!

Jack, blushing, depicted himself as a suitor in cotton suit and silken necktie, golden cufflinks and a golden watch.

Then, he claimed, I'll get a bird.

Mother sawed at the crust of celebratory pie and hushed. She was put out, not by his earthy term for her sex, but by his hastiness to leave her bedroom.

She, Emmeline 'Emmy' Wedge, was bedridden in anticipation of her bowels' decline. She had moved from Father's armchair up to her attic bedroom, pessimistic about the restraining powers of her sphincter.

Hearing of her only Jack's good fortune, she made a shopping list: a finer bed, a finer gown and finer curtains to keep the sun from her. She felt the change immediately, ordering prospectuses so now that they were millionaires they could view a millionairish house. She told their tabby cat of how a wealthy tabby cat must not forget his friends and not crow about his rise in the world. And she felt a twang of nostalgia for the olden days, when life was simple, when you knew where you were and only needed two hands to tot up your savings.

Jack's bounding-in and spouting of his find had quite thrown her out of sorts. He had no right giving her such a shock in the majesty of poverty. He should at least have waited till her Sunday morning trot. Then, she was more resilient.

Each week, she indulged herself. A turn about the yard restored her torpid veins to thudding life and rearranged the solids in her gut. She had not shat for sixteen weeks. She entertained a notion of this being holy.

Jack, contrarily, relocated himself on a stool in the Queen's Arms. He downed two and one half gallons of yellow beer. Fizzing with optimism, he plied bored barmen with tales.

He told how he, an honest loafer, had come across a vein of ore in them there hills while on his stroll. It had come to him, he retold, quite out of the green! One minute khaki grass and molehills, the next an explosion of sunny gold! He could barely restrain his intake.

Later, he kneeled about the altar of the loo to let yellow spirals of the beer flash golden in the pan.

Like tales, this vomit came unprompted, with warning only given to get him to a receptacle in time.

Mother, as was her way, pronounced that night her last. Mr Wedge, despite his state, hurried to be near her, to press his nose to the counterpane.

I'm your boy – I'm your boy – don't you go now, don't go – just sleep – there's a dear!

And Mother, lulled by a song of tomorrow's spending, snoozed with snores and farts that threatened pristine sheets.

It had been his plan to marry Miss Arabella, Emmy's sixty-six-year-old widow friend. Of all the women he knew, Arabella was the only one who was not his mother.

Arabella had passed the postwar years in bed. She found in Mrs Wedge a distant consolation. And love could not but blossom as Jack Wedge scuttled from bedside to bedside, bearing friendship books and pamphlets from invalid to mother.

When Arabella went to hospital to have her lesser-needed inner organs out, Jack set up a plan to wed her the day his mother died. A simple juggling of his daily route, and he could move from mother's grave to Arabella's bed with ease, without disturbing his routine.

His millionaire's fortune came into his mind again the following morning. Woken by his mother's scream for bedpans, the memory returned.

And being a servant to his long routine, Jack moulded a pillow over his ears to dull the recollection to a whimper.

It's going to change everything, Mother had solemnly said. And she repeated the truism for the benefit of history.

He had not cared at that moment, his discovery having just been made, his elation still causing him to jig from ball of foot to ball of foot.

Now, with the clarity of half-consciousness, he recalled the calm monotony that had been his youth and wished, with no little enthusiasm, for a return to ignorance.

Mr Wedge, who sits peering over this page as I write, nodding, shaking his head, correcting correctly-spelled words and accurately-written lies, has requested I describe him.

As the reader knows and Mr Wedge does not, words are one thing, Jack's flesh and few hairs quite another. It would be folly to set down annotations to the skull that cranes to see what it looks like to another's eye. Mr Wedge needs a mirror to lie to him, not a ghostwriter.

However – to persuade my patron to cease his weeping (his desire to know himself is immoderate) – I shall set down the impressions he has made on the soft plastic of my brain in our short, honeyed time together.

He is, like most men between the senility of youth and the dementia of decrepitude, hopeful for the marvels of marriage. He is adoring, yet loathes all women not his mother. He is calm, yet subject to murderous tempers. He is pious, but irreverent. His self-command under mockery is admirable, his misery at comments on his person suicidal. He is possessed by daemons and angels who between ceasefires produce those vacillations of decision for which he is beloved. And he is beloved, by the three who know of him. He is also envied, for his majestic imagination – men like Wedge burrow at the biting edge of civilisation's tunnelling machine. His utopia sees mankind enjoying the first-fruits of his philanthropy while he enjoys the harvest of their absence. He values his own company above all others. He cannot be reduced to scrawl. But, in his munificence, he is grateful for my modest attempts at portraiture. He smiles, as if I were his mother.

Miss Arabella, foretold of Mr Wedge's desire in dreams and in a note from his mother, was overjoyed by word of his ascension in the material world. She was to be wife to a millionaire! The lifestyle! The clinics! The prosthetics!

While Mr Wedge, 'Love' to her, was young, he was also wise. His foresight had relieved her bedsheets of nasty accidents on more than one occasion. He was not unbecoming, in low light. And he was selfless, given up to the service of her and his mother, a priest to her Diana.

Without her non-essential inner organs, Arabella felt fifty years her junior. However, she saw no need to rise from her bed. Fear of losing Wedge's ministrations kept her supine in that dip of mattress quarried by her limbs.

After his announcement that he'd come into money, Jack's afternoon visits stopped. Miss Arabella did not fret. He was preening himself for her, arranging affairs to perfect their imminent coming-together.

It is a fortunate thing for a woman in the last chapter of a life's imbecility to find a lover. And one with the discretion of Jack Wedge could not be found in any institution. Good gods had plotted their paths to cross.

Jack – he admits with saintly candour at past transgressions – was meanwhile passing his time among the looser women of the town.

His reputation spread with swiftness, his name from brothel to bar, his particulars venereally from woman to employer.

The newly nominated millionaire, despite each morning's desolation, found it impossible to keep his trap shut. No sooner had he vowed to renounce wealth and return to happy penury than some woman interrupted his broodings, asking after his desire:

Want a shag love? Looking good today!

Distracted by the beauties of nature, Jack postponed his renunciation for an hour.

Sensual pleasures indulged, he found a bar to ruminate his plight. No sooner had his rump kissed stool than some loon came forward to congratulate the reluctant millionaire:

Tap you for a fiver mate? Jack, me old buddy!

The miseries of fabulous wealth soured his drink, he ignored the suppliant and staggered on his way.

He was not disloyal to Arabella, not unfaithful in his skull. But no sooner had he turned his steps in her direction than some new distraction threw him from his reverie. Man's progress from mother to wife is complicated by there being a choice of the latter and only one of the former.

I was born to me mother, moans Wedge at my elbow. Why can't I be born to me wife?

I have paused to first absorb then praise the erudition of this comment. I include it in this account to edify the reader.

Mr Wedge was a man of few initiatives, many habits. Without money, his shuffle from Emmy to Arabella was a rite not to be thought about, a nothing to be done.

With the gross intervention of wealth, Jack was forced to think, to decide, to weigh the plaints of the townswomen.

Mrs Baggs caught a hold of his lapel with violence and demanded to know why he, in his recently elevated position, had not called round to seduce her.

Mrs Beggs, a brilliant alcoholic, tripped him up. As he sprawled inelegantly before her, she interrogated this 'right rude millyenear' as to why he had not organised a soirée where they might be alone together.

A certain Theodore Biggs had, in queenly fashion, requested information on why the enriched Mr Wedge Esq. had not called at his town address, summoned him – Mr Biggs – to a waiting sports car and driven them to fleshpots in the South.

Jack, being of a timid make, had answers to none of these questions. Answers are, like mother-lodes, difficult to come by, named after their finders, and most commonly stumbled upon by misfortune.

Jack, being of a forgetful cast, could never recollect what answers he had been instructed in, nor when to say yes and no. His mother masterfully took charge of the Answering of Questions Large and Small.

And on his return, later that week, she beat him while he bowed, for not visiting his betrothed.

But but but –

No buts, just go!

But she's not –

God didn't give you a mind to make up he gave you a mother to make it up for you – now go!

He went.

He travelled scuttling to Arabella's, dressed in greyed twill finery, penitent.

His beloved greeted him with a shriek.

My love!

My 'Bella, he returned.

En route, Miss Minna Ecks lured him to a bus shelter, mocked his wealth, doubted he had ever found a penny, laid bets on his having broken banks to get it and rammed her palms deep into the sack of his thermals. Drawing deeply on the succulence therein, she giggled at his chicanery.

Oh why oh why can't I be in on it? Trust me!

But, determined, he scuttled on. Only to be met by a second tradeswoman who solicited under the pseudonym 'Zandra'. Beneath the grey gold of the dock gantries, she pestered an old client for trade –

Oh come on, Jacko, a quick one!

And, in sympathy for her eternal lot, he paid and withdrew himself.

Got a girlfriend yet? she asked upon receiving him.

No yes no, he replied at intervals.

Run away, Jack, come with me, come.

He deserted her, the ferry coughed its bilgewater to the port and left for Ireland. On, on, he scuttled, faithful to his laid-up Bella.

Jacko! whooped a gaggle of lads, rejoicing.

'Lo, he returned.

Pegleg! Billionaire! Give us ya money! Where's gold?

In dread for his suit, Mr Wedge turned tail and hobbled as fast as one good and one game leg could take him.

The hecklers jigged about him, a pack of Pharisees to his Jesus. He had known them at school, they had known him at streetcorners, they were not intimates.

Show us your willy! Where did you get your money? Kill mummy?

Mr Wedge suffers from many ailments, not least a reputation as a slow-wit and buffoon. His physical disabilities, his retiring calm, his drunkenness, his idiocy and his close attachment to a mother, draw hilarity from contemporaries and only admiration from myself.

Forgive the impertinence of an opinion.

While Miss Arabella looked with only honey eyes at Jack, her juniors nominated him town jester, village idiot, the national clown. That he had, they heard, come into millions did not deter them from scorn. As rich men everywhere will echo, wealth attracts malice like

71

interest. Good fortune, like talent, makes detractors out of friends, confirmed antagonists from enemies.

Arabella listened to a censored version of the above and, testing out the role of wife, soothed the trembling Wedge with murmurs.

He glanced to catch her eye. Beneath a slipping wig, she gazed with wondering lust at his dusty jacket.

Come here, she purred.

He came, having no wit to disobey. And they snuggled as one flesh. He sobbed. She sighed and smoothed his hairs.

No matter, she murmured. You got me.

Wedge winced. He untangled himself from the tubes which sustained her excavated torso.

Miss Arabella – we must talk!

For ever, Jack.

He paced, in imitation of men who have made up their mind. He spoke about his wealth, how it was a fiction dreamed up in a reverie above the town, how to win a wife he had seen himself as a millionaire, and how that fiction had been so desired that it had seemed granted. He stuttered on . . .

Mr Wedge has asked me to inform others – while he addresses Arabella in terms too personal for the common ear – that, in addition to a game leg and a blind eye, he is tormented by a stutter which on occasions of extreme fright accelerates in frequency, rendering him silent, mouth agape.

. . . And, he continued, he thought it only right, his reading in the English novel had taught him, it was only polite, etc. etc., to tell the woman whom one is pledged to marry of your reduced circumstances.

That was what he had scuttled to tell her. Now, ashamed, he would do whatever she commanded.

Drying her eyes on the hem of the sheet, Miss Arabella proclaimed she had not heard so beautiful a speech since the time her Eric had gone down on one knee and proposed.

Mr Wedge, reversing through the door-frame, had expected abuse, oaths and curses. He had foreseen a total break.

His scheme, to counteract the plots of Mother, had been to tell a fresh tale. Then, without waiting to see her explode like Mt. St Helen's, he would leave.

The truth would surely persuade her that the union of a sixty-six-year-old imbecile and a derided pauper (whose lying ruined so many lives) could not be blissful.

Instead, she threw back the covers, sat bolt upright and spread her arms cruciform with joy.

My own! she shrilled, shrilly.

Mr Wedge lowered his eyes to where a stomach's crater crawled with serpentine tubes, a fat black bag and numerous electrical devices.

He was not given to prejudice, his judgements being slowly considered and remembered by his mother. At this revelation, however, he was forced to loosen his necktie and take a turn about the room. He peered from the window.

Don't open the curtains! shrieked Arabella.

No?

The light!

He stared about in perplexity. It was high time he left, it being neither day nor night.

I must get back to me mother, Bella – don't think we can be seeing one another again, do you?

Arabella took several minutes to detail her differences with Mr Wedge on this point, using all weaponry within her grasp.

He had not intended this to be a final rejection, merely a staging-post to such a break. He knew, from long experience of his mother, that women were best when handled gently, when dealt censored truths, when led by the nose, tug by teasing tug.

His words had come out all wrong.

And he dared not tell Mother how it was all fiction, she would hit the roof and more besides. Mothers, photophobic plants, were best left in the dark.

Thinking this, he informed Mother that negotiations over his and Miss Arabella's future had been stayed, she being unsure about the money side of things.

Mother undertook to write Miss Arabella at once, requesting she explain herself. She had no right fiddling with her boy's heart and feelings that way.

Mr Jack, being the carrier of all correspondances, did not worry himself at this. He censored Mother's letters.

The loss of youthful monotonies demanded he sleep, he was exhausted by his eventful life.

He dreamed Miss Arabella at his throat, all tubes and electrified chairs, throttling him for the family's failed affairs. Loss of their fortune would leave them on the streets! As her husband, he could not bring a charge of rape against her though she clambered over his pale corpse and bounced and bounced and bounced . . .

He passed the following day away from Mother on the pretence of seeing solicitors, investment banks, government officials. Mother fretted.

Desultorily, Mr Jack walked the fells.

As he walked, he planned what he would tell Mother: how hasty investing and misappropriated funds had wiped his entire fortune from the earth in one of those stock-exchange things you hear about, but no matter all was for the best and we were happier when . . .

He came upon the spot where it had happened, a shallow dip in the fold of moor. Here, he had danced Eureka!

The city streamed a belch of fog to dim its outlines, the valley curled encrusted with roofs to the sea.

It seemed the gold lay thinly veiled by turf. It flowed molten, soft like grass, from active volcanoes and cooled to nuggets in the steel sea. The mist was steam from its condensing, a breath of relief as it sunk to solution in the waves.

Kicking at the turf with his one good leg, he leered for gold. A dust of sand and earth rose to stain his trouser-hem. He crushed the chalk-white skull of a finch beneath his heel. He wished against his own imagining.

Miss Arabella, made anxious by her escaping fiancé's tone, had risen that morning not to return immediately to bed. She dressed and hobbled about the room, assisted by a frame.

Mother, made miserable by an inability to press anger into words, gave up the letter to Arabella and also rose. It was not Sunday morning. But the emotional ruin of her beloved son called for direct action.

The two old dears embarked on collision course at three, it being habitual among them to devote six full hours to toilet, dress and wiggery.

Mr Jack limped sadly to a hummock. He deposited himself on the earth, rump first. As his feet flung heavenwards, he saw the mists lift, involved with their selves, and bodily aspire to become a cloud. And heavily, he rearranged himself, to observe.

As if afraid it might burst to rain, the base of the condensation hauled itself above cathedrals, cranes and spires. It hovered, then, rejuvenated, swirled to prominence, obliterating the homeland, veiling the city in lunchtime secrets, hiding his mother from view.

Mr Jack felt uncomfortable – he grows dissatisfied with sitting too long and is, even now, pacing about the room while I set down this boring bit. He is coughing between lugs on my cigarette, splattering moisture on the window-glass.

The cloud ascended to the noon, boiled for a while, then rose further, wary of the sun which threatened to disperse it earthwards.

It moved to the hill on which Jack sat and, wearily, sat also. Embracing the wanderer, it nuzzled him and brought a tear to his one good eye, blinding him. The finch's skull, ground to soil, seemed to reassemble, grow, sprout golden feathers and wink.

Mr Jack became agitated and paced downhill, anxious to gain his bearings. Sightless in cloud, he stumbled limping across heath and gorse.

The cloud, refreshed, suddenly rose, a balloon released to the stratosphere, loosed of its load, heated, growing, air.

In his flurry of fear, Mr Wedge had chanced upon inspiration. While he is seated, no new ideas torment him. When in motion, his brain becomes infected with curious pictures. In this he is, as far as my researches can discover, unique.

He conceived a plan to oust Miss Arabella. She had become an irritant and, spurred by his own hallucinations, a curse.

He would argue that, despite his promises, he was unable to marry because – he breathes deeply – he is to devote his life to philanthropy, the gentle act of throwing his money away.

Mr Wedge could not marry for two reasons – to concentrate fully, to remain devout, he must live alone.

Mr Wedge has, at present, forgotten the second point. He assures me it was a clincher.

Mother would be displeased at first. Grudgingly, she would benefit from his continued attentions.

As to giving away non-existent gold, well – no one had been suspicious at his getting invisible gold, why should they query his giving it away? Who knows, they might receive a gift from the anonymous philanthropist! So, at peace with the world, he would be happy.

He rejoiced at the genius of it all. Mother's mastery over all he said and planned and dreamed had eclipsed this fecund brain of his, this brain which on mountains and in mists spawned such fantastic yarns!

Mr Wedge, my employer, became quite excited while expounding his romantic sensations on the hilltop. He has stepped outside to take a turn about the yard.

He descended from Sinai with his renewed covenant, ebullient. The wind seemed to restrain him. Then, strong to his face, it all but lifted him to flight between each leap from good to game leg.

Mother welcomed Miss Arabella into her kitchen. The two had not met in twenty years, though living but one half-mile apart. Despite their hostility as rivals, they embraced with tears.

Miss Arabella set out her concerns.

The mutually adored Jack was vacillating in his responsibilities.

Mother urged her to take a chair, the tea would only be a moment.

Miss Arabella, diamond-eyed with yellow hands, took considerable time shuffling her feet to a cringing chair. She plonked her butt to rest and set off once again.

It's all well and good him coming and saying he's having second thoughts – what about me and mine? A woman's got to think about her future!

Mother nodded gravely and stirred the golden tea to ferment in her best china.

Arabella, she began, Arabella – what with all this money, I'm a little apprehensive I am – a-pprehensive – milk?

Miss Arabella frowned. She had forsaken one of the conversation's many strands. She cross-examined Emmy on one small point, telling of Jack's morning story.

Our Jack's been telling his tall tales, has he? He has his ways – telling howlers is one – the money's good as gold – *is* gold!

They vied to laugh the loudest, the dissonant cackles diverging to separate frequencies, terrorising the cats in the yard, icing the heart of

Mr Wedge as he turned to limp over scattering moggies, as he thought of exile.

There he is now! Now Jack, what've you been telling our Bella? Another one of your stories?

About? Jack replied, sick with guilt.

About you and me's fortune, said Arabella with a grin.

Mr Jack had not previously enjoyed a view of Arabella with teeth. He took one moment to savour the sight. The two women twisted turkey-necks to admire the millionaire.

The telltale stared at the teapot snout and dreamed of escape. Like a cat, he knew that running only landed on your back those enemies you most wanted to avoid. He decided to crawl by imperceptible degrees, and out of sight to run.

He made noises resembling explanations but in mid-phrase was struck down by speechlessness, his mouth locked open, a crater with gold sparkling in its back teeth, his tongue a prospector's flag.

Mother giggled it off, Arabella leered wide-eyed.

Jack gargled.

His mother, ignoring him, recited her grand suggestion, one she had been mulling all morning, a wonderful idea – why did not Arabella and her Jack stop wasting everybody's time, get themselves married quick sharp, and move into the nice room at the front until Jack had bought them all a mansion where they could, like queens, die in splendour?

Arabella seemed, in the telling, to expand, to inflate like a cloud, her measly features to distend and sprawl. With joy, she breathed out her pride, ruffling all five hairs plastered to Jack's scalp.

Mother beamed, a visionary.

What do you think, Jacko? she asked.

Ossified, he turned a shade of buff.

It did not much matter, the women established the habit of ignoring him whether he uttered words or not. And as he stood, two pictures popped like grapes in his mind: one, of himself revolving clockwise, strung by the neck from a light-fitting in the lounge; the other, of two girls flapping about his weary corpse laid out on the carpet, preparing ointments, salves and perfumes, two girls whose ministrations were all he had wanted from life, two girls who paid no attention to the volcanic tales spewed from a mouth with a mind all its own.

And in the yard he saw a golden cat explode to figments of a diseased imagination, a calf made from the jewellery of a nation, a silly god to calm the restless soul.

WOMEN

To Annia

I

Annia is walking the dog. She is gadding over the hill in the drizzle to sit at the foot of an elm. The trees cluster on hummocks of soil. Their roots have expanded the earth to large molehills, the tunnelling roots have created drumlins on which the trees sit, haughty as poseurs. She runs the last bit, giddy with her hair sodden. In the drizzle she can imagine the sea. A man loiters by the pond. In the water, his dog flaps and breaks the surface. Annia's dog races to bathe the mud from his flanks. Annia sits, exhausted, in the shade of tree. She can smell the odourless elm. She pats the old feet of the tree. She listens to it thud with every slap. The man looks up, conscious of her solitude. He thinks about her. He mulls the idea of threatening her with his company. He changes his mind, half-heartedly. Annia breathes the drips away from her nostrils and closes her eyes. She can feel the man and she can feel the tree. The dogs thrash for the mud at the bottom of the pool, eager to smell the other. The man whistles for his dog. His dog ignores him. Annia starts, then brushes the dark hair from her eyes. She can see the forelock of tree at the top of her vision. The tree shivers and a rain of droplets falls to burst on her upraised knees.

II

The doctor had called her in and announced it: she was pregnant. There was no question about it. Without thinking, she knew – she must lose the child. He had not cared, only shrugging shoulders to rid himself of feeling. She booked in to a clinic. Even now she cannot stop weeping, imagining a bruise within. But there was nothing for it – she had a life to live. He wasn't important, the spot of matter that was the father. But the baby, secretly she cared for the baby. In her mind it was a boy, full-grown and waddling behind her as she ran.

The man, the father, he had been a crush, an insensible crush, an infatuation. He was no father. He was an inseminator. He hadn't the guts to father. So she booked into the clinic. It was necessary. Had she lived in the eighteenth century, she told the doctor, she would have dug up some back-street witch to do the job. He stared. He did not say anything.

III

Annia worked in an office, a newspaper office, selling advertising over the phone. She loathed the futility of it, the futility of flogging *space*, space that would be vacant again tomorrow, space to be filled with adverts, adverts for spaces in industry. She became angry at the emptiness. She had been born to fill spaces so they might be emptied! She may as well work in a supermarket, stocking shelves.

The job paid for the flat, it bought space for her, a small walled space sealed against a vast noisy spacious world.

And it paid for a car, so she could drive at evening to a pool or to a bay and bathe. The car was a godsend, a shuttle out of the valley of the city to the flat-topped hills and gorse.

It was on blocks at the moment, raised up, its wheels removed, its bonnet up, yawning with boredom. Annia was infuriated. Now she must walk everywhere, and could only make it to the park of an evening.

IV

Annia wanted a child, she wanted a marriage, she wanted to live alone. She could not find a man who would give her all three. She had found a man who gave her the first, but not the latter. She had found a man who wanted most of all to marry her, but he loathed children – they would keep him from her – and he asphyxiated her with his love.

So she chose the latter, having no alternative. Or rather, she elected not to change what she had not chosen.

V

How difficult it is to laugh when you are alone!

She told Ellen, her best friend. Ellen said that was why she chose to dig out people, mix, get to know them. Laughter was then always a possibility. Ellen said this was why aloneness got muddled with the sad word loneliness. The woman alone never laughed. And although she may not have been depressed, she remembered that time as a sad time.

You should see more people! Ellen said. It's not good to sit and brood. You think too much.

But Annia said you could never think too much. Ellen said she was wrong and Annia ignored her. She added that if you could not find people who made you laugh, then mixing with dull-wits was a waste of life.

You never *look* for people! laughed Ellen. How can you say that!

I do, Annia answered, but she knew Ellen was right. She suddenly hated herself for being stupid. To think she could stay alone! What stupidity!

Ellen adored Annia and envied her stability, her calm acceptance of her own company. She would ring Annia or call at her flat and there would be no answer. Ellen knew in her heart her friend was in, she knew Annia was sitting in a stupor, self-involved. It made no sense to keep ringing. She was happy. It would be like disturbing her with a man, she was so complete. At those times Annia did not need her. This irked Ellen, more out of envy than self-pity. It would be so nice not to need anyone. She told her.

I need someone! Annia retorted.

No you don't! You said so!

I did not – I didn't mean that – I meant I didn't want to *need* someone – you know.

They sat in mutual incomprehension. Annia feared knowing herself dependent on a man, or even a friend. What if that friend should die! What if that man should leave?

You're not living, Ellen said. Not properly.

Ellen had several boyfriends, most of whom cared little for her, acquaintances whom she dated. On dates, they would laugh and squabble, drink and sleep together. Ellen was lonely, but she had no alternative. She only said she did.

VI

Annia did love being with Ellen, it soothed her to sit in the same room as the maternal girl. And so for Ellen – both women behaved as mothers to the other. It was no secret between them. Their motherhood was nearly upon them. They hovered in limbo, awaiting the hope.

I got a letter from Jack, said Ellen.

Oh, Annia smothered her fright and stared at her lap. What did he have to say?

Nothing – he's met a girl – but he's unhappy.

Bastard.

You just say that, Ellen chid warmly.

Annia slumped to a temporary sulk. She rose and undressed. Ellen ran her a bath. Sometimes Ellen stayed over. Annia lay in the amnion of the tub. Ellen sat close by, playing with shampoos and perfumes, conditioners and salves.

What's this one?

I got it in Cardiff – it's gorgeous – try it on.

Ellen squirted rich, pungent oil to her neck. She leaned into the steam so Annia could smell how it went on her skin. Ellen watched Annia bob up and down, softly in the water.

Good, Annia advised. You should get some.

And Ellen told how she had met a friend of a boy-friend, and how this friend had said he liked her hair and how he had gone now but it was nice to get compliments. Annia nodded and let the girl speak on, watching the disturbance of the steam as she spoke.

She rose and fell in the water, feeling the scalding water peel the skin from her legs and arms and stomach. She sank to a reverie, Ellen's voice jabbering somewhere distant in the fog. Then, pinching her nose, she ducked underwater. For seconds, submerged, she thought how nice it was to be immersed, to stay immersed, to have a twin to play with in the soft thudding deep of the water. She rose, cleansed.

VII

Annia met Jack at a bus-stop. Annia tore the accident down to its components to see why it happened that time but not again.

Jack offered her a sandwich from his lunch-box. She took it, watching how he ate. She hated the way men ate.

She chewed cautiously on the beef sandwich. She was anxious not to mimic his horse-like munches. He loitered, unselfconsciously chomping the meat. He did not say much. He caught her eye. They unintentionally moved in circles about each other. It was as if he wanted to see her from every angle before going further. She wanted to smell him and to hear him speak.

What with the wind and his silence she did not find out much about him. She wanted to feel the dark of his cheek, just to see what it felt like. But she did not dare.

He asked her casually, Would she meet him – later that evening? He was a scientist, a biologist – he studied tiny organisms.

Annia nodded, thinking he had offered another sandwich. And even though she did not want either a second beef sandwich or a drink with this presumptuous oaf, she said yes. He told her where to meet him and clambered aboard the Dunvant bus. He was absorbed into the drizzle.

She panicked. She vowed not to go. She rang Ellen who said she must. Annia insisted. She would stay in.

VIII

She was only five minutes late. Jack sprawled on a pink sofa in the Rhyddings bar. Annia shuddered with self-doubt.

He looked up at her, his dark eye seeming to grin and mock her weakness. He held the stare, mockingly. She broke away first.

He jumped to his feet.

What are you drinking?

She wanted so much to say, Nothing, I've just come to tell you I'm not coming. But an ice-black shimmer in his eye, so close to her, made her curious to stay awhile.

She sat in a tremble, watching him at the bar. She had an odd idea that he was not real, that he was an angel, good or bad she didn't know, but an angel offering beef sandwiches to girls who just wanted to be by themselves.

The barman chattered to Jack. Annia forgot the idea.

IX

She gave in to her curiosity to know the feel of his cheek and let him kiss her. It was smooth, razored. He had shaved since the afternoon. He smelled of cold smoke, an aura brought into the house by a visitor from London once, way back. His voice was low-pitched, a hovering tantalising sound which demanded you stoop to catch it. He held his fingers before his mouth as he spoke. This irritated her. She wanted to rub her fingers on his two front teeth.

Under one light, in a restaurant, he looked old and craggy like the town. Under another, her orange-shaded bedside lamp, he was a boy, soft-skinned, an ointment she could dab and soothe herself with, a pale moon. Under the sky he was white-faced, a clown with full red lips and dark-circle eyes, a wig of spiral-curled hair and a big pink nose. He was hilly and sprawling over the sand-dune of her sheets. He was a rock in a soft place, a block to sunbathe on, a mooring.

She preferred to be with him in the dark. To see him was a dampener on her other senses. With no light, she could concentrate on silently sniffing, on mapping with her fingers his stony warm body as he slept.

And in the dark she could lie, distant from him, and concentrate on the undertone in his voice, tune to the bagpipe drone of meaning below the unimportant words. She listened to him, not to his words.

X

Ellen had mothered him from the start. This riled Annia. It brought a cool wind between the girlfriends. They must be apart while he was with her.

He tolerated Ellen, unsure what her game was, quietly pleased by an excess of mothers, irritated by Ellen's chatter.

She bores me, he complained.

And me, she had treacherously agreed. Let's be alone – just us.

Fatally, he had suffered this. Annia forgot her oaths and vows, she neglected her promise to remain within her citadel-self. It didn't seem to matter. Love was giving, and she gave up herself. He noticed.

Although he bored her with his chatter and sermons about micro-organisms and invisible world, she loved to hear him talk, to talk to her alone. She held his gaze as he talked, wishing the light would go out so she could rest her eyes and listen in other ways. But he prattled on and she half-listened.

Course the amazing thing about the world, he stated breezily, is the invisibility of it all. We only see the impression of a whole. But it's millions and billions of tiny tiny unseen little bits. What we see is a blur of bits – like a dot painting!

A Seurat, she corrected.

Yes – and all these little pumping throbbing cells, they're all down there – around us – in us – trillions of bits – that's all we are – trillions of bits looking for company.

What about explosions?

Explosions? Not my field, to be precise. But I guess that when the cells and atoms and neutrons get sick of one another they just bugger off – bang!

And what about implosions?

Don't know what you're talking about.

Where things can't get close enough – so they squeeze and press and – bang!

He shook his head, clueless. She could be obscure, only the tremulations on the surface showing, a deep detonation giving little idea of its cause, its origin, its aim. He changed tack.

What's your favourite animal? Mine's an amoeba – it's not really an animal, a protozoa – a fat soft cell which only has a skin, a filling and a nucleus. Bit like me really. Ha, ha! What's yours?

I haven't got one.

She somehow knew, knew he was making it all up, pretending. How she had no idea – but it was all so inconsequential as not to matter. But she had not detected it before. The hint chilled her. He was capable of awful things.

And she stared for a while at his hands as they gestured in accompaniment to some detailed description of amoebic feeding habits. Those hands, those skilful agile hands, that dextrous delicacy, could turn to violence, a savagery she almost wanted, so great was her erotic curiosity.

In fact, he blurted, an amoeba feeds by totally absorbing its food, swimming round it, extinguishing it like a fire, dissolving it into itself.

Shall we go?

She was tired and sad. He was full of shit, he was a fraud. The magnificent deception was a boy's disguise, a mask played with to see if it would fit. She lusted after older men, she deplored youth.

XI

When she looked back it was the first days she remembered, the times before she discovered his sham, his fabulous forgery, his untrust-worthiness.

And the time she recalled was less a continuous stretch than flaring moments. Images, not of him, but of red cliffs and yellow gorse-flowers, the cool deep of the bay, the autumn leaves on Mill Lane. And she realised it was not him she was nostalgic for – he was a zilch, a nothing, a wart – it was the flashes of heightened being which he made possible. He would so charge a time and space with eroticism that she could not – despite her will – forget it. He had been a catalyst to that ability already within her, to connect herself with the immensity of trees and cliffs and sea. After the process, he was redundant, unaffected, left as he was before. She, she had been connected in indissoluble union with the red cliffs and bobbing yellow gorseflowers with their fluffy revealed hearts, she was forever the autumn waste on

Mill Lane. It never was but it was her. He had made this possible. And she tried to be grateful. But how could she be grateful to a skunk?

XII

The one organism with which he had not connected her was himself.

He took Annia to Tenby. They stayed in one room of a lime-green Georgian house. Standing at the silvery net curtain, Annia could see the distant Gower, she could watch the sea rise and fall, covering, then revealing, the yellow crescent of sand in endless mutability.

They walked the cliffs. It was here that he pointed out the red stone of the cliffs, the burst hearts of gorse, the sludge of sea thrashing the rocks. She stopped to finger the golden, exploded gorseflower. He blundered on, immediately bored once he had seen. She loitered, bearing the bloom in her palm, memorising it – no, not memorising – just bearing the bloom in her palm.

They swam at Manorbier, stripping to be with the sea. He bounded in Y-fronts to the tide and leapt to the depths without a pause. She waded, trembling with cold, to knee-depth, then on, step by step, letting the water gradually take her. Then, suspended, she dug the thick sea with breaststrokes. She broke the surface, the skin of the surface, and plunged voluptuously into the thawed ice. She ploughed to the bed.

It was not there. In panic she drove for the air, seeing his legs bicycling against the green sky. Suddenly airborne, she shrieked with laughter and clasped his shoulders. Down they passed together in dual snotty baptism.

He shook her off. He struck for the shore. And cast down, she turned to wander restless in the open sea. The sun shattered on the waters. The waters tried to penetrate her.

He sat drying himself off, sullenly. She flopped beside him, her bared breasts an affront to him. He threw her his towel.

You trying to drown me or what? he asked savagely. I nearly died! What?

She stared in astonishment. He was angry, angry at her play – she scowled at him, scornful.

Give it up, she advised. But it was dangerous and he simmered, then rose and collected their things.

She sat in utter bewilderment. To her, this was play, a gambolling in the waves. But he could not swim, he could not swim! She had forgotten, or wilfully not remembered. And he was angry, but he couldn't let it get to him! He couldn't take it the wrong way. She was only playing. She ran after him, penitently.

He was furious at her carelessness. She was an abandon of senses, luxuriating in a nonsense, seeing wonders where were only facts. He stomped angrily. She caught him up but he was wishing for the dull monotony of an Ellen, the realities of anyone save this mad, luxuriating sensualist.

XIII

She soothed him, but only by accident. Days later, frustrated and depressed, she left him alone for a week.

He was jaunty with half-freedom. He forgot about her, he forgot her oozing, smothering love. He idled with his mates, he worked in an invisible world. For a while, he was content.

Then he called her, and she succumbed. He came round with wine and fruit and noodles, and they ate and she listened and he smouldered with desire.

His desire for her was a sporadic, occasional event, a volcanic explosion, cracking up through what he called his weaknesses. He grew aroused by her mysterious breasts and her odd thighs. He needed to see them bared. He undressed her, overwhelmed.

She rejoiced and wept to be reunited with him. It was over and it had started again. She let him paw her breasts and thighs and strip her to see more and revolve about her studiously. He seemed to be memorising her, not becoming part of her, but memorising her, his finger to his lips, circling like a valuer totting up the worth of an Aphrodite. She shivered, cold, and went to him, forcing him back to the floor.

It bewildered her that he seemed content to watch, to observe, as if she were an image on his electron microscope, a configuration of video dots. He seemed in no urgency to have and hold her, only to memorise an external image.

Whereas she, when embroiled bodily with a lover, strained to bind, to mould them together. It was what it was all for. To erase the membranes that separated, to merge organisms. She strained and strained, breathless with the trying. She urged him to push and squeeze only to make separation impossible.

He broke away with his orgasm gained. That was sufficient. A blast, an explosion for him, a squirt in the loins for her! And he was content to lie back, a scorpion, and giggle and breathe inanities and sleep. How could that be enough?

Ellen said it was usual for men to turn over to sleep because they were bastards. But men who didn't want it, wanted just to look and leer? Best to send them to a therapist or a whore.

Annia winced, and blinded herself to Ellen's wisdom. Jack could be got, she was sure. And in a fury, she calmly announced she wanted children. Not with him of course, she added – just generally.

Nightmare, he slurred from half-sleep.

Jack, don't you? You sure?

Sure as hell – this is the end of the line.

And Annia knew she wanted this man utterly, totally within her, to leave no trace of him on the earth. He would, all of him, be Annia.

She came off the pill.

XIV

Jack had already decided to leave. But what with one thing and another he had not got round to telling her. Annia was not to know, she pressed for him more and more. She prepared dinners, arranged dates, devised a party, booked a distant holiday and planned their move into a joint flat.

In all this she forgot herself. For a brief while, Annia forgot Annia and tried fanatically to be Jack. She muddled her plan, she tried to merge them by becoming him. Jack grew nauseous. It was plain to him, so ugly and plain.

Yeah – we're kind of together, he mumbled to a mate at her party. You know what it's like!

And both men howled hyena laughs and cast their eyes to the ceiling, swigging beers. Annia hovered, frantic for Jack, wishing guests anywhere but her flat, manic with desire for him.

Sometime later, she told him of the holiday – a fortnight in Mauritius, she had spent her savings. He winced. She noticed and blinded herself to it.

It'll be marvellous – imagine!

He was already imagining. His desperation mounted. Her arms were winding about him, the poison ivy hampered his step. He smothered his instinct, he lied.

Marvellous – how much did it cost?

And she lied, but it still shocked him. He reeled at the complete encirclement. To bow out now would be savage, to leave it till afterwards, parasitic. He was distraught. He went to a mate's house for a weekend.

Annia knew, but busied herself closing the deal. She left a newspaper open at the flat adverts. In work, she sifted out the notices of new accommodation and viewed properties. She planned the lay-out of furniture. She put his desk and microscope under the window. Her curtains would match. There was a room for the baby. But how to break it to him?

He returned from his friend's and asked her to go out for dinner. She could not accuse him of being tight. He had given his all but she wanted much much more. It must end.

XV

Annia is pressing her palms to the knees of the tree. The man is blurring in the drizzle, walking away. His dog and Annia's dog are embroiled in the mud, gleeful. She is grieving for her son. She is laughing as the drizzle becomes rain. And she is wishing she had the guts to jump into the pool and immerse herself in water so her atoms become the mud, then evaporate with the steam and rain down on the leaves of the elm and on the man's hair and into the soil to pass up through the filaments of tree-stem and out to the green veins of a leaf, each leaf, and be uttered up to air. And then again, maybe she is wishing the pool and the dogs and the man and the rain and the elm and its hillock would give themselves up utterly to Annia.

Our Marya

I

Marya and her mother sat idly talking. The loaves were browning in the oven. Father was working in his study. In imaginative laziness, the two women slumped at the table. Marya chattered, Anne laughed and set up a tale of her own. Marya watched, her eyes wet with excitement. Anne spun the tale of Joachim's, her husband's, folly. Her daughter gagged with laughter. Her father was so funny!

And – wait! wait! Anne cried, And then he took the bucket of water round the front and – with all the neighbours watching – him in his dressing-gown – his little white knees bobbing across the lawn – his glasses on the end of his nose – this scowl on his little face – and he poured the water on the beds – then back he goes – not a word to us! – we're all watching him – back to the bath – fills his bucket – so as not to waste our precious water – we paid for that water! – we're not going to waste it! – and out he plods – dirty water slopping all over his slippers! – all to water the michaelmas!

Marya doubled with hysterics, the laughter hurt. Her mother wore the face of a jester, the mock-simple expression of the comic. Marya slapped the table with her palm and jigged her legs to kill the laughter.

My loaves! My loaves!

Anne leapt to her feet and gadded to the oven. Four black square-tins she drew out of the smoke.

Oh me and my chatter! Look at these!

Marya calmed and comforted her. The loaves would be fine inside, no matter. And she made her mother a sweet tea. The women reclined again, wearied.

In the warm, they thought up something else to talk about. Marya lured Mother to tell again how it was when she was born, what it was like to be pregnant. She listened, familiar with the tale, comforted by repetition.

Marya had left home years before. Her mother had grieved. Joachim had disapproved. He raged but it did no good. Marya went her own sweet way. Unbeknown to them, she set up house with her lover.

John Jordan owned an antique shop in St James's Crescent. She took Dad's gold crucifix to him to have it repaired. Jordan kissed the heavy solid figure three times and smoothed the metal to a gloss. She waited to watch him work the soft metal into place, to nail hands on to the ebony backboard. His hands carved a new niche for the loose nail, his hands tapped the broken nail home. Then, with oil, he rubbed the wood cross to a deep shine, the gold figure to a gleam. She watched in wonder.

Jordan was twenty years her senior, a mute, cautious man with a soft fleshy face. Its lines and silver-flecked brows and temple reminded her of Joachim, his silence and obsessive industry of her father's secrecy.

She returned again to hear him murmur. In the back room he massaged her with yarns. Gilt mirrors were framed portraits of the stacked tables and of them. She burned for him, she asked him to take her to an auction. She wanted to buy another crucifix or an icon or a statuette. He quietly agreed. He was a sad, insightful man. He knew her purpose.

II

Quietly, he adored her. He took her to his house, an odd crumbling mirador high in Ffynone. She flitted amongst the shimmer of table-tops. She was ghosted in the varnish of wardrobes and fenders. While he distinguished a modern dresser as a genuine Regency piece, she chewed her nails in the shop. She did not work. It was not her nature.

He was fitting out his house. It obsessed him. The antique business was a front. It let him search out perfect furnishings. It paid for his redecorations. He tried to enlist Marya. She was not interested. But to calm him, she painted a wall – then cycled to be with Mother. She

95

hung two strips of wallpaper so badly he had to strip and rehang them. She fled to have lunch with Elisabeth, her friend.

Elisabeth had a crush on Jordan – it was an affectionate gesture to her Marya. That way, she showed how much she approved. Marya sparkled with pride. But she could not tell Anne or Father.

III

She had been with Jordan two years, and she was mad with boredom. Not with him – oh no, she was hypnotised by his distant, still stirring in the workshop, his silent pacing about the kitchen as she chattered, his presence over her in the black.

It was the subsistence at his side. That bored her. She did not want a grand project of her own. It was not how she thought – of grand projects and ambitions, murderously chasing achievement. She let Jordan do that. She wanted to idle, contemplative and worshipful. She wanted to sprawl on a sofa, munching chocolate digestives, watching the black-and-white romances on the telly, humming songs to herself. When she got up, she wanted to nap in the afternoon. She liked to rise late. She liked to be in bed by midnight. She didn't want to work in the shop.

But Jordan and her father, ignorant of the other, urged her to get up! do something! And she put it off and put it off. It was not worth the bother. Better to pass the days with friends or a book or a short walk round shops. Why all this hurry?

She half-heartedly sewed curtains and fittings. She displayed the calico drapes in his shop. They sold well and she was happy. That was enough curtains.

She bought and sold jewellery, marvelling over the trinkets and bracelets, necklaces and brooches, beaten from bronze and pewter and soft brass. In a case in the shop, her chosen jewellery grew dusty in the sun.

And she collected old 78s, thick discs of waveforms which, under a stylus, gave up muzzy operas, sonatas and quartets. She could not bear to part with them. Jordan frowned, this was bad business. She hoarded them in her room, playing them rarely. Just liking to know they were there.

She grew tired of all this business, this horse-trading. There was no drive in her, no urgency, no need. It was wasted time. When there was so much else to talk about, how could you fritter hours in haggling! She talked to Elisabeth about babies.

IV

The doctor announced her pregnancy in April. Her heart leapt.

And as she grew bloated with Jerome, she told her mother. Joachim screwed his brow and peered in fury over his half-moons.

What do you think you're playing at, girl? he blurted, incomprehending. Who is he?

She told them. She told them lies and half-truths, a patchwork of anecdotes – all to pacify them, to please them. She was so over the moon, she was so ecstatic, that they couldn't fail to be infected!

I know that scoundrel, snarled her father. He's a pirate, a shark! Don't want to know.

Dad, he's not! He's mine! Don't!

But he grunted and stormed out.

Anne soothed her, murmuring how he didn't mean it, he would come round. But why didn't she go and see a priest about getting married? Joachim would pay, she would do the eats. It would be lovely.

And the two women sketched it with vibrant colours, daubed the marquee in the garden, the confetti outside St Mary's, the cars, the horse-drawn carriage, the dress – her mother's dress – and how Father would look so funny in his silly topper!

Together, they wept. Anne held her and placed her palm across her daughter's belly. She swore she felt the child kick. But it was early days.

V

Jordan received the news impassively, his eyes like coals barely glowing with the breath of her telling. He was laying marquetry into a worthless table-top. His scalpel shivered, then steadied. He turned to his work.

That's marvellous, he said without tone.

John John John, she cried, her hands as duckwings clapping her thighs. Please – hug me!

He laid the scalpel down, reluctant. He was so cool, so restrained, so strong! He kissed her, to shield her eyes. She did not know him. He broke free.

How long?

Two, maybe three weeks past my period. A month.

Sure?

Doctor said so.

You happy?

She exploded with glee, slapping her palms, jigging with elation. He watched her without moving. She told how she was oozing joy, how she had never imagined, never thought it could be . . .

She was lost for words, she hung about his neck.

His mind was a storm, a sea-storm thrown into wild sky-reaching frenzy. How had it happened? It was not his! It couldn't be! He froze, his heart deadening to her. At the prospect of her infidelity, he boiled.

Marya, he tersely said, untangling her from his neck. When – when can it – when was it. . . ?

You know, you remember, *then*! You forgot!

He had forgotten. He stepped back in a pale faint. His hand flapped for support. She rushed forward, urgently.

The telephone box you silly! She laughed, crying.

VI

She had told him to meet her at two. They would lunch at her favourite restaurant. She flitted off, to shop.

Marya loved to shop, to buy or not, to fly from tiny shop to tiny shop. She loitered, soiling goods with her criticism, lighting on them only for a moment, rubbing a blouse between fingers, smelling it deeply, imagining herself as the blouse – no, it was not her – and suddenly dissatisfied, she flicked her eyes to another shop, on the far street, and danced to be with the books or the jackets or the carpets or the ointments. A bee, she worked the shops with their blooms in clusters, then raced on, on – buying frivolously, imagining herself everything.

She met Jack at the corner of Whitewalls. She had not seen him in years! He looked so different! She embraced him. He looked white, dead, his dark curls a plume squirted from a dead scalp. He eyed the ground, surly and restrained. She enthused over his presents, he had sent her flowers and books and music. He shouldn't have! He *was* naughty!

He wore black. He reminded her of a whale, a grampus, white blotches for a face in a shining black mass. She told of Jordan.

He scurried away, mortified.

He always was a bit strange, she calmed herself. She knew he had once had a bit of a crush on her. But that was all over. Crushes do not last.

But she could not shake the whale out of her mind, the lunging surfacing spouting killer – sudden, then gone. And she chattered to Jordan about other things.

They lunched all afternoon. He whisked her to an auction in Sketty, then to a friend's. They drank gin and she grew dizzy till all the flowers looked like ice-cream sundaes thawing to reflections. She staggered home, clutching Jordan, singing inanities. And as they passed the telephone box on Walter Road, he tucked her inside and removed the bulb. Stuck, they rutted like two dogs. She loved it all. She raised her knees against the glass. They were visible on three sides. Doused by the sweep-lights of cars, they were together under one name, daylit, nightlit, moonlit, sunlit, passing time, a whore and her client. Then she dreamed she felt the telephone box tire and lean backwards to rest her gently on the pavement but it was only Jordan laying her out in the soft snug of the duvet, a snowfield of duckdown. And he licked her all over, worshipfully, like a dog.

VII

A reporter from the *Post* sidled into Jordan's shop, incognito. Jordan enthused over an inlaid desk, an orange silk ottoman, a Victorian fauteuil. The man was impressed. He asked after their value. Jordan pitched high.

He grew flushed at the prospect of a sale. He needed to raise money, the baby was due at the end of the year. The top rooms must be done out. He had not paid that month's loan-instalment. The rent was late, the mortgage was strangling him. The man was a serious buyer.

He asked many questions about many things. In trepidation, Jordan fluttered about, drawing him into the back of the shop – there was a dresser, two hundred and thirty years old . . .

The man paid £2,100. Jordan sat shuddering in a sweat.

VIII

Marya told Elisabeth all about the sickness.

It was horrible, a loathing of the baby woke her and she stumbled to the loo. Wrapped around its neck, she vomited nothing, though the wish to throw the baby up was secret in her. It felt like the little blighter was working free, going up the wrong tube and rising, rising up her throat. Only nothing came. She couldn't wait.

Elisabeth sat with arms folded to contain her yearning. Her Simon had raved against babies. He never wanted them. She so envied Marya. She wanted so badly . . .

Elisabeth – tell him! Go on!

I can't – I mustn't – I won't!

You can, he'll love you! Take no notice of him!

And the women charmed themselves with the prospect, how wonderful to know, deep within, a secret coalescence of cells was clawing to be free! To know the certainty of your own fertility. What a relief! Marya gasped in bright beautification. She was already a mother. She was already swelling with a second soul. How she had always wanted to lie down and be the world, to become it, and now a new world was becoming within!

You're so silly, Elisabeth snorted. You and your bun in the oven – you'll rise and rise – and bang! Pop goes Marya!

Simon overheard their blarney. He traipsed in, mocking, from the dusk. He teased Marya's rapture.

Fucking nightmare, all this baby nonsense – can't you women find something useful to do!

We're making the world, Simon, so shut up!

You and your bother – let my wife alone – she's bad enough without you inciting her to rebel against her tender loving husband, aren't you, Beth!

So, Elisabeth told Marya and Jordan first, leaving Simon to his cars and his oily rags. She stood and shook with tears in their kitchen.

I don't know whether I'm coming or going, she sobbed. He'll freak!

He'll be fine, Jordan advised sternly. You just go home and tell him. He'll be made up.

And she brought her husband round to Marya and John's, shivering with fear, him dark and sarcastic at her side. They poured beers and the men screeched and hollered in the lounge. The women nuzzled each other in the kitchen, Marya whooping with shrieks of pleasure. Elisabeth was due a month or so after her.

We'll be together – we'll be together – Eeee!

Stop it, Marya, they'll hear! Shsh!

John solemnly told Simon how it got worse after the first week – a baby in the room and they weren't the woman you knew. Sex? Out the window. The next time you get a shag it'll be because she's bored with the first and wants three more, all at once.

Listen! Listen! hissed Marya. He says – he says he's going to strangle you in your sleep! He did!

He didn't, he didn't! whispered Elisabeth, crouching to hear. Did he?

You want it really – come on, admit it, Jordan pestered. Things'll never be the same – you married two women – one you see now – the other, she comes with the sprog.

And the girls clung to each other, infected with giggles.

IX

Marya had become so immersed in Jordan that, while it was happening, she felt his retreat, degree by imperceptible degree.

She had sunk herself in him utterly. While seeming to gad on the surface, she swam deep and low to the depths to be with him. She forgot how distant was the world! She rose to the surface again but, bored, delved back to where he worked noisily in his woodshed.

But he was cool to her, cooler than ever – his head bowed in adoration of a chessboard and pieces, carvings which he delicately restored.

O! she wanted to be his icon, his idol, the object of his passionate litanies, to be the mother of God and adored by all men everywhere, but most especially by him – if only he fondled her heart as he worked his effigy of the Blessed Virgin! If only she were a virgin, if only she had never been with any man – then, then he would want her! And she could withhold herself.

And at other times, overcome by the wearying wait for the birth, she would collapse to the sofa. She wished herself a trollop, a whore, wished he would treat her as he did that night in the phonebox – picking her off the streetcorner, reclaiming her, redeeming her, letting her wash him with her hair, letting her flaunt her bared buttocks to the moonbeams of cars.

But she grew tired of imagining – she wanted a security, a concrete root, a fastening. She could not bear the swell and fall of his mood. She needed to know – then she could relax, contemplate, be lazy and watch him work while she waited.

The doctor said her mood swings were normal. She had not felt suicidal? She had not wished to abort? Was she happy with Jordan?

She lied, but felt solidarity with an invisible community of pregnant women – 'pregnant', that ugly word, that ugly state, that's all she was! It would pass and she would have the child. But still she was restless. She grew tetchy and spoke her heart.

John John – I want to be married, I do.

She watched his brow furrow, his silver eyebrows shiver.

Of course.

She breathed deeply out. She curled into him and felt his shirt like licked rice-paper vanish. They pressed one to the other, she squeezed. He clenched, but it was to extinguish a terror in his heart.

He had married once, flippantly, thoughtlessly. Now, the request, the proposal, the idea, could not leave his mouth. He could not suggest it. He did not know his mind. Best to let her will take them both. What did it matter? She was insistent, she was devoted – what could he offer as a counter-argument? Nothing. If she needed marriage, she could have it. And when she ran, when she fled him, he would let her fly. She had wanted a child, she had got a child. Child and marriage – he felt himself vanishing before rivals.

They married in October, not soon enough for Joachim. He spoke at the reception, darkly referring to 'extended families', 'the seal of God upon a union' and 'the passage of time eroding barriers'.

Marya winced. Jordan ignored the father-in-law. That was all he was – a legal ornament.

X

They returned from Venice as the winter clasped the town. And as it thawed, her brother was killed on the Severn, his body washed out to the Atlantic and never wholly found.

She grieved with Mother. Joachim retreated to his study. Jordan softened to her, hauling her stuff about as she waddled from friend to friend. He smothered financial concerns with a dogged attention to his wife.

Barely had she mourned than the waters broke. In the spring thaw, Jordan whisked her, skidding, to Singleton Hospital.

Jerome appeared, without his consent, on a Sunday, under Capricorn. His moaning began and was to continue, with few pauses, for the next eighteen years.

She held him to her and secretly wished him back inside, where she could keep an eye on him – but the burden had worn her quite out, and besides, she would never have seen how like her brother he looked.

XI

Jordan scarcely had time to sort his worsening affairs – the newspaper blew the whistle in January.

He had been dealing in fakes for five years. The assiduous reporter had informed over one hundred customers of their bad fortune.

Jordan immediately closed the shop. He drove the remaining furniture to his father's old place in the mountains. He evacuated his wife and son.

For spring, they huddled to keep warm in the cottage, never answering the phone, Jordan receiving newspapers and summonses with equal despair.

XII

Marya shivered with outrage, conserving all her warmth for the boy.

Jordan loitered, white with shame, superfluous.

He explained: first he told half-truths, then a history he had not told before.

He was fresh out of jail, Swansea jail, somehow fortunate to get another shop. His father died while he was inside, the money paid for six months' rent, a down-payment on the Ffynone house and the stock, the fake stock.

And – and why were you – what had you done? She dared not look him in the eye, she was not in judgement, she was not.

Same sort of thing.

She could not believe – the stories of his past jostled and rivalled for attention, a million bits of anecdote, smudged to seem plausible. She wanted a clear, crisp story – one she could easily remember. She was unconcerned with morality, she only wanted a plausible truth, a proper tale, a past.

But he was shifty where before he had been shy. His dark coal eyes flickered one way and the other, scanning the fir-forested hills, not her. He could not be trusted, never. She stalked away to bathe the baby.

Somehow, in the smouldering rubble of the man, the headless

spineless chicken flapping with court orders and newspaper-cuttings, she could see an ember, a glow to adore. Only for a while, but she needed something for the while – to see this out. And they barely noticed the beauty of the mountains and the valley and the river.

XIII

Jerome laughed at Easter, his first giggle. It came from behind his toothless smile, a gurgle like the splutter of a plughole. It rose to border on a cough, his whole fat face screwing up to wheeze the chortle to his mother.

Jordan was not home to see it. He had driven to Swansea for the court hearing. He stayed away a month. Her mother came to stay. Elisabeth visited. But mostly, she was alone with Jerome.

Mother was a saint and Elisabeth was a dear, prophesying it would all come well. Talk was, he would be cleared, having only to fork out compensation to the unfortunates.

They climbed the hill at the back of the house. In the wild wind, Marya burst to hysterics. Her mother clasped her. Elisabeth carried the children to a distance, staring south, silently blessing Jerome.

Marya, overcome with grief for her brother, furious against her husband, urgent for her son, struggled to remake a history. She told her mother long stories of how it had been with him, as if telling it over and over would engrave it on the soft warm wax of her brain.

Mother returned stories, telling how 'your father' had been a rotten apple till she had made him good.

It's not true what they say about barrels, she warned. A bad apple can always turn good – just look at your father – he'd be in hell *now* if it weren't for me – and never a word of gratitude!

And slowly, Mother teased laughter from her. Elisabeth left with her son. The bracken blasted from the brown hills a pungent green.

XIV

Jack called, a whimper vibrating at the other end of the line. He had read the papers, of her marriage, of the fall. He was most terribly sorry. Could he come and see her? The verdict was on Monday.

She despised him for it, the gall rose in her. She curtly declined. The voice shrivelled to a whisper, apologised, then blurted insanities.

I did, I loved you, you know you do and it'll never be the same, you could have! you could!

She replaced the receiver. The ugliness of the man, the aged ugliness, the way the weather had torn him down. Such a beautiful boy! And he was a filthy, decrepit man! Ageing – how it ruined! She drew her son to her breast and squeezed.

His call threw her back on a memory of Jordan, a memory of his touching the crucifix with clean, white fingertips, and the clutter of the back room where in a mirror she had seen the two of them, overlapped. How hard it was to see a man! She revolted at the thought of Jack, his desire for her seemed a poisonous ambition, an amoral business move, a vulture's wheeling.

She was too hard on him, she knew. But his quiet sneaking, his covert lust, his snooping – oh, she had seen him in St James's Park, huddled on the bench, leering up at her window. But she had not thought of it or felt it – it was a nothing.

And she despised her husband for his deceit, his dark hidden conspiracies. What would leap out at her next? Another wife? A thousand step-children? A fake name? A false age? Who in hell was he? She drove maniacally back to Swansea.

Mysteriously, he was acquitted. And when he told her, she could not believe him – she bought a *Post*. Even the newspaper was a more reliable source than her husband. He had been charged to pay recompense to one hundred and eight customers plus undeclared court costs.

He sold the Ffynone house, the Powys cottage and the two cars. In a house sale, his furniture raised four thousand pounds. Valuers from the town oversaw the pricing.

XV

After the birth of their second son, Marya took the boys down to Swansea to visit their grandmother.

Joachim had retired, he sat in the garden staring sullenly at the michaelmas. Jerome hassled him, the old man stirred.

Anne asked after Jordan, Marya tutted, looked to the ceiling and explained. He had chanced upon a 'scheme', a way to set them up again. She never asked questions, she never saw him – the business got the best of him, the boys the rest.

All I see is a corpse – laid out on the bed – exhausted, he is – James is the last of the kids.

Oh, the next thirty years'll be the best – then it's monotony – look at *him* – he's mulling whether to have a bath so he can water the flowers – without a job he's nothing.

They walked the path to the beach. Joachim manoeuvred a grandson to a dune. They set about rearranging the beach to a castle. Jerome took the ramparts, building them before Joachim had scooped the walls from the moat. A drawbridge was found, thrown up by the sea.

Marya linked arms with Mother, nosing the buggy across the hard wet sand. The sea moved threateningly, then, distracted, retired. Distant moths of yachts trembled to steer about the rust smudge of a trawler. Bait-diggers shovelled mud in search for worms or gold. Low among the marram grass, mauve trumpets blasted their flossy stamens to the heat. Nothing was steady.

Look at the men – taming the beach.

It'll be the sea next.

Then the sky.

Their shrieks reached the man and boy. But they were too busy to care about scoffers. Ridicule always assailed the builders of fantastic projects. They must not be put off.

Anne walked Marya as far as she dare, till the boys were just a blur, then they turned, following the tracks of the buggy, back to a civilisation.

Martha

I

The dog was dead by sunset. Shot through the belly by an airgun, she crawled, her back legs nulled, to the sill fronting the door, and there expired. The Saducees' boy, sighting through the net curtains of Number Twenty-Four, had taken a potshot at the bitch as she snuffled bones.

Our Joey found her propped against the door. Nose upwards, as if to sniff the draught, she stared with dead yellow eyes. The black blood matted the fur about a shrivelled teat. Flies clawed the soft scabs to no resistance.

Joey was a carpenter, employed at Marriot's, tooling door-frames for two hundred a week. His callused hands daily fed white wood to screaming saws. He bore the dog's carcase to the children and their mother.

Look how her tongue is gone yellow! Ellen wauled.

Mother eased the girl back from the carious teeth. The dog was laid out, wound uppermost. She closed the mouth. She eased the eyelids down.

Now get yourself off – bath time – then bed – go!

Ellen scarpered, chattering death and resurrection. Joey shrouded half the blanket over the body.

How's it done that, then? Joey asked.

The cat peered at the dog's indignity with yellow-eyed disgust. The question was addressed to Martha via the cat. Both turned away without words.

Joey dampened a cloth, folded back the shrouding rug and wet the wound. Dabbing the scabs made them gleam bright. It seemed continuous application would warm the blood till she rose again.

Did you not bloody think she'd get done in? – did you not bloody think at all? – damn fool to let her run wild!

He picked at the dried haemorrhages. Taking an awl from his coffin-wood toolbox, he dug out a nail – a pewter-grey head lay buried in flesh.

The woman looked in horror, she felt the twisted metal missile.

How do they do it? she croaked, splitting the words.

Easy – already told you – because some fools let their dogs run loose in this place.

Joey rose from his haunches and placed both awl and nail in the sink. Martha knelt to lay the blanket over the body.

Should've kept the damn bitch in the house, like I said – not let her fend for herself!

He turned on her with snarling contempt, hating her shrinking. She cowered, expecting a blow. Ghosts stared at one another in the black glass of the window.

Drunk, Joey watched television. The lounge accumulated a carpet of beer-cans and ashtrays. He hated this house with its skinny walls. The cracked, skinny walls could not keep out the stink of the world. Decomposing, he sat lost within himself.

Martha moved about him, insulated. He ignored her for some hours but with the onset of bedtime became more hostile. She was incapable! A willed hatred seeped up through the fissures in him. He plotted against her. He recalled the sleeping children. It was no good. There were no excuses. There were no explanations.

Where will you put her? the woman asked quietly.

Outside – isn't that where we put dogs?

Joey leave it!

Leave it! I leave it! And look what happens! I'll leave you, more like!

.Stop it! Stop it!

She shrieked in mania. He really did blame her. She disbelieved it at first. But here it was dribbling out of him. Bile! – he hated her! She couldn't believe it!

I'll bury her in the morning – in the garden – where else?

Butbutbut – you can't do that – every dog in the neighbourhood'll be round scratching her up again!

You should've thought of that afore you let her run with every gang in the place, shouldn't you – go to bed, woman!

After dawn, Ellen woke him on the couch, telling how the cat had eaten out the heart of the dog and dragged its entrails all the way under the fridge.

II

They were only passing through. The council had placed them in the town with a promise of a nice house. That was two years back.

Joey was thirty years old, a master craftsman forced to abandon furniture-making for the steady wages of a sawmill.

Wood boards and planks stood splitting in the shed at the end of the garden. He had always planned to set up his own workshop. Now he would have to wait.

On the mantelpiece, among the ornaments from his first marriage, stood the carved head of a dog grooved by the awl with which he had later dug out the nail. He dug the head out of solid oak, sitting at his bench in the corner of the lounge with one eye on the dead beast and the other on his restless hand.

Each afternoon, Martha kitted out the children, put Jack in his pram and set out with the dog on a leash. They walked through the backwoods that butted up to the house. It was a regular thing for her. An escape into the thickly wooded country from which the estates had been hewn, thirty years before. Their estate was the most dangerous, yet, as if for consolation, bordered the woods. Forests filled the Clyne valley and flowed to the sea in the south.

When he was home, Joey took the dog out. He found the toppled oak in this forest. Returning with an axe, he sliced chunks from the soft tree. With ambition, he dried them in the outhouse.

Now, the trees were marked with fat red crosses of paint. Each cross tagged a doomed tree. Lumberjacks would hack the glades to timber, and bulldozers mow the roots to rubble. Two hundred and fifty homes would rise, wobbling, from the wet soil, one thousand more council tenants move in around them. They would be surrounded.

Their afternoon walks became more anxious. Martha memorised each sensation. She wanted to keep this world within her. She wanted to mentally map the entire Eden. Life in Sketty Park was made bearable by her ancient garden.

Martha spent her days wishing for the future. The council permitting, they would move to the Gower. She had heard of houses in villages where there would always be woods and hills and fields. Stories were told of cheap rents, sea views, friendly neighbours. She had been born at sea and longed to return to where she could see it and breathe it. Every week she pestered town-hall clerks. Every week Joey's pessimism deepened.

They'll never get us outta here – d'you think we're top of their list? – d'you think we're that bloody important? – wise up, woman!

He began to drink at the Fox in the winter. He escaped at eight o'clock and stomped in when she had gone to bed. Fumbling in the dark to strip his jeans, he clambered beside her and snored. The drink allowed him to bypass sex with her. His terror of getting more children was intense. She knew that. And it strangled their sex to a monthly affair.

I'm twenty-three – unmarried – with two kids – and living with a man who can't leave me – can't marry me! she moaned to her mother.

The older woman looked down at her, yearning to straighten out the daughter's life.

Didn't I tell you!

You told me love would be enough – I love him – it isn't enough – he'll marry me – you know he will – but he's got to get a divorce and she won't divorce him.

Oh! – if only you'd waited – why can't young people wait?

They had met in the Fox of all places.

He left his first wife on his twenty-fifth birthday. She admitted loving her brother more than her husband. His disgust sowed in him a suspicion that women lacked any morality whatsoever.

Money was owing from the house she had sold. The hope of eight thousand pounds did much to buttress his life with Martha. She had spent part of the fortune and planned the allocation of many more times that which remained.

So, indebted to the tune of four grand, they struggled through two years of home-building. A dralon suite was borrowed from a friend and never returned. Her mother donated two wardrobes. Joey built a vast bed from stolen pieces of teak. A table and a box of wedding presents were all he had salvaged from his first marriage. And for a time, they were happy.

With the child, Ellen, had come the accumulation of babystuffs and the job at Marriot's and the wistful longing for childlessness. Separately, they suffered.

III

Then, the letters began to arrive. Martha intercepted them. Joey was always out of the house in the morning. And so, for a while, he knew nothing.

Katrin, his estranged wife, had found the Lord. And in her earthly bliss had known she must reclaim her marriage.

She had moved to Bradford with her brother to escape public vilification. A powerful Church in the city heard of their iniquity. Elders had visited, prayed over them, and God entered their lives.

This was all told to Martha in a series of letters. Each one was ritualistically burned at the sink and flushed to silence, so regularly that the children thought it normal for mothers to incinerate the mail.

She removed the ornaments from the mantelpiece. Over a period of months, she replaced his old clobber with new clothes. She advised him to cut his hair quite differently. That was *her* haircut. She forbade any talk of Katrin or his life without her – enforcing the ban with black moods. Talk of his work enraged her – it was a place she had never seen and could only imagine as dangerous to her life with Joey.

In her heart, a fury raged. An obsessive lust to keep him insulated from whispers of his wife. Mention of marriage wreaked rage in her soul. Other women's unions became the object of her private envy.

He had not asked her to marry him. He said their relationship was different. It did not require the sanction of the state. When it was possible to live well without the legal ceremony, when the council did not view you any differently from married couples, it was better not to ratify the attachment.

Doesn't mean I'm going to leave you – I'd never leave – how could I leave the kids?

They were her children and they were his. That bitch up north could never obliterate that – she could never make them equal. She, Martha, was the mother of his children, the caretaker of his life, the companion in his thoughts and that made her his wife.

Still, the terror remained. No amount of walking the children through the woods could soothe her. And Joey's careful elision of their sex life fuelled a growing conviction that she was not safe. She watched the dendriform crack sprawl a grasp across the magnolia lounge wall, and waited for the house to crumble.

IV

Joey followed Ellen into the kitchen. The light was off and the blue dawn illuminated little. For a moment, the sapphire windows of the houses opposite seemed faintly beautiful. Then he remembered that he was living his life and he remembered the dead dog.

A smell of rotted meat merged with stale smoke. He flicked on the striplight. He saw how the wound in the dog's flanks had been opened up. The cat had been fiddling. No entrails trailed under the fridge – yellow liquid coursed across the linoleum, reeking of urine.

Back to bed, Ellen, and don't wake your mother – let her be.

He drew on his boots and collected up the dog. The garden and all in it was blue.

Between the outhouse and the flatboard fence lay a patch of unworked earth. It was here that he planned to lay the grave. He gathered a shovel from the shed and dug the soil. Distant, a moorhen called. Swallows cried invisible in the beeches. At the upstairs window, Ellen breathed an oval of condensation on to the glass.

He worked hard, drawing off his shirt and jumping into the pit to thrash at the cold earth. The body of the beast lay stiffening. He was three feet down and the sun was a red circle of fire on his cornea.

Ellen appeared, draped in an overcoat. She watched the silent worker. Bored, she plucked snot from her nostril. She peeked under the shroud to see the corpse once more. Resting, they marched inside to swig orange juice.

It was his daughter who ran to the front door to catch the tumbling letters. He flicked idly through them and plucked the envelope with Katrin's hand. The sun scorched the Saducees' bedroom window blood-red.

V

Martha lay beneath the duvet in a fug of half-sleep, that third state, quite different from wakefulness or sleep. Buoyed up as on an air mattress, she flung her thoughts about in fantastical imagining. She dreamed the sea.

If she attempted to wake, she could not. The state persisted just so long as she relaxed. When she did not think about waking, but rather tried to further the state deliberately, she would stir to regretful consciousness.

Most mornings she was automatically awoken by her rising lover and so deprived of this blissful interlude. But Saturday and Sunday remained special, most for this momentary scamper with the angels. Yet both days were scarred by that daylong wistfulness, a tremulous sensation of losing an unremembered world.

So, on balance, she preferred weekdays.

Joey stared at her pale body. He felt neither hatred nor desire. The sight of one breast lolling flat against her arm stirred nothing with him. He was another man. He moved forward and recalled the letter.

The fury swelled. He hated the cocked legs that coiled the duvet about themselves. He despised the tumble of brown hair smothering her face. For particular vitriol he singled out her mounded buttocks, raised out of their impression in the sheets.

He could not think what he wanted to do. Should he wake her with condemnations, beat her, or leave her be? If she had not seen the letters, he would stoke up a situation that might wreck everything. But, surely, it was best to confront her? What else could he do with the letter?

She stirred and dragged a hand across her brow. Cold, she tugged the duvet up to her neck, so vanishing all but completely.

He drew up a pair of her knickers from the carpet and turned them in his hands. He could not leave the room without some retribution.

These were her favourites. Black silk strands that seemed incomprehensible when held in the hand, but adorned luscious white flanks with inkiness, impossibly slender yet incurring the most excessive of lusts to strip away.

He took them with him to the garden.

Working quickly, he broke up a forklift pallet he had been keeping for some unknown use. He laid planks across the base of the grave. Stabbing with the shovel, he squared the hole and laid down the blanketed dog. He stored the pages of Katrin's letter and the stolen underwear in the blanket. Ellen moved from the shadows of the house into the orange light of early morning, murmuring to a plastic rose held as if it smelled sweet to her nose.

He assembled the hefty one-inch planks of unplaned pine into a crude coffin for the dead dog. He piled sticky soil in a rough pyramid over the grave. Ellen hummed a makeshift requiem and scattered plastic rose petals amongst the clods.

Burn out, he stamped down the surface. He tried to forget his fury. It was no good. With adoration, he paused to eye the leonine head of the young girl. He rejoiced in the living colour of her hair, the lambent blonde giving up its pigments easily to the risen sun.

Make a cross, Daddy – make her a cross!

He plucked two lengths of oak from the shed and swiftly nailed them at right angles. He plunged the foot of the length into the soil. They stood with hands clasped before them, unsure of what should be done at such a moment, yet confident, silence was the best way to follow a death.

VI

On Sunday, Joey took his usual walk through the woods. Unable to walk the route he would have taken with the dog, he trailed up through the beech woods to where one of the great highways slashed a corridor through the woodlands.

He crossed to the estate on the far side. Affluent houses stood adorned with teak doors and aluminium window-frames. Proud owners strolled with leashed dogs and rolls of fat newspapers.

Among the houses were set a supermarket and a church, constructed from matching materials, said by the architects to attribute the colony a sense of community and place. Joey felt no sense of community and place. They had spent two years trying to get their neighbours to say good morning. Wheelless cars sat beached on the streets, kids stole any movables and assassins shot two-inch nails at your dog.

He sidled to a noticeboard, abstractly wanting an excuse to pause. He would buy a newspaper but he was penniless. Saturday night had cleaned him out. He could only obtain money now by stealing it from Martha's purse. Payday was a week off.

He stumbled to the light and turned a circle on the tarmac. He wanted to destroy the world. He took a token kick at a litter bin. Someone shouted out of the white light. In controlled fright he revolved to face the wall.

The wall was the wall of the church. A large cast-iron outline of a fish drew the faithful – a Pisces, an Ichthus, a secret sign. The noticeboard happily advertised services celebrating the glory of God. Joey looked for the glory of God. He saw a clean-shaven man walking straight at him with outstretched hand.

Morning – good morning – you joining us? – hallelujah – my word what a wonderful morning!

Joey had not answered his question. He found himself steered gently into the foyer. He did not much mind: he had subconsciously been wanting to say a prayer for the dead dog. He was unsure as to how.

A woman with golden hair stepped majestically into his vision and, with half-born thoughts of punishing Martha, he followed her shimmering mane to the inner sanctuary. A spray of chrysanthemums bloomed from an urn. Distantly, a piano jangled and someone tapped a microphone.

A black cross was fixed high on a whitewashed wall. Joey thought of the dog. He passed the next hour in a trance, obediently rising or falling with the small crowd. Volunteers danced an enthusiastic amateur's jig in aisles. A flame-haired pensioner angrily thrashed a tambourine against her thigh.

Go up if you feel moved, whispered his caretaker.

Joey was not sure whether he felt moved or not – a movement in his stomach urged him to eat. And when the shouting minister mentioned the bread of life something curious seemed to draw him upwards and propel him forward to the plastic smile of the frontman.

Martha giggled when Joey earnestly told her he had been converted by a man with a hairpiece and, for years after, that fact adorned his proud testimony, raising smirks wherever it was heard.

And so, in Joey's mind, his entry into the kingdom of heaven on earth was indissolubly linked with laughter. Mockery stamped his rebirth from the outset. And at his death, many years later, it was said many were still sniggering at the unlikely fact of our Joey giving his life to the Lord.

VII

The first casualty in his war against the Evil One was their sex life. He carried the spare duvet into the guest-room. Clothes were hung in the wardrobe that stood on the landing. Martha was solemnly told that he was reviewing all aspects of their life together.

That evening, he visited the toupeed pastor who schooled him on his peculiar situation. He stressed the validity of his first marriage.

Persistent unfaithfulness is the only grounds for divorce – the word of God says that much – you must contact your wife – see what can be done.

Martha suffered a good deal. In a white panic, she scurried about the house, searching out tasks to do, inventing jobs, busying herself with the two mystified children who found unfamiliar attention lavished upon them.

In her heart, she disbelieved him when he said he wanted the best for her. A tumultuous fear swept through her, stopping her for moments. She paused, grasped a handhold and steadied herself. It was as if he had walked out the door, died and a new, wretchedly cold man had appeared, claiming to be Joey. This was not the man she had said she loved. This was an alien, a guest, a temporary resident.

And she knew he would leave, that he would have to leave, that staying would demand her submission to that faith of his, and she would never do that. It would not last and she could not trouble herself with things that would not last.

But what if it should? And as he happily chattered to her that evening, she saw in his eyes an ignorance of her. She had not known this before. He was an unreachable distance away. He had no idea who she was. How could he say such things if he actually knew what she was? And to herself, she admitted that if he did not revert to life again, it would be she who left him.

The week passed in an agony. She stuttered through each day, tracing out a barely remembered routine. Homecoming had been a mild pleasure – now she dreaded the return from the shops, from the library, from her mother's. And his homecoming became a terror enacted in the dying of the day, a living hell of frozen selves floating in a flaming mire, unresponsive, deaf and blind.

She endured it, focussing on the children's heads, drawn to them in a crushing, continuous embrace of souls. Slowly, she eliminated every other aspect of her life. She must wall herself up with them.

Her mother looked archly across the family dinner-table. She took Martha to herself and raised eyebrows to the ceiling.

Whatever next! – you silly fool – going and having the children of an idiot.

He's not an idiot – he *wasn't* an idiot – not when he used to be – alive.

Now you just look after number one – just make sure you and the kids are OK – you could move in here if it gets too bad.

And her father looked on in vague disgust. He matter-of-factly declared that she should leave that young fool as soon as possible – she could return to her old room. They would be only too happy to help . . .

She dismissed the idea. She committed herself to victory over Joey. He became an icy enemy floating in the same environment as her, a demon possessing her whole body. She must dig him out. The exorcism must be swift, she was dying while it lasted.

And soon they lapsed into silence, moving about the house in the evening, as if she were landlady and he tenant.

You sure you wouldn't be happier paying a rent? she asked.

He returned a sanctimonious smile that claimed to understand her better than she knew. But in fact he was mystified.

118

He wrote a letter to Katrin, explaining how his Damascus road experience had made him a new man. Martha sat with arms folded, watching the television, sipping a glass of gin. The fury mounted in her until she could suppress it no longer. It was pointless to keep silent when your life was being slowly sapped.

Just what do you intend to do?

Her voice shivered with the tremor of anger and sorrow. She would stop herself from crying, she would not cry. And to staunch the tears she focussed maniacally on his nose and learned how to despise it.

I am seeking the Lord on the matter . . .

You and your bloody Lord! And she flung the gin glass heavenwards so it swooped in a wide parabola to crash on the seated man. Gin splashed the scribbled letter, glass exploded about him.

He rose with dignity and collected each and every fragment. With finger and thumb he peeled the paper from the board and carried it ceremoniously to the bin.

Our children are upstairs, he said. Now, by all means have your little tantrums – that's your way – but think about your soul and their souls – that's what's at stake.

Oh they've really got to you, haven't they! – brainwashed you, good and proper.

I'm a new man – yes – born again.

Well, I can't live another day with a new man – I loved the old one – and if he doesn't come back bloody quick, I'm out – and I'm taking your children with me.

He sat for some hours in dark misery, praying urgently in a whisper. If he left and rejoined his true wife, the two children would be irrevocably damaged. That would be a sin. If he stayed and divorced Katrin, who had now repented her crimes and pledged herself to him, he would have to marry a woman who refused pointblank to submit to his authority. He would watch as she carried her own soul to eternal fires in hell.

With decreasing optimism, he thought on, circling round and round, until a tremor from his soul told him to rejoin his wife. In haste he dubbed it the word of God. And with new zeal he embarked on a systematic destruction of his life with Martha.

VIII

First, he consulted the head of his church and spent a morning with a solicitor. With religious and civil law ratifying his actions, he returned to Martha and the children.

We must stay friends, he announced to her laughter.

She folded her arms beneath her breasts and turned obliquely away from him, nodding to his specifications.

I'd like to take the children with me – I accept that it's not possible – you must have them – come and live near us if you can – we'd love to see you.

She winced at the pronoun 'we' – that was the stamp of separation. The entire break rested within one syllable.

When you've squared it with the council, he continued, I'll bow out of the arrangement – it'll make your life a whole lot easier.

She boiled with rage. She rolled one fat lip to stop her chin shaking.

This whole thing is a mess – I wear it on my conscience for ever – but we must right a wrong – you know that.

She could not follow this logic, but could not counter it either, so held her peace. Stolid silence was the best way to survive irrational tyranny. To engage a madman in discussion was to dub oneself an idiot. She marked a cross in the condensation of the teak table-top. And he could take that bloody bed back with him. She would move into the guest-room – an alien in her own house.

I'll get this sorted as quickly as I can – remember Martha, the Lord loves you – and I love you – as a sister.

Just one thing, she began with deliberate meekness. Permit me one favour?

He smiled an oily grin with closed lips, his eyes mapping her face as if it were an odd land.

Leave my house tonight – I can't bear another night in your company . . . Her voice began to oscillate, as if between control and madness. Leave tonight if you are leaving – get out quickly – strangers scare me . . .

He paled, his skin the colour of the cream wall. He seemed to vanish, leaving a propped jacket and jeans. Then, without a word the ghost turned and left the lounge. A faint draught created in his wake cooled her brow. She clasped the back of the sofa for support.

Four hours later, he was gone. He hired a van and loaded the bed, table and his clothes into the back. He anointed his children with a kiss. By midnight, Joey was embracing his wife in Bradford.

IX

That afternoon, they walked the woods. In the haze, the howl of chainsaws blotted the birds' cry. Blue smoke ascended into the canopy of spring leaves. Ellen found a track that led up to a high place from where a ring of stones rose to mark an earlier city. Entering the ancient temple, she catcalled to the nested swallows and danced in erratic flying circles. Mother followed, at a distance, her son strapped in a papoose to her breast, her face bright with the climb into the heavens.

Beneath them, the town stretched, a recent phenomenon for the mossed beeches, a crenellated sandcastle, designed on one drawing-board, years ago, and precisely laid out for the dogs to die in.

So rarely did she get out of the town that Martha had forgotten the view of pale hills, greyed in the distance, and the expanse of land, and on all horizons, the sea. She was thrilled by the prospect of distance, the view of the sea. It was possible to move, to sail, to swim. The walls of the town were not impregnable, she could up and out. She rejoiced in the few illimitable freedoms she possessed. And with a sudden grief she missed the yelping of the dog and the moaning of the man, but it was final grief and it passed.

Some time later, a letter arrived from Katrin and the Reverend Joe telling of the miracles with which God had most wonderfully blessed them, and as was usual with her, she torched it in the sink to cheers from Ellen and to yawns from the cat. And the flame climbed briefly in a yellow tongue that licked the ceiling black.

Of Saphira

I

Saphira died today, peacefully in her sleep.

As she sank to sleep, Saphira dreamed of all those she had known. In a doze, she recapped.

While a young woman, she had loathed her name. She must rid herself of it – 'Saphira Goytre', a cancerous growth of a name, all the sugary ambition of her parents in that forename. What had they been thinking?

And she set about finding a husband, a man with a fine, clean, musical name – an exotic, perhaps foreign name. After her operation, she worked for an estate agent. Stan Brass had changed his name to leap to the top of the telephone directory listings. His business was growing – he struck out on his own: Stan Anias Agents & Financial Services rented a shop-front in Walter Road. He hired the most attractive of his interviewees. Saphira accepted the job as secretary.

They married the following year. It was a tax move. Stan needed a partner, a wily accomplice. He co-opted his secretary. They bought up land in the Mayals, selling it to developers. A single deal – proposed by his wife – grossed one hundred thousand pounds. Their share bought the house. They lived in separate rooms. Saphira could count on one enamel-nailed hand the times they met for sex.

It was futile of course – to strive for children. Stan neither could, nor wanted, to have them – his wife was barren, stricken as a young woman with cancer. Cured, Saphira quelled the wish, the want. They were too busy to adopt. Business was all. But still she yearned, darkly, secretly – as if her wish was an illicit fetish. And it gave her a rush to think of it as she grappled with one or other of her lovers.

Stan never mentioned it. He never got the chance.

II

Adam was the first. Oh, she had been with men many times before, but Adam was the first in the game, the long-running wicked sport she delighted herself with.

He was the first to be told to meet her at the hotel. She took a suite, once a week. He was stopped in a bar on Oxford Street. She used her favourite tactic – stun the man with outrageous desire, tranquillise him with candour.

Would you mind coming to my room?

She gave the number, the name of the hotel etc. She spoke sternly, correctively. It always alarmed – but she adored the alarm, the terror. Men were so easily terrorised. She stalked away, clasping the fur jacket to her breasts.

And they would always appear, all except one. And she had her suspicions he was deaf. Not gay – oh no, gay men were fair game. Adam was gay, his olive-black hair long, his face a plastic mask, his left eyebrow permanently raised in queenly haughtiness.

He had told her his name – that was regrettable. She never let it happen again. And if she met them on the street, well, she ignored them. She never commandeered the same man twice.

III

It was Adam she remembered most clearly – a curse on her – as if he had been the only one. He had not been perfect, far from it. She had not mastered the technique, so early on. The key was to play a part. That time, she let the mask slip.

She met him with a drink. It was best to calm him, indulge him in familiar rites. Then, curled on the sofa, she instructed him.

It was quite simple – he must utterly forget himself, improvise, be another. To help, she placed a dolly on the bedside cabinet. For her it was her husband. Stan was overweight at thirty, cumbersome at forty, immense at fifty. The mannikin sat squatly under the conical lamp, a wax Buddha.

For Adam, it could be anything – a fetish, a totem, a think-piece.

Just concentrate on being the blubbery oaf on the table – forget Adam.

And later, she removed all mirrors and shining surfaces and reflective objects – nothing must put him off. The one problem remained: how to forget the object of her body and his material form? She lowered lights and on occasions – when she was particularly down – wore a blindfold. Better to hear and smell, to taste and touch. Nothing then distracted the imagination.

IV

One had been a policeman, an officer on duty in the precincts. It was remarkable – she said so herself. How easy it was to seduce a man! But this was not so much *seduction* – she thought of it as deception, self-deception, a magnificent theatre, staged in a temporary coliseum. A mock-gladiatorial rite.

To her mind, sex could only be thrilling when you did not know *that* person – you were free to make him (or her) what you willed. Actual personalities – those shifting facets of a jewel – were such an inhibition.

When Adam offered his hand and said his name, she shuddered with revulsion. Had she known better, she would have turned him away. His worldly presence drifted like smog into the pristine room – all in a name! that dirigible under which we insist on hanging, huddled in a basket with our past.

She shunned naming – but while prancing naked about a prone boy, imagined herself with thousands. She composed them as he gasped over her. Muttering girl's names, boy's names, god's names, soothed her – sent her out of herself, up to float about the distant lamp.

That policeman – stern, officious, then abandoning all prurience – stripped off his uniform. But he must keep his hat on, she giggled. He must keep his hat on! Then he was no longer a bobby, he was an erotomaniac with a bobby-fetish. And he looked so stupid!

She loved above all to laugh – anything they could do to make her laugh, that was a treat. And she got one boy standing on one leg on the dresser, clothed only in a scarf, twirling in a pirouette, holding an inflated condom over his head, as if suspended from it in mid-air.

That she could pluck men from the city streets, undress them, instruct them and persuade them – for an hour or so – to clown and jest, she did not see this as odd. She gave herself no titles – 'therapist', 'whore', 'frustrated housewife' – she was none of these. She could be anyone.

V

Once, to make herself cry, she co-opted an older man – to survey her, to walk round and round the bed, scrutinising her – she commanded him to describe her to her face.

She had seen three boys sniggering in a street, pointing and sniggering: They pranced behind her, mimicking her walk, nose in the air, hands on hips. They were mocking her! Her panic barely restrained, she stumbled to a bar, necked five gins and asked a grey-suited man to help her.

He was a little agitated but paced about her – fully clothed, frowning. She lay on the bed, utterly revealed and yet not so.

A mole inside your thigh.

A birthmark! Not a mole!

Shoulders: fine, bony but fine – can see the tendons in your neck – loosen up – arms: good working order.

Be honest, be honest – my legs!

Legs! – your legs are good – a little heavy – perhaps too white – hairy – I like your feet . . .

What are they like! What are they like?

Like feet – the line of heel, the line from shin to toe – very impressive – almost perfect.

Thighs?

Good, not so good but good.

Good this, good that – say something imaginative!

She turned over, lay on her front.

White and fleshy – like . . .

More! More!

Buttocks – personally speaking – you have good buttocks.

Describe! Describe! I can't see them from here!

She was torturing herself. The man was no help. Words told nothing. But she pressed on. His judgement was in a way final.

What I like about buttocks like this – they're like hills, like round hills. They rise here –

Hills? Hills? Hills!

He moved in to show.

Don't *touch*! I said – don't touch!

He retreated. She giggled.

Sorry – I want words not prods.

They start here – on the back of the thigh rising from a fold – they climb – steep – to a soft mound – lovely.

I believe you – God knows why – what about now?

She leapt to stand, to turn and twist before him.

Yes, not so good – full, perhaps too full – the price of looking good when you're lying down.

What a stupid thing to say! I never paid – I got landed with this! What about tits – you said nothing about tits!

No – a big-tits man myself – another man would say different – they're too small for me – nothing really – only one opinion.

Like this?

She pressed them together.

Afraid not – it's nothing to do with that –

Oh you're no help – describe!

Small, drooping . . .

Drooping! Do they droop? They don't droop!

A little, a little – no, on second thoughts – pert!

Better, I like pert. More, more.

Nipples, large. Cleavage (under pressure), fine. Profile, indistinct. But not drooping.

Now you've got the hang of it – belly?

Yes – flat, good and flat – have you kids?

None of your damn business – please leave – thank you ever so much – I don't know you – if I see you, we are strangers – but thank you ever so . . .

He traipsed out. She was left with herself. She was none the wiser.

Best to forget altogether the cumbersome body to which your soul was tied. Best to run from it in the dark with the hard, nameless body of a boy.

VI

It gives testimony to the essential goodness of the human spirit that not one of her boys – before this one – ever sold his story to the hungry news agencies. There was enough fodder here to set up a youngster for years. A snitch could humiliate this city councillor, scupper her career and launch his own. Somehow, her empress manner sealed lips, somehow the mutual humiliation kept chattering traps shut, somehow the spell worked – stripped of their names and histories for an afternoon, these men forgot the woman. The hours were bubbles out of time and space hovering on the seventh floor of the beach-front hotel.

VII

One afternoon, she commanded a woman to follow her. Occasionally, Saphira was overwhelmed by female beauty – by the power of female beauty. A dark, solitary lady crossed her path. Afraid, Saphira followed rather than approach her straight away. For an hour, she assessed the woman. Then, in a sudden stab, she paused her. She let her eyes flame to hypnotise the other's. The woman cowered, eyelids shivering, pupils dilated.

Please come with me . . .

Alarm animated the woman's face. She followed across the streets into the foyer – speechless, stumbling on high heels and mini-dress. The receptionist nodded. Swept up, up, up, Saphira glanced down at her stunned victim.

And, unlike her men, this woman did not need instruction – she opened her mouth only when Saphira's lips forced her. She murmured only sounds. She worked in the dark with this seductress, obliterating themselves.

True to form, Saphira never learned who she was – she felt a twinge of regret. The woman was extraordinary – rather, her effect on Saphira was extraordinary. Utter silence! where man can only chatter, ask questions, quiz. And the inscrutable face, its soft flesh barely moving. So silent, so hidden a woman – Saphira dallied with giving up the game, giving up the men, giving up Stan and his business and running to the hills with that dark, humble woman.

She laughed at the fancy and smothered the lady's bewitchment with a boy, a shrimp, a puny startled kid, brought shivering under neat hair to strip to boniness in her lair.

VIII

She asked another to give her age, to guess how old she was. The man laughed and jumped about the room, his soggy member banging on his thigh.

Twenty!

Wrong!

Thirty!

Oh! Wrong!

Forty! A hundred! A million!

So, so wrong!

She was lying, and she was not. He named her age according to legal records – not the age of her persona: a three-thousand-year-old priestess at the oracle of Diana at Ephesus.

Forgive her imagination.

There are no allusions.

IX

Saphira loved to adorn herself, to dress in costumes, jewellery, make-up, cars, houses, gardens, sky. But most of all she loved to adorn herself with others' things.

As a child, she danced in Mother's wigs about the house. Under a cake of face cream and deep black eyeliner, she hid from Father.

As a grown-up, while entertaining men in her suite, Saphira carefully maintained a disguise. Naked, she needed a prop, a toy, a mask – to complete her cover-up. With a wig in place, or thick eye make-up or coloured contact lenses, she felt as covered as a corpse.

This was less to conceal her public face as businesswoman and city councillor; than to aid her histrionics. She hid the vacuum of herself from all. She did this most effectively by appearing to reveal the lot.

She quickly learned how a man can be altered by the view of a woman stripping. All disapproval, confusion and resistance vanished as she unbuttoned her blouse, or loosed the shoulder-straps of a dress. He stood stunned like a struck elephant, sweat anointing his brow.

The art was to strip without self-consciousness. She tried the mannered performance, the pout, the fluttering lashes – the man blushed and looked away. But if she simply disrobed while she talked, flicked off her shoes as she stirred drinks, unzipped her skirt as if he were a disinterested husband, then he would stare. He was altered.

Naked, she was utterly hidden. They looked and thought they saw. They heard her stories and thought they understood. They heard a name and thought they were acquainted.

Once, she made the mistake of elaborating on her own misfortunes – how a bastard of a husband, tripping all over the world, ignored her for winsome girls. He never loved her! she wept. He never loved her in the way she had just been loved! Oh, she needed love like that all the time!

The man had crassly fallen for her, declared his intention never to leave her side, to fold his company and with the gains lavish her with attentions.

She gasped in horror and bustled him from the room. That sort of thing must never happen again. She stuck to stories of an emotionless cast. She insisted that this meeting was a one-off. Men believed what you told them. They were stupid creatures, beguiled by a demonic stare, led by the nose, deprived of their trousers at a woman's whim!

Contrary to popular wisdom, promiscuity made her happy. Twenty-three hours of each day tottered to black depressions, the fear of which scared her on waking – one hour was an afternoon heaven. She was perfectly herself. If you suffer – as I do – from an anxiety to know Saphira, then look to these dusky afternoons, these secret salons, where the thousand facets of her soul sparkled to the walls.

For she had no character, not worthy of mention. She was only the stage for a thousand divas, a platform whereon ten thousand dissimulators could prance to dupe us.

X

She got to know Jack, hence she never invited him to the hotel room. He lusted after her, he sat in her office and bought land. Had she seen him characterless in the street – she might have controlled him.

But Stan and she chattered the inane dialect of business – told how they met, how they had fallen for the other – you wouldn't believe how well they worked together on *every* level!

Jack pestered her with calls, offering dates – telling how he knew she was not satisfied by her husband, how he could see it in her eyes, in the way she ignored him. He proposed dinners, he invited her to operas, plays and the ballet.

She was weary of him when she met him – by the time he had revealed himself she was irritated. Eventually she insulted him so grievously he never called again. It was regrettable, to lose a customer. The man was irrelevant.

He followed her, watched her, made notes on her movements, contemplated rape and wept at his fantasies of their affair.

Her contempt for him worked in the end. In pursuit one afternoon he was distracted by a look in another girl's eye, a look which promised interest. He smothered his obsession. He spoke to her, he barely remembered Saphira.

Saphira never gave him another thought. He was a nonentity.

XI

It was their habit in business to divide investments into small lots, stored with many banks, to guard against both a bank's collapse and the taxman.

With this policy in mind, Saphira distributed herself among her men and boys. What short-sightedness to desire one man! To attach yourself to one shifty unreliable man! She squabbled with friends.

I know this woman, she exclaimed – she has hundreds of lovers – never sleeps with any more than once – never asks their names – she loves the world – she wants to be part of everything –

Huh! what a tart!

Imagine – her poor husband – she does *have* a husband?

Oh yes – she says he's wonderful about it – pays the hotel bills – has the men driven around . . .

She was getting wild with the story, telling tall tales. She clammed up. The mob of pious friends chattered and muttered, tearing the woman to shreds. How unfeeling! And a woman – behaving like a man! She'll do her soul an injury!

Saphira looked on, highly amused, swearing for ever to keep it a secret. To hide herself was so wise. Who – if they had a self – would give it to this pack of baying dogs? Honesty was stupidity, make-believe was the way to truth. She left the room.

XII

Most men were hasty, shoddy in bed. Sex was a discharge, an excretion. Once done, it could be left for hours, till the stewing juices again demanded release. They could only be used once.

But occasionally, she chanced upon a woman of a man, a lusty athlete who would never tire, never dry. She kept him on and on, until it was urgent she left. And now and then, she wanted to see that man again – but she desisted. It would do no good, it would not be the same. It would take as long for him to be wonderful again as it would for her to find the next stud. A man was not intrinsically but accidentally good. Like a favoured food, he delighted – but the continual gorging numbed the palate.

What she would have done without Stan she never knew! Could it all have been possible without his ignorant support? Alone, could she have divided herself between ten thousand lovers, given herself up like the sun on the sea to uncountable fragments? How could she thank him?

It came to her that they had not had sex – as man and wife – for ten years. It was their tenth anniversary! She cloaked herself in a transparent negligée and welcomed him to her bedroom.

He was enormous, a bloater under the worn shirt and pinstripe – he wobbled on the plinth of her, dangerously insecure. He could not get it up. He could not get it in. He could not come. Somehow, they negotiated an orgasm. And put off similar terrors for another decade.

So it was a relief to have them put him in the city jail – charged with corruption. There, he remained completely ignorant of her shenanigans, there he was relieved of the torment of feeling he should sleep with her. When his parole was cancelled for bad behaviour, she was quietly happy. She knew where he was, they had lovely chats each Thursday, she could manage the business – or rather, her managers could handle the business.

She threw herself into her vocation. She took the suite full time.

XIII

Her theatre grew ever more sophisticated. She accumulated a permanent store of outfits, gentlemen's and ladies'. The victim was ordered to select a costume from his wardrobe, dress, think himself into the role, and stride in when he was ready.

It was of course always a seduction, a bed-scene. She taped the bedroom sequences from several films and played the erotic collage to the preparing male. She combed them for new ideas. Her imagination flagged with age.

Once, she was Julie Christie, he Donald Sutherland, the room Venetian, the dead girl her unborn daughter. Then she was the voyeur's girl in *Man of Flowers*. Later, she was Jean Seberg, he Jean-Paul Belmondo, sprawling before his death on a ruffled divan, clothed in vests, smoking Gitanes.

But it was too specific, too limited. She needed to play in the fenceless fields of her imagination. It could not be scripted, this was improvisation.

132

So, she wrote a cue on a card, left it on the table and, from that starting-point, they would wander as the whim led – but it must end with her absorbing him wholly – this was what it was all for – the reverse birth, the baptism into herself.

Then, disgusted, she would banish him from the gloom to collect his strewn suit and twin-set undies from the lounge. She curled into the sheets, clasping her womb.

XIV

The *mises-en-scéne* grew more elaborate, the roles more far-flung. She played everyone – there were not enough documented women in history, there were not enough types. She needed to know the world, she needed to travel the world, she was a permeable membrane, the game an osmosis, the succour the universe.

And she grew a little mad with it – friends noted her obsessive need to be alone, her business managers kept consultations short and restricted press and clients from seeing her. Madame would write, she might call. She did not take visitors.

She moved to an isolated house on the Gower, she almost wished herself in solitary confinement in a cell next door to her Stan. But no – how silly – what would she do without her boys?

Yet her boys did not need her. And on terrible occasion a man laughed in her face. His girlfriend sidled from the shadows. She darted away. And the one who did accept that afternoon, she was more than ever tempted to keep, to foster their attachment – but he was Mark Antony and she Octavia – and she knew how that tale ended. Besides, she was already attached.

And she rushed to visit Stan, to stare at him with fervour, to see if she could see the strands binding them across the table. They were imaginary, but she felt happier imagining them than not. That was what marriage was for, warm attachment.

XV

As her desire for sex ebbed, she took to playing only short games – often clothed, they would pace out a dinner in a restaurant, a walk by the beach, a stroll in the park, decorating the house – all in the controlled universe of the suite.

Her partners she took from the older men of the town, fearing more and more her deep wrinkles and dusty skin would lure jeers from lads and boys. The gracious, well-heeled greybeards treated her with calm interest, a gentle curiosity – and she told them the tale they wanted to hear, to warm them.

Less and less frequently did she take off her dress. She didn't want to see another flabby stomach. Better to sit in silence and watch the afternoon film, or snooze in separate armchairs after a cup of coffee. And once, quite by mistake, she had a visitor stay overnight. They were dozing after the late film, pretending to be a retired long-married couple and the next moment it was dawn!

She pitied him, ordered breakfast and they played the couple rushing to eat and talk before he flies to work. He vanished, he had touched her only once – to peck her cheek with a goodbye kiss.

Wearied with organising her domestic life at home, Saphira moved permanently to the hotel. She took the same suite.

And she drew her stock of dance-partners from other residents, the traffic of guests who lolled bored in the bar.

The hotel-manager tolerated her custom with amusement – dear old Miss Saphira! nabbing all the crumblies in the place! He came to regard her as an establishment facility.

Her business managers maintained her public face. Grants and gifts were distributed as palliatives to a faintly curious media. The ostentation of her giving was no less than a distraction, a mask to shield the decomposing Madame from a nosy, busybody world. She was grateful. Increasingly, she needed a back-up, a support team. It was less easy to manage a theatrical career, ageing under the spotlight.

She had not received a visitor during the last six months. She always meant to – but it was so difficult to entertain with indigestion! Best to put it off till tomorrow. She found it difficult to walk without a stick. Accosting men in the foyer was all well and good – but you wanted to look your best! A snapped daffodil is never so alluring, even if it has a prop.

Stan came to see her when he got out. But the hotel-manager had been instructed to fend off the curious. She was out – she had left messages with a certain Mr Smith – Stan raced to see his business manager. Indeed, Saphira had put the lot in his stained name. He took on the job with gusto. He didn't get a chance to call again, he was so busy.

XVI

Saphira spent her time rehearsing. Each day she changed costumes at noon, again at three and for dinner at six. After she had worn a costume once, she had it burned. So, while her memory filled, her wardrobe thinned.

She requested the manager have her mirrors restored. They hung faint and magical over the fireplace, over the dresser, over the bath. And wherever she went in the suite she carried an oval handglass, just in case there was a knock. But the manager obediently ensured that never happened.

Saphira anointed her face and body with oils – to separate her from the profanity of ugliness. She larded on the creams and lotions, thick plaster casts of clay, layering a flesh over the bones. For an hour, she coloured the mask with blues and oranges, greens and pinks, a death-mask in brilliant colour. Dressed with the aid of trusses and ties, concealed wires and drawstrings, she emerged at twelve.

A mirror was waiting.

By half-past twelve the face needed remaking. For two hours, she renovated the façade. Then, for her matinee appearance, she stalked back in from the wings at three.

And so on, utterly taken up with the sculpture of herself, the Diana at Ephesus. For she had absorbed into herself all the world and the world was nothing, it was a superfluous gallery and pit and gods, spectators to her command performance for the queen of Saphira.

And dozing on the brink of a fresh life, she remembered all who had been and were now within her, and she felt herself swelling, pregnant for a life, bearing a hive of worker-bees, airborne about the superfluous streets. Dying, she shrugged off her name, she forgot herself.

XVI

TRANSCRIPTS

I

I have an ache beneath my breasts, right across my front. Not serious, where they kicked me. Oh, they didn't hurt me. They are my friends. No. Father liked this, this music. The umbrella plant is Mother's. She brought it back from America. I'm lying. You'll never guess what happened: I went shopping. Last Wednesday, no actually it was yesterday – it could have been Monday. I'm hopeless with dates. The shops are good here, good clothes. I left in the morning, followed the yellow line along to the corner. You know, the corner on the hill above the station. From there you can see the dock, the dock where Mother didn't come back from America. And I walked along the yellow line past the house where we got the cat. There's an old couple living there now – I don't know their names. My head hurt, but it didn't matter. It was a hot day, it was probably the sun. Mother always said you should wear a hat – that's bollocks. Mother was full of bollocks – no, that's nasty. I was full of bollocks. What are bollocks? Daddy said he had bollocks and I didn't – he said I was afraid. I never knew what bollocks meant. The problem with this cat is that he crawls all over just as I'm beginning. Where was I? The shops, the shops. I'd got this idea of a dress. I couldn't see it for all my trying. They had red ones, red ones with satin patterns down the front – ruched arms, great ball-dresses that women wear, wedding-dresses. They had yellow dresses as well. Yellow's my colour. I'm pale and I have yellow teeth so it matches. They say I have yellow eyes as well but I haven't seen a mirror in weeks. The blue dresses are nicer. If only I could wear blue. I just haven't got the figure for it. There was this man who offered to show me all the good shops in town. He said I didn't know where they were. He was probably right. I haven't been to town for God knows. It's one of those things. You can live in a town

139

for ages and never really know it. I've stayed inside and cannot bring myself to go out. But this was a special day. I thought I'd treat myself. I had to sneak out, mind. They wouldn't like me just wandering off on my own. You know what they're like. Anyway. This man – tall, brown hair. I could describe him. I *did* describe him for them. They never found him. Took me in one shop, then in a bar and stole me a drink. Very nice, oh very nice – immaculately dressed, lovely teeth, smoked a lot, and he had the most enormous bulge. I couldn't keep my eyes off it. And when he went to the bar his two buttocks were pressed tightly, tightly together. Anyway. He took me out the back. I shouldn't have gone. But he took me out the back and started undoing my shirt. He said he had a dress he wanted to show me. I couldn't see any box but he said he had a dress in a box he wanted to show me. He said his name was Fischer. We've got a Fischer here. He lives downstairs. He likes jam roly-poly and frankfurters. So do I. This Mr Fischer – I don't think that was his name but we'll call him Mr Fischer with his brown hair and his nice teeth and his chain-smoking – he had got half-way down the front of my dress when he said he knew my father. It was impossible. No one knew my father, really knew him, knew him at all, except me. And he got to the fifth button – I was counting – the fifth button. He was fiddling with it. It wouldn't come loose. I freaked, suddenly freaked, just lost my rag. I do it every now and then, smash the place up, always feel sorry afterwards. I can't help it. I lost my rag and grabbed his balls, his bollocks. I have felt bollocks before, loads of times. Fischer downstairs is always letting me feel his bollocks. The point was: these were not bollocks. I know bollocks when I feel them. This was a wodge of something. And as I was screaming and he was putting his hand over my mouth and trying to do the buttons back up again, I squeezed even harder and he started to scream. Then we both shut up and left – not together. It wasn't much but it ruined my morning. I decided to make the best of it, seeing as I was in town. I went and bought myself some lunch. Well, I say bought but there's no point in buying something when you can steal it is there? I managed to get a pack of ham from M&S and a tomato from the greengrocer's in the market and a roll from the baker's, the one in Dillwyn Street. And I went to sit on the beach and make myself a sandwich. I always carried this knife with me. Gorgeous day. I had chosen well. Father used to love this music. He used to dance. I was sitting on the beach, thought it was time for my afternoon nap. I lay back, burrowed myself into the sand, didn't want to be disturbed. There was no one on the beach. And I'd just dozed off when I felt this hand. A big hand pushing my head back into the sand, down, down – like they do in Japan, the hot sand. I thought it would scald my scalp. I wasn't wearing my wig. I had my hood but somehow it had gotten mislaid. I could feel the sand in my ears and up my nose and in my mouth. Then this hand scratching between my legs. It was quite painful. Somehow it all ended. I fell back to sleep. I felt sick. When I woke, Fischer – this man with the nice brown hair and good teeth – sat beside me smoking. Course, I asked him if he had seen anyone. I said I had been done over. He didn't seem to know what I was talking about. He didn't seem to hear me. He looked a bit like Fischer downstairs – black curly hair. But I said he had brown hair. Black curly hair, brown straight hair – much of muchness. Fischer downstairs has got a big nose. This Fischer had a small nose with a ring in it like a bull. And I don't think he could hear. I'm sure he was deaf. You never know with people. They're always putting it on. I was telling him all about Mother and how she didn't go to America. How she came back to the docks and worked her way up. He wasn't listening. Then I realised I was in love with him. It happened in an instant. And it went away in an instant. I think it was something to do with the tomato. These things are very strange. Anyway he wandered off in the middle of my sentence. I followed him at a distance. I didn't want anyone to think we were together. He just kept on ignoring me. We walked for some miles. Very nice the beach. You get sand in your shoes, in your knickers, in your ears, but nice. On a nice afternoon to take a stroll. Can you hear me all right? We got to the end of the beach, miles it was. He turned and asked me why I was following him. I said I thought we were together. We walked out on to the rocks. We walked on to the next one. We swam on to the next and sat by the lighthouse. It was all blue, all around. The brown rock and the white lighthouse. We shouted to ask them to put the light on. There wasn't any need but it would have been nice. I say 'we', though we never really worked together. But it was nice. We lay on our backs. Some distance apart, mind. Every time I went near him he moved away. But we lay on our backs and took our shoes off. I took my knickers off to empty out the sand. He watched me but he didn't seem very interested after that. Come to think of it I know who he reminded me of – but I can't remember. It's one of those things. No sooner have you got a hold of a thought than it's out of your hands like a jellyfish. Eventually this man came out. He asked us if we were staying. We didn't know what he meant but we said no anyway. He put us in his boat and rowed us back to the rock. Very nice young man in a big blue jumper. There was a lot of blue around. Yellow's my favourite colour. We got back on the rock. The sea was high. On all sides the tide was in. That's what he said. We waited on that rock. Fischer seemed unhappy. So I talked to him for a while. He didn't say anything. I rubbed between his legs to cheer him up. It was tissue-paper, wodges of tissue paper. And I pulled it all out and he got very angry. He put it all back in again. I wonder if he could speak. Now you mention it I don't remember him saying anything, anything I could understand that is. He made noises. But it was as if he couldn't speak the language, any language. You get some people like that. Mr Malkin upstairs from Rampton – he's like that. He makes a lot of noise. Sometimes he never shuts up. But he never says anything. I can hear him now. Mr Fischer wandered off for a while. He wanted to be by himself. He jumped in the sea. He didn't take his clothes off. When he came out, the tissue-paper was trailing out of the bottom of his trouser-leg. I told him he looked ridiculous. He ignored me. Long pink tissue-paper trailing behind him as he walked up the rock. I took all my clothes off. Then I went for a swim. It seemed a lot more sensible. I've got this mark on the inside of my thigh. I don't know where it came from. It's a big red mark. It looked like a jellyfish under the water, shivering. When I got out it looked even worse. It had a green centre. I asked Fischer to kiss it better. He didn't even look. It's right at the top and it hurts. It gets better if I scratch it. We ended up having to swim back to the land. There was no man with a boat. We walked up to a building, a bar. It was closed so we tried to get in. Fischer threw a bench through the window. I climbed in and took two bottles. Whisky, I think he called it, or was it written on the label? I've got such a bad memory for names and places. We drank that bottle walking along the front. By then it was evening – or morning. I get the two muddled up. It was getting a bit cold. His clothes were wet. I was soaking. We didn't care. Vodka warmed us. People shouted at us but it didn't matter. When you're with someone it's OK. It's when you're alone that shouting hurts. Then it's nice to have a place like this with walls and windows to keep you in. And people to keep the shouters out. It's nice to have the select few around. Do you know what I mean? I shouldn't say that really. Do you know what I mean? People always nod. Do you know what I mean? They never know. Do you know what I mean? The cat has come in. We saw this yellowhammer in the park sitting on the oak while we played on the swings. You don't see yellowhammers these days. They were Father's favourites. He used to go into the country to look for them. He trapped them and brought them back. He had ten stuffed in his bedroom, tiny little yellow birds. I remember looking at them when he, when he was with me one time. Fischer couldn't catch them. He tried. We were getting on a bit better by then. When he kicked me I kicked him back. When he pulled my hairs I pulled his. Nice to have a mate. I'd love to be able to play the violin. Father always wanted me to learn. He said it would be good for my arm. Did I tell you I have a bad arm? I can't move the thing. Bit of therapy would have sorted it out. But we never bothered. I had this dream. I always connect it with that day. Father and a yellowhammer, mother and an umbrella plant. And somehow Mr Fischer as well. Not the one downstairs, the one with brown hair and nice teeth. Funny how people merge in your mind – not in reality, if only we could. When you're trying to sort them out and tell other people about them they smudge together. Well, anyway. In this dream we all took our clothes off and went for a swim. In the thick water we scooped jellyfish and dragged them to the beach. They stung us but it didn't hurt, not till later. Maybe that's where I got my red mark from. Father laid them all over me. I lay on the sand. Mother shouted commands. Fischer passed them to him and Father laid them all over my body. I was a shivering mass of jelly. Then with a pole he shooed them all away. I felt all red and raw and stung. Fischer said we ought to get something to eat. So we – what did we do? – I can't remember what we did for tea. See: living in a place like this you never have to worry about tea. It's always served up on a plate. Marvellous they are. Fischer – I remember – took me to a little place he said he knew, run by an Italian. I asked him if he knew Mother but he just shook his head and asked us to leave. He probably had known her. But no, my skin's too pale. We finally got something to eat. Fischer said he knew a good Chinese restaurant where the bins were always full of chicken. We went round the back. And sure enough all these legs and ribs and wings. You wouldn't believe! It's worth bearing in mind. If you're ever hungry in the town centre late at night, check out the Chinese. I tell everyone I meet. Good piece of advice. Best thing Fischer ever told me. Funny I don't remember him saying anything. But he told me a lot. He must have been good with his hands. We went to the cinema but we couldn't get in. And then we went to a club across the road. But we couldn't get in there either. They started shouting at us but when you're with someone else it doesn't matter. Fischer got in a fight with some men in black. They kicked while he was on the ground. I stood and watched. It didn't really matter. He had all that tissue-paper stuffed down his trousers. It can't have hurt. He got up and walked away. His nose was broken. But it was only small. I think his jaw had snapped. He didn't make a noise. He lumbered on as if nothing had happened. You meet people like that. It was dark by then. We went and sat on a bench to finish off the rest of the chicken. I had kept some in my pocket just in case we got hungry later. We met a man who seemed to know Fischer. And he sat down on the bench with us to tell a very long story. It was very boring without a pause. He couldn't tell a story to save his life. He wasn't very funny. I didn't know what he was talking about. It was full of rude words. He kept talking about sex while we were eating! The tree next to the bench was a cathedral. It had a clock trapped in its branches. The wind made it moan like a jellyfish. Fischer hit the man after a while. He went away. We walked back to the sea. At least, Fischer did and I followed. He was quite angry now. He kept turning round and coming up to me and pushing me away and pointing in other directions. That wasn't very nice. I knew he wanted me to follow him really. We had become very close. We walked to the sea and jumped to the beach. He started running round in circles. I stood in the middle of the circle. He ran round and round screaming. It didn't matter. No one lives down there apart from Eddie who sleeps on the top of the dunes. There are no houses and the bluebottles never bother you. Fischer ran in circles until he was tired. He collapsed and

I lay on top of him and we did it. Fischer downstairs has a dong as big as a salami. He put it in me once to see if it would hurt. It did. I didn't tell Fischer with the nice teeth. It wouldn't have been nice, would it. Then there were shouts. Someone told us to leave and I couldn't find my dress. So we went anyway. I was cold in my knickers and Fischer wouldn't give me his coat. We walked along the streets trying to find shadows. Somewhere to lie down, do it again and be warm. We knocked on some doors. No one answered. It was cold and neither of us could tell the time. Fischer ran off twice. Later I found him. He tried to hide in a yard amongst some bins. I crawled up next to him to keep him warm and he hit me in the mouth. That's how I broke my tooth, I found a blanket and carried it with me. I didn't want to put it round me because it was dirty. In case of emergency I thought I'd better hold on to it. Fischer hit me one more time. That was how I got my bruise. He hit me in the stomach so hard I was winded. I staggered about doubled up in the middle of the road and a car nearly ran me over. Because I was winded I couldn't shout for him to tell him how I felt and because he was deaf he wouldn't have heard and because he couldn't speak he wasn't able to say he loved me. When you can't express yourself it's a bummer. I couldn't find him. I looked all night and all day for weeks. And then I didn't. In the town centre the man was still on the bench. The clock was still in the tree. The men in black shouted at me again. I was happy to have someone to talk to. We talked for a while. They seemed to understand me which is always nice. They stood in a ring like disciples. They were very nice. One of them took the smelly blanket away. That made things a lot better. Another pointed to the mark on my leg and the mark on my chest and asked where I got those from. They laughed with me. They pushed me around. But it was only friendly. Not like Fischer. They liked me really. They asked me how old I was. Funny that – I thought it was obvious. After I had the treatment, people said that I looked twenty years older. I'm twenty years younger really. And then they left. Somebody shouted. The bluebottles turned up in their van. They were really violent, really horrible. They threw me in the back of the van. Two men came in with me. We rode to the station. It was light. I could see their faces under big hats. I asked one the time. He didn't seem to know what I meant. He said they had been looking for me for an age. I asked how long an age was. Then I might have been able to work out how long I had been away and how much of a telling-off I'd get at home. He wouldn't tell me. For a long time we were at the station. I couldn't find Fischer anywhere. They put me in a white dress in a white room. A lady came in and prodded me. I thought I saw Mother but I was wrong. I don't know if Father's dead yet or whether he's come alive again like he used to. They say he's dead but you can't rely on people. That was my day out. They've had me in here since Thursday or was it last Saturday? I've lost track. The cat is snoozing. He's not listening. The umbrella plant needs a good watering. But they only give enough for me to drink. That plant'll die if it's not careful. It's been knocked about. No one looked after it. I dreamed of a bull. The one good thing is – they've given me a view. I can see the sea from here, the rocks where we played and the sand where we did it and I can even see the cinema. But I can't see the man on the bench or the clock in the tree. Do you remember when we were in America? Oh no, you wouldn't – we weren't there, were we? Father used to write to me when they put him away. He blamed it all on me. It was nothing to do with me. It was all his own fault. It was a bit of my fault. I shouldn't have worn short skirts – still his fault. I've got plans for the summer for once in my life. I'm going to find Mr Fischer. We're going to have some fun. We might go away to another beach further down the coast where there aren't many people. Where we can sleep on the beach without anyone bothering us or shouting at us. Funny thing about adventures. They make you love home. It's so nice to get back to what you know. To the family chair and bed and table. To the cat and the plant and the view. It's very good of them to give me a view. And on the ground floor so I can't jump out. We're supposed to be free to go out. I don't see why they got so angry. I thought we were free. That's what they tell us. You've got to keep your own mind on these things. I'm convinced of it. I dream of bulls and balls and bollocks. I used to have good conversations with the lady who lived next door. They've moved her to another wing. There's Elsie who comes in and cleans. She lives down by the sea and tells me how many holidaymakers there are. They say I'm a danger to myself. How can you be a danger to yourself? Only other people can be a danger to you. Or is that silly? Father says he has friends who gave the umbrella plant to my mother. They lived in a yellow house. That's where we got the cat, near where Fischer comes from – Fischer the one who likes jam roly-poly and frankfurters. Not the one with nice teeth and brown hair. And Mother, Mother hated Dad's yellowhammers. She put them in the bin. That was when he threw her out. I think he did the right thing. Difficult to say. He said he'd have nothing more to do with her, that she was a bad influence, that her craziness had to stop. He was a wise man. Funny thing was, when we were in the town centre and those bluebottles threw me in the back of their van, do you know what I thought? I thought for a minute Mum and Dad wanted me back. Self-pity's a sickness. I'll stop my whining. It's nearly tea time. I'm done with all this chattering. One more time? I'd like to go. My tummy still hurts, it does. I'll hush . . .

II

Curious, I've just seen her, wearing a suit, a hydrangea dress, standing in a room downstairs. She has yellow hair. She has hard flesh on her face, hard skin around her neck and shoulders. She stands about six foot two, slightly too broad at the hip, small breasts (did you catch the lascivious tone as I licked those words?), and moderately beautiful. I admired her for – no that's not quite right – I adored her from a distance for upwards of four years. I only recently had the misfortune to become her friend. Misfortune – our attachment is organised. It is occupied discussing her happiness with an imaginary boyfriend. And me, lying about my happiness with an imaginary friend. She has the kind of yellow hair which speaks of health and happiness. It is enough on its own to reveal she is quite different from me. Any dating-agency which put us together would have to answer for it. So much for my opinion. I wonder what her knees are like. This music always reminds me of an afternoon when I thought it was going to happen. I had followed her some miles as she walked around town looking at shops. She was fingering jackets, dresses, jewellery. We walked, with about fifty yards between us, from the centre of town along the beach. She didn't get a bus. She sat in the park reading a book. I sat in the park reading her, about seventy-five yards away. Finally she noticed me. We talked for a while. She had come over. And we talked for a while. An hour, maybe two. She, she – it's enough, *she* – all in the word. No, let's get closer – because I have the facts. I have information. I have followed her and watched her and filmed her and drawn her, written about her interminably. A laborious well planned classification of the genus, rather the sub-genera, the species. I would imagine she finds life an easy, rather enjoyable ride. She's been going out with him for, well, as long as I've known about her –

four, five years maybe. And in that time they've been to France every year. As she once told me: it was their habit to do so. But she's not all shallow. She likes to think of herself as a reader, as a thinker, as a talker. She regards me as her, her intellectual friend. The chap with whom on occasions she can sit and talk for hours, asexually. If I could tell you the, describe the, capture the, no – if I could *transcribe*, if I could transcribe the look in her eyes when I say something which alarms her, if I could set that down you would know her. It is an alarm, momentary, then gone. Important. As if she was a little girl who has found herself through the mischievousness of a distorting mirror taken to be a six foot two, full-grown adult woman. And on those occasions when you say those key words, unscriptable, unpredictable key words, the little girl is suddenly revealed, the mirror reverts and you see the little frightened girl, sexed, but alarmed and most magically vulnerable. Vulnerable – shouldn't use the word really. It implies some sort of predator bearing down on her. And I'm nothing of the sort. I'm quite a, I'm a very shy, hidden, concealing figure who, on those occasions when she sees me before I see her, is trapped into a conversation with her. I would rather never speak to her again in my life. The sad fact is, she regards me as a good friend. Oh him! Yes he's that nice person I speak to about clever things! I'm no predator and she is no prey. If anything, predators are within me, prey is myself. She is just a catalyst. But what sort of catalyst? When I have caught her in the middle of our conversation and glared deep into her tiny brown irises, searching out some narcissistic me, leering as if that picture, that silver reflection, might tell me what she sees while we talk, while that conversation pauses – then have I wondered if she is impregnable to everyone, whether that blonde fool (six foot four) who walks beside her has ever penetrated those brown irises, whether she conceals anything behind the varnish in those eyes. I am being too literary. I must try to be restrained. This is a scientific exercise. I saw him once. He towers over her. She once told a short, stubby friend of mine that if only he were another two feet taller he would be attractive, she might go out with him. The man she is going out with is two feet taller than my short stubby friend – and so she is going out with him. He is elegantly balding, with a skull like a ram's and a pine-hued tan all year round, glistening – no not

149

glistening, not glistening at all – just a pine-hued tan. With pale yellow hair sprouting like the tint at the base of a lily petal from his scalp. Sometimes I can see what she sees in him. Sometimes I am privy to what women see in their men. It is a strange kind of insight – as if you've been admitted to a masonic rite, the story that they tell themselves. And there he was, shoulders broader than hers, straighter than hers, leveller, overslung with jacket. The jacket flapped against her pelvis, as no doubt his pelvis had flapped and flapped. I wonder what her knees are like. He had patent boots on, a mark of tastelessness. But, then, she is no fashion queen. She prefers tracksuit bottoms and T-shirts and cut-down sweatshirts, bumbags, odd scarves. A horrific mismatch of colours. And the committed use, the *committed* use of trainers. She wasn't wearing these today. A relief to my eyes. Today she was attending an interview. She caught me afterwards. She glowed with that excitement you feel for no good reason other than being released from the tyranny of being observed, scrutinised for what you are and what you're worth. She was wearing, as I may have said earlier, a dress patterned with hydrangeas. A thick bodice made up the top part of it. This clasped her midriff snugly. I wondered if my hands place thumb to thumb, finger to finger, would circuit, clasp that waist without squeezing. No, of course they wouldn't – she's not a small girl. And she was wearing black stockings. I wonder what her knees are like. What do the stockings do when they pass over her knees and calves? What keeps them up? Does she have fleshy legs? Stocking band constricting the blood of thigh. And do her buttocks sag? And as you pass your hands up across her spine is there a continuous channel, a shallow trench lined with down? For there is the faintest, most fragile down lining the cleft of her neck. And I watched her voicebox as she spoke. The stud of oesophagus shivered as she generated sound to cover the silence. The silence might tease the alarm from her eyes. I could smell my breath – a vicious tang of dung curling under my nose. I breathed in swiftly after each utterance so gases might not cross the gulf and clamber up into her nostrils. And yet, what a pleasant thought! To mingle gases! Or was it her breath? Maybe, deep in the forest of hairs that line the throat behind the stud of oesophagus there is a nervous mucus which emits a foul stench. This stench is then carried across the short gap to

150

tickle the hairs in the back of my nostrils. An equally delectable conceit! Impossible. There was glass between us. She wore velvet braid which I can remember more clearly than anything else. For no reason. Plaited velvet braid, about a centimetre in breadth, lining the seams on the shoulder and the black lapels of the jacket. The jacket was short, cut short to the waist so the bodice lining of the dress, sorry the skirt, would show. What this matters I've no idea. All this waffling and not a picture of her in sight. Externals tell us nothing. Apart from the speed and thoughtlessness with which she dressed this morning. Or perhaps their value lies in letting me get a purchase on what I think I saw. I know nothing. And her hair was pulled back into a clasp of some sort which I couldn't see – all the more erotic. In her nervousness she had shaken free the finest filaments of hair. Thousands of them had come loose in the hour since she sat in front of a mirror and hastily arranged it tight. And these plumed to form a halo. A cheap image, a halo. Her skull: faced with flesh, an ugly nose but the most perfectly modulated eyebrows. Short forehead, no deeper than two inches. Two inches above the eyebrows and the forestation of the scalp begins. Beneath the eyebrows – which provide the marvellous balance to a whole head, a head held high, central, equipoise – beneath these eyebrows, varnished brown irises and faint ochre lashes, small eyes, not too small, but small. Eyelids blink to conceal her alarm. And the alarm when it comes, those unforgettable instances when she lets the girl show, is signalled by a momentary dilation of the pupil. The brown iris vanishes, the lashes raise, the eye is a pool of white with a black heart. And then the iris swells again. The lashes close and blink fast. Way beneath, the mouth, momentarily open, closes without a sound. A blush begins beneath each temple. It skirts over cheekbones – does she have cheekbones? Do I remember nothing? On one occasion – many many weeks ago, months – I followed her again, as was my habit. At a distance to protect her, you understand, not prey upon her. All the way from town to Mumbles, this time. She lives in Mumbles. Mumbles is a fishing village to the west. No – Mumbles is where she lives. And we walked round the curving bay. On the coastal path in the gloom of evening. Her ponytail, like a pony's tail – a poor simile – shivered behind. She walked and hummed and thought on how . . . Ah, the music! How the music holds the history! I have lost my train. Mumbles – the bay curls round. So, from where I sleep, Mumbles can be seen. Normally misted, with its roofs and gables, small odd-shaped fishermen's houses clambering up the cliff from the wharf. Why am I telling you all this? Description! Description! It describes nothing. In one of these houses she lives. The one thing I have never had the courage to find is her address. Oh I know her surname, her parents' names, the measurements of her corpse, her wealth, her poverty, her – no, not her. It would be impertinent to presume a man might know everything about a woman. There are some things she should have all to herself. Besides – to know everything! I would have nothing to do with my idle mind. And who knows what could have come of it? I might, I might have started leering through her window. I'll be honest. They have asked me to be honest. I know her address. I have been to her house. Never inside. I took a room on the opposite street. I scanned the windows day after day – to discern which was her bedroom. This took some time. You can imagine. You have an imagination? The occupants drew curtains for much of the night and day. But eventually, I determined that none of the windows facing south were hers. So, I moved. This time to another terrace, to an attic flat, to the north of her house. This time, to scan the other windows with binoculars and a camera to hand. Hers was the window, as you looked at the house, on the top right. A high small window at the back of the house. A back of a house like the face of a die with six windows for dots – a poor simile. A back of a house like a back of a house, with six windows. A long, thin, tall, pinched house with a raked roof above her window. For some curious reason she never closed her blind. I could see this obliquely suspended at the top of the window, never let down. I moved rooms to gain a finer vantage into the room itself. Once my angle of sight was perfected, I sat to wait. I saw little, the lie of the land, a picture by El Greco, a black-and-white photograph of a nude male. One time, I saw the boyfriend, six foot four, smoothing his hair back on to his ram's scalp, rub palms the length of his naked thorax – and then drop to his knees to continue whatever unspeakable act he was committing to her indignity. I would see her walking absently, fiddling with her hair. Or pluck a book from a shelf, then disappear out of sight. I presume the table

152

must have been on the left-hand side of the room as I looked, the door on the far right-hand corner – upstage right, so to speak, or is that left stage? God knows. Damn the stage. And a bed in the far left-hand corner, or perhaps under the window. Such a room cannot have been more than eight foot square, perhaps deeper than it was wide. And the window was not more than four by six, higher than it was broad. Occasionally and most tantalisingly, I would see her stare from the window. Not in my direction, oh no – she never suspected I was there. Staring with a pained, wistful look. And this gave me the idea that she was not the happy-go-lucky fool I had credited her with being. Here was a darker side, a crease to her hard face, a sullen moodiness. A disfigurement I welcomed at first. And then it occurred to me – this was more than probably a pining for the man who had disappeared for a few days, a memorialising of the feel of him between her thighs. Or of his cat's tongue licking her breasts . . . Did I mention her breasts? Yes, I did – small, but once revealed to me. Oh, it's hopeless trying to pass the news on to you. But imagine saucers upturned – small, yes, small. Perhaps . . . no. I was going to say breakfast bowls. Curse these similes. Once, she caught me at lunch. With an appearance of glee at seeing me, she knelt by my side, squatted down. Her loose top fell forward. There they were. Extraordinary – I didn't feel the slightest twinge of desire, merely scientific curiosity. You are in the hands of an objective observer. And, of course, that is what this is all about. Not a desire for the physical object. But a scientific curiosity, motivated by a desire for her *in absentia*. Most of all, I would like to be a sculptor – at this moment – my ambitions change with the hours. A sculptor – pah! this coffee's cold – a sculptor who could pay her an honest day's wage to stand upon a plinth and pose. The governor, my landlord, would not allow it. And then, in stone – another element, not words, useless words – mould and carve and chisel and hack an impression of my inner sense of her to stone. Of course it would not be her. It would not really be a representation of her. It would be a memento, for me alone. A coded message to my future. And it might stop her visiting. It would do me well enough – it would replace her. Imagine the skill: to craft her again from stone, a stone so large it could not be moved from where you had hacked it out. It would have to stay there, peering over me like some great

153

Aphrodite in the Colosseum – or Parthenon or Acropolis? A splendid immovable symbol – for I believe in symbols. I symbolise everything. I cannot look at a chair without seeing what it is standing in for. That one for instance is standing in for her – see the knee? Not to worry. My mind is diseased with associations. This is like that, that is like this, she is . . . quite unlike anything. Perhaps that is the fascination. Perhaps this is a failure. A life's work – a failure! Perhaps not. I record these annotations to show the futility of ever trying to annotate. To her happiness, I feel desolation. To my desolation, she feels happiness. We could be desolate, we could be happy. There is no relationship. Of course, killing her would deprive me of nothing. Oh, I could tie her up and keep her here. No. No, I have no desire to do that. Besides, the governor would never allow it. My battle is not with her will. My battle is with another stubborn animal which refuses – sorry – which cannot bring itself to think of remaining with me. Each time she visits, it is to leave. So, if I could extract the animal but leave the rest: the down in the neck, the velvet braid, the halo, the dung breath, saucer breasts, the fleshy thighs, the sagging buttocks, the stud of voicebox – if I could keep all of these, sprawled upon the couch, untied, unrestrained, quite quite dead – well then, I might be able to get on with something important. Instead of this futility, this postponing of an end to this transcript, this transcript of nothing. I can't think of anything else to say. Is that enough? Do you see? You see nothing. All I can testify to is a powerful feeling, a powerful feeling: what does that matter? It matters for nought. So be quiet, silence. Shall we try it again? I think it would be best – I didn't quite get her that time. One more thing . . .

III

I'm locked in, that's the first thing. The second is – I've not let them get to me. I'm not sure who she is but I've got plenty of ideas. It's a woman all right. Only a woman could think up something this wily. I have heard her creep away in the mornings, like a thief. She gets in and out without waking me. She is the only one with a key. It's the creeping away that always brings me round. I jump up, run to the door, but by then she has locked it. And she is padding off down the corridor. She comes in every morning to change the pot and put food in the other. And she sneaks around so as not to wake me. I stayed up one night, determined not to fall asleep. I stayed up all night, all the next day, all the next night. I dozed off for five minutes. I wake up. And she's creeping away again. There are two clean pots sitting down by the mat. One thing I can't complain about is the view. Most people wouldn't like it. But it has everything I could want. Except yellow. As you look out the window you can see the sea. There are houses in the way but we are high up here, higher than most, most of the cubes that infest this prison colony. And the sea leans up to the sky between two walls. Down there is an alleyway. I would have jumped by now if I thought one of the dustbins would catch me. But they always leave the lids on, thoughtless gits. And it's a long way. I had bars put on the window years ago to stop fools climbing in. That's a laugh. Unless I slim down to bone I haven't a hope of getting out. I have broken a pane to let the breeze in. Well if you're reading this you'll know what the room is like. One day I will have covered all this white with black. White is the colour I hate. I can't stand white. It is the colour of the ill, the colour of the sick. The walls are a huge mirror, spreading me cuboid. That's why it is so nice to have a window. When she first got me I kicked up a right fuss. I shouted and screamed the place down I did. You wouldn't believe the racket I made. I kicked at that there door, booted it for all I was worth. It would not budge. I reckon she's had steel put on the outside. The outside! I'm not sure who she is but I'll bet I know her. You know how it is with tormentors – they are always known to the victim. White paint, white skin, white nails, white, white, white. I've done my best to cover most of it up. The white sheet is brown now, covered with me. My skin has come off, my hair is falling out. And I lost control a couple of times. But no matter – anything to get rid of the white. Brown is a far healthier colour. I have ripped up most of the carpet. There is black lino underneath. Highly satisfying. I got a couple of letters. That was a good day. Wake up to hear her shuffling down the corridor. And there's two white envelopes leaning on the pots. It is nice to get letters. I left them for a couple of days to savour the feeling of being remembered. One was from my mother – strange, she's been dead a while. It must have got lost in the post. It was a very nice letter. She never could write very well. Full of emotion and soppy stuff. But it is nice to get a letter from your mother. Telling me all about how she had been to the shops, seen her friend Maggie, decorated the house and made me a shepherd's pie. The other letter was from the manager. Telling me as I hadn't been into the bank for six months this was 'formal notification of termination of employment'. I put the letter in the pot of shit. You work, you slog your brains out, give them all you've got, sit in their offices and rot. And what do you get in return? Contempt. You think they would have a little bit of respect, wouldn't you! A little bit of understanding. We all have our problems. It is not my fault I have been stuck in here for God knows how long. They could have got a replacement in – two temps could clear my desk each morning. It gets me. I can see a boat. I wonder where it is going. He always was a fat git, that manager. He had no respect. He never cared. Penelope always said he did not respect anyone. He had taken her on for a laugh, she said. Once he had got her in his office he did awful things to her. My ink is running out. I will have to mix some more. I have got this cough. It starts at the bottom of my lungs, works its way up and explodes in balls of flob. They go out the window. I have got to keep up appearances. Yellow is my favourite colour. That irritates me most. There is not a spot of yellow in here. Oh, I have tried to make some yellow, believe you me. But how do you make yellow? The walls will take five years to fade. That is the problem with white. It hates other colours. Other colours leave. It would be nice to be able to see a tree. I wonder if I could get them to plant a tree, down on that bit of beach. I can see a square of sea. It is a little square. But of course it isn't a square. I can't explain. I cannot write about that. It scares me. I hate horror stories. A snail is on the wall. He has just stopped. He got half-way up yesterday and now he has just stopped. I cannot reach him. There might be some yellow in his belly. He is stuck about ten feet away. Crawl this way! Do us both a favour! There is some green – I think it is green – about three miles away, just before the beach. And there is some brown on those buildings and red on the roofs. And the sky changes its colours all the time, never satisfied. But damn me if it is ever yellow. Mother used to say that colours told you about yourself. I never knew what she meant. After I had stopped shouting at her to get me out of here, I decided – she was not going to get the better of me. You feel like you are being told off for something – just so you know. There are plenty of things I should be told off for. But I am at the age where you expect to be treated like a grown-up. There aren't many ways I could get my own back, though. So I am going to deface her walls. I am a quarter way through it now. Scribble all over them, wipe out the white, write me on the wall. I will have to mix some more ink. Once, I took a walk on the beach. I must have walked across that bit of grass three miles away. Who would have thought it? If I had turned left I would have seen this window. It is possible to see into the future. Be vigilant. And I might have seen another face leering out, trying to see me, yellow on the beach. It is possible to see into the past. Be warned. I went swimming. I think that was what did it. There's all sorts of shit in that water. Everything comes out of the water. Every now and then she leaves me a bucket full of water. It is cold by the time I get to it but I give myself a good sluicing. The sheets keep me clean most of the time. You have got to wash every once in a while. You never know when you will receive visitors. The two pots are white as if to mock me. They never give up. White this, white that, white the other. One has this food in it: a stew, a stew with stringy bits of lamb and discs of carrot and a sludge they call potato. They weed out the yellow bits. They employ someone to do that. I have not seen a bit of sweetcorn in twenty years, maybe five. I lost time. My watch stopped. I never was very good at telling the time. My watch stopped within hours of me getting locked in here. I alter it now and then to give me the feeling of things moving on. There is something quite nice about still time. Oh, sometimes I tell myself that it is midday or four in the afternoon and time I went for a stroll. You know how every time has its feeling? It's that six o'clock feeling, blah blah. Then again, I was sick of time, working at the bank. In at nine on the dot, out at five. You would watch that clock hand creep up the face until it banged into place at the twelve. And we legged it. But you have got to have a job. Look at me now, vegetating, spewing up guts on these walls. Oh, I tried that once. When I was a kid my vomit was always yellow. But now it is just a stringy brown. That is what comes of having a food censor. No yellow one end, no yellow the other. I try and get all sorts of vile things in that pot for her of a morning. There are little ways you can get your own back for this life. She has to empty it. She has to carry it along the corridor, making sure it doesn't slop down her pretty little dress. It serves her right, the shit they serve up in here. One pot, two pots, who's to tell the difference? Eat from one – shit in the other. The food chain. I asked her for some books. I left a big message scrawled by the pot so she could not miss it. Did she respond! I tell you – being in here is like being in a cafe, ordering chips with flan to follow and getting someone else's order. Eventually she left me a bit of paper. But no pen. What is paper for? To wipe my butt? So I wiped my arse on it and popped it in the pot. A love letter. I have not seen paper since. It would be nice to have some books, some fishing books. I could learn how to fish for that snail. I could learn a language. At first, I was sure it was a demon out there. You take a room in the city, you hate it, you put up with it, you wander to work, you wander back, you look at women, you cook your meal, you look out the window and wish you were in a world elsewhere. You despise the place and go home to mother at weekends and then some joker goes and locks you in and mother dies! A nightmare, it had to be a demon. A man possessed. Mother said demons follow you around and trip you up when you are happy. She was full of things like that. I cannot shake them off. I keep blurting them out. It is like she is in here with me. I figured it wasn't a demon. A demon could not feed me. Not

158

unless it had possessed everyone. Or just her. I do like food. No. And then I thought maybe I had been kidnapped. Always happening, you hear about it all the time. Terrorists and all. But no, my family hasn't got any money. Or any members, come to think of it. After screeching and shouting and booting the door for days on end, I lost my voice. I haven't seen it since. I open my mouth and all that I get is a squeak. They have even taken that away from me. So I am writing, scribbling all over these walls. I am not going to let them get away with it, you know. There's a law in this country. They can kick the little bloke to the ground but he can always get the donkey of the law to kick them in the balls. I used to think I had a saviour, a guardian angel. A sort of ghost of a mother who followed you around when you left home in the morning, making sure you did not go under a bus or get done over by big boys. It seemed to work. Nothing ever happened. A nice nothing of a life. Now they lock me in here to do nothing where no one can see. A guardian angel could not let it happen. I am a hostage, a hostage for no ransom. And that is what gets me – I do like to have a few reasons. Just to keep me warm. And if there aren't any, well, you make them up. Like that time I was asking Penelope out and she told me I was hideous and she felt sick to look at me. Of course she did not mean a word of it. It was the heat of passion, Mother said. We did not speak for three days but we are friends now. Well – there were reasons for all that. Mother gave them to me, true ones. I hadn't had my hair done in months, hadn't been looking after myself. Course she was not going to find me attractive, was she! You have to work for a woman. There are reasons for everything. When you think about it. Why does the sun rise in the morning? Because we are going round and round and round. Why does it rain? Because the sea is going round and round and round. Simple. Why? Because, because, because of the wonderful things he does . . . So there must be a reason for all this. I am damned if I can think it up. That boat has stopped moving. They have dropped anchor. Who would stop still when you can move? There is a cat outside. Maybe he can help. A siamese, blue eyes, setting up the most awful yowling. Not a yellow hair on his corpse. Is bile yellow? You would think she would plant flowers outside, wouldn't you! Nasturtiums or daffodils or alpines. Just a spark of yellow in the grey. I have not seen the sun in months. It passes overhead and shyly

159

avoids my gap of sky. To think I never paid it any attention when I could stare! Sometimes I hear noises. There is someone stamping upstairs. This is funny because I am on the top floor. They must have got the builders in. I can hear this bloke shouting. I cannot hear a word he's saying. He hollers and hollers and then he quietens down for a while and then he sets up again. It is very far away but unmistakably a man trying to get himself heard over the silence. Maybe she's got him locked up as well! Caged lions trailing round and round and round, roaring their little hearts out! A veritable zoo! I can see chimneys stretching away into the distance, slate roofs – least I think that is what they are. This window if filthy. It is smeared with oil. Only I cannot get my hand out to wipe it clean. I almost don't want to. You need something between you and the world. I've got a bed in here. It is just about all I've got. I spend most of the day on the bed, saving energy. Just in case I catch her out. I nearly did a while back. I was burrowing through the wall. I had broken a pane and saved bits of glass. I was digging away at the cement. I finally got down to something that resembled yellow in between the red. Digging away like the Count of Monte Cristo trying to get through to the next room. I figured there must be a next room. Even if someone is locked in there as well, it would be someone to talk to. I set up a bit of a Morse code but never got any response. She must have heard because suddenly there was a key in the door. I heard it go, this beautiful clockwork sound of bolts shifting and sliding and the click as it dropped. And I looked up, ready to pounce. The door opens an inch and then – slams again. That is the only time I have ever seen her. Well, I did not actually see her. I got a feel of her. I saw what she can do. The rest of the time, one pot goes, another pot comes. Occasionally the light goes on for no good reason. At any hour of night or day. Damn it – haven't they got any respect! Television would be nice, a line of comic books, a yellow carpet, some black paint to brighten the walls, a couple of pictures, a telephone even! But no. I have tried writing all this by the door. Do not think I have been idle. I am a workaholic. I have made a long list of every one of my demands. I could even do with some real ink. And a cat. Something to talk to, something to make a noise back at me. All I can hear is the deathly echo of my own rasping ringing from corner to corner and down on to the floor and back up to the ceiling and deadening on the bed. And all I can see is my own rasping scribbled all over the shitty shitty walls. I tried smothering myself with a pillow. It is very difficult. You need someone else to do it for you. That is why it is nice to know people. And I have toyed with slicing my veins but it is a terrible way to go. Sitting here while you dribble all over the floor. I have done enough dribbling over the walls. When I go I am going to go with a bang, an explosion, a splat! I am going to make some noise. I am not going to let them forget me. You think I am going to let them forget me? You've got another thing coming. When they come in here, there is going to be an almighty stink of shit. Me, exploded all over. They are going to read the writing on these walls, the tiny delicate handwriting, the twisted mind, the perverted words, the bile. And they are going to remember me and regret. You can control other people's memories. You cannot control your own. But others' are an open well. Don't think I do not know that. I was in control of statements at the bank. I had a plan to marry Penelope. It was a good plan. I am good at plans. It was devious, cunning, wily. I learned all that from my mother. The best way to treat people. She was a nothing of a girl. She would have made the perfect wife. She did not have a personality to speak of. Not pretty, broken nose – her father had knocked her about, terrible case. Anyway, they gave her a job at the bank. Out of sympathy more than anything else. She would come and talk to me when she needed a bit of intelligent conversation. I helped her with this and that. You have got to, really, help the new kids and the women. Once I put it to her that we should walk home together. She lived on the other side of town but I lied and said so did I and hers was on my way home. She did not take up the offer while I was still there. But I am confident she was mulling it over. On one occasion when I actually did accost her, like I said, she told me to bugger off. But I saw that look in her eye. You cannot mistake it when you see it. Absolute lust. I am not much to look at but lust is nothing to do with the outside. Everything to do with instinct. Even I know that. Today I drubbed for hours, perhaps many, on the door. No response. I would like a newspaper – to see how they have reported my case. I am a fan of sport. That cat is still yowling. I wonder what he wants. He is a trapped lion. Someone ought to come. There is a line on the sky going from east to west, or west to east depending on which way you look at it. I think it is a telegraph line or a crack in the glass or an ink-line. There is a bird on it, a fat pigeon. Maybe that is what the cat is singing about. I could do with that fat pigeon. You never get a bird on this window ledge. All they tell you about prisoners and birdmen is crap. That telegraph line – there's people chattering to each other on that line. Seems impossible that they can't hear me yelling or that cat yowling. It is a thinner line than I could draw. Oh, did you see my pictures? I did a self-portrait by the window. That is so I will not forget what I look like. That bitch will never give me a mirror. Mirrors are, after all, dangerous things. It is a flattering self-portrait: 'As I Used To Look In My Youth'. I put the title underneath so I do not forget. I have always had a bad nose. My mouth is good. And I have got a squint in my eye but some people say it is rather becoming. I haven't much hair left now, but then – what a thatch! I mix the ink in one of the two pots. I have tried getting more than one colour but it is very difficult. I got this brown shade, good dark brown. It will last for a good long while. There is no danger of that fading. Even the early work over there by the door is as brown as the day it was written. I have got a good hand – angled slightly to the right, leaning. And my line is good – see that line going down the cheekbone? Nothing like reality – but this is a line, not reality. Lucky all my hair has fallen out really. A devil to keep clean. No idea why it did. Must have been something in the sea. Unless she has been doping my broth. I wonder what Mother is up to. God – this white! I might get a letter tomorrow. Of course I might actually be getting thousands of letters. But my jailer – she is not going to let me get my paws on those, is she! She doesn't want me reading the thousands of letters of support, the seditious plotting of my liberator. Oh, I have tried writing letters. On the bits of Mother's note. I left them for her but they are still here. Looking at it another way – she *is* my protector. I have nice thoughts about her as well as evil. I am a fully rounded man. I have glopped over her, I have married her, I have killed her. All in my mind, you understand. She is keeping the world from my door. My mother did it for years – very successfully. Kept all my mates away, never answered the telephone –had it put in for decoration. Said she couldn't not have a line for all the neighbours to see – one of those telegraph lines. You need a woman to filter out the scum. I love women. The light has just come on. If I put my hand in front of my eyes and peep through my fingers I can see a bit of yellow. That is highly refreshing. I feel born again. I cannot stare for too long. I might damage my eyes. Like staring at the sun, a great refreshment. My sight is very important to me, even though there has never been much to look at. The fortunate thing is, I do like being by myself. They picked the right man when they locked me up. She is not stupid, that woman. I am one of my best friends. And frankly, if you are going to have a conversation, best to have it with someone who isn't listening. That way you can get on with it. I have spent most of my life in my own company, never listening. I love music. That is one conversation I can listen to. That is one thing I do hate her for – depriving me of music. And what with my voice going I cannot even make my own. Sometimes I think I am dying without music. I used to pass evening after evening lying on my bed, hands behind my head, humming away to myself, making them up as I went along. I never sang them to anyone else. That's not the point. The point is to soothe yourself. I do not know many ways of soothing myself. Oh, you can always glop yourself off but it is not quite the same as a good sing. A good song, hollered at the top of your voice. I scrawl song-words on the walls so I do not forget them. And when my voice comes back I will set them all to music. I forget the tunes but that keeps you making them up. I cannot think of anything else to say about the past. It is best forgotten. I have told everything I know, everything I can invent, except what I am going to do when I get out. After I have killed her, I am going to find Penelope. They will not give me my old job back. But I figure if I can just get to Penelope I will explain everything. That really hurts. She is out there, wondering where the hell I am, blundering around in ignorance. Oh I have shouted for her out the window. It is the only thing I can do. She is not going to hear me, though. What is she going to think of me? Wait till I get my hands on that warder of mine. Anyway, once I have explained everything to Penelope and once she has forgiven me, I am going to persuade her to drop that job at the bank like a hot potato. It is time that manager stopped getting his maulers all over her. He is a dirty sod. And then we will take a cottage out in the middle of nowhere. A cottage with lots of windows and lots of doors. Doors that can stay open all the time. Where you do not need

163

clocks and you do not need to keep writing your shitty nonsense on the walls. She will listen to me so I won't have to put up with myself anymore. Nice to have somebody else to do that for you. And she will never make me lamb stew. And we will paint the house yellow inside and out. It will have a little yellow roof and a little yellow door – built by me. And I will make a table out of yellow wood and the taps out of gold. And we will have a boat and we will sail from the bay, out, out, out into the square of sea that I can see as I write. And we will sit in the boat and I will tell her my history. And we will look at the window through a telescope and we will laugh. That is the only thing to do when they have locked you in a cube. Jump out like a jack-in-a-box and giggle in their faces. Ha! Bloody Ha!

IV

I met Jesus on Monday, walking on the beach. He asked me who I was. I said I couldn't remember but if he gave me a moment I'd have a think about it. I asked if he had come down from the sky. He said, Yes he did come from heaven. He came from the dunes to where I slept and kicked me awake. I am not very good with words, I am not very good with speaking. I am a public speaker – on buses and in marketplaces and up by St Mary's in the precinct. People do not listen. No matter how many times you say it, people do not listen. I am writing this down so as people will listen. When I speak they do not understand. I was talking to this boy on the bus today. He turned his back on me and stared his ginger head out the window at the sea. I told him he did not understand the sea. He was looking but he did not understand. They do not know, I said. No one knows anything – over and over. He pretended not to hear. Jesus says he has this problem all the time. He said it was just the way I say things. He understood perfectly. He listened to every word I said. He laughed. He asked me if I believed in him. Believed in him? He was standing right before my very eyes! I have been sent away. I told him that. They kicked me out. So I took up fishing on the beach. You do not catch much here. The sea is dead. They told me not to come back. So I stayed on the beach. They cannot touch you here. They are tyrants. And the sooner we get rid of them the better. You know what we could do with? A good ruler, a good king. I could not see a thing that afternoon. My eyes go funny sometimes. It is the sun and the heat. It blinds me so it is all haze. But it gets hazy round here. And when Jesus kicked me awake, all I saw was this shadow standing by my boots. Behind him nothing – above him nothing. Just a shape. No outline. He reeked of drink. He said someone had thrown it all over him. I believed him. He knelt beside me and that way he became clearer. He touched my eyes. At once I could see him. That was a miracle. He rolled a cigarette. A second man stood in the distance. He said he was with him. I did not believe him. He said he was a rock, a real pal. I could see the rocks and the lighthouse and the man, clear now, then hazy. He started playing with my bits – my bits of driftwood, the odds and sods I collect from the tide. You can make a few bob that way, flog them in the market. I put a scarf over my head. That way they never recognise me. It pays for my food. We keep fishing, me and this boy down on the harbour. About a mile down the beach we sit on this wall and wait. It is waiting really, not fishing. When I called him Christ, he jumped. I asked him if it was all right to call him that. He said it was his surname. I suggested Mr Christ. He said he preferred to be familiar. But I had to keep my voice down in case anyone was overhearing. He did not mind, then he said. He asked if he could borrow some money. I fished out a pound I had picked up. I gave it to him. He called me a hero. He said I was the Prince of Wales. He kept talking. I was not really listening but he said something about the 'present tyranny' and 'wretched usurpers'. I believed every word. I did not listen to most of it. I could not understand any of it. And while I was not listening I stared at this boat way out in the middle of the bay. It seemed to be sinking, then rising at the same time. I looked away, watched Christ again and he told me some more about 'overlords' and 'underlings' and how the 'syndicates' ruled from that big white palace over there. I looked back at the boat. It was still sinking. Just as it was about to disappear, it rose again. They seemed to be fishing from the prow. I shouted to tell them there was no point – the sea was dead, chock-full of poison. They carried on fishing. It was difficult to see. Christ said he was new in the city and would I show him around? I stood up and walked down to the sea. I said how I was not allowed back in: I had been thrown out. I showed him all the landmarks, how the houses start at the top of the hill and flow over the brink. How further down they start again and fight in the centre. He compared it to sugar and then he said it was like a volcano, all the lava chucked over the hills into the causeway. He talked nonsense if you ask me. He pointed to the roofs and chimneys and said how they looked like a castle and how every castle had to have a king. He asked me where the king lived. I said there was no king, that there was a board and there was a council and that was that. There were some policemen and they caught me and slung me out and caused a lot of bother. With that he started talking about 'the seventh sign' and 'overthrowing governments' and 'false kings'. He made a lot of sense. He asked me if I wanted a drink. I said I had only just had my lunch. He had some fish on him. And a bottle of something. So we walked backed up the dune. He hailed his friend Saint Peter. Saint Peter staggered over. He brought some bread. We ate even though I was not hungry. He told me how they had wandered along the coast – ten, twenty, a hundred, a thousand miles. He had lost track. And everywhere he had been he picked up a bit of this and gave a bit of that. How he got in fights and nobody believed what he was saying and called him a liar and a thief. He was moved on and I nodded and said, Yeah I was much the same only I was not a god and I had moved on to the beach. We stared off and looked at the boat rising and sinking and them fishing from the prow. He asked me if I wanted to take a walk. He seemed to quite like me. Saint Peter did not say anything but that was his way. Christ said how I was half fish and half man, how I reminded him of a salmon he had once seen landed on the shore by its own stupidity. I did not quite know what he meant. I had not seen a mirror in years. And he added that I reminded him of a liquid – I cannot remember its name. He was a queer fellow. We walked along the beach not saying much. But everything he said I remembered. And everything I said he seemed to understand. But I don't think he did because later on he gaffed a few times. It gets me when people do not listen to you. We saw this girl with spots on her legs. I said I had seen her before. And that now she had picked the spots on her legs. He said she had the air of a 'virgin waiting'. I said, What is a 'virgin waiting?' But he did not say anything. He must have smelled her. He went over and asked her if she was bored. She screamed at him. Girls do if you go up and ask them questions. He did not seem to get the hang of it. We saw another one. And he went and sat by her. He started to tell her off for wearing such skimpy costumes. Saint Peter and I just stood and watched. Christ started prodding her. She started screaming at him as well and then slapped him around the head. We did not know what to do. He said he had been beaten up before but this was a girl. We carried on

167

walking. I saw one of my friends – the boy who I go fishing with. He has got flaxen hair. He was carrying one of his bundles of fishing-rods and a tackle-box on straps over his shoulders. He had these huge green wellington boots on, flapping round his legs. Jesus told him to go bugger off and said he would catch fatter fish in his boots. The boy swore and hissed at him. I cannot remember his name but we are good mates. Jesus told me this story about a man he knew who had done a murder. The police could not pin it on him. They knew he had done it but they could not jail him. So they waited outside his house. He was walking about inside. They could see him talking to himself. I said I talked to myself all the time but he did not seem to hear. That is why I talk to myself – so someone will hear. Anyway. For a lead they bugged his room. And it turns up he was walking up and down making up stories, trying to cover up what he had done. In every new story what he had done got twisted out of shape. By the time the police had sorted all the stories out – there were hundreds – they figured they had got the murderer. The judge would not accept any of them as a confession. The murderer is out there, running loose! At that, Christ looked at the sky and rolled his eyes down to the ground. Then rolled his eyes back up to the sky again and flicked his lips so they made a smacking sound. We stopped after that. We were worn out. We must have walked half a mile. I continued to tell him about the city, seeing as he had just arrived. I pointed out the two rivers – how the city took its name from one and dumped its shit in the other. So it took from one and gave to the other. He did not laugh. I think he had fallen asleep by then. Saint Peter said he did the odd bit of fishing as well. So we talked about that for a while. But he was very drunk. I could not figure out what a drunk was doing with a god. But gods attract all sorts of loons. Suddenly Christ woke up and suggested that we murder the king. I told him again that there was no king but he carried on, said that we should find him, kill him, dress ourselves up in posh clothes and take his place. I said again that we could not do this because there was not one king, there were hundreds, in fact there were thousands, there were probably hundreds of thousands. Everybody was a king. Leastways that is what I had been told. This did not put him off. He had drawn a plan in the sand. He got his notebooks out. I got my notebook out. We scribbled ideas. Saint Peter did not say much. I think it was his turn for a sleep. Anyway, Christ stands up and he's jumping around and his greatcoat is swirling in the wind and I don't know whether I am coming or going and he has got me carrying the gun and he is going to take his stick. He is going to hit him over the head and I am going to shoot him and Saint Peter is going to take his crown and I keep saying, There is no king! There is no king! We cannot kill a king! We would have to kill everybody! Then there would be no one to rule! And what would be the point of that? But he did not hear a word of it. He was getting excited. I asked him again if he had really come down from the sky. But he was not listening. Seeing as these were gods, how come they could not figure out there was no king? They should have known. Gods know everything. Maybe they were just playing with me. People play with me all the time. And seeing as I liked the idea of living for ever, I played along. Christ said that was the nub of his job – to hand out loads of lives. It seemed like a good deal. So I took it on board saying, Well OK, I come along and kill the king so long as I get to hang around for ever. He said it was not that simple. I was starting to lose him by this stage. But he blundered on. The point is, he said, you are the real king! I said I did not want to kill myself. Besides, how did he know this? I had known it for years. He went up to a man on the prom and shouted, There's the real king of Wales! Bow down! What do you think you're playing at – worshipping false gods? He was quite a character, this Jesus. His friend did not say much. Then again, gods do not always say things, do they. Most of the ones I have spoken to have never said a word. Nice to meet one who will hold a convo with you and knows a bit about your previous. Anyway, I said if I was king of Wales, who was he? Oh, he said, I am the king of heaven and any other place I choose. Only he did not have the time – took up your time being a king. By this stage we were getting fairly excited. Both bottles were empty. Christ advised we walk up to the town. I said there was no way he was going to get me in that town – not without my scarf anyhow. And I said I could not put my scarf on as it was too hot. He took no notice. By then it was cooler. A wind was up. He nagged me. I gave in. I put my scarf on. I tied my rope round my waist. I put a trilby on my bonce. I put all my relics in my bag. He stopped me and said he was giving them a name and he said these are the 'components collected by a victim from his master's table'. I have never forgotten that, I might have got it wrong. I haven't a clue what it means. But it is a nice name for a pile of junk. I have forgotten pretty much all else he said but I have never forgotten that. He scratched his beard and he sucked his fingers and he bit his nails and he looked as if he was about to say something awfully wise and then he just farted and strode off ahead. The two of us followed. Of course it changed everything, that did. Up till then my life, well, was not much to speak of – bit of fishing, bit of beachcombing, bit of snoozing, bit of shoplifting, getting evicted, saying goodbye to me mother. Not much. And I like a bit of excitement now and then. This was excitement. Off we trudged in his shadow. I could not see properly. My eyes were going again. So I chased up to him and said, Here touch me eyes again. But he blundered on, scratching his beard and mumbling about how we were going to 'unseat those rulers' who had 'tyrannised an innocent people'. We walked into a bar and got slung out. We walked into an off-licence. He went up to the man and head-butted him and asked for a bottle of Scotch. Or did he ask for the Scotch first? I have got such a bad memory. Anyhow we got ourselves a bottle of Scotch. That fortified us. He said gods needed fortification like men. We headed for the council offices. They are built of sand, hard sand. Sand built up to a clocktower with this dome on top. A very ugly palace. He goes up to the big steel doors and starts a hammering on them and saying as how the walls will come tumbling down and he is going to throw them all out of his father's house and turn their tables on to the grass and ransack their secret files. There was no one in by that time, of course – they had all gone home. He wasn't to know that – he had just arrived. We soon tired of hammering and kicking at the doors. So we went and sat on the verge and planned our next move. I suggested that we should find a token king and kill him, instead of looking for the real one. As I said, there is no real one. He did not seem to understand so I wrote it down in my notebook. I always carry a notebook – very valuable. When I showed him what I had written he nodded. Off we trudged, him walking ahead with his stick like a divining-rod finding the way. He led us down streets and down back alleys and over the hill and into Brynmill. Finally we found a pub, walked in and lynched a bloke. He started kneeing him in the nose. I was not having any of this

170

– you do not know who this bloke is – so I starts legging it. And Saint Peter's running after me. I think he is escaping too, only suddenly he collars me and drags me back to Jesus. And Christ starts nutting my head against this poor sod out of the bar. I could not believe it. Anyway, when he has knocked him unconscious he says, That's enough miracles for one day – we will find another king tomorrow. Off we go. He has got blood all over his fists and feet and we are feeling like another drink. He said how he could get into this and I was thinking how can I get out of this. Then he told me about this man who used to steal suitcases for a living. How he emptied them and sold anything he found, then slung them away. He worked on the trains, walking down the carriages grabbing a suitcase, getting off at Swindon or Crewe or Exeter, opening the case, emptying it and flogging the stuff to buy himself an honest lunch. Only one day he opened a case and found a dead baby. Christ looked at the sky. He did not mention a moral to the story. Then he rolled his eyes down to the earth, then rolled them back up again and started chewing on his rollie. I did not know whether to believe him. I half expected him to get the dead baby from under his greatcoat. He had all sorts under that greatcoat. He said he would give it me when he had finished his mission on earth. Anyway we ended up back on the front. I said I was a bit worried. If they caught me in town I would get an awful kicking. He gave in and said, Yeah, let's go back to the dunes. There we sat, watching the sunset over West Cross. He said he wanted to go to church. I said, It's a Monday, no church is open. He said, There must be a church open. So we walked along the beach towards the dock. He pointed to churches and said, What about that one? What about that one? And I had never realised there were so many churches in that place. I said, That one is no good, it's Anglican; that one is no good, it's just a poxy little chapel. Finally he pointed to St Mary's in the centre. We loafed up there. I put my scarf on my head. We wandered in and sat at the back in this pew, me wondering what two gods wanted in a church, Christ muttering how this was his mother's place and he had not visited her in an age. It must have been the heat because it was only then I noticed the smell. It was a funny smell. I am the sort of chap who likes to keep himself a bit tidy. With a fresh bit of rope around my waist, clean my nose out now and then, I feel spruce.

But him – oh, he stank of piss. I suppose gods can choose any old carcase. It does not matter to them – finish the day's work and whoof! hop off back to paradise. But you would think he could clean himself up a bit before stepping out to work. He started muttering about some girl who was sitting at the front. I thought it was that 'virgin waiting' we saw on the beach but it was another one. Long brown hair, nice to peer at. She got up and walked out. He hoiks both of us up and we have to follow. Off we go at a canter. She is striding across the precinct to catch her bus and he runs up behind her and says he knows her! Of course he didn't – he had got the wrong bint, but he presses on. She tweaked his beard, slapped him off, shrieked and clouted him. Usual response – made a right song and dance. It did not seem to bother him, though. Maybe he could not feel. She finally kneed him in the bollocks and that got him mad. So he took her behind some bins and started doing her in. Well I was not having any of that so I started running again and Saint Peter he started running to catch me up. He got me by the scruff of the neck and dragged me back to watch. When I got back I pulled Christ off I was so mad. It did no good – he did her in. We were in deep shit whoever he was. I could see that. It was time to do something big. So I told him I did know where a big-deal king lived. This was to get him off the girl before he did her in. But I think he had done it. We ploughed on up the hill and out of the town. Big fancy houses line up to look at the sea. They do not understand it, though. I pointed to a house and said it was the king's house, his palace. I had a quick look round just to check there wasn't a bigger house. This was the biggest. It was called something mansions. He blunders inside and Saint Peter follows at a pace and they hammer on the door and some poor bastard in a dressing-gown opens up and they knock him for six. Well, I was not hanging around to see anymore. I legged it back down to the bay. I found my stone, my stone altar. I decided I'd had quite enough for one day. There was a bit left in the bottom of the bottle so I necked that. It sent me off to sleep. That was not the end of it. I was woken by voices. It must have been dawn. It was them again. They were sitting some way away. Chattering, arguing, sober as judges. They did not seem to have seen me. But I could not work out why they were sitting there. I started to crawl away. Seeing as I was awake, he bounded over and said how he was sorry for last night. That sort of thing was necessary if we wanted to overturn the state. They had killed the king. I was king of Wales. The ship was still out in the blue. The fishermen were at the prow. The rocks were still in place. Mumbles was grey – it always is. You would never know it was crawling with lice. Jesus started to say as how he had never existed. He was being very nice. He waggled his finger under my nose. He rolled me a fag and said how I was to remember one thing – that I had seen him and he had told me he had never existed . . . No, no – that's wrong. Something like that. You work it out. All I could remember was that I had seen him. You cannot forget some people. I do not know whether he did not exist or what. He just was. Anyway, his face was shaking and gurgling as he patted me on the head. He was saying as how I knew I had never seen him and You just remember that my son! You just remember your high birth, that you're king of that there city and they are not and now he had done over the false king I could take my throne. I was king I said – but I still cannot go back into that city. He nodded. I think he was praying. They staggered off about midday. They spent a while telling me my story. We said our goodbyes. He cried. Saint Peter dried his eyes and we all embraced and I gave him my trilby and he gave me his rope and Saint Peter did not give me a thing. They walked away looking at the women lying on the sand. I watched and watched until I couldn't see them anymore. They became mist and sea and haze and heaven. And then I went blind again just like I always do in the afternoons. I lay down for my nap – always a good idea at my age. And while I slept I had a dream – that I claimed the land he said was mine between high and low water and that the king who stole it from my dad was butchered on my stone. And that my father came and kicked me awake. When I woke he was not there. I decided to leave. I walked in the opposite direction so as one day thousands of miles away we would bump into each other going round and round the island in different ways. And we would holler and whoop and hug and weep at how glad we were to see each other. It was a long walk. That day I left my bay and my city and on my rock I carved my name and I carved my song, my national song, a song I have sung for a very long time:

> Listen to my last words anywhere
> Listen to my last words anywhere
> Listen, all you syndicates and defenders of the faith
> Listen to my last words anywhere!

I wrote, I did.

THE PRINCE OF WALES

a novella

The Mystery of Birth

The land of Britain, a batch of lands, lies beached in the Eastern Atlantic, a triangle of turf and bog moored to the bed by the weight of its sixty million people, among them many Kings. Delusions of greatness have not yet taken these kingdoms of heaven skywards. So they remain, grounded on a sandbank.

These peoples have good reason for their delusions. For the fields of this Isle of Apples are a luscious green. The forests froth from the bogs, and are pared back to make way for eighty-eight cities. Roads, great Roman avenues, speed a King's passage through its settlements. And Kings there are. Millions of them. Each one King of a mudpatch. And great wars follow one on another as King after King tries to get all Britain into his hands. And all of these Kings (some less ambitious than others) envy that family paid to act as figureheads for the lot: the Windsors, temporary tenants of the throne.

One of these fancy-beridden men, Jones, dreams himself more chock-full of blueish blood than any rival. And with thuggery, pillage and much letting of red blood, he seeks to impress his mark upon the planet. But the planet, an unripe peach, resists his thumb-squeeze. Even when the boyish King makes his way across impressionable sand, the planet resists his footprints. And the sea, the giggling sea, sludges on its westerly, erasing these certificates of presence.

Jones digs a triangular map of Britain from the mud. He chains the ocean. He carves a channel from the big sea to his little sea. The Atlantic bubbles, chewing his map's cliffs. With an erect pencil-finger, he marks the four great rivers: Severn, Loughor, Tywi and Tawe. In descending order, he marks the four great cities: Swansea, Rhossilli, Port Eynon and Gowerton. He builds the mountains of the unvisited North. The principal motorways. The great cathedrals of

Three Crosses, Llanmadog, Oxwich and Bishopston. And he marks his birthplace and gives it a new name: Jonestown.

Satisfied with his handiwork, he kneels on Norway and places a hand on Troy (the homes of his ancestors), imagines himself an angel, airborne over turf and bog and triangular land. And he knows it is his. Even as the sea rots the moorings of Jones's Britain, he knows this is his land. Dozing, Jones thinks he sees a woman, reminiscent of his unknown mother, hovering inches above the map. And this woman prophesies that if he fights for his divine right, then he will become tyrant over his people. Failing that, he will be condemned to blunder about its borders until God takes him up into heaven.

For now, Jones blunders over sand and turf and bog and mountain. Off he goes, hunting believers and a Queen and, to clinch the deal, a necessary father. For without a royal parent, what is a man? He is, for one, no King. His mother is by her own confession as common as muck. Jones must find his royal father. Mum said he had one. So he must be found.

I

King Jones is born, without his consent, as the sun enters Capricorn. Of this we can be certain – with reservations. The story has been passed down by the thieving hands of Kings and Saints and Queens, interested parties all.

Stars and moons wheel to view a rude conception. His mother, that wavering sun to his chaotic system, has taken a room near the Docks. She sits preparing herself for an evening's business. Before a mirror, she lacquers life into her face with a dust of Pink Rose. She is broke, work is scarce. She zips up a capacious satin dress, towels her hair and sets it in a queenly bouffant. She fixes home-made jewels on to her egg-yolk perm. A blue satin sash crosses her breasts. A plastic orb sits gleaming on the sideboard. Easter 1953. And on the three nights of one Queen's festivities, she services the needs of twenty-six subjects. Twenty-six men answer an advert placed in the city's telephone booths – QUEEN OF THE NIGHT HOLDS COURT TO ALL COMERS, CONFIDENTIAL SERVICE, TEL 465995. And twenty-six good men and true are so inspired by her monarchist pose as to contract her for half an hour.

II

Messrs Malgo, Bun, Pelham, Morgan and Tar are booked for the first night. A remarkably good Friday. Each man announces as he takes off his coat that if she is Queen then he is most definitely King. Singing 'Lavender's Blue Dilly Dilly', Mr Malgo sows the idea of a royal child in her mind. Meanwhile, he attempts to sow a child in her womb. He is and is not successful. She vanishes to the toilet, to flush out his seed. He lances each and every one of her condoms, ready for the next bout. Elaine returns, looks at her watch and throws him out, She has a full night's work ahead of her. He must wait in the queue. Why not book Monday night? Mr Bun arrives, drops his kecks and, nude as a natterjack, announces he is the Archbishop of Canterbury. He has come to crown her. She laughs him out of court. A Mr Pelham arrives in coronation mood. He is decked out in a maroon overcoat, a paper crown and waves a sceptre of pink champagne. Her advert, like the imminent Coronation, has quite caught the popular imagination. So much so that Mr Tar, for want of a crown, stretches his Y-fronts about his scalp and, as he thrashes away, lustily croons the National Anthem.

III

Easter Saturday: Messrs Gareth, Jones, Jones and Jones appear one by one, void their scrotums, and to Lainie's irritation, pillowtalk of how their claims to the throne have been persistently ignored. And the investiture of Elizabeth Windsor in a distant Abbey so excites a Mister Bore that he demands Miss Elaine provide what she has advertised. Sit in a chair on the bed holding a gigantic plastic penis in one hand and pair of vinyl testicles in the other! While she perches on a shaky throne, he dances naked as King David about her, angrily enquiring why she has not greeted him by his full title: Crown Prince

Philip Bore Augwitz NigNog Hanover Glyndwyr. He crowns her Queen of Australia, of Canada and New Zealand and Empress of all the World, and places about her head a tiara woven from three inflated prophylactics. Messrs Trahern, Leir, Pir and Garnish arrive together and, under the influences of strong spirits, help each other to orgasm by laying hands on buttocks and pounding them to climax, singing with fine Welsh dissonance 'Rule, Britannia!' So it is that, given the chance of a few days off, a nation celebrates its monarchy.

IV

Easter Sunday 1953, Elaine receives the custom of a Mr Ban, a Mr Bin, a Mr Bon, and a Mr Bun, a Mr Accolon, a Mr Damas and DC Jones. Their antics blur in her memory, though she quite distinctly remembers a thin fellow with an outsize dick insisting she sing in time to his thrusting: 'I'm The Queen Of The Swing I Am, A Jungle VIP!' A second client gains much satisfaction by being addressed as Emperor of Haverfordwest. And another fellow, fat, with no dick to speak of and bright yellow hair which she thinks must be a wig, whispers throughout that he knows she is really Elizabeth Windsor (disguised) making the most of her freedom before taking the throne in six weeks' time. Detective Constable Jones, the last in line to the throne, has his way with her, then reads rights and arrests her for solicitation, offences under the Trade Descriptions Act and for imitating a royal. Incarcerated, Elaine warms to the idea of being mother to a Prince. When, three months later, the prison doctor says Yes she is pregnant, the mother decides one of those pokers must have been a King! Chances were, if one could get a child on her, they all could. And from a gene-pool to which they were all donors sprang this prince, a kid with royalty written into his genes. Besides, Elaine was of the mind, and still is, that if there can be one Prince of Wales, then there can be a million.

V

For his tutelage, Elaine leaves her son in Care. A State Institution (St Bedlam's of Cockett) takes in an heir to the throne. For fifteen years, the son of Lainie and an unnamed father is held in custody, runs away, is caught and promptly runs away again. After each escape, Officers of the Law find the boy on a beach, somewhere on the Gower Peninsula, squatting on the sand, refusing to move, so they must drag him to a van and take him home like a dog.

Tender loving Care cossets the King. Yet he is deprived of a surname and he is deprived of a mother. His contemporaries at St Bedlam's instantly make up the shortage – calling him Dick (vulg.), Bastard and Son of a Bitch. So, the seven-year-old lad assembles around him a gang of loyal boys who kick the shit out of any scoffers.

He is watched with sympathy by Mai, an astute boy of extraordinary powers. The Prince of Wales ignores Mai. He is useless, weak, lily-livered, tiny. But Mai is wanton for friendship. So, one night, he slithers down corridors to the Warden's Office, drags a chair beneath the window, clambers aboard and breaks a pane of glass. He reads the only file headed by a number (00101). Footsteps, and the pointed face of Child 00101 appears, sniffs out filing-cabinets and peers at names. Mai reveals himself and hands him the file. Mother: Elaine Lot, father: unknown. The shivering bastard feels first glee then desolation.

Mai envies him. Mai has no known parents. Mai has no file-card. Rumour has it Mai has always been (hidden under a set of disguises), that he has no beginning nor will he ever end. Mai is sighted in Gorseinon, imitating the oldest man in the world. He is seen selling newspapers in Oxford Street, got up as a seventy-year-old war veteran crying Po! Po! And precinct prophets and party magicians appear only when Mai is on walkabout. And in his most famous feat, Mai vanishes utterly while in polite conversation with a policeman. Mai the Magician is a wonder, a useful friend.

VI

With the address of his mother, Child 00101 and his accomplice, Master Mai, plan escape. Mai engineers it so, miraculously altered to the likeness of Social Workers, they pass through the main gates unchallenged. Elaine, duped by their disguises, invites them in for Garibaldis and a cuppa.

What d'you two want – is it my Wanda? Is it? Is it my Wanda? – I'm a mother me – got responsibilities, a reputation!

Mum! You're me mum, you are! Mother does up her dressing-gown, extinguishes her cigarillo and bursts into tears. How d'you get out? she wails. Bitch! he says with affection. What they done to you? She strokes his bruised and crew-cut scalp. Mai plays reasonable friend. We only came – he begins – we only came to get his dad's real name! not move in!

Come here, my love, my ickle highness! And she blurts out: he'll never guess what but he had a King for a Dad and his line stretches back centuries and it's a crying shame he's been treated this way. What's his name then? Whose name? His name? What him? His dad! But there ain't just the one! Queen Mum leaps up and digs about in a laminate sideboard. My black book! She bites her lip, then spits them out, the possible fathers. Mai scribbles them down. The Prince of Wales sweats. He loathes his mother. He has known her five minutes and already he loathes her. The loathed Queen Mum is in a tizz, what with all this raking up the dead past and deader men.

In the civic library, Mai pores over the Electoral Register, collecting Christian names to match the patronymic surnames. Child 00101 picks the most popular surname and all of the first names. So it is that these sperm-donors contribute to a name-pool from whose muddyish depths leaps a Hero: Crown Prince A. B. C. D. E. F. G. H. I. J. K. L. M. N. O. P. Q. R. S. T. U. V. W. X. Y. Z. Jones, King as shall be, Heir to the Land Of Ower (European Sovereign State), Divinely Appointed Defender of the Faith. He is at five nameless. At ten, landless. And, aged fifteen, he is not unoptimistic.

VII

Mai wheels the King in the chariot of a shopping-trolley through his capital city. Crowds scream laughter. Jones gives voice to his lust for a woman. It is high time he lost his virginity.

Mai's job is to find him a fuck. Not an easy quest.

As they march on, Mai spews forth a prophecy. His life's work divides happily into three: Juvenile, Major and Late Mad Periods. This, the first of his Major prophecies, tells Jones that his eldest son, born of an incestuous union, will chase him to a grisly death. Jones bends an ear to all this, pronounces the bits he likes splendid and the rest hokum, shouting about how he is not the sort to go rutting with a mother or a sister or a grannie or his kids. Besides he can't even find his father! Mai smiles and elevates an eyebrow.

VIII

Balin Savage, Barmey and Bob pull over, cooped up in a stolen Ford Anglia. They suggest King Jones and Mai join them for a spin about the Gower. The royal court jumps at the chance. Jones has not yet viewed the wedge of planet he plans to call his own.

Balin Savage steers the joy-riders along the centre of the Mayals road at speeds over thirty-five. When the Anglia clobbers a septuagenarian and flings him to a ditch, the King in his wisdom cries Step on it! Balin guns the Anglia over forty m.p.h. knowing such a mishap could land them quicksharp back in Queen's Custody. Avoiding the charming village of Pennard, they pass at speed through Parkmill, Penmaen, Knelston and Scurlage before reaching their destination, Port Eynon. Jones whiles away the journey by screeching obscenities at pedestrians. Mai sulks. The King skins up. Bob drums on Jones's head and, to great popular acclaim, performs a cover-version of *Vedan Fleece*. Meanwhile, Barmey rhapsodises Loraine, a renowned beauty, a waitress in Gino's, the ice-cream parlour on Port Eynon beach-front. It is her they have come to molest.

The Boys bundle into the cramped shop, boisterously speaking of Barmey's desire. The girl blushes the colour of pomegranate seeds.

183

Barmey sticks out his chin, his chest and then his hand to maul her. Steady on! cries Balin – wait till you're offered! But Loraine is not about to offer, so Barmey must take. The Boys thrust him forward, loosen his belt and restrain Gino The Manager who has the insolence to disturb the molestation. Jones announces his annexation of the shop. With majesty, he thwacks Gino on his oily wop scalp (royal words). Plan is, to feed him through the ice-cream dispenser and serve Tutti-Fruttis to the queue of sightseers.

The King stands upon an elevated point (the Manager's skull) and promises the crowd that he will feed to the ice-cream machine all greasy Eye-ties, Pakis, wogs and yids until the thing only runs vanilla. Mai pours himself a weak tea, eats part of an orange sorbet and interprets the patterns on a Custard Cream. He borrows six hundred cigarettes and £200 sterling from Gino's counter as a souvenir of the annexation.

Barmey has completed his rape. Bob and Balin release Loraine and, with a broom, Jones sweeps The Manager under a table. He announces to the crowd that now he, a Prince of Wales, rules this ice-cream parlour and all that is in it. Barmey chooses to stay behind, to comfort the bruised girl, and later that evening is arrested by the local Constabulary. Under questioning, he gives up the names of a Mr B. Savage and Mr Rob V. Morrison. Officers of the Law cannot trace the fourth and most dangerous fifth man whose indifference to the outrage suggests he is barely human. Barmey dies in custody, valiantly. Jones cries There's the Windsor's Justice for you! Balin Savage and Bob B, loyal to the King and to Mai, breathe not a word to their interrogators and pass much of their adult lives in the city jail keeping company many of the King's men who await the coming of his kingdom and the bliss that it will bring.

IX

The King and his henchman meet Cuthbert, Dibble and Egg, boys who live in a red-brick tumbledown squat on the St Helen's Road. They thieve from the Docks and sell the booty at a stall in the Market on Wednesday afternoons and so scrape a modest living from the sea.

Mai introduces Jones as His Royal Highness The Prince of Wales. The three hosts introduce themselves as God the Father, God the Son, and God the Holy Ghost. Jones, he of the hot temper, screeches with anger. Mai takes him to the beach to cool off. It will take time, take time to convince the wooden-headed locals of his Claim. He must be patient. Meanwhile, take a stroll by the sea. You know how it always cools you off!

The River Severn is the longest river in the lands of Britain, flowing from the Shropshire hills to carve a path between warring Devon and the fractious states of southern Wales. The Gower peninsula, Jones's land, was carved out by this firebreak of a river, hewn from the sandstones of the Black Mountains longer ago than anyone can remember. Jonesie's land is outlined by the confluence of the Tywi, Tawe, Loughor and Severn rivers.

On the extreme south-east corner stands Mr Mai and his scowling fuming King. Mr Mai takes Mr Jones and, like a custard cream, dunks the whole of him in the tea-coloured river. To bring down the temperature of his blueish blood, he says. The three gods, Cuthbert, Dibble and Egg, stand cautious at a distance, impressed by royal anger, almost believers.

Flung beyond the driftwood, the King does not sink: he floats on the river's skin. And the three witnesses declare this a miracle. And so it is that King Jones gains the first of his loyal retainers. And, to further cool his nerves, Mai takes the King on a weekend break, off over the Gower to be alone for a while, to steady his character.

X

Left alone on Sweyne's How, the King twiddles thumbs. He snaps finger-joints. He counts clouds. A bird settles nearby to chatter. Jones chatters. Alone again, the King curls to sleep away his vacation. To tire himself, he takes a turn about the hole. Then he sets to reorganising it. He tears up the bracken and piles it at the head. He excavates the twig of gorse and repots it inches to the north. He rolls a rock to shield him from the insolent east wind. Half a mile distant, he thinks he can see Mai – a head on a hole, a badly buried man. All day he is left alone, to try and form his character.

Mai brings food at sunset and sees the King's redecoration of the hole. This is good government! hammering the earth and nature's mistakes into shape! The two celebrate this with a hug and set to refining this theory of political government. Good kingship is good gardening. The King takes no backchat from the twig of gorse so he must take no treason from oiks on the street. He relocated the gorse-twig, so should shunt immigrants from his state. A King should impose the patterns of his mind upon the whole and, Mai continues, because this King's mind is a beauteous crystalline thing, so too will a subdued Britain be a beauty, a glimmering jewel expressive of a King's spirit.

Understandably, Jones becomes emotional over Mai's words and, consequently, most miserable over Mai's departure. The next day, King Jones cannot see Mai's head in its bed of gorsy grass. Neither can he see the wizard limping at dusk to feed him. After nightfall, terribly alone, King Jones tiptoes to Mai's crater, finds it empty and panics. He runs a figure of eight about the heath. He calls Mai by a range of vulgar names. He lies face-down and thrashes the turf. Then, tear-stained, he retires to his hole. He cannot sleep, he cannot dream. In the rainstorm, he shivers and recites MaiMaiMaiMai. He thinks he's caught hypothermia, so mumbles the last rites. He thinks he sees great branches of lightning over Cornwall and fears with trembling the prospect of a great bolt uniting him with heaven.

With dawn comes the last rain and a shout from Mai who grins as he hears how the King secretly wanted a lightning bolt to burn out his brain, how he wanted to run and jump from the distant cliffs into the Severn gorge. But he resisted temptation. And he learned that his life is a wheel of fortune on which he is racked, passing from trauma to bliss by way of tedium. Mai nods – this is what grown-ups call growing up. But more importantly the King has passed the test! Not once, Mai shouts, did he doubt his Divine Right! his purity of race! his destiny as King! his origin as Prince! And over a breakfast of bilberries, Mai announces that, aged eighteen, King Jones has at last found a character.

XI

They walk home, renaissance men. Mai, short and balding at eighteen or thereabouts, in a tweed overcoat and several scarves, large leather boots and a trilby. The King, with hands clasped behind his back, garbed in a primrose-yellow leather greatcoat and a large Dutch hat. As they walk, Mai wishes the King a Happy Christmas and the King wishes Mai a pleasing Boxing Day. Mai thinks it an appropriate time to make a speech.

Jones, it is well known, is an ambitious imperialist. He is not one of those Kings who are happy to rule a little backyard and leave it at that. No, Jones is of the snatch, grab it and rule breed, the pillage, plunder and burn variety. Jones has designs on lands neighbouring his own, lands neighbouring his neighbours, lands on neighbouring continents – and this all before he has so much as acquired a House he can call his own! Jones is, Mai told him, a born world-leader, an empire-builder, a good old-fashioned barbaric colonist. And when he has annexed his own land, why, he should strike out and colonise greater Britain! make Britain as India to his Victorian state, a crowning jewel! But first, but first, Mai reminds him, we must think up a name! – a name for the land that is ours by right, the land we saw from the peak above your hole. Let's call it Ower – use an old word that everything knows – shorten the English Gower to a battlecry, a name for a nation among many tiny tiny nations! Our nation!

For the moment, Mai consoles him, he is but one among a million Princes of Wales. He must assert his right with force and terror. Jones nods solemnly and stoops to tie his bootlace. Mai thinks he is bowing so cries: Rise O Worthy Prince of Wales! This is his investiture. The testing is over. The King of Ower has gained his maturity. And to celebrate his eighteenth birthday and the one thousand and nine hundred and seventy-first birthday of Our Lord, the two boys re-enter in glory the city. And, it being Christmas, they find a wench to take the edge off Jones's desire. New Year: they lie dead-drunk on their backs and imagine how it would be to be buried for ever and ever in the mucksweat of earth's holy embrace.

XII

The rightful Prince of Wales spends his nineteenth year touring his land, speaking before large crowds, addressing businessmen on how to cut deals in the European Community, giving seminars to historians and academics on the Historical Precedents For The Independent State Of Ower, The Fallacy Of The Holocaust And The Reality Of English Brutality, The Racial Purity Of The Welsh, and Ower: Arthur's Chosen Kingdom.

Teenage prodigy or several Jaffa Cakes short of a pack? Those court reporters who write up his public appearances certainly veer to the latter opinion, their headline-writers penning such fictional wonders as LOON HARASSES JANUARY SHOPPERS IN DILLWYN STREET! MADMAN LASHES OUT AT ROYALS! RACIALIST REARS HIS UGLY HEAD IN UNION STREET!

Jones, characteristically, ignores bad press. His mind is on a higher plane. He is practising his walk, he is cultivating his wardrobe, he is taking elocution lessons from the fanatically well-spoken Giles Gstungadung.

Mai observes that all Kings worth the name evolve a Style which thereafter takes their name: Edwardian, Georgian, Arthurian. He adds that the washed-out Windsors had conspicuously failed to acquire such an appellation, either Windsorian, Elizabethan, Charlesesque. No! Mai shouts through a loudhailer of toilet-roll – this is the Jonesian Age!

And even now! he shouts, the usurped monarch is upstairs, weeping in his bed. This man Jones, King among us, is even spurned and reviled in this his refuge – 33 St Helen's Road!

For, despite Mai's oratory, mockery of the Crybaby King continues. A crown of used teabags is nailed to his door. The King is told of letters addressed HRH PRINCE OF WALES and rushes to the doormat to find bank statements for JONES ESQ. When Egg shouts that a crowd of naked women are mobbing the house wanting to bear the child of the real King of Britain, Jones jumps the first two flights of stairs and, airborne over the third, becomes entangled in a Hoover flex. He is hung three feet over the hall-carpet and, staring at an encyclopaedia salesman, he swings south and north and back again.

XIII

He is saved from death. The quick-thinking salesman manoeuvres a stack of *Britannica* volumes beneath Jones's galloping feet and builds a stairway down from the noose. Having conferred upon the traveller a Knighthood, Jones shows him to the door and goes in search of culprits. He finds his housemates huddled in the back kitchen, catatonic with laughter.

With a range of domestic utensils, the King disfigures his disciples. He beats skulls out of shape, slashing leg muscles and snapping forearms. Flab, Fuckhead, Gary and Garison come to the rescue and full-scale battle breaks out. To Cuthbert's ear he applies an awl. To Flab's belly he affixes a fork. And, with the flat of a cast-iron saucepan, he decks Gary and Garison.

The King ascends to a small red formica table and, clutching an egg-beater and a large spoon, says You fuckers ever badmouth me again – fucking kill you, I will! It is a stirring, eloquent speech, rolled from the tongue with majesty, delivered with florid waves of spoon and whisk. Make treason a capital offence and few subjects will mock their King.

Mai and Jones bathe the wounded, carry them to beds and administer lemon tea, digestive biscuits and Elastoplasts. Around midnight, the two victorious squatters share a nightcap and, enthroned in an armchair, Mai declares King Jones of Ower the Absolute Ruler of 33 St Helen's Road. Kings win land bit by bit, Mai reassures him – like trench warfare, territorial acquisition is a tortoise crawl.

XIV

Therefore the King must be patient, be good-tempered, calm in the face of insults. Most especially when in public . . .

Mai arranges a Public Meeting outside Marks and Spencer's on Saturday morning. Garison, Gary and Dibble form a band for the occasion, acquiring euphonium, drum and trumpet to catch the public ear. To catch the public eye, they paint on large signs the

King's full title. Jones is anxious that even the deaf should get his message.

Mai is careful to train the King in the use of good manners, rhetorical flourish and public-address systems. The megaphone, a bright red voicebox, is connected to a small battery unit, an amplifier and the speaker on Cuthbert's National Panasonic transistor radio. The King holds the scarlet cone to his nostrils and points it at his subjects.

From the cone comes his prepared speech, extolling the virtues of monarchical regimes and damning the present abuses of power, a speech vitriolic against British Imperialism and passionate for indigenous rule. But the script gets lost.

Accusations are levelled against Flab who holds the record for eating balls of paper and swallowing them. Whatever – the speech gets lost and the King improvises to great popular amusement. A fantasia on the theme of kingship starting with the words: In this land of Britain there are loads of lands – Oh! my people, me people!

This opener catches the public imagination and a crowd of minors gathers to hurl the contents of a litter-bin at the orator. The King stoically disregards the wave of missiles and turns his attentions on a gaggle of imbeciles under the guard of a nurse. Jones gains much encouragement from the interest in their watery blue eyes. At least these people understand him. Look at the fucking state of this country! Our land! Diseased, it is! Under the rule of loonies, it is! Any fool can nick our money, he can! We'll boot them out! All furryners!

Tourists take photos, police officers circle warily. The juveniles on his left go in search of a second litter-bin.

Tell you wha. . . ! Jones starts, with great promise. A palpable silence follows. Breath is held. Even Flab looks up from his takeaway. Tell you sunnink for nuffink . . .

And the sentence ends there. Band music blurts from the transistor radio. A march, a military march. The King falters, opens then closes his large mouth and starts goose-stepping on the milk-crate, as if the musical interlude is all part of his order to service. He closes eyes in reverence to an imagined crown and murmurs Pom-Pom! Pom-Pom!

Flab, Fuckhead and Mai stare in horror, unsure whether to run or join the one-man march. Garison, Gary and Dibble play their instruments, trying to keep in tune and time with the band. Cuthbert drops to his knees and fiddles with his radio. But when he switches it off, Jones waves him to switch it on again.

To the music of the Royal Grenadier Guards at the Trooping of the Colour in Whitehall, King Jones and his reluctant men perform a sideshow which, for an hour or so, makes the lives of the townspeople a good deal happier, puts smiles on idiots' faces and gives a hundred housewives tales to transport home with their durables. And so it can be said Mai's plan most spectacularly succeeds. The King is famous.

XV

King Jones is mighty pleased with his performance and his fame. He tells his boiled egg how it brought his People together under a common flag – a flag! a flag! – someone must design a flag for next time . . . There is to be a next time? Mai enquires. Course! the King blurts – can't let a good idea go! Someone might steal it!

The Boys are too cowed to rebel. The King offers rewards of land, great territories for each of them, and titles, titles till they're coming out of their ears, and women, the women of the land are theirs for the taking . . . ! Jones vanishes to his quarters to write speeches. Subjects are written on posters and Dibble and Egg are sent flyposting at two in the morning. THE PRINCE OF WALES WILL ADDRESS HIS PEOPLE, SATURDAY MORNING OUTSIDE MARKS & SPENCER'S: On Our Land: The Land Of Ower, The Devil And Charles Windsor: A Friendship? On Immigration Policy, Who Will Lead The Uprising? and, one he in particular looked forward to: Why Me? And each of these Public Meetings is as successful as the first.

By Christmas and his twentieth birthday, Jones is weary of the heckling, the treason and the raining rubbish. He decides a new way must be found to enthrone himself King.

XVI

The house on St Helen's Road is tottering, falling down, the slates on the roof are coming clean away and threaten to slice in two halves a passer-by or, worse, the King himself. The Boys place buckets under leaks and plug draughts with rags. King Jones grows ambitious for a large, suburban property, a many-roomed mansion where, of an evening, they can relax in comfort with great distances between them, where they can hold parties for visiting ambassadors and receive Heads of State in a style befitting a Royal Court. Jones refers to this desire in his final speeches to the populace in the winter of 1973. But Britain is in the grips of a depression. Only the Windsors and their fops enjoy luxurious habitats. Dibble and Dragon are sent scouting for a new squat, one with a meaningful title to adorn letterheads and visiting cards.

Jones has his eye on Mumbles Rock, the one set with a lighthouse far out in the Bay, a lighthouse he would convert into a Camelot which no walker on the sand could ignore and without which no ship could safely sail. But by lunchtime, he has gone off the idea, thinks it a waste of valuable resources and the Rock too confining. Dibble finds properties in St James's Crescent, Prince of Wales Road near the Station, King Edward's Road, the Kingsway, the Queensway, Princess Way and Jones Terrace. The King and his retinue view them all, turning their noses up at squat after squat, pronouncing them all lowly. Around candles lit during blackouts, the Boys pass tales of future glories with a cider bottle, cooking over a fire in the garden and banking earth to prop the house.

As the house collapses, Mai is lying in a heavy doze, dreaming up a prophecy to cheer the King. He hears the roof go, the main beams give, and rushes to wake Jones. A storm has torn loose the majority of slates and tossed them to the garden. Treasonously, winds have inflated the loft and wriggled under beams. The structure starts to slip. As the Boys tumble out to the pavements, the gable drops through an outside wall like a guillotine, carving through soft brick and window-frame to the yard. On a grey Sunday morning, the entire Court of King Jones watches the house of a god descend to the cellars. No one rushes to save the house or its contents. The group of pyjamaed revolutionaries waits, watching with tear-filled eyes the irreversible end of an era. Then, to get spirits up and warm the blood, Jones starts a round of the national anthem 'Ower Land, My Father's Land!' and commands Dibble to get out his list of properties so they might find a temporary residence. From there, they will make the assault on the usurpers in Westminster and the counter-revolutionaries in Ower.

XVII

The city railway terminus cringes under the winter sky that rolls down from the heights of Mount Pleasant, a sky that slips like glass through Townhill streets and flows over the gable of the Palace of the Prince of Wales. No. 6 Jones Terrace is of more solid build than 33 St Helen's Road. The leads about its tiles and cement parapets have survived bomb-blasts, sixty autumn storms and the acidic seaspray that blows over the Tawe and wrecks the complexion of brick-skinned terraces.

Jones and his men pace about the property in an orderly fashion, steel heels rapping a march on cobbles. The King has them three abreast for fear of attack. They Ooh! and Ahh! and Imagine! (We imagine.) Jones climbs a wall, falls and climbs again. The Boys stand in siege. The King shouts, I'm over! I'm in! Stay where you are! Come when I tell you! All safe! Get the fuck over! Dibble is first over, Cuthbert follows, Garison raises Gary on his shoulders, Mai is helped by Egg, Egg is helped by Fuckhead, Fuckhead is helped by Garison, and not forgetting Flab for whom Garison is not enough so Fuckhead must clamber back over and the two of them hoik the fat jowly fellow the height of the wall till he tilts on the top and, after wobbling, drops, stonily, to the back-yard.

It is a triumphant entry into a conquered castle. Mai cooks beans and fried eggs on toast for all. Jones expects an assault in the morning, Monday morning. And sure enough, up turns Roth of Llethrid, landlord of Jones Terrace, owner of Roth's Knockdown High Street Hypermarket and Snips Coiffure in Picton Arcade, and demands the whole unruly rabble leave his prize show house this instant. Jones declares war.

XVIII

By sunset, under a wafer of moon, Roth has No. 6 under siege. His mates are, with power tools, driving a breach through a side wall. Neighbours mill in the street, coughing up the blue dusk, sweating for both sides, serving hot chocolate to the engineers. All is silent in No. 6 – no gob from upper rooms, no boiling tar from parapets, no jeering at the surrounding army.

Roth's men work into the night, cautious, methodical, hammering great gaps in the damp-course. Must be upstairs, snarls Roth, pacing about with a telescope, fucking hippies! No sign of life, only a rising moon and the kack-kack-kack of drills. Then, a tea-break. But Roth loses his temper, curses slow progress and backs a mate's Ford Transit into a side wall. First, the front of No. 6 peels away and flattens both Transit and Roth of Llethrid. Second, the roof folds like a tablecloth into the centre of the house. Last and loudest, the sides collapse like pieces of toast, dropping over the tumble of beams and tiles and Ford Transit with Jericho's ease.

Ambulance-men pronounce Roth of Llethrid dead at three in the morning, his stomach proving most resilient to the crush: protecting its load of pickled egg, saveloy and munched chips from the garlic-press of collapsed No. 6. By contrast, the Court of King Jones is most definitely alive, though sound asleep, in No. 4, Jones Terrace – two doors down. Only Mai is sufficiently conscious to laugh at the crash and at the story of how a landlord lost himself and a house in a night.

XIX

Number Four, Jones Terrace, is, despite the change of digit on the door, quite as well appointed as Number Six. Aside from modern kitchen units, a posh bathroom and a landlord, the only lack, in the King's opinion, is a fitted woman.

So, the King orders Mai to find him a Life Companion, a Better Half, a Queen no less. He needs more than ever a little darling to cradle in an armlock, to suck dry, to have canoodle with him of an afternoon. While Mai searches for omens, for guidance and thereby a woman, Jones lies on his back on the floor of his State Room and groans. He is terrorised in anticipation. What would he say to a Girl?

Mai sits cross-legged in his room, casting stones, making mugs of tea to read the leaves, shitting in a pan to read the stools, spying on stars to read a horoscope, praying to the sun. He sneaks to the Palace Theatre, but five hundred yards from Jones Terrace, the only gay nightclub in the southern Welsh states. He takes a stand at the bar, jostled by Queens, Leather Kings, Sisters of Perpetual Indulgence, Androgynes and Bishop Beaters.

One youth has got himself up as a Girl of considerable beauty. He loiters near Mai, daggered desire in his eyes. Halloo! he croons, egg-eyed at the wizard. They flirt. Mai quickly does the honourable thing, admitting he is as sexless as a sweet potato, but tells of a friend who, as we speak, is clutching his stomach and groaning for want of a good rogering. This is Faye's kind of talk. The two men come to an agreement.

Mai leads Faye (né Colin) to the King's Chambers. Wha? mumbles the celibate, wretched within. Your Majesty, murmurs Mai with the greatest of respect, winking at Faye to indicate some vast chronic delusion. A young lady greatly desires your attentions . . . The door swings open: big King in bathrobe, little hairy knees and bare chest poking bottom and top from towelling. He jigs to see over Mai's shoulder. Hello! Hello! HRH, Faye – Faye, His Royal Highness!

Faye poses (organs denoting gender well and truly strapped to pubic bone). Such beauty! The boygirl has high ivory cheekbones, arched brows and pursed lips, all carved from a lump of chalk, wrapped in a black mini-dress – a black mini-dress! – and sure as he is King, black suspenders peeped under hemline! Mai backs out, sealing the door. Faye, né Colin, twirls centre stage. Strip, bitch! Mai returns with drugged mixed drinks. The boygirl kneels, rises, rides an imaginary male, smooths breasts to ribs, grinds fingers deep in groin. He/she teases and flirts, fingers cheeks, courses nails along lips and tips drinks to his mouth. Impatient, the King draws the child to the pillow and kisses . . . But it is too late, too late . . . And over his boiled-egg-and-soldiers the following morning, Jones can only remember an undulation of breast, foraging between thighs as if he'd lost something – then nothing. It must have been heaven. And, as is the rake's way, he tells the Boys of a night of unprecedented passion, a delving for flaming pearls, a torrid mucksweat of a fuck – love! love! – the girl had been born a woman . . . And Mai hides his smirk with a hand.

XX

The Court of King Jones is short of cash. Social Security payments lapse in between moves from No. 33 to No. 6 to No. 4, and with the harsh lightless winter comes penury.

When a Royal Court is broke, what does it do? Promptly declares war, so to raise taxes. But on who to declare war? And from whom to extract taxes?

In a black rage, the big King (over six foot now and may have ceased growing) jumps up, storms out, grinds the Ford Zephyr into town and rams through the plate glass of Moynihan's Electrical on Oxford Street. Filling the back seat with eight Grundig music centres, two JVC televisions and a job-lot of vacuum cleaners, he can feel the giggle choking his throat till he can hardly breathe, but he is half a mile away before he has to pull over with tears streaming down his cheeks and tickling his beard. He wipes his eyes, but cannot stop laughing, laughing at the sudden revelation of a Plan, a taxation plan! Why suffer poverty when you can rob?

He joy-rides back to Jones Terrace, wheezing with hilarity, chortling Eureka! Before dawn, three more ram raids, raids on wholesalers, retailers and warehouses, ramming doors or windows or walls, plucking booty from within. Tax the bastards! Find some furryner's gaff and have him – go, Boys! Exhortations hurtle from his car to stolen getaway vehicles, until the sun bubbles in the east and the scream of sirens rises with the mist to glut the dawn.

At Number Four, Mai leads a team of experts in the clean-up operation, polishing bruised veneers, peeling labels from undersides and scratching out serial numbers. Before the stores open with patch-eye boards over shop-fronts, Jones has sold on half the stock, knocking on doors in Waun Wen and offering tellys for £30, hi-fis for £25 and hoovers for a tenner. Mai tots up the takings and finds they've made a round £500 for ten hours' graft!

Celebrations are general. The Boys go in all directions and by nightfall half are in police custody for terrorising the borough. At nine p.m., King Jones gives a stirring speech, condemning the brutality that led to so many arrests and commending those still at large for their heroism in the Field. He speaks of the Future, the glorious iridescent Future, with its hundreds of thousands of televisions, and millions of hi-fis and tens of millions of cars – all, all theirs, by right, by lawful right, a tax upon the wealthy to subsidise wintry poverty, a tax extracted with necessary force and redistributed to the poorer areas of his capital city. This, shouts the King, backed by a mural of news bulletins, is our age, the age of Ower!

XXI

The new tax is levied at intervals, waves of raids extorting valuables from the merchants of the city. King Jones appoints a Minister of Finance to his Court, to administer the taxing of the state. Raids continue. Extortion provides increased revenue. Businesses need protection from thugs like the Prince of Wales's Militia. So, gasps the King, we protect them from us – fucking charge them for it!

The P.O.W., as it is known, strains to an illustrious future. A future in which King Jones falls head over heels in love and Dibble and Egg, Garison and Fuckhead rot in Swansea Jail, warriors who lacking a leader can't seem to get themselves organised into a force of any power.

Quite enough fortune-telling – the future, like the past, is known only to the flame-headed pentecostal few, while we Britons marooned in the present strain to wallow in the future, can only sip at the Atlantic to come.

The Adoration of Vera

From a nothing of beginnings comes the royal marriage of King Jones and Queen Vera, its origins in the void at the heart of a zero, its offspring a dynasty: a river of atoms, genes, numbers and names, a string of Princes of Wales, enough to pack a library shelf with hack biographies and a jail with hack biographers. King Jones, with origins in a Coronation Year bordello, has, we have seen, built from the most atomic of beginnings a cell of terrorists and vigilantes, all activists on behalf of his Claim. His Claim: a lunge at the Crown of Britain, at worst a request that his bit of Britain be returned to him, a land he has called Ower, a land in his family for centuries, a land colonised by the British longer ago than anyone cares to remember. Indeed, there is too little remembering going on. What of the events as seen by those who lived them minute by interminable minute, chained up in the prison of the present? Tell, tell how Jonesie meets Vera and Vera meets Jonesie and of the almighty rows between them, the war years at home and abroad, those wars to begin all wars, wars in the kitchen and the diner and the loo, wars in the bed, wars over who's the fool who brought them together in the first place.

I

But there is no first place, no *ab ovo*, no egg nor sperm, only a crash as the two meet and meet without recognising each other, a meeting only I know about – an abortive coming-together, one treacherous January morning, on the ice.

King Jones, a magician astride a stolen bicycle, finds to his distress his trouser-leg caught in sprocket-wheel. He curves between hectic cars on the Walter Road, bumps over kerbstones, dodges pedestrians but cannot avoid catastrophe. Streets collide at right angles, paths touch fingertips and Jones crashes into iron railings at speed. At the feet of his wife-to-be, he sprawls, cursing the day of his birth.

Vera Velindre, girlfriend to Police Constable Arthur Idris, cries Whoops! and titters to her Beloved. She steps graciously over the prone stunned King and strides on up the hill. King Jones sees only silhouetted colossi: legs picking a path among his limbs. A woman! He struggles to his feet, straightens his overcoat and dusts off boots. He smiles and tut-tuts and hums 'Oh What a Lovely War'. But Vera doesn't see dignity in the face of humiliation. She licks her Beloved's neck and gropes his genitals and whispers, Tonight, tonight, my lovely . . . King Jones lifts his bicycle to its feet and, perched upon it, voyages by a circuitous route towards his Beloved.

II

1975 begins well. New Year's Eve is celebrated in fine form in the King's Arms on the High Street. All Boys gather round to sing God Save Our Gracious King! As they make resolutions, Mai delivers a stonker of a prophecy. He predicts an upturn in Jones' sex-life, till now, a succession of downturns.

So, as spring churns the soil, optimism churns the King's belly. He sets off to visit a neighbouring King, Ernest, Dictator of Neath. Ernest's Court sits in perpetual residence in the lounge bar of the Welsh Bard, 1 Commercial Street. Jones misses one train, the 11.32 leaves early. He must catch the 12.32. With uncharacteristic good humour, he waits.

The 12.32 is late departing, a fact which raises the temperature of royal blood. Still he does not lose his rag. But when, at 12.35, his InterCity collides with the 12.02 from Carmarthen on sidings a mile out of Swansea terminus, the King at last explodes.

He does not explode in the way we have come to know and love. In sheer fright, Jones dives under his seat, whimpering. His sphincter relaxes. Unsolidified excreta squirt to his undergarments. So, Jones fills his kecks, and the InterCity contracts the carriages of the 12.02 from

Llanelli to one third their railworthy size. Inside, Vera Velindre, travelling from her father's house to her Boyfriend, is thrown against a bulkhead, bruised, shocked but intact.

Within the InterCity, her future husband gathers his trousers close about his waist, stemming the flow. He totters to the air, to the sidings, to the long grass. Here the sight of his projectile vomit will not upset the ladies.

Vera Velindre, staggers also to the grass. Trembling like a roe-deer, she gags but does not vomit. Jones approaches, to comfort her. She shakes with new horror. A monster is wending its way through the grass, its arms outstretched. It is going to embrace her! Shock piles on horror. She backtracks, spasmodically gagging air. Nah nah nah . . . ! But the King cannot be stopped. He is struck by this woman's likeness to a picture of womanhood carried in his head since puberty. He is, in a word, possessed.

III

After an eternity of this shuddering, crawling and backing away, Vera turns and runs. She trips, she stumbles, but she runs, straight into the arms of an ambulance-man. She is unquestionably a victim and victims are his stock in trade. So he wraps her in blankets, clutches her to still the shivers and wheels her to a yawning ambulance.

Jones, stopped in his tracks, a stunned buck, wants to boot the ambulance about the panels, he wants to lance the tyres, he wants to clout the impudent ambulance-man.

But he does nothing. He knows full well that decisive type of girl, the maniacal woman who, once seduced, would give up that wondrous reward of being maniacal for him! For the moment, he lets her be. He believes, as you see, utterly in predestination. She is to be his Empress. The two of them are sweeping forwards on a collision course. He is, if nothing else, a character in a romance. He knows they *have* to meet.

IV

It is a short walk back to Jones Terrace. Spring wind is iced water thrown against his face to bring him round. It comforts him to feel the shit dry on his trunk and trousers, so the legs of both crackle with each step, crackle as he lumbers up the hill with a raging optimism in his gut.

Mai greets him at the door: Back early! Where've you been?

Up to Hafod to look at the Queen, replies the King – Seen her, Mai, I have . . . His voice trails to a whimper, his eyes to the ceiling and he topples backwards, knocking himself out on bare boards.

Mai undresses him, burns his trousers, and has three Boys bear him to a bath. From within steam, the Emperor talks. Mai sits on the closed toilet. Amazing Mai . . . Bang! there she was – so simple – couldn't've arranged it better meself! Bang!! Mai listens patiently to Bangs and Crashes and he nods. For he has known of this all along, but hates to reveal endings to those who are trapped in the present. It so spoils a journey to know where you are going. He stares into the mist, but the King is immersed to his beard in scalding water. So, for once, Mai must be content with listening.

Course I went for it, the voice continues. Fucking went for it, I did – know what I'm like – given a chance I don't take it – but this one, Mai – this is the one – like you said – Bang! So, Mai asks, what next? Well – the King begins. Optimism surges to his throat. I know it's going to happen so I can like sit and wait for her to come to me, can't I? – but if I see her I'll have her, I will, kidnap her – grab her – if I see her – I will! But but, interrupts Mai. How do we find her? Easy, replies a voice. You tell me.

V

Mai does not tell. He is not a coin-in-the-slot prophet. He does not perform magic tricks to order. He is a strictly spontaneous magician. Magic, like romance, comes unsought.

Reluctantly, the King agrees, grumbling as to why he pays a sorcerer a wage to work no tricks for him. But off he goes, as soon as he is dried, lurching about the streets in search of an accident. At high speeds, he steams round corners, hoping to bump into her. He buys a bouquet of scarlet roses, just in case, just in case . . . In Debenham's, he anoints wrist and neck with aftershaves. On the corner of Union and Nelson Streets, he bumps into a woman of Vera's proportions and instantly launches into a speech praising her choice of clothes. The turn of her heel, the dimensions of her breasts! She marches off. Jones kicks a wall. But his optimism is irrepressible. Up it surges and off he charges, stomp stomp stomp. Women scowl at his scrutineering. Wha's your farking problem? What you farking looking at?

A Boyfriend takes particular umbrage at the King's peering. Jones stops, hands behind back, bends forward to squint up a girl's nostril and, from behind her, comes a six-foot-seven Boyfriend, fist first. Jones is toppled at a blow, without a hope of returning the gesture.

He rests on his back for a while. The pieces of Vera coalesce in his memory. Minutes pass. Up he jumps. And off he plods, serene in his vocation. And as he travels, so he thinks he knows those breasts better than any. As he travels, Our Jonesie comes to regard himself as the High Priest and rightful curator of Vera's breasts. She is his inheritance.

And everything about Vera comes to seem familiar. Hence the shuddering recognition, the paralysis that grips him on Oxford Street when he is damned sure that it is her . . . and chases and chases, taps the likeness on the shoulder. She turns, it's not her . . .

Sunset, and the King is exhausted. His reserves of optimism are run down. He skulks to his room to lie on the carpet, turn up his Led Zeppelin tape and sing along, fixing the mental photograph of his wife-to-be in the darkroom of his mind.

VI

This mental photograph is at last brought to light. Mai, some days later, brings Hoel to pay homage to the King. Hoel is an art student at the Institute, hair down to his arse, encamped in a poncho, carrying a portfolio so big he could be buried in it. He speaks of Art with a burning joss-stick clasped between teeth, championing his talent at representing human forms.

Hoel has offered to draw Her Majesty, Mai announces. The King leaps up: You can draw? – get your brush out – get this – brunette – or is she blonde? Mai? – small head, small like this, long legs . . . perfect tits.

Jones pins the picture to the kitchen wall and writes above and below: WANTED: THIS BIRD, REWARD: A DRINK OF YOUR CHOICE, BY ROYAL COMMISSION, OWER. The 'Wanted' sign yields many woman, none of them Vera. Twenty-two women are brought by hooks and crooks to squirm on the linoleum. The King shakes his head and the shrieking rejects are released like minnows into the street.

Day after day, Jones paces the streets. He is leaner now, the fat has slid from him. His pacing is swifter, his boot-soles have been thinned to wafers and the leather barely skins the feet that hurry hurry hurry after a ghostly woman.

And then he meets her, bangs into her so to speak, crashes into his wife-to-be despite her better wishes and his best efforts.

VII

The ninth of August, 1976. Six months have withered since on spring ice one train mashed into another. Six months have been endured since the King of Ower first saw his Beloved.

And he is morose, he is inconsolable with the waiting. A noose is permanently tied to a staple in the ceiling. He sets deadlines for his own suicide, stands on the chair, grits his teeth, lifts one foot, then loses his bottle.

A baking summer cannot raise his mood, the summer that raises a mirage from tarmac and a heat haze from the sea and an army of bathers from neighbouring lands. Out of the sun, on his bedroom carpet, the King moans and blubbers for his love.

Come dusk, and Harry, Hoel and Herb want to go kick the stuffing from a beach-party of coons on Oxwich Bay. Will HRH come and help? HRH says No, then Yes, then No again and finally Yes! The ride will do him good. It's time he got a bit of exercise.

He drives alone. It has become his habit to talk to himself. He spends all day and all night talking as if she is there. Lovely view over there, he cries to the car – fucking caravans ruin it – have them off there – you're farking gorjuss you know that, don't you – so glad you came – makes it, it does – no fun without mah bird cheering on the sidelines – give those black fuckers a kicking! Kick the black shit out of 'em!

He slaps the steering-wheel, then imagines she has gently criticised him for his violence. What? Don't be a silly cow – a kicking's the only way to get the wogs out – fucking snivellers whine and get to stay – ask government to boot them out, no one fucking listens to us, do they!

And he smiles as she contradicts him. She loves him really . . . He follows the South Gower Road over sun-bleached moors where sheep cower beneath gorse out of the blasting sun.

In a moment the mirage on the rise ahead becomes an orange car and it is in the wrong lane and though he tries to steer off-road he can't help and – BANG! Stunned, he feels nothing. The royal chariot rolls into the gorse. It groans, he groans. He wriggles, he squirms. He crawls through a window.

The orange butt of a car pokes the sky, bending to peek at a celandine. Jones limps over, rehearsing outbursts. The orange car is mashed real bad. The driver is bent over the wheel. The King raps knuckles on windows. The driver does not stir. But a window is open and he can pull the head back to check for wounds. And if there aren't any, well, he'll add some . . .

The nose, the little bobble-tipped nose! and the curve of linen over breasts, and the mouth, the eyes, the ears, oh the hair, the hair in his hand! He is startled to see her, unconscious, eyes of stone, utterly passive. And he holds her head just to feel the blood rattle at the back of her neck.

He lifts Vera's body through the window and lays her out on the grass. For a while, he cannot move, save to grope her. He is as unconscious as she. But then he must mend a car, one of the two. He rolls his Zephyr back on to its wheels. But he must hurry, he must race against her coming to consciousness.

VIII

Vera is strapped into a passenger seat. A wire is noosed about her wrists and he is driving off west when she comes to. What the. . . ! She cries and wriggles and squirms and, seeing him, gasps. For Jones is not a pretty man. She gags at the snarling grin and bonehead crop, the bull-rings in nose and ear, the hairy hands moist about the steering-wheel. Please – don't . . .

Oh, no worries, he says cheerily. S'all right. Jones can be a most reasonable and sensitive man at times – at all the wrong times – but sensitive and reasonable none the less. Vera takes this as weakness and reverts to outrage. Just stop the fucking car! Jones frowns, wounded, slows the car, then remembers himself, his rank, his mission. D'you know who I am? he asks stiffly. D'you know how fucking lucky you are? Evidently not. She repeats her last command, adding expletives.

I, he begins, I'm fucking King of all this . . . He sweeps a free hand across the windscreen, waving at the smoking land. A bush fire blurs the horizon, scorching gorse to black bones.

King What? – Vera retorts – you trying to impress me?

He mulls his next move. King and Queen in stalemate.

I know you! You're that loon at the train crash!

Jones takes a deep breath, to stop himself clouting her. He launches into a dull speech, a monologue painting a vision of their future. He elucidates his claim to be Prince of Wales. He tells of his businesses, his belief in strength and his hatred of undesirables, the English and their settlers, colonising this the West Bank of the Severn.

Vera does not listen. She is fiddling with the noose about her wrists. He is mad as well as repulsive. As to dangerous, it is stencilled across his brow: AGRO. She will calm him down and get him to a Crown Court a.s.a.p. Let Justice handle him.

Anyway, the King continues, then I saw you – the most wonderful woman in my fucking country!

She smiles, endearingly. The noose comes free and she goes at him with fingers and nails and screeches, trying to erase his name AGRO. Once again, the car plunges nose-first to the gorse and on impact they are flung together on the dash, arms and fingers locked about neck and ears, lips smeared against each other in a sort of royal kiss.

IX

A 1974 Ford Zephyr is unrivalled among its peers if only for its boot-space, giving the reluctant tenant more breathing space than any coffin. The woman who is thrust feet-first into such a boot can complain about many things, leg-room is not one of them.

Just to be difficult, Vera complains about little else. And as Jones motors on to Oxwich, the muffled screeches and screams do not let up, though he stops the car twice, leaps out and thumps on the back for her to shut it. Vera, in more ways than one, heats up. The temperature inside the boot threatens to stew her in her own sauce. And not knowing where they are going nor how long it will take, she keeps up a protest, listing his war-crimes against her royal self.

Jones hums loudly. He opens all windows so a breeze raises a din. But still the small voice comes clear and crisp. He tries to shout back: Keep it down, love – I'm driving . . .

But she shouts, Not listening – got me fingers in my ears – can't hear – dah dah dah – can't hear! – Little Dick Who Can't Get A Girlfriend – if I had to go out with you I'd kill meself, I would – yeukh! – 'magine! doing it with you!

Jones swallows, recognising the ingredients of a prophecy. But they are pulling on to the glaring white sand of Oxwich Bay and Hoel is running to the car to report how they kicked the fucking shit outta hoards of niggers and chased a load a English bastards from the Hotel bar but now they're banned from there, so could HRH go get them drinks?

Dusk, and a moon hangs from the Cork ferry, the boat trawling it through the heavens. The beach is deserted, the Boys having spent all day clearing it. Jones congratulates Hoel and slaps Herb on the back and tells Harry to open up the boot, only be careful because he's got an *animal* caged up inside . . .

X

The animal is too tired to run or to scratch and fight. She is limp and hot, a faint soft bundle of flesh that the Boys carry to their fire on the sand.

Jones returns with cans of cider and lager and ale, and drags Vera away from the milling Boys. Twenty of them loiter orange about the fire, ragged Nazi insignia festooning arms and waists. Vera watches them, coming to consciousness. They are obviously subservient to this grotesque. But she can't quite work out why. She stares at him as he talks to her. He mutters about 'Us' and 'Our', Terms and Conditions and Contracts.

She repeats that the thought of him turns her stomach. But she is quiet now, dishevelled and exhausted and quiet. The sea is rushing to be near her. Arthur Idris is a million miles away, pacing about a flat, probably calling his colleagues at Alexandra Road Police Head-quarters. But no matter, for it is nice to be here within spitting distance of a warm fire, with these men whom she is sure would protect her if she asked, or throttle and roast her remains in cider over the flames if she was silly. So she lets him kiss her and tell her all about his being King. His royal face is long and bat-eared against the furnace, the upturned smudges of eyebrow picked out as shadow, his skull a bristled dome, oddly naked without a crown.

Course we want the Pakis out, and the fucking wogs while we're about it – two million unemployed and guess how many wogs? – so they can fuck off home – and the fucking English.

She shivers, but loves the jaguar's purr, rasping words and tossing them to her. He doesn't look at her. He looks away because he is in love with her. She can see it in the Boys' behaviour. A conspiracy is afoot. The Boys stare at her for a moment, a worshipful leer, then look away. He's so strong. She'll forget this afternoon and be nice to him, just till morning. Then see . . . riding a wheel of fortune.

XI

She is sleepy with the smoke and when he says he won't fuck her on the beach but will take her home to his Terrace she murmurs but not words. They are in the car and spotlights of cars are Arthur combing the peninsula for his lover and the moaning engines are sirens squealing for her to come back to life. The bed is big and soft and his hands are hard, callused hands and he hasn't shaved so she gets stubble-burn but no matter because she will go in the morning and though he doesn't use a condom she doesn't worry because her period is so soon it can't do anything bad besides he's actually a good lover. Finally he lets her sleep though not before telling her she is Queen and he is King dilly dilly.

XII

She decides to stay – just for a while, mind. She tells him over breakfast, a nice breakfast, brought as she ordered to her bed. She is Queen and Queens get what they order – fruit chopped into cubes: Granny smiths and bananas and Conference pears and a pink grapefruit, all in yoghurt with sultanas. Porridge doused with skimmed milk with nuts and more fruit and as much coffee as they can carry up the stairs and across the hall and into the large bedroom with its views over the parapets to the distant grey.

At first, she is afraid to go to the loo. But then she must, so she pads across the landing in his fencing-shirt and races to the cubicle to pee. She can hear the house moving about her, a small solar system with ambitions to replace the larger one. There are shouts and commands, there are knocks and bangs and she works out that in the morning they train – One, Two, One, Two, and A-bout Turn! – and thuds on floorboards.

She tiptoes part-way down the flight of stairs, but a boy with golden hair angrily waves her away. So she stays in bed, then has a scorching bath and preens herself. Every time she tiptoes downstairs, they wave her back up. Then at midday, he comes, King Jones – the only name he'll give her – lacquered with a sweat, tanned with being out in the sun, his shirt sticky on his chest, his arms ropes by his sides.

How you? he grunts, eyeing her for damage. Fine, you know, she replies breezily. And he kisses her, and they are as married as they'll ever be. Married, for they elect to spend the foreseeable future together, loosely yoked in affectionate hostility until the next test. Then they will marry again. Can she leave? No. Can he leave? Nope.

And he is so made up by her apparent willingness to stay that he skips along the corridor. But the floor is polished and he trips down

208

the stairs. Once more, he fails to notice a loop of vacuum-cleaner flex hanging from the landing. Entangled about his neck, the noose tightens. His planned suicide is happening despite his altered luck. The King, strung up like a ham from the banisters, strung up till Vera comes racing out of the bedroom and takes him on her shoulders so he can loosen the wire. They collapse to the hallway and in a shivering embrace giggle at the foot of the gallows.

XIII

Queen Vera is settled in Jones Terrace. She leaves the house only at dusk, to walk on the prom with the King. This is their time together. They pop into the Adam and Eve or the King's Arms for a couple of pints, and mooch home.

But this is risky. Surely it is only a matter of time and ill-fortune before they bump into Police Constable Arthur Idris, much worried by his lover's disappearance.

The King himself becomes concerned at this, sharing his worries with Mai. He, in the hermitage of his attic, casts Cards for enlightenment. But the Card of Death emerges time and again. He is loath to tell the King, so says the Cards are dumb on the question. Jones is frantic, suddenly unsure of his claim on Vera. And what has been calm assurance within him turns to rancid paranoia curling in his belly, a tapeworm coiled about his intestines, so he can only shit liquid.

The King summons Iain, Jack and Kit to his rooms. He tells all he knows about the wretched Constable and commands they get an address, stake it out and call him when the man is there.

Idris! he tells the servicemen, he's dead meat he is!

Together they find his lodgings: a small flat in Winch Wen, a flat with double bed and Vera's clothes in three drawers, portraits of her in the bedroom. Iain finds and confiscates explicit cine-films starring the Queen. Jack spray-paints swastikas on the magnolia walls. With a nail, Kit etches OWER and AGRO into the bathroom plaster. The King arrives within minutes, closely followed by the police officer: Arthur Idris thinking of TV dinner and two cans of Heineken followed by a look at his Vera video.

209

Iain and Jack and Kit wait outside while the King lays the ghosts of the past and later, in the Bird in Hand, they listen to Jones's excited, nervous account of how, on the bedroom floor, he garrotted the traitor with his own coat-hanger, plugged his fingers in the mains and stuck a lampfitting on his penis. Sadly, the traitor hadn't lit up like a Christmas tree.

At home, presented with clothes and underwear and the cine-film, Vera gets a quite different account. But then, she was a friend of the deceased.

XIV

A brief interlude – to talk of myself. This is loathsome. Vulgar, to prattle on the subject of 'I'. I have been ambitious to write myself out of existence. Please excuse this lapse.

Soon after Jones moves Vera into the royal suite at Jones Terrace, I am recruited into the P.O.W. The occasion: a Public Meeting held on the move. Police officers are ranked moustaches with truncheons and tear-gas. They move us on, on.

I am addressed by a charming fellow with a head like a peeled chestnut and a gold ring in his nose. He wears a yellow paper crown about his scalp. A bright flag is tied as a sash over his shoulders. He shouts OI! and Agro! and Charlie Charlie Charlie Out Out Out! Twenty or thirty similarly dressed thugs repeat the cry. This man, with his royal poise and royal hook to royal nose and royal hands held royally behind back, asks me my name. I stammer. He stops, he starts, he stops again.

Why, that's my name! he cries with alarm.

He seems about to accuse me of plagiarism and shout Stop thief! But his henchmen are restless and distract him.

I'm King. Follow me or I'll kick you to fuck!

This seems eminently reasonable, so I, reasonably, follow. And I befriend a shy, podgy, clear-faced fellow who insists his name is Mai. He introduces me to Gary and Herb and Iain and Jack and Kerry and Lance and Mick and Nic O'Cairdubhaïn and many more whose names I forget.

I troop alongside them, learning the chants, borrow a flag to tie about myself and I hear how they are marching against the English and the French and the Africans and the Asians and against all American influence and I ask the podgy fellow how I can join because right now I'm in between religions and looking for something to do in my spare time. He tells me, following this King requires I sell everything, swear allegiance and move into his palace, putting himself at his service.

Being an impressionable man, I get down on my knees before the jackbooted King and swear fealty, loyalty, allegiance, etc. The King asks what can I offer to the revolutionary movement? And I reply that I can write this language, read a few others but find speaking troublesome. He places his hand on my shoulder and gives me a new name: JOE BLOW, meaning Dopey.

He takes me to Number Four Jones Terrace, shows me the many-roomed mansion and the magnificent views over his capital city and says all this will soon be his. I am given a box-room at the back, a room which has no view save that gained by crawling up and into the attic, wriggling six foot south and peering through a ventilation grille into the bathroom below.

Here it is that the beautiful Queen Vera bathes at eleven each morning and eleven each night. At night the King accompanies her, and like seals they roll in the soap-greyed water, and so it can be said that I have seen King and Queen from all sides and all angles in all positions and in all situations and am therefore eminently qualified to be the royal biographer. Many others love to scribble about our monarchs but none work so assiduously as I to give an impartial many-sided and factual picture of our turbulent times and the personalities who shape them. I, celibate, teetotal, bookish, dull, devote myself monkishly to observing, to not involving myself. I am a nonentity and, so, we will hear no more of the insignificance of me, only of Kings and Queens and Princes . . .

XV

To teach a King to eat – to rid him of all British dietary habits – to forbid he touch all red meats, full-fat dairy products, sweets and cakes, to bar him from beers, to do all this Vera must utterly displace all prior mothers. All those mothers who schooled his palate and nurtured his sweet tooth, the cooks at St Bedlam's, Mr Mai, Mr Kerry (proprietor of a chip-shop on the corner) and the devilish Lubb of Ystradgynlais who nightly prepared beans, bangers, mash and brown sauce for the King of the house.

She establishes herself Queen in the kitchen. She banishes rivals from the linoleum. She sends cack-handed Boys to the exile of the lounge. She keeps cookers, fridge, units and utensils all to herself. And she rules autocratic over pots and pans, controls the flow of natural gas, limits the import of ingredients and forbids public assemblies in Her Kitchen.

Her cooking is Vera's most substantial contribution to the body of the King. It is her ambition to clean him out, to refill him, to shunt bits around, to relocate the royal belly on the royal chest. And she succeeds: ounce by ounce, seven pounds of fatty tissue are hoisted skywards and flattened across the ribcage. Tentatively, colour returns to his chops. Teeth are strengthened, eyes empowered and every cell in his hot corpse nourished by the throughput of Vera's cuisine.

Chicken is named the Royal Bird. Not a day passes without a roastie spluttering in the oven or a carcase rotting in the fridge. And fish: salmon of course, squid, bream, shark and crab are netted in Severn and Fastnet and trawled to the icebox at Jones Terrace. Briny anchovies and capers, olives and garlic are stirred into a Napoli sauce. Chicken-breast fillets are sautéed with mango, garlic and coriander and served up with a Vera Salad: julienne carrots, red and green and yellow peppers, finely shredded lettuce, parsnip, lemongrass all in a ginger and lemon dressing. And remember the calamari? calamari slithering beside a Greek Salad: lettuce, cucumber, tomato and feta cheese in a garlic and fennel dressing, or stirred with water-melon balls and spring onion. Bananas stuffed with pineapple and baked to bursting in the oven. Pumpkins done all ways – mashed as a pasta base, pumpkin pie sprinkled with nutmeg, pumpkin scones and pumpkin scooped out and stuffed with herbs and vegetables, baked and served with, yes, Vera Salad.

Why can't I have what they have? he gripes. What's so good about bloody garlic?

Garlic cleans you out – washes the gobies out of your system – whoosh whoosh – gets the devils out of the innards of a King it does – now get out, give me some space!

Every ounce of his food passes through Vera's fingers. Every lettuce leaf, every wedge of cucumber, every slice of peach is processed, scoured for offending bruises, checked for overripeness then stuffed down the King's neck. All this to show how a Queen may make a progress through the guts of a King. She inseminates every cell of him with life, her oversight breeds him again. She mothers him – quite literally mothers the man – gives him a mothering, remakes him into a man. Strength of body, she preaches, and strength of character – and you want a character, don't you? Most of all, this caricature wants a character.

XVI

He pooh-poohs all this cant but loves to watch her preach. To watch her tick him off, then soften, come close, mould him to her, gain a purchase with thighs on hips and moan as he kisses – mother, sister, wife, all in one.

Add to these, boy, man, animal, and Vera is all things to one man. Her small bust (becoming, a small bust), her small bust allows her to impersonate the male sex. Naked, lying back, breast-mounds flat on pectorals, cropped hair, she is brother-son-father to him. Sitting up, tits akimbo, she is sister-daughter-mother-wife. A world, a family of a woman. Ah, how he adores her. And the adoration cannot bring itself to words.

She rearranges his inner organs, modifies his heart, slows the rotting of his liver, reinforces his colon's wall, she improves his cognitive faculties, slows the shedding of memory cells (in irreversible decline), heightens his sensory response to touch and extends his

213

staying-power pre-orgasm. She redresses him, getting him up in a green bomber-jacket with orange lining, buying new eighteen-hole Docs, twenty-two white T-shirts and scarlet wool socks.

Adroit with needle and cotton, V. stitches together her own designs, kitting him out in homespun clobber, she gets him a new skin. So grateful is he for this total overhaul that he bequeaths to her his own skin, ordering she fashion it into bra and knickers to be worn every day after his death. She passes many hours caged up in Number Four, fiddling with seams and hems, her mouth pursed with pins, a sewing-machine clattering as it turns out flags and black shirts for the Boys.

And the King takes on the intonations in her speech. She has the stronger accent and the stronger will. Records, tapes, books and posters belonging to Vera far outnumber his. He has favoured a minimalist approach to interior decoration, having only a mattress and, reluctantly, a rug in his room. Vera imports a bazaar to this echoing space, a market town collected from a thousand markets, odds and sods which clutter every horizontal surface and scar the King's bare soles each morning.

To him it is a sacrilege in the house of god, to her a tidying-up, an unstoppable feminisation of the world. And she has been with him a year now and can dictate what he does and when he does it and with whom and where. She selects who might pay homage and who gets knocked back. She creates this man in her own image and this is her way of adoring, this is the adoration of Vera for Jones, the love of a beautiful woman for a malleable man.

XVII

Jones, ever conscious of his malleable life and mindful of the biographer's task, foresaw the need for a story to his life, a beginning, middle and end to impress those students of monarchy who will crawl through every cranny of his corpse. How to structure the slopping river of a love affair? Why, marry!

Royal weddings provide a focus for the gaze of millions. Royal weddings give crushed masses a model by which to fashion their own grotty unions. Royal weddings come every eight years or so – celebrations for a nation to revel in. All eyes peer beneath the veil at what a King has chosen to fuck.

Jones mulls the wisdom of announcing his marriage in the Society Column of the *Evening Post*. 'The Prince of Wales will take in wedlock Princess Vera, daughter of King Vaughan Velindre of Johnstown and St Clears, on 29 July 1981 at 11 o'clock in the City Registry Office.'

But he cannot do this until he has gained Vera's 'Yes', so he sits dreaming of what he will say to her and how he will say it and how it will be. She will be the star to his sun, they will have children, armies of them, great battalions of sons with no doubts concerning paternity, daughters who can strut in Gstaad each Christmas, the Rue de Rivoli each Easter and St James's at Pentecost. Yachts will be theirs, films stars their lovers and Swiss accounts stuffed obese with fivers, all, all theirs.

Vera hears snatches of this reverie, guesses she is expected to hogbreed these millions and sits firmly and squarely on the idea. Who d'you think you are? A bloody maharajah? A wedding! And who's going to marry you?

Why – you, you old horse! Me? You!

She has thought of this affair as anything but permanent. Each day she wakes and decides to leave, then stays another day and wonders why Arthur never rang. Marriage to this brute? Unthinkable. What if they should produce kids? The poor mites!

See, V. – it'll rally people round, won't it – focus on us, give a bit of a speech – papers'll be there – bit of publicity, bit of publicity. And he nudges and winks. And yes, Vera's eyes ignite with anticipation. She too is power-thirsty, and the suggestion that she might take on formally the title of Queen, well it does odd things to a woman.

Announce it in the papers, the King advises, invite a few stars, get the Boys at the BBC organised – it'll be a right carnival.

You just think you can get me to say Yes to anything, don't you – we'll see! And she storms out, is chased, rugby-tackled, brought to heel with a good thrashing and made to say it.

Yes, all right then, yes, get off!

XVIII

Secretly, she is relieved. But a gold wedding-band won't go with her purple crew-cut, or with the swastikas tattooed on each hand, the pewter rings armouring fingers from tip to knuckle. And can a bride wear a nose-ring and knee-high DMs?

Her fiancé is looking forward to having a wife. He is twenty-seven going on twenty-eight, that age when a man gets itchy for a little marital instability. So, as they sit over a pint in the Swansea Jack, he makes positive suggestions:

What about we get Mai to marry us! – set the chairs up in the living-room – get a load of cider in – dress up posh – have a bit of a party afterwards? Eh? Eh? Eh?

And the King gets the Boys raising taxes and Mai writing the vows. Vera makes a wedding-dress, a baby-doll nightie cut in white chiffon, to be worn with white DM boots and a full set of white lace lingerie. The Boys clear £2000 net profit from a raid on the betting-shop in the High Street and a further £600 nicking a Ford Transit, driving up to Manchester and selling it to a mate of Ludo's. And £1500 is donated by ten shops and two 24-hour petrol stations, buying round-the-clock protection from P.O.W. Securities.

Jones celebrates his engagement by spending the £4000 yield on a white Rover V8, and a stagnight in the King Arthur Hotel in Reynoldston.

Police officers turn up to protect the King and wish him well. Fifteen Boys pass the night in custody. Happily, they are released the following morning, just in time to pile into the lounge where Iron tells us he is strumming Mendelssohn's Wedding March on Mai's guitar. Mai stands in black robes between two candle-stands, beneath a large picture of the King.

At eleven a.m. on the dot, Jones draws up in the white Rover, out steps one steel-toe-capped DM boot, then another and by degrees the royal bride emerges from the car. All eyes are pinned on the 34B lace brassière fully visible beneath opalescent chiffon. The King waves the Boys into a welcoming party. Bride and groom walk between. All sing a round of the National Anthem, under the eye of the neighbours.

The King is majestic in a too-small suit, trim with pink satin hankie, mixed-and-ill-matched with tie-dyed drainpipe jeans and his favourite neon green Doc Marten jackboots.

The Boys follow King and Queen-to-be into the lounge, moving nervously from boot to boot, and cheer when the King says 'I do' and the Princess of Wales says 'I might'. Mai, Archbishop of Wales, lowers a crown on to the Princess's head and at this solemn moment, as the Archbishop pronounces Prince and Princess, Man and Wife, Jones drops his trousers, bends double and moons for the benefit of the Boys at the back.

XIX

For their honeymoon, the Prince and Princess of Wales take a tour around the land of Ower, staying at the Caswell Bay Hotel, the Oxwich Bay Hotel, the Rhossilli Bay Hotel and the Britannia Inn in Llanmadoc.

Royal watchers might find such facts edifying but others find such stuff intolerably dull. We will cut it short and say only that on their honeymoon Princess Vera and Prince Jones fall utterly and irrevocably out of love, and on that honeymoon the Princess conceives her first child, the father of whom is unknown but is thought to be the village punk in Overton, an anachronism by the name of Zee who visits her while King Jones is marooned on the Worm's Head having gone adventuring there in between high tides.

Princess Vera decides that she loathes her husband when he insists that they do not drive around his land but walk instead. He is, he says, the sun going round his world. Vera is grumpy, plotting ways to spite her husband. Jones, forbidden to shag her, plays the tour guide, pointing out defence establishments, inventing histories for Iron Age fortresses and tumuli.

Dead kings under that molehill I'll bet, he points.

People take more notice of them than you! Vera stares at the back of his head and mulls which shaved lobe would be least resistant to a bullet.

XX

I'm pregnant, Vera announces glumly at the New Year's Eve Party in Jones Terrace. The opportunity to abort has passed. The swelling beneath her fat leather belt can no longer be dismissed as water retention. She must face judgement.

Whose the fuck is it? shouts the King, leading Vera down Princess Way in winter daylight. They are handcuffed together. The King is red-faced, his entire scalp coloured vermilion. And he bawls the facts of her infidelity to the city. Vera trails at the end of his wrist, leaning back so they create a 'V' which the January sun projects as a shadow on the paving-stones.

Jones has a thing about fatherhood, an obsession with identifying fathers. Vera cannot see what all the fuss is about, but still she is dragged along behind him like a bull terrier yapping and squealing on a leash.

Why d'you want to know? Because – he nearly loses his voice – because I'm a fucking King, that's why, and if he's my kid he's a fucking King as well!

Jonesie! she shrieks, let me go an' stop shouting – everybody'll hear! And he turns off the pavement into the Duke of York's, Vera skidding like a waterskier, Jones yanking her inside, chipping walls and denting paint. He orders drinks, sits her down, and convenes a Court of Inquiry. He starts accusing every man in the Duke of York's bar of being the father of his wife's child. One takes umbrage, and in place of the Court of Inquiry starts a boxing bout. The King's nose is broken with the first blow and his jaw with the second. Vera is inextricably involved, a half-pint of stout in one hand, digging fingernails into Jonesie's wrist with the other, booting marauders in the bollocks as they come within range, shouting abuse at a colloquium of Asian businessmen seated in the corner. A spunky lady, this Vera.

And the attack brings them both together in a new way, revivifies their relationship for an afternoon. They are ejected from the Duke of York's by the landlord and his friends, with Jones shouting, I'll have you, you fat bastard and your fat English friends! Vera quite loves him for this and feels all soft and gooey inside.

XXI

The world adores Queen Vera – the world, that is, of Number Four, Jones Terrace – the only world to me. And as she blooms with a Prince, as she lies back on a couch and feels a royal family swell within her, we gather sweetmeats and crisp vegetables from delis across the city. Silently, we adore.

And our adoration is only disrupted by the sudden, arrival of a visitor, a visitor who leaves his stamp on this world, a visitor who stays for an era and rivals the King in the arts of love-making, war-mongering and child-rearing. The new recruit is one of those men for whom Life is made, in whom Life catalyses a brilliant reaction. And Vera adores him the moment she sees him, as he is when he enters the lounge and sees her, knees raised, supine under a swollen belly and a plate of chocolate biscuits.

If you mashed Jones and this newcomer into one gigantic blob, the resulting Superman would rule the land of Britain for decades, he would dominate mythology as Odysseus, Alexander, Charlemagne, Arthur or Caesar. But so often our great Kings are divided among many Kings and the pieces fail, generation after generation, to coalesce into one, two-legged, two-armed man.

The Death of the King

How does King Jones die? By degrees: a chain of mock-deaths, heroic wrestles with the Reaper, tangos dance-stepped at the end of a rope.

But Mai has paid close attention to the royal palms and is there at each attempt with a stepladder to cut the King down. When Jones discovers his wife's adulterous adoration for Napoleon, he freaks and strings himself up like a joint of pheasant.

To get the worms out! he tells Mai – to get the worms out a me belly! Mai cannot see if tapeworms are coiled in his belly. But Jones none the less pronounces himself bad meat. And bad meat is best strung up from the rafters where kids can't get at it and it can't get kids.

Talking of which: another King Arthur, one whose limbs are forming from water, young King Arthur, resident of Queen Vera's womb, chooses this time to stage an entrance. Bad meat or not, the embryonic King bursts from his tomb before time. His poor mother is rushed to Morriston Royal Infirmary. Puny young Prince Arthur, titular Heir to the throne of Ower, blinks at the light, smiles at Mother and expires.

The royal family goes into shock. Jones feels, once again, suicidal. But he cannot organise a second royal funeral so hard on the heels of the first. So he postpones his own death and declares that day a Public Holiday. And in the city streets he rails at the bank-clerks, solicitors and shop-assistants stupid enough to go to work on a national day off.

Napoleon the Rival consoles the Queen. Rumour is she doesn't need much consoling. But that's gossip.

Napoleon is a fine figure of a man. With iron-black hair (faintly rusted), long and beaten into curls, a low forehead, slugs for eyebrows and a turbulent beard, Des Napoleon cuts a dash. A friendly alliance of cells formed in him a heart-stopping vision of Man . . . hell, just say the Man is beautiful and leave it at that. And that he and Vera commence relations at once.

I

Four o'clock of an afternoon: the hour when Napoleon feels the second of the day's sex-urges well up from his scrotum and rise to tickle his fingernails.

Meanwhile, Mai, the Magician, sweats over Tarot cards, dealing again and again in the hope that they will tell some story with a happy ending. Mai has foreseen the death of young King Arthur, the death of old King Jones, the love of Vera for Napoleon, seen all this in the tumble of a deck of cards.

Mai sits in his attic, hiding from the glare of an Indian summer. It is a quarter-past four. Dissociated moanings and groanings, thumps and squeaks rise from the Queen's Chambers below. At least Mai is free of Desire which makes all men's lives miserable. His only desire is for the next life. And he swears he can feel his arms beginning to swell and his thighs ballooning and his belly bloating and jowls drooping beneath his jaw, as if all the prophecies to which no one pays any attention are speech-balloons trapped within him, swelling and swelling until it seems he will pop with an almighty release of gas.

II

Napoleon, royally appointed to the Household Cavalry, quickly distinguishes himself in the ranks. Jones elects himself regimental Field Marshal and Napoleon his General. He nicknames the ten Household Cavaliers 'Jacks', and rivals his General for supremacy over them. The Jacks spend all their time in training for the war which their King says is imminent, and in imitating Napoleon, which the King says nothing about.

During morning training-sessions it is General Napoleon who beats his eleven compatriots at road-running, at unlicensed boxing and at wrestling, at shooting, and in round after round of British Bulldog. The P.O.W. has, as one man, fallen in love with the brilliant and ruthless General. Napoleon is talked about with reverence, mimicked in all he does and showered with titles. He is Big Boy to the Jacks, Cocktail Sausage to his lover, Desmond to his best mate, Jones, and Dickhead to Mai. He accumulates names, names by which he is refracted into bits, names amongst which the one he has chosen gets lost. Napoleon becomes a half-remembered term, a gold standard with which historians assure themselves they are talking of the same figure.

For her part, Vera comes to associate Cocktail Sausage so closely with all foodstuffs that she regularly forgets to eat. Under normal circumstances, she slots him in between meals. On special days, he is her diet, her three-course meal taken thrice daily. While her husband gads across some patch of Ower pointing a wooden Lee Enfield at gorsebushes, Vera takes down sufficient protein and essential minerals to sustain the entire Household Cavalry. Napoleon cannot object. His penis is too narrow a tool to pleasure the Queen in the normal way. Circumstances dictate they top-and-tail: Castor and Pollux, Geminian twins in a sixty-nine figure, head to tail, arse over tit, mouth-to-muff resuscitation.

Cocktail Sausage, oh my Cocktail Sausage!

Ah farking bwilliant! shrieks General Napoleon at four-fifteen every afternoon.

On and on until, one afternoon, Vera permits Napoleon to poke his bug-fucker's equipment into her rectum. Ah, there – no, up a bit – down a bit – ahhh! Vera clenches sphincter muscles, holds him there and the great General Napoleon is to be heard howling as he limps behind our High Priestess. Lemme go, Ver-ah! Lemme out!

These howls are at their loudest when, after an hour's training, the King himself marches into the bedroom and sees his best mate conjoined with his wife, hopping behind her as she, doggishly, crawls away from her husband. Jones slaps Napoleon about the head, then grabs his shoulder and heaves. He holds his General about the waist and he pulls. But it is no good. His wife and his General are not to be parted. They must wait until her muscles relax. The King leaves the lovers alone to tear themselves apart.

III

A typical Capricorn, King Jones bottles up the jealousy. He stumbles from the house, and wanders through a blue dusk to hide. Alone, he sits in the King's Arms, persuading himself he is pissed and retelling the story of his meeting with Vera.

He goes over and over the text, establishing time-schemes, chains of cause and effect, indicting scapegoats. Why was he so unfortunate as to *want* Vera, then to *meet* Vera, then to have Vera want *him*? – the insolence of fate, to give you what you ask for! Not to see the impossibility of his making a mark on a person, let alone on a whole land!

And a chill spreads through him at the immensity of his own delusion. He can see, staring into a dark pool of beer, a gnat paddling on the skin of the liquid, thinking itself the only being on the waters. With a royal forefinger, he drowns it.

He is vanishing – by degrees, he is vanishing. No one pays attention to him any more. So, with violence, he will impress himself more indelibly on the planet, with violence against the anonymous. That is the way to be remembered. Elevate yourself by lowering those around you. He has a handhold on greatness. He can see the path ahead. On, on, down to the river, into the dark, the dark at the edge of the town.

IV

A Monday night – day-night of the moon – the Emperor goes for a lunatic stroll. Along Dyfatty Street. Loitering about the old Palace Theatre where Mai met Faye. Strolling onto the Prince of Wales Road (a street named after him! he would not be forgotten!), down to New Cut Road by Jockey Street.

Here the platinum serpents of rail-tracks entwine in grasses, here the soft iron of lifelines knotted in grasses, here trains collided and entwined to hug in the mud. If only he could spool back through time, return to disentangle lifelines!

Under the Quay Parade, crossing to the east bank. The river scrapes a broader gorge here. On its flank runs the King's Road.

Jones spends several minutes reading the road sign, letter by letter. Then he rejoices that his name is written all over this land. It must be his!

The King's Road separates the river from the King's, the Queen's and the Prince of Wales' Docks. (He is amply venerated, the whole world is named after him!) A city of warehouses with containers for cathedrals and gantries for spires. He dreams his engagement, so many moons ago. And he dreams a fuck with Vera, envisages it, gives it face and body: King and Queen forging a Prince of Wales in the gloom, royalty breeding royalty, long lines of watery bodies lying flat, sweating moons.

V

Midnight has passed, in real time. He wanders along the dock-walls. Here the eastern breakwater noses out serpentine into the Bay. As if to extend the length of the River Tawe, two walls were built in time immemorial – been there as long as any can remember. But their arms fail to catch the escaping snowmelt. Then the arms of the Bay have a go, reach in a wide hug to hold the waters back on the earth. But the river pours free into the Atlantic.

The King hops and skips to where the river snaps through delicate walls. Here is the confluence of rivers: Tawe from the north, Severn from the east (Severn and a million others, unnameable rivulets merging to swell a King of a river). He peers into the black to see the seam of flows. Where do two rivers meet? Can they meet? Where does one name end and another start? Or is there a fading of a name, then a nameless stretch, then the growing influence of a new name? Or is there war between ATLANTIC, SEVERN and TAWE? a battle fought along a fault-line, a trench moving inches forward and inches back?

Were he King of all Ower, throned, acknowledged by world governments, empowered, he would have the pier walls joined, a weir constructed, lock-gates imported and a customs officer installed to man the sluice. Two large signs would name the water to the north TAWE and the water to the south SEVERN. But how to treat fairly the million streams building the longest river in the land? Sod them. A river, like a King, is the sum of a million nonentities. His name erases all others.

Jones! he cries, King Jones! Kingadingaling Jones! From here, on the tip of the breakwater, he can see the city, a vast fortress, glowing embers of neon, well defended yet unruled – leastways misruled by an emasculated Englishman who paints bad watercolours, talks out his melancholy with hack philosophers and avoids the land over which he is named King.

The true Prince of Wales stamps his feet in frustration and screams at the city that won't recognise him. The city does not reply. Somewhere deep within it is his true rival, a man he has at last learned to despise, a man whom he will kill at the first and best opportunity.

And that'll show the Bitch! That'll show the slag! Teach her who's boss. She's mine – my fucking land!

VI

As the King crawls into bed, the earth revolves and lays bare his kingdom to the sun, dragging another day to reluctant birth. Inches away, he feels the heat of his wife's living body. He looks at her, but can only see a bristled scalp, bedded in the pillow. He lifts the sheet and there she is, her back to him. Her buttocks slope towards the sheet. He can see discolourations about their heart where, like a dog, his deputy waddled, stuck. He strokes her without touching, running his hand millimetres above the pale clenched skin. She is laid bare on a white bed, a victim on a sacrificial plinth. He stands over her, anxious for a total view. He shuts one eye and covers the other with a ringed finger. This is his territory: Vera and a border of white that may be sheeting. She is curled, knees to breasts, and the pose reminds him forcefully of an embryo. But as he takes the ringed finger away from his left eye, he sees that she is part of a room and part of a world. He stimulates himself with fantasies of investiture at Harlech so his penis comes erect. He eases his wife on to her back, moves thighs apart, coats his knob with spittle and injects her. She wakes, most definitely does not give her consent, but he comes inside her. And once again she is ovulating. Eggs are lining up to slip down fallopians.

225

Her thrashing cannot get him off. They are lovers. He relieves himself, stakes his claim, marks out his territory, reasserts his power over this little sunlit patch of Ower.

VII

Napoleon leads a march on the City Hall. Behind him, a throng gathers around a corpse of Jacks. Ned and Nero, on the wing, hand pamphlets to curious pedestrians. The pamphlets call for the immediate replacement of the powerless city council with an intermediate government and the true King of the city.

Napoleon has organised the march himself. The King is not present, he is sulking at home and receiving the homage of his hairdresser. Napoleon doesn't mind, this is his chance to redeem himself. He leads from the front and his chants are carried over heads in a wave of sound.

Councillors have come out of the Guildhall, barristers are huddled close to the County Court cynically eyeing the demonstration. A glut of tourists snap shots of the angry skinheads thrusting fists at an aquamarine sky.

Your time's up, Napoleon shouts at the councillors. The shout is passed back to the stragglers and fades to a whimper. No more laws from London! This land is our land!

A police van pulls up outside the vast white council building and vomits its load on the pavement. A squad files on to the road. A battalion of Marxist activists, warned of the march, storm across the lawns. Jacks start battle with the socialists and steal their placards.

Otto, a visiting dignitary from a German neo-Nazi cadre, has misunderstood Napoleon's instructions. He snatches a policeman's helmet, puts it on his head and prances through the crowd shouting, Chews out! Vogs out! Yanks oot! English hoot!

He is bundled into a police chariot to keep three other Jacks company. Napoleon manages to get the march to the steps of the City Hall. From there he delivers a speech setting out the aims of the P.O.W.: We're not into all your crap, so no elections – the true King of this city will come soon – he'll get rid of the imperialists – and the fucking immigrants and the Nips. Long live the King! Long live Ower!

And with that, Napoleon runs with his flock of jackbooted camouflaged Jacks across the main road and into a side-street. And the crowd is left on the Guildhall steps, blinded in the sun, desultorily blundering in search of the storm-troops who will lead them to a promised land.

VIII

Phil Ridgeway, By Royal Appointment Hairdresser to the King, cloaks His Majesty in a shining robe, snaps his scissors' jaws, and senses HRH is not in the best of moods.

How'd you like it, sir? Jones lowers his chin to his chest, scowls and thinks. Napoleon has had all his hair shaved. All Jacks followed suit and now have crew-cuts. The King should have something a little different, a distinguishing mark, a rallying-point.

He has been growing his hair. Teak-brown strands an inch long lie flat on his head. The hairdresser rubs them between fingers. Not a lot I can do with this, he murmurs – how about spiking it up? The King is suddenly excited, he sits up, chews his lip and paints a portrait with his hands.

My aunt went to America, the hairdresser interrupts – all her teeth fell out.

Got to watch those Americans.

Put your head back a bit sir, better –

There's thousands like us, Phil – got mates all over the place – it'll happen it will – we'll take over – clear out the furryners – it's well defended, our little land is, see – got natural resources – fucking loads of the stuff – survive here for months, mind – take Scotland – there's nobody in them hills – flood the place with beer an' 'ave them while they're pissed.

Never has the King come out with so many words in one go. The barber nods, though he has a Pakistani record-dealer friend and doesn't want anyone giving him a kicking.

He has finished the King's hairdo, the reformation is complete. The King shakes himself down and heads for the mirror. In the glass, an oval head appears, dressed with rings in every ear and nose. Large irises stare at yellow peaks of hairsprayed hair, twelve ringed about his scalp. A crown sparkling vivid yellow, with red tips high over a bleached scalp – a crown! The King smiles. Two of his teeth are blackened from the Wars. But his smile is pleasing. And the tiny barber smiles back, happy with the coronation of the King.

IX

The moment she sees him, Vera laughs a violent, screeching laugh that scrapes at his eardrums.

A crown doesn't suit you! she cries between giggles – it's ridiculous! Wash it out, dickhead!

But he is damned if he's going to do that! He clouts her and storms on to the street. Vera runs to the window, though she's laughing so much it hurts to walk, but she gets there in time to see him stalking stiffly down Jones Terrace and on to Dyfatty Street.

A cloud of children gather in his wake, following, pointing, waving others to look. He's got a wanker's haircut! He's got a wanker's haircut! Passers-by mutter – Look at 'im then! Well I never! 'Oo does he think he is, then! King Kong? – and the laughter is passed like a baton from pedestrian to car-driver to child to woman – and the murmur travels with him along Dyfatty Street to the roundabout, under the subway and up on to the Kingsway.

The sun glares down, intensifying the colours so more may enjoy the sight of a crowned King on the Kingsway no less. Striding through the centre of town with a crown on 'is 'ead! Jones concentrates on a spot at the end of the road. There is a glint on a window in which he fancies he will find a most flattering reproduction of himself. But it is a long time coming, and when he finally reaches the glint at the end of the Kingsway, late that afternoon, the sun has sunk behind the office-blocks and the shadows are long on the concrete and the reflection is nothing more than a smear. His wonderful crown has collapsed to twisted rat's tails and the yellow dye has given his face the pallor of a corpse. He despises humanity for seeing him. He will live as a hermit.

X

The Jacks sit in celebration around a large table in the Full Moon, Napoleon at the head, Vera on his lap. Napoleon is smart in a trim, tight-fitting khaki jacket with a round collar. He has taken to wearing circular glasses with gold wire frames. By tomorrow night, these will no doubt be replicated on every nose about the table. But for the moment all eyes are on the only pair of glasses present, beneath which a mouth holds court.

Napoleon outlines Step Two: flyposting, pampleteering, the release of Otto Klapp, organising the Public Meeting at which he is to speak, drawing up maps to post about the city just to show everybody what we mean when we say 'Ower'. And and and, shrieks Vera – you forgot, you forgot! Boys, have you got to see this! You know who's only gone and got himself a crown!

And she stands up, hands spreading fingers on her head in a coxcomb, face contorted to capture the King's peculiar repulsiveness, and she does his snarl so well it ignites the mob of Jacks to bright, hilarious laughter. Vera starts a chicken-walk the length of the bar, her arse wiggling outrageously in skin-tight vinyl trousers. As she turns, she trips – but it is only pretending, then on, on, with the ridiculous wriggling walk and the swinging head and the crowning coxcomb.

And she goes on a little too long, and the laughter dries, and Boys turn back to their drinks and wait for Vera's contortions to finish, so Napoleon says,

That's enough Vera, who's getting the next round in?

But she is put out by this, and stares sullenly at her cider bottle, waiting for her lover to apologise. She sits in a black mood all evening, then to cure herself she wheedles her way into Napoleon's lovely big bed at the back of the house. In his celibate pit, Jones hears his distant wife. She has an agenda all her own. She is wheeling Fortune.

XI

Not for her the unimaginative physical violence in which men so love to indulge. No, Vera is much too sophisticated for such brute brutality. She is above fistfights and bottling opponents. She is far far above breaking noses and spines. And, as for kicking a man when he's down, well that's for truly uninventive thugs. Her violence takes on a much more serene complexion. So who is the stronger? Ding, ding, round eleven.

What a night! she smirks.

He rises deliberately, slowly. And she knows what's coming but she doesn't move. She weakens herself so when it comes the blow will knock her to the carpet. He takes a breath, swings his arm and the clout sings in the air. There is a crack and a BANG as she hits the skirting-board.

Look at you, she giggles – just look at you!

He sits on the bed. She stays firmly on the floor. There is, for a moment, peace. The embers smoulder. Possible moves occur to him. She mulls an escape route, then waits.

You know I'm going to kill him, don't you? the King whispers. You know I'm going to have him? And this becomes a scream, escalating to a shriek as he comes at her, head down. She wriggles sideways. Crack! as his crown of horns hits the wall. Another snap! His nose breaks in two halves, clean-cut down the middle.

Animal! We're not married and we never were! Want to know why I stay? He won't leave you – and I won't leave him!

He stares at her, as if she is the ghost of his father or whoever condemned him to a life of inconsequence. The bristles of her head catch light and cast a demonic halo about her smile. She is laughing now, it is so funny.

XII

During these War Years, my adoration for Vera is left to rot in this, my hermitage. My hermitage, my perpetual hermitage – a cage from which I leer at an indifferent hurly-burly, from which I leer at an indifferent Vera.

I have adored her all my miserable life, a life made more miserable by my meeting her. So I am inclined to be sympathetic to good King Jones. Despite his manifest faults, he is one with me and I with him. We have both watched adoration turn bad. So, in my hermitage, I attempt to make an image of Vera.

With inks and watercolours, cotton and needles, pastels, charcoals, limestones, clays, photographic paper, song and, of course, fat reams of A4 paper and felt-tip pens, I set her down, make her up, build her from memory. And in bad poetry, laughable sketches, wretched sculpture and dissonant choruses, I prove not only my general disability as an artist but the general disability of art. But I press on, compulsively redrawing the woman.

I have been a writer since the age of three, when my mother cursed me to a life of scribbling, inserted a pen between squirming inexpressive fingers and requested I draw her. Draw her I did, and my self, and my god, and beneath each representation, I scrawled the words MOTHER, ME and GOD. The gap between word and picture and thing has been troubling me ever since. And the gap between VERA, ME and JONES, between those things and the words skating on the ice, troubles me now.

I write of Vera, I write of me, I write of Jones. I have planned hagiographies, biographies and autobiographies, serialisations, film adaptations and a mini-series. I grew ambitious for a cult musical – the T-shirts, mugs and West End billboards – I sketched in opening numbers ('A KING HAD A FLING WITH A BRIGHT YOUNG THING'). I designed a poster. I have painted royal portraits. I sculpted Vera from a Zanussi refrigerator with a chainsaw. I designed ermine garments for a coronation. And here, at Number Four, I have become house poet, advertising my services on the kitchen noticeboard – WRITER PENS LOVE NOTES, BIRTHDAY/CHRISTMAS CARDS & VERSES, LETTERS TO RELATIVES & POLITICAL PAMPHLETS: 10P A LINE, 10% TO P.O.W. FUNDS.

So you see, this humble Jones is admirably placed as chronicler of the Court of King Jones, chronicler of the War Years, the brief Peace, and the Death of the King. The Boys view me with much scorn, as they do Mai and any who concern themselves with books and not with women, multigyms and brawling. But this obsessive compulsive disorder provides my tin-can brain with blessed relief from its rattle, rattle, rattle. And I sit and listen to what I have not managed to say, what you will never hear: that lost library of Jones Terrace, that unwritten History of the Prince of Wales. For the King dies when put into words.

XIII

Napoleon is lying awake, unusual for him – to remain in bed after he has awoken. Rarely has he had anything to think about.

He is regretting his lost friendship with the King. There was sure to be trouble! He coughs, as if to throw up the nagging guilt. And as he coughs, the door inches open. The King's head, the body of the King, then the King's boots.

And to Napoleon's surprise, he is smiling, forcing a smile but smiling. How you doing? says the King's head. All right?

Yup, says Napoleon. Jones eyes the tumble of sheets, the dimpled mattress, the damp pillows. The General sits up, laying bare great pectorals, and scratches his crew-cut.

What d'we do next? The King says, seeing a naked leg, the naked torso over which Vera regularly crawls. He turns away. Napoleon swallows, surveying the battlefield.

Got a few ideas – you know . . .

A pause, while Napoleon reaches for his trousers, pulling them under the sheet and drawing them on.

I've got an idea too, the King says. Thought we could occupy the Castle – what d'you think? He turns, eyes flaming.

Napoleon has his jeans up about his waist, the fly a wide gash. A tiny penis shivers in the wind. The General flicks it inside his jeans, blushing brilliantly.

The King stammers about the derelict Castle in the city centre. The occupation will be an eyecatching spectacle for the Press. But the sight of the offensive organ has put him off his stride. He muddles the rest and makes to leave.

'Course Boss, course – great stuff – start right away?

The King pauses, the fury damned behind clenched teeth.

Yeah – one thing, Des, just one thing. The General stares, beautiful in raw light. The King blinks at the sight.

This one's just you and me.

XIV

Doctor Otto Klapp rises to speak at five-past eight. A long-winded introduction from the General of the Prince of Wales' Private Militia, Desmond Napoleon, describes the guest speaker as one of the most distinguished of modern German historians, and a great politician. Herr Klapp, it seems, enjoys majority support in many of the German princedoms.

He stands sixteen feet high on an eleven-foot-six-inch dais, and peers down at his audients through wire-framed glasses oddly reminiscent of Napoleon's. As promised, these have appeared on many noses and now stare up at him, some misted, others rose-hued and a few icily clear-sighted.

Brothers and sisters, cries Herr Doctor. We are subjects!

Applause resounds obediently about the hall.

Subjects of many Kings and Princes – leaders we are learning to revere – despite the wars waged on our intellects by evil Imperialists –they, brothers and sisters, would have us believe, not in our Kingdoms and our Kings but in corporate states, amalgamated Kingdoms, which they give names, names we do not recognise – do we, brothers? – what is Britain? brothers? – Britain is a convenient short-hand – it lets them off the hook – it is a lazy man's way of saying the Kingdoms of Britain – and what of Germany? – a plasticine ball of Kingdoms, multicoloured, pressed in the Imperialists' hands into one colourless mass – where is Saxony, where is Bavaria, where is Ower? (To this, cheers, whoops and wolf-whistles.) Yes – where is Ower? You sir, yes sir, yes you, where is the Kingdom of Ower? It has a King, yes it has a King – I have met him and I revere him – it has land, on a map – and the Kingdom of Ower has a people – Imperialists will tell you we are sitting in the country of West Glamorgan of Great Britain

233

– and yet, and yet. I am a guest at the Court of your King, a King the Imperialists obscenely refuse to recognise – despite his reported claims to represent his people, despite his bold demonstrations and marches and speeches – even his people refuse to recognise him – the Great are not recognised in their lifetime – but why leave history to recognise this King? Hoist his flag over the Guildhall! Enthrone your King within – make this land truly your land, truly OUR land!

At this point, Doctor Klapp pauses. He makes them wait. He stands absolutely still, staring from the podium, transfixed.

And how do the Imperialists manage this obscene cover-up? Well, let me tell you, people of Ower, Kingdoms are beaten into corporate states – their people are beaten into submission – and the clubs that you are beaten with? – the clubs of silence, the batons of non-recognition, the truncheons of indifference – for the best way to subdue a people, to strip them of their rights, is not to beat them up – no, the best way to oppress a people, as the people of Ower are today oppressed, is to ignore them – to turn a deaf ear to their requests – the evil American Empire ignores your cry and so takes over this country of Ower – Imperialist puppets in London have moved their agents into your streets and avenues and terraces, in the shape of Englishmen and women, of Pakistani families, Indian gentlemen, and Caribbean youths – a Trojan horse, brothers! – these people take your houses and push the prices of houses up and up and up – they take your jobs and push your wages down and down and down – their houses are kibbutz settlements – oh yes, they are – fronts for a vast Jewish and American conspiracy, diluting our blood and poisoning our soil until we too become a wandering people – and the diaspora of the Kingdom of Ower will be forced to settle all over Europe – you, your children and your grandchildren will wander with your possessions across Belgium and across the Austrian Kingdoms and the Hungarian city-states and you will search for a place to lay your head and you will weep, weep because you could have instated a King where he belongs, a King who would rule you fairly and justly and protect your race and your nation – brothers and sisters, this King is among us, he is moving among us and he will take your command to rise and rule over you – well, ask him, just ask him, call out and ask the true Prince of Wales to take his place, to topple the clown who sits in

London, Charles Windsor – can you go to him with your concerns about the tidal wave of aliens? Can you? – we are an ocean, brothers and sisters, and though we lie tranquil at present, we too can rise into a tidal wave, a vast wall of water upon which the frail craft of American industrialists and Japanese colonists will never survive – and together, brothers and sisters, we can found a new order, a new order to last a thousand, no, ten thousand years – heaven here on earth – heaven in the quiet fields of the Kingdom of Ower!

XV

The King is borne on shoulders to the podium and hoisted eleven feet six inches to his place beside Napoleon and the great historian. Dr Klapp bows, the King weeps. Napoleon announces that Dr Klapp will be in the Swan on the Kingsway to answer questions and to receive gifts of pints. Tomorrow he will return to the Hall to give a speech which has received ovations across Europe, entitled The Myth Of The Holocaust.

And the King's head finally rises to stare into the throng, but he can only dimly see the crowd. One face is shining bright, a vivid map of features, a beautiful pale land, her eyes diabolic, her mouth cheering and her gaze stubbornly fixed on the General of the P.O.W. Militia.

XVI

The King carefully chooses the day for the assault on the city's ancient house of gods – Midsummer's Day, June 21st, when Gemini meets Cancer, the King's Official Birthday.

Plan is, to plant Napoleon on the top of the castle keep, then have him haul up the King, and together they will keep a vigil. To get the ball rolling, General Napoleon and Crown Prince Jones spend the night of June 20th acquiring a 120-foot mobile tower crane from Victoria Avenue. They cannot work out how to dismantle the crane, though Napoleon has claimed to be a bit handy with a spanner. And they have a high old time, just as in the good old days, manoeuvring the crane along a route avoiding low bridges.

The General dare not stop the transporter, so lumbers on with Jones scaling the vertical. Up, up, up to the cab, ninety feet above his head. Jones is possessed of a sudden desire to see the city from a height, to look down while it is moving. He must see his capital city with an angel's-eye view. Far below, the rubble of office-blocks gleams phosphorescent in the dawn, and, still higher, the promontory of Townhill makes a crater-rim about the city. To the south, far out on the black, the sweep-light on the Mumbles Rock blinks in recognition at him.

Napoleon manoeuvres the transporter as close to the Castle as he dares, and from the cab the King can see him lowering jacks. Then his voice comes through the intercom: See if you can make it go!

Lines start hissing and the whole shebang turns clockwise. The great nose of the jib swings through the air, apparently flying in circles. He lowers and raises the winch. The great hook drops fifty feet, then rises. And, largely by accident, he has it rest close to his Deputy. Napoleon attaches their kit to the armature. Then, according to instructions, he straddles it and is hoisted ninety feet into the sky and swung over the parapet.

XVII

It is a simple matter, releasing the levers so the steel hook plunges into the keep. And the load falls ninety feet earthwards to dent the soil deep in the Castle. When the King sees the line go slack, he reverses the motor, raises the hook ten feet or so, then releases levers once again.

He pauses, breathless, and the cab seems too small a space for a head which is pounding with a lust for power and blood and land. So he clambers out and walks the full length of the jib. He is high over the cylindrical keep. He had not meant to do it, not in quite that way. He had envisaged mashing the beautiful head against a parapet. Or turning the great crane into gallows and noosing the evil General on the jib.

He cannot see into the hellish hole. So for reassurance races back to the cab, hoists the hook into sight and breathes at the sight of it, dangling without a load over the fort. He labours until the stars are all out, revolving, round and round, one hand holding the lever as the great cross of the crane rotates. He is tired, so tired, what with all the excitement, and he must traipse home to sleep, sleep with his detested wife. And he dreams a Castle as a skull on a hill, opening jaws and coughing up a bone.

XVIII

The newspapers report how a crane was moved from a building-site in the west of the city to the Castle in the east. And they write up the events with jocularity, as if comedians are at work needling the city to laughter. And reporters tell of a body found buried in the Castle. A squad of officers under one D.I. Jones is assigned to investigate the Castle murder, the death five years ago of a police constable and the two men found dead in the Docks. Suspicion centres on extreme nationalists whose pamphlets threaten supporters of the Windsors with death.

The King is understandably overjoyed at such publicity. His wife closets herself in the bedroom to grieve. She retrieves from newspaper-articles a history of the last five years, a history which she edits into an indictment to throw like acid in her husband's face.

She faces him. He holds her gaze, then drops his eyes and stomps angrily around her as if deciding which bit to thrash. She fires words like pellets to lodge in in his ear. He stands with his back to the sun and stumbles through the tale again. He is trapped in a corner by the second-floor window.

Whatever, murmurs Vera – whatever. Oh, by the way, your mother visited – with some news – about your daddy – your long-lost daddykins. The King moves quickly about the room and it seems to move quickly about him. Gyroscopic, his head spins within a spinning world. He struggles with a cigarette.

Don't you want to know? She fiddles under his chin, pats his scalp and pulls his red braces so they snap on his chest.

He grabs her throat, trying to stem the flow of words but up comes her laughter, her irrepressible laughter at the commoner who thinks he's a King. And her mania drives him from the room.

XIX

Mai knows what will happen next. He sits atop the house and sees down as if floors are glass, and he sees the King racing to the ground floor where the Boys are gathered, and Vera following, choking on laughter, and the two of them bursting into the lounge and speaking together, vomiting rival histories at the multitude. The King grabs her again by the throat.

Careful, careful, she cries – I'm pregnant, careful! And Mai, dismayed at the coming-apart, reshuffles the pack and deals again and I pass him a glass of gin.

Vera fights her husband and her husband is restrained, though more by the gaggle in his head than the gaggle in the hall. Pongo, Queer and Runt chant Fight! Fight! Go! Go! Go!

The King who is not a King barricades his wife in the kitchen and turns to the Boys, great beads of sweat slipping from brow to cheek. Did she come – my mother? – did anyone see her? Heads shake, eyes stare bewildered at him.

And Mai sees him enter the kitchen and accuse the Queen of lying. And the Queen replies: Maybe, maybe not! The King kicks out at her, to kill the last of Napoleon. But the Queen shouts It's yours, it's fucking yours! She is wild against him, and rises, clutching her stomach, oozing tears. He leans back into the wall. Mai crouches, afraid this will bring another house about their ears. But the mortar holds and only the King collapses, desolate to the tiles. Vera hobbles from the room, makes for the telephone and dials.

Police, she murmurs – yes, er Vera, Vera Velindre, Four Jones Terrace. The King cannot hear over the din in his skull, the demonic parliament in revolt. But there is a scuffle in the hallway and it seems Sid Scurlage and Tim Tycroes are attempting to wrest the phone from her hands.

She's called the pigs – run Jonesie! Run! Run!

238

And Mai sees the King scramble to his feet, lurch to the back door, and skid as he clambers the back steps. For a while, from the back window, we see the King climb the incline on all fours, the incline that rises from the back of the house to the heights of Townhill, and when he reaches the promontory, he turns, dusts himself down, spits, and lumbers on, absorbed into the sun.

XX

Vera staggers about the hall, tear-stained, in some agony where he has kicked her. Boys mill about, Tim blurting: What d'you go and do that for? Vera struggles to a couch, winded. He killed Cocktail Sausage!

What we going to do now? cries Sid Scurlage.

S'all right, she says – I'll see to Plod – you're fine!

Knocks at the door, and she answers, white-faced, faint, in shock. Police officers. And she spills her tale, how her husband beat her when she was pregnant, how he ran out when she rang them, and how she has friends to look after her, protect her from him, because he will surely come back and beat her.

D.I. Jones listens with less emotion than his namesake, acquiring descriptions and hearing an account of the years during which the leader of a reputable and popular political organisation took great advantage of his powers, slaughtered any who crossed his path, lied to his closest advisers and friends and brutally turned on his good and faithful wife.

Dutifully, his good and faithful wife supplies information as to any places he might choose to hide, and, with great emotion, she is taken to identify the body of her dear, dear friend, Desmond P. Napoleon.

XXI

Does this mean the King escaped Judgement? Of course not – none of us do.

The murmuring Boys take to trading stories of his disappearance.

One, my favourite, has it that the claimant to the throne of Ower cut a balloon from yards of stolen silk and double-stitched it on Vera's Singer. Knowing he is soon to go away, he borrows Ted's blow-torch for inflation and stows the lot at the top of the hill. Then, in an urn-shaped laundry-basket, he steers himself to the moon. Plausible, this tale – King Jones once commented to me that, had the American and Russian Empires not done it first, he would have relinquished all claims on Ower and colonised the moon. He was an Imperialist, so when things went badly at home, he looked abroad for backward states to annexe, there to enact his fantasy of tyranny. Another account tells how a wandering Jack finds a cairn of stones on cliffs over the Knave, in the bottom left-hand corner of Ower. Leaning on the stones is a large flat tablet carved with the words: SICK OF THE SIGHT OF MYSELF – GOING GOING GONE – THE RIGHTFUL KING OF OWER – GOING TO BE WITH THE SUN – JONES 1953–1986 MUCH MISSED.

A Sunday afternoon drive is arranged, five to each thieved car. Jacks comb the promontory till dusk finding many piled cairns but no rhyming stone. The tale survives more than probably due to man's love for the story of a King who, too much loved, seeks silence in the envelope of the Severn and Atlantic, or in the sun, the moon, the stars or the concrete on the new M4 interchange at Cwmrhydyceirw. We shall never know – for, as with all tall tales there are no certainties together with the desire for many, and an embarrassment of improbabilities together with the hope for none.

If only this were an end. So comforting to have a Hero who dies without ambiguity, who lets the yarn wind to a hasty close. But this one shies total obliteration. He has to keep coming back. Endings, like beginnings, are regrettable and so there is nothing to do but procrastinate, to put off a last word.

The Resurrection of the Dead

And the rains fall on the tin roofs of Townhill, bringing to a shine the slate tiling and steep cobbles and attic windows angled to stare at the stars. An anonymous figure, a figure without a name, plods down the incline of Constitution Hill, a figure grey as the slate slabs, as the slate tiles, as the slate that lies, unmined, beneath the tarmac. He looks up from the pavement when a passer-by draws close. But there is no flicker of recognition. His eyes drop back to the shining slabs. He is a nonentity. He merges with the background.

From the slate-grey clouds come slate-grey rains to watercolour the slate-grey city. And yet, upright and walking, he feels he is again part of things, quite as if he had never gone and left. He is, for a while, allowed to re-enter the atmosphere. And he grows to hoping for a familiar face, and a familiar gaze to rest on him, and a familiar voice to say 'Lo!

But no – for all the recognition he receives he may as well be in an alien city-state. Weepy, he tries to define the word 'home' – place of rest, memorial gardens, a quiet spot . . .

I

He is ignored as he fords the river of Walter Road, paddles through gutters and soaks crimplene trouser-legs. And as he pads down Nicholl Street, no one notices him begging for attention.

Along the St Helen's Road he requests alms and is ignored for his troubles. And at the Guildhall, opposite the Crown Court, he urinates as a mark of his respect for the present regime. His urine, a poor rival to the rains, erodes no foundation blocks. He passes on, shadily.

He is at the beach-front, the sea is warring with the sand. A perpetual struggle, a conflict without a peace. The boundary of the city is the sea and as mutable. Back, forth, up, down, hum drum, a nibbling corrosion of a line on a map.

The prom – a battlement fortified against an imperialistic ocean. On the grey sand, an endless siege. Forces retiring in late afternoon to return at dusk. Sand battlements rucked up like a carpet, cringe, fold, then collapse.

In October, Council men bulldoze the cowardly dunes level. And all year round, the industrialists of Port Talbot and Margam avenge the onslaught on the city-border by poisoning the sea, killing it stone-dead.

II

The sea is dead, has been for years. And its net of fish is thrown up, uncaught, each evening. Silver-bellied, dealt a dose of mercury, they lie in mass-graves with detergent foam, condoms, an arm and a leg.

The anonymous figure kicks a path through the detritus. He walks along the Front, the battleline. Trenches move one step forward, one step back between matins and noon, dusk and evensong. The city lies like a slagheap, coals glowing in the fug of evening. Like a drunk, it totters on the edge of tottering, and somehow stays on the shore.

The man walks, swinging one leg out and up, away from the other, and plonking it sandily down. He repeats the gesture with the opposite, rival number. So it is that he seems cheerful, celebratory, on the verge of happiness – or, would if any clapped eyes on him.

But, as has been the case, he goes unnoticed. Walkers on the prom peer into the gloom to enjoy a view of the Rocks. But they see only a monotony of greys, a drizzle of whites, not an outline worthy of mention. The man weeps. But the rains upstage even this, sluicing across his cheeks, a weir of waters regardless of tears. Surely someone will notice a little boy crying! – a woman concerned for my well-being . . .

He bends to write his name in the mud. He pauses, pencil-finger held wet in the wind. What name should he apply to himself? There

242

are so many. Oh, to have a Birth Certificate locked in County Hall! Why, he could break in now just to have a poke at it! The luxury of sauntering in of a Monday morning and requesting a fellow in a tweed suit with a bald head and mutton-chops to go get it.

He recalls that he is between names. He plods up the raked stage of the beach. A cutting wind navigates a path to his armpits. In the lea of the War Memorial he sits, sheltered by a standing-stone. War Memorials are, after all, gravestones for the unforgotten, unknown soldier.

III

At Pentecost, Mai delivers the greatest of his mature prophecies. Seen as a thread in the tapestry of these times, Mai's Prophecy LXXXVIII is a devastating blow to the sceptic. Mai forsees how the P.O.W. will grow, absorb hundreds of eager members (female) and mutate into a popular force within the local community. He foresees the autocracy of Empress Vera and how she copyrights the name Jones and uses it for her own ends.

He foresees the canonisation of good King Jones, he foresees the publication of *The Wit and Wisdom of HRH The Prince of Wales* and its huge American sales. He foresees the T-shirts, the junk mail, the telephone canvassing and the funding gratefully received from other far-right-wing groups across Europe.

Babbling, brookishly, Mai tells of the P.O.W. assaults on local parliamentary seats, the returned deposits in 1987 and the twenty-two votes gleaned in the 1992 election. Most remarkably of all, Mr Mai sees with great clarity a decade in advance, he foresees the revaluation of the European. For Mai calculates on the rear of an envelope that, if an individual equals 1 divided by the population of that individual's fatherland, then in a Europe of, say, 300 million people, the individual is reduced to 1/300 millionth of the whole.

Compare this with, say, 1/3,000,000 of Wales, or 1/300,000 of Ower, or one-quarter of his own household. And Mai foresees that homelands, like families, will divide upon growing too large. And he foresees how the European mainland will divide into 300 million homelands. Each will protest its right to self-determination. 300 million Kingdoms! Imagine the multiplication of borderlines! the friction! the griping over where a garden wall is to be built!

And Mai forsees the explosion and disintegration of the globe, how like a boiled egg rolled in hands, its shell will crack into innumerable shards and on each piece will stand a King.

IV

To close, Mai takes the deepest of breaths, screws up eyelids and peers deep into the future, deep into the night, out to Cornwall, and thinks he can see how this race mothered by a woman shall die, millennia hence, and leave a man staring at a ewe, wondering.

So he sees that humanity, unsocial ants, will swing through cycles, yin then yang, mothering then fathering, doing each as badly as the other. Mai is not a pessimist, he simply doesn't believe things will get any better.

And anxious to be one step ahead of the pack, he fills suitcases, borrows Tommy Tackler's caravan and says his goodbyes. He hands his P.O.W. membership card to Vera, wishes her all the best and makes for a distant plot of Ower. There, he jacks up the caravan, raises the awning, cooks himself jacket potatoes and white cabbage (buttered and peppered) and prepares a mixed vegetable salad. With his meal inside him, he smokes a cigarette, sups a mug of coffee and, to the gnats, declares the Empire of Demetae (the caravan-plot) established.

V

Evening on the beach. Yachts tremble on the light of the waters. A rust smudge of trawler pulls against the drift. A rugby club in shorts and coloured tops jogs on a patch of sand. The trainer blows a whistle and like ascending gulls they cloud to run for a line in the dust. A grey silhouette is a man and he bows to etch a map in the sand.

Pensioners giggle and nudge nudge wink wink over a game of

boules, flirtatious under mauve-rinsed scalps. A girl with a river of hair wades at the shore collecting what? from the Severn's rubble. Diggers in boots shovel for bait or gold on the flats. No swimmers, it is evening and the sea is acid.

A low sun flares the Cork ferry to golden battlements. The blast furnaces pile clouds in the heavens. The silhouetted man who could be a boy jumps in and out of the land drawn on the sand, playing a round of Tom Tiddler's Ground, all on his tod.

He sings: Here we're on Tom Tiddler's Ground picking up gold and silver! No one watches, save ourselves. Even the sun is indifferent and slips to light other adventurers behind the West Cross hills.

Anxious for attention, the silhouette pads to the waterline and, mixing among fishermen and beachcombers and walkers, he hollers and stamps his feet. No one attends to his tantrum. So he runs to the girl with the river of hair and requests she marry him. She too ignores him.

Snarling, he patrols his borders. Vigilance preserves a Princedom. Stand firm he does – by God, yes – though he detects mockery in the tones of the rugby-players, beefy in a mucksweat, yards from his borders. They are more than likely sniggering at somebody else, a man who deserves a bit of healthy abuse, a man in ridiculous clothing perhaps, maybe a lunatic.

So he will snarl a little less ostentatiously. He wants to draw attention both to, and away from, himself. He wants to be visible and invisible. He wants to be both man and angel. But it seems he is neither. He has neither ascended nor descended. He is stuck, pig in the middle, a parcel passed between heavens. Ghost is too trim a word – the light in these parts makes all men ghostly. A forsaken pope, he waits.

VI

It is six months since Vera began celebrating her late husband's disappearance. And she is pregnant in a big way. A seedpod on legs. She waddles till she can waddle no longer, then collapses on a sofa.

Ulick Trostre, it has been noted, is particularly assiduous in soothing the Queen's brow. Ulick is as smitten with Vera as any of us. He snivels up to her, flattering her with gifts, waiting on her hand and foot. But he hasn't got a hope in hell of bedding the woman.

For Queen Vera adores the calm, diminutive Una. Una with the naval ring, Una with the purple-laced jackboots, Una with bee-sting breasts and iron-black hair. Una seems the reincarnation of Napoleon, cast in bronze and steel, making her entry as King and General make exits.

So the Queen loves Una, but Una loves Ulick and Ulick loves the Queen and waits in adoration upon Her Majesty. All three lovers dominate lounge society, sprawling on sofas to watch afternoon television, consuming choccy-biccies by the plate, Ulick and Una rushing to turn channels or brew coffee or buy fags or mop the Empress's brow.

And Vera switches her mind between lusting the echo of Napoleon and despising the absent King. Hospital specialists have shown her the scan of her belly. Obstetricians have solemnly announced the presence of four little hearts setting up a military tattoo. On the screen, quadruplets like kidney beans turn slow somersaults in brine. Vera demands the balding scientist clean his glasses and his blessed screen and look again.

Sure enough, four embryonic Princes of Wales clutter up her womb. Yes, she is to have quads – his quads! She is horrified, raves and rants at nurses, kicks doors and refuses to renounce cigarettes or drinks. She has half a mind to kill them, then softens, even though they are that ruffian hung, drawn and quartered, seeded inside her and left to incubate.

The cheek of it! sending a cloud of semen up her insides just as she has one fat egg clogging a fallopian! That egg subdivides, angry against itself, then, civil war raging in each nucleus, divides again and creates four variations on a theme of Jones Vera.

Ulick suggests she call them Matthew, Mark, Luke and John – seeing as they are to be reminiscent of one world-changing King. Vera huffs and puffs, says she has no idea what he's talking about – besides, what if they are girls! And, one more thing, they are her quads, not some fly-by-night scumbag's!

Like a bug stuck on its back, she thrashes on the sofa, waving limbs

246

in all directions, and eating enough pasta to sustain a division. Pasta is brought in by the caseload – pasta shells, pasta tubes, pasta bows, conchigli, tortellini, canelloni, gnocchi, ravioli, spaghetti and all manner of spiced tomato sauces.

This is served so often, Una declares when the quads appear they'll only need heating-up, smearing with cheese sauce and Vera won't know them from lasagne.

Then, one two three four, the Boys drop like eggs, nurses keeping a careful count as to who drops first, tying a red thread about the forefinger of the firstborn . . . But does she get it right? A lifetime's squabbling and fraternal rivalry begins with a nurse questioning her knowledge of reef-knots. And the Boys are carted by the armload to four incubators, being underdone eggs, and are laid amongst a spaghetti of drip-feeds.

And when they wheel the museum-cases before Vera, she sees four relics of a father, she sees a father's face ghosted in each blob of fat and fibre. There he is, equally apportioned among four of them – piggy eyes on Victor, honk of a nose plonked on Vincent, flapping bat ears on either side of Vivian's head and on little Valentine's lower jaw that succession of chins. There he is, refigured in bits, back to haunt her. She asks they be wheeled away so she can get a bit of peace and quiet. And the pieces of King Jones are borne away in incubators, wheeled as if journeying from funeral to christening via the mother.

VII

He is away from the city now, away from the terracotta-tented roofs, the untidy loveliness of breeze-block parliaments, away from the anthill subjects. Clockwise, he beats the bounds of Ower.

This is his route – skidding, in so far as he can, between high and low water, the land a monarch may call his own. The Severn has notched the southern side of Ower with caves and cliffs and promontories, hewing limestones as the river meets the Atlantic (where does a river meet the sea?). A path hugs the cliff-edge. His feet, booted, hug the cliffpath.

The runaway stoops low and hurries as if seven devils are on his tail. His hood is drawn high over a squashed hat, a cowl to hide him from passers-by. And observers they might be, these passers-by – the anonymous cannot be too careful. A passing mind might start describing him, setting his features to words, applying names to the already misnamed. Whenever possible, he makes their task easier, sighting them a long way off and clambering to a hole.

This is his stomping-ground, where he traipses through a life looking for a father and his father and his father, back and back and back, round and round the perimeters of a fatherland. Madness, to ever start this.

And he quivers. On a promontory he stands, and is shaken by a wind that slips from the Black Mountains and speeds over forts and lakes and settlements to whip the Severn to meringue peaks and slaps his buttocks with coat-tails. He breathes out, contributing to the wind that blows a maddening gale, a wind making mad the seas about Rhossili, Pembroke, Cornwall, Ireland and distant New York, a gust blown like a fart as a King declares his right to rule wherever and however he chooses.

VIII

To pay for his caravan palace, Mr Mai places advertisements in local periodicals and in the *Evening Post*, notifying the subjects of King Jones of his gifts in Acupuncture, Aromatherapy, Allergy Counselling, Ayurveda, Bach Flower Remedies, Fortune-Telling, Herbalism, Holistic Health General Practice, Homeopathy, Horoscopy, Hypnotherapy, Iridology, Jurisprudence, Metamorphic Technique, Naturopathic Medicine, Palmistry, Reflexology, Shiatsu, Tarot Readings and Zen.

He has read up on most of these arcane disciplines, but for those of which he has no knowledge, he invents practices, collecting and drying flowers and herbs, selling them at exorbitant rates, applying pressure to any available body-joints and declaring that person fit and well and free of the National Health Service.

And the revenue generated by his quack remedies and hack curatives more than pays rental on a caravan site and buys him a meal a day. Mai forsees how the overdue decline in English Christianity will leave a greater hunger in the belly of British nations, a hunger for any story so long as it tells of primal energies, alludes to gods and angels and offers the hypochondriac the hope of a cure. He foresees how the entrepreneur might invent a faith, replete with mysteries, holy spots and annual subscription fees, and make himself a mint. He foresees how the craze of the imminent millennia will be the invention of religions. And with this, as with popular monarchism, he aims to be in right at the start.

IX

After masturbating on the grass above Three Cliffs Bay, the grey figure rejoices to see himself ejaculate. He is routinely testing his bodily functions. Good to see limbs in fine fettle.

Hard on the heels of his orgasm, he holds his penis dripping over the earth. He is anxious to urinate. The urge is there. Talons grip his bladder. His urethra wriggles in anticipation. But the earth remains dry.

He swallows, sniffs, mourns the drying of his loins and replaces the organ, half-cock. No sooner has it slapped his thigh, than a stream of piss soaks his long-johns.

It is a precious moment, tempered only by misery at the prospect of clammy thighs. He savours the joy, clicking tongue on palate in celebration. There are few sweeter pleasures than the confirmation that a digestive system is in tiptop condition. He walks on wetly with renewed faith that gods order the ways of men. Time passes, and at last relenting, he gives in to misery at his damp cold thigh.

He walks and he walks, miserable, then ecstatic, mourning, then rejoicing. And by and by, the fellow finds himself by happy accident at the door of Mr Mai's caravan. He enters and fervently expresses his pleasure at meeting an old friend. He glosses their times together, their times apart, the colour in Mai's cheeks, how well the old wizard looks despite putting on such weight. . . !

But Mai does not raise his eyes. His hand rests on an upturned glass. It shudders as the visitor talks. An alphabet is arranged on the table-top in front of the sorcerer.

Suddenly, the glass shunts about the table. The fat hermit seems to wake up. He scribbles letters on a pad, collecting words. The visitor doesn't take offence at such rudeness – Mai has his ways. He makes a cup of tea, chattering about the troubles of the past, the joys of the present, the bliss to come. The glass scratches on the table-top, moving from letter to letter, chattering to the druid.

The visitor paces about the tiny mobile home, commenting on fittings and pictures, books and bric-à-brac, reminding the host of their lost love.

We met, we met! he yells, running in a tiny ring. Remember!

He is beside himself, he is inside himself, he is all over himself, he is barely himself. He grows quite frantic with the insisting, but still the wise fat man sits there, inscrutable.

The visitor moves closer, waving in front of Mai's eyes, peering over the notepad. His words written there! His cries are bunged up in an atmospheric log-jam of sound. Pieces filter through as lumberjacks clear the flow, pieces that by a circuitous route emerge inscribed on Mai's pad.

And, as time passes, a smile, a beam, a grin of the largest order spreads across Mai's mouth. His pudgy face is mangled with delight at noting a familiar voice. The visitor falls silent so the remains of his monologue may drip through.

Then he speaks again, this time more slowly, speaking each phrase many times over so its many parts can all, all of them, get through, be passed by the lower spirits working to relay a chat long-distance from speaker to scribe.

X

The Queen is in residence at Number Four, and is hard at work adoring Una. Una, meanwhile, is feverishly adoring Ulick.

Vera is far from pleased. To have the object of her desire rutting with that scamp Ulick Trostre is bad enough, but to have it go on in her realm! it's a crime against her state. She takes immediate action, devising a plot against the offending Boy. She drafts in female members. And, within a week, she has switched the balance of power within the P.O.W. from Boys to Girls. It is time to redefine the state.

In the cellar a coffee-bar serves Danish pastries to victims of male violence. Earnest feminists provide counsel. On the ground floor, a telephone line is installed, a Crisis Helpline. And the back room becomes a reception for the flood of women escaping the evils of patriarchy.

To purify the haven, Vera purges the remaining Boys, some who have served the P.O.W. for years. Ulick is her target, Ulick who accuses the Queen of betraying the late King's ideals. Fortune's wheel spins, the Purges of the Eighties follow.

The Ulick Faction of the P.O.W. moves into a vacant property on Jones Terrace, breaking-and-entering in time-honoured fashion. From there, they start their propaganda war against Number Four. Somehow, I avoid eviction. I keep my manhood close to my chest.

Vera busies herself with raising a new P.O.W. from the dust: the Parliament of Women Party, a pressure group that oscillates between right and left, fighting for a chamber of representatives peopled only by women and ultimately for the elevation of Vera to a position of power within her husband's Land of Ower, or as she put it to me, to put the P.O.W. back into power.

To do this, she searches for a new property for the growing Women's Centre (that parliament in embryo). In the process, she retells the history of her husband's decade-long fight for his throne. For, she says to me, they who control the histories control the present, and, *ergo*, the future.

XI

Seven o'clock of an ungodly evening. Port Eynon, the sandbar like a lemon-twist sucked clean by the sea. The granite sliced and racked against a turquoise hill, the village a smuggler's ramble to the waterline.

A man hangs out on the prom, nondescript. He floats towards Gino's, a coffee-bar hidden behind bleached billboards. Within, plastic buckets and spades hang from an invisible ceiling. Sweets and foodstuffs are raked up to a wall. He has some memory of the place. He may or may not have been here.

He stuffs Granny Smiths into his coat-pockets, as souvenirs. He examines the cash-girl's breasts, impertinently close. Outside, he loiters, awaiting a decision.

He walks the beach, patrolling his land. He yells at two adolescents, buried in the sand, wrestling with each other's clothes. Filthy buggers, mauling in public! Yelling does him a lot of good, gets it off his chest. They take no notice, so he cranes his neck for a closer look, willing the boy to have the shirt off her back.

The man moves off towards the Head, past the rotting Salt House and on to Port Eynon Point. Squatting between two rocks, he lays two lengths of shit with care. He feels the intensest of pleasures at his continued ability to excrete. He gazes at a tanker's lights out on the water, markers of life in the black, the outline of spars and lines and masts splayed over sleeping men, moving softly south with the drift of the river.

He completes his ablutions and heads up into the cool air trapped in the nook of the cliff. Weary, in the Culver Hole, he polishes all four apples, buffing them on the hem of his overcoat. If there was light, he would peer to see his face, dim and mutant on the globe of fruit. But there is no light, so he takes a bite from each apple in turn. This way, he commits himself to eating all four. An apple turns brown if left in an overcoat pocket for too long, so he must keep himself awake until four nibbled cores have been extracted from the apples.

He takes a fifth, sixth, seventh and eighth bite from each apple, and to his horror, hears one of the apples – he does not know which – roll thudding from its perch. He curses, for this will wreck his Method. Order is everything when ailing.

With the greatest of pleasures, he discovers the apple in the crook of a rock. His pleasure is, as ever, tempered by misery, and by fears that this is a fifth apple inserted into the dark by a maleficent spirit, and that the crook in which he found it was the crook in which, minutes earlier, he laid shit.

These thoughts troubled him throughout the night, infesting his dreams, waking him before dawn with the symptoms of cholera, convincing him that the rediscovered apple has sowed within him some gruesome disorder which could spread epidemic throughout mankind.

XII

Being the only man of marriageable age remaining within Number Four, Jones Terrace, I approach the Queen with a generous proposal, suggesting she might find the company and affection of this like-minded soul beneficial to her health.

She replies, not without discourtesy, that she has no desire to remarry. The concerns of her late husband's estate have convinced her that to marry once was youthful stupidity. To marry again would be farce.

I point out that I have no estate, no Kingdom, no title, no prospects. I will, almost certainly, live life in utter obscurity. Neither do I mind her new-found sexual appetites.

Perfectly natural, it is.

This is an elegant attempt to say the unsayable. None the less she beats me soundly about the skull, tells me to mind my own business and find somewhere else to stay. The Party requires my room, not a man to write its histories for it.

This is not how I had hoped the tender moment would develop. Instead of the reward of my Beloved weeping with gratitude, I receive a boot to the nuts, a summary eviction-order and copper-bottomed evidence that Vera does not, in any shape or form, desire me. I may as well hang.

Instead, I leave my hermitage of seven years and move to less salubrious quarters. And, to mark my departure, the Queen plays a hilarious practical joke upon me. Even I laugh, and I am not known for my sense of humour.

She telephones Officers of the Law with information concerning her criminal husband. She says he has visited her, stolen a suitcase, beaten her and her children and is making off at an unhurried pace along Jones Terrace, heading west.

Indeed I am – heading west, with a view to lodge at my great-aunt's bungalow on Caswell Bay. A pleasant verandah it had, between the Wars, they said.

Fortunately, mine is a speedy trial and a lengthy incarceration. I am well received in Swansea Crown Court and entertained like royalty in the City Jail. I have no complaints to file concerning my gentlemen-in-waiting. I have a pleasant room, a large window and a view over the Oystermouth Road to the sea and the rocks and the south.

I have many visitors, the Queen included. She apologises most graciously for the manner in which she refused my proposal. Her love for Una overcame her propriety. She adds that the late King must be laid to rest. So disrespectful to have grubby police officers crawling all over a royal grave.

And, she continues, the best way to stop policemen is to give them somebody to lock up. I was the obvious candidate. For I am, she tells me, disturbingly reminiscent of the King, so much so that she could barely stand to have me around the house. So I am he, as far as any in the Judiciary can tell.

She promises I will receive my reward after the revolution. With this knowledge, I languish happily in one Queen's custody, living for the land promised me by another.

XIII

From the tip of Overton Cliff he can see Cornwall, a wedge of grey, crisp in the November light.

The path is a crunchy snow of dust under boot-soles. It is deeply marked in the earth, cut by his many circuits about the Kingdom. An outline, it teeters on the brink, hugging the zone where the rocks decay. Sea shatters on the cliff, rattling on the nation's walls. And with pieces of shrapnel torn from the bluff, he piles a cairn. He passes an afternoon etching a poem on a flat stone, a suicide note, and leans the tablet against the cairn. He warms to the idea of it serving as his tombstone.

He picks a meal from between his teeth. He cocks a leg to ease the passage of a fart, letting it escape without ostentation to the outer air.

He is tranquil, thinking of death, a little bored by the waiting, but calm.

He contemplates the fall. Prince of light, he peers from the precipice. Rocks are stained with prior suicides. But he knows too well the regret of falling. He has dropped on a rope often enough to know that nostalgia for the diving-board.

For three days and three nights he camps out in his coat, entranced by the idea of the drop. After much reflection, he concludes it is best to let death come to him, to end his wandering with serene exhaustion rather than impetuous flight.

He has thirty, perhaps ninety, years left in him. He is an old man in new wine-skins. He is both young and old, though I forget whether mind or body has the edge. Either way, the sooner he gets walking the sooner the walking will get to him.

He takes up his coat, gets into it, dusts down the tails, buttons up the front and kicks waste matter from his boots. He smooths what remains of his hair, picks his nostrils to ease respiration and takes a lungful of the autumnal sky. Using his right leg, he steps forward. His left leg is slow to follow, but soon gets the picture. And within minutes he is off, firing on all cylinders, gulping the air, flapping coat-tails trying to lift him from the earth.

He must speed up, he must rush on, on, on, stamping down the stones. The land is built of stones, stones carved out by the sea that is now trying to swallow it whole.

Territory, a body, needs defending. For, without territory, as without a corpse, a King is a nothing. He must hang on to both body and land. But a runny nose is bothering him, as if his brain has thawed and is coursing out each nostril. And his dick is sore, feels like any minute it will drop off. And in the last few days or weeks or months, all but fifteen of the hairs on his head have moulted, leaving him as good as bald.

XIV

The P.O.W. Militia (P.O.W.M.) moves into Number Four, Jones Terrace when Vera and the Parliament Of Women Party (P.O.W.P.)

move out. The Militia has an all-male cast. Yam takes over from General Ulick. Expelled, Ulick sets up a third splinter group, the P.O.W.P.A. (the Prince of Wales' Private Army). The Army proclaims the Militia an illegal gang of terrorists. The Militia calls the Army thugs. Vera's P.O.W.P. dissociates itself from both. Wars break out between the Army and the Militia.

Throughout the late eighties, the Army commits a series of outrages against Militia servicemen. The Militia retaliates, hanging three Army soldiers from lampposts on the beach-front.

The Army famously defeats the Militia at the battle of Blackpill. The Militia rises again, moves premises and operates successfully for many years from secret addresses across Ower.

The Party, under Queen Vera, condemns all terrorism. The Army, under Ulick Trostre, condemns violence. And the Militia, under General Yam, condemns the Queen to death. Tedious details, I know – but necessary, to show how a King can be refracted into a thousand Princes of Wales, each one zealously guarded by a Faction, insistent that their piece of the portrait is the real McCoy.

XV

Nine a.m. – an unearthly hour to awake a man – but on the causeway between the mainland and the Worm's Head, the sea gallops in on a late high tide and rudely sluices over a fellow sleeping in his overcoat.

He awakes, swearing. And at a faster gallop, he leaps from his bed of rocks and makes for the high-water mark. The sea nibbles at his ankles. He dances in the surf, yelping. Then, with great relief, he reaches the dry land. Here, the river's detritus lies in banks awaiting beachcombers.

He lays his overcoat out to dry. He's going to grill some fish, perhaps mackerel. He hunts for firewood. Wary of the sea, he keeps an eye on the gap between ocean and unguarded overcoat. He walks fifty paces to the east, one hundred paces to the west and fifty paces back to joyful reunion with the coat.

The sea, cunningly, waits until he has walked forty-nine paces east of his precious overcoat. Then, it hurtles inland, rising up the steep shingle, boiling with anticipation, pacing itself against the man who runs.

The sea reaches the overcoat first, douses the piled driftwood, drags planks and coat back out from the shallows, and holds them there, as debris. All a man's possessions, far, far from the high-water mark.

He is forced to get his trousers wet. And his knees seize up in the cold. His feet freeze in his boots. He slaps the sea, correctively. He wades, commanding that the waves return to low water. The sea is the devil about the godly land.

With no thanks to the sea, he at last retrieves the coat. He climbs above Rhossilli to Sweyne's Howe, a Welsh King's burial chamber. The man pauses here for a cuppa and a biscuit on each of his rounds, to pay respects to his ancestors.

He whiles away a pleasing afternoon, sitting atop the gigantic grave, trying to pick at blisters between his toes. His knee has seized up for good or bad. Getting at his toes is nigh impossible. He fondly recalls a youth when he could indulge such luxuries as crooking his knee to get at his foot. Then he doubts that it is his youth he is recalling. It might be another's, carelessly picked up on the way. Histories are so plentiful a man muddles his own with the rabble's.

XVI

And at the risk of muddling the reader, I must tell of the goings-on in Number Four, Jones Terrace, the right royal racket as Boys tell of sighting the King.

In General Yam's Militia, there are as many tales as tellers. On a Sunday evening in the Prince of Wales bar on the sea-front, General Yam himself tells how he sighted the late King in a queue at Sainsbury's, bearing a basket of exotic fruits, corn chips, a four-pack of Stella, tubs of cottage cheese and a large pumpkin. The King is wearing a grey pinstripe, is clean-shaven and has a head of mahogany hair. On his VISA card, General Yam sees the name A. IDRYS.

I said nowt, says Yam. He'll come back in his own time.

Corporal Yaw bounces up and down – Please, sir! Me, sir!

And the Corporal tells how he is walking one Sunday in the town centre and who should he see lying asleep on a bench under a copy of the *Post*, cuddled up to a bottle of Jack Daniels?

But Private Yup offers a tale finer than his, a tale of the King in the gents in the Mayfair nightclub. The Corporal didn't want to disturb such a private moment, so turned his back and – guess what? He vanished – up in smoke!

The Boys have no qualms about such a crop of tales. They are devotees of that theory of fastbreeder reincarnation (FBR) which teaches how a migrant soul hitchhikes through many hosts.

Sergeants Yack and Yuck stand to recite the favourite tale, the tale of how they sighted the King on Overton Cliffs where the famed Overton Stones and Tablet, inscribed with the Last Testament, were found. This has become, in the years that followed the discovery, a holy site, revered by rival Brotherhoods who clash when they meet at the spot.

As they walk the road out of Port Eynon, Sergeant Yack is the first to notice him – a hooded figure at a distance, talking to himself, picking a path through the sea's waste.

For some minutes, all three figures walk parallel paths. Then, with a shout, Sergeant Yuck notices him. The King! And the booted overcoat and hood takes to its heels, hobbling with a stiff leg to vanish into the Salt House, the house of a god.

They spend an evening picking up stones, hunting for concealed tunnels and shouting the King's name at the top of their voices. But they come away with only the tale. And as the Boys of the Militia listen with awe, a ghostly figure passes the bar's sea-facing window. But the Militia are too intent on hearing the last lines of the Sergeants' Tale to see a shadow stamping his boots and soundlessly screaming at the sea.

XVII

Imagine the land of Ower as a dog's dick hanging from the belly of Wales. Rhossilli Bay is the tip of the knob. On the tip of Burry Holmes, the tip of the tip, sits a bubble of semen.

This man sits midway between the ruins of a fort and a chapel. He sat down, having little choice in the matter, when his left knee, following the example of his right, seized up. His eardrums' fluid imagines the earth is leaning at a 45-degree angle. With rigid legs he must fight to keep his balance. But over he goes, flat on his back. He sees stars.

And he fears he will be marooned there till gods come like dustmen to collect him. But, as is their habit, they don't turn up. So he turns his head to the heavens.

The sky is a brilliant grey. Light scorches his eyes. The Worm's Head is a sea-monster with its tail tied to the land, straining to get out to sea. To the north, the warring Welsh states are adrift. He yawns. He bores easily, this man. He is anxious to get on, to be done with it.

So, by a process both ingenious and ungainly, he hoists himself to the vertical. Then, with steps short, long and middling, he rejoins the beach at Broughton Bay.

This is most satisfying. The sand is soft, fat, wet and takes memorable impressions of his boot-soles. Though his neck is stiff, he can turn to see the plod plod plod across the beach. As ever, the sea gets the last laugh and, as he lies at an angle on the dunes, he watches, not without cursing, the rubbery water erase every bootprint. It must be done again.

XVIII

The north shores of the peninsula are particularly difficult to follow. Marshes stretch from a path on dry land to the Loughor river, a distance of two kilometres between high and low water.

The grassy flats are nibbled to a crew-cut by the sheep who rival wild ponies for the pasture. The flats are dotted with unexploded mines, laid during one of the many battles in these parts. And a passer-by – hauling himself forward with hands and elbows – is very moved, moved almost to laughter, by the sight of a sheep stepping on one of these devices and disintegrating – BANG! – to mist.

He half wants to be blown to atoms in this fashion. For the most tantalising of pauses, he would know himself to be solid, palpable, resistant to the touch – then, nothing.

Instead, he is lost between states, neither solid, liquid nor gas. And he crawls, a vagabond, around and around, clockwise about his land.

The slacks, dykes livid with spiders, threaten to bog him down. Houses, dabbed like white paint on the green, tempt him. But on he goes - on, on, on to the sweet end. But now, his arms, with a crack, treacherously secede from the rule of his head, and, like snakes, they drag astride his torso. Not to worry – his heart is good, his mind is sound, and his jaw still gives up a rattle, a dry-tongued rattle to the midnight moon.

On the southern horizon stands Arthur's Stone, a gravestone erected in memory of a King who, it is said, corrodes in these parts. The graveyard of ambition.

He looks north, he can hear a sound. No sight of anything – then again, no sight. He peers south and all points east. Zilch. Bugger all. Then, that sound again – a murmur, rising.

He wriggles about till he views, without vision, the west. A lady stands bulky against the night, blotting out the moon. She holds a bag in each hand. He makes sounds. She stops, peering down. You again! a voice cries. He thinks up a reply, plans a sentence in every detail, reorganises it for best rhetorical effect. But when he speaks, it refuses to come.

A stutter stands in its place, an inaudible stutter. The bag-lady speaks – telling him to get off her land – he is a trespasser and she, the Queen of all Britain, is landlady with dominion over all land between high and low water. He gurgles a challenge. But with a kick, she says goodbye, indicates who's boss and announces that she doesn't expect to see him there on her return.

The humiliation of it! the cheek of the woman! and him, incapacitated, bellied like a snake in the dust – not able even to spit in her face or tear off her beard!

He rests, he cools, he waits.

XIX

Detective Inspector Jones is hard on my heels, having assembled the facts of the life of a King and raced through that past, stumbled over discoveries, tripped over concealed contradictions, and finally, almost finally, arrived at an end.

His diligent researches, costing hundreds of thousands of pounds of public money, lead him from Elaine's little black book to Vera Velindre's quadruplets and on, on the trail of a man who posed as a Prince of Wales, then had a man pose as him.

For DI Jones has rumbled me – he knows I am not the real Prince of Wales nor am I the real Jones – whoever he may be. But he cannot prove it.

The Inspector is mad for the truth of the matter. Many times, he tells the story, vicariously living in present tense the life of his quarry. On the Gower coast, with a telescope, a rifle and a camera, he scrutinises the shore.

He is, he tells bewildered friends, looking for a hunched renegade who is plodding round and round the coast. When he has the energy, the Detective Inspector plods off by himself, with sticks thick and slender, one for walking, and, he tells his poor wife, two for bringing him in.

The Inspector visits me regularly and has quite taken my plight to heart, pledging to get me released the moment he catches his Suspect.

XX

Distant now, and fading, he blunders, galloping on shoulders and pelvis, making over the dry ground to the wet ground.

He has come a long way in all these years. From Weobley Castle to Dalton's Point is a distance of five statute miles over land rough then smooth, dark then light, barren then fertile. But he is a tough muscle, a brazen little bugger, crawling over the face of the earth, anxious for a long-promised judgement.

He wants nothing more than a hearing in a court before a god, and he wants to ask a few bloody questions like – Why can't a man with a parched throat get a drink between the hours of eleven in the evening and eleven in the morning in this unruly Kingdom? There are more – oh yes there are more – questions turning over in his head like worms, burrowing through the mud of his skull and oozing out of eyes and ears and nose and gob, questions hungry for answers. Why?

Perhaps.

XXI

The end of this world is nigh, an end to all this death-rattling, this chatter, this drone of a voice in a jail, a voice telling its own story of the Prince of Wales, of how father led son a merry dance and son raced after father and the two wheeled round and round a roundabout on opposite sides, busting to break free of the fact of the present, of the limits of the land of Britain, and I think it's true . . . true as I can make it, though there will be proof-readers and libel lawyers and police inspectors crawling all over this corpse checking for offence caused, offence taken, offences committed and offences unpunished against persons living, dead, half-alive or unburied, and the Kings will squabble over who is misrepresented, who is under-represented, who goes unmentioned, who has been ruined and who shot to stardom, for Kings need publicity, they need to be made public, they need to own a public and have a public own them, to draw a land in the sand and stomp their jackboots into the earth, to define and redefine, for there is no worse fate than vanishing before your very eyes, fading out of existence, greying to a ghost, especially when you are a Prince of Wales whose middle and beginning have no end.